ISBN 978-0-243-48583-3
PIBN 10801137

1 MONTH OF FREE READING

at

www.ForgottenBooks.com

By purchasing this book you are eligible for one month membership to ForgottenBooks.com, giving you unlimited access to our entire collection of over 700,000 titles via our web site and mobile apps.

To claim your free month visit:
www.forgottenbooks.com/free801137

English
Français
Deutsche
Italiano
Español
Português

www.forgottenbooks.com

Mythology Photography **Fiction**
Fishing Christianity **Art** Cooking
Essays Buddhism Freemasonry
Medicine **Biology** Music **Ancient
Egypt** Evolution Carpentry Physics
Dance Geology **Mathematics** Fitness
Shakespeare **Folklore** Yoga Marketing
Confidence Immortality Biographies
Poetry **Psychology** Witchcraft
Electronics Chemistry History **Law**
Accounting **Philosophy** Anthropology
Alchemy Drama Quantum Mechanics
Atheism Sexual Health **Ancient History**
Entrepreneurship Languages Sport
Paleontology Needlework Islam
Metaphysics Investment Archaeology
Parenting Statistics Criminology
Motivational

Books by LeGette Blythe

CALL DOWN THE STORM

LeGette Blythe

HENRY HOLT AND COMPANY

NEW YORK

For Will and Nancy

HOLLY GROVE

Out of the corner of his eye he must have been seeing all along the rectangle of lamplight on the carriage-house wall. But in the ferment of his thoughts he had been unmindful of it.

He sprawled in Alexander Cardell's battered heavy armchair, his heels hooked on the railing of the front verandah's iron balusters, his lank frame outwardly as relaxed as the moonlight-flooded evening, his stomach burdened with Sarah's excellent supper.

If only Alexander Cardell could be sitting in his chair this calm night, the turmoil in his son's mind would fade out as quickly as the rasping shrill call of that male cicada in the towering water oak near the road.

Claiborne Cardell loved the song of the cicada. Like the gentle, sad call of the mourning dove from the deep woods, it was a sure sign that the heavy stillness of summer had come. Somewhere he had read that the harshly grating cadence of this blatant insect was his way of attempting to attract the attention of female admirers, and that the crescendo of notes was produced by vibrating membranes of certain sound organs on the underside of his stomach. The Negroes called them July-flies or dry-flies. "When hit gits hot and dry, dem flies starts rubbin' dey laigs together and makin' dat pow'ful fuss, Marse Claib," many a black had assured him during his childhood at Holly Grove. "Dey's callin' fer rain." It was the same sign, they said, when they heard the plaintive distant cooing of the mourning dove or the *keow-keow-keow* of the shy yellow-billed cuckoo, which they called the rain crow. "Ol' rain crow's th'oat's dry," they would announce solemnly. "He beggin' fer water."

If his father were living, Claiborne would not have to concern himself with the problems of the plantation. He could devote his energies to building up a medical practice, and to a more concentrated courtship of Melissa Osborne.

Vividly now he recalled the morning in '61 when his father rode off to war. He was nine and Violet was almost twelve. Eph, Uncle Stephen's son, who would accompany his father as body servant, had saddled the horses for the ride to Charlotte, where Alex Cardell would join his Mecklenburg regiment.

Never would Claiborne forget the moment he had come upon his father and mother in the hallway at the foot of the circular stairway. They were standing in silent embrace, holding each other closely, his mother smiling up into his father's face. And then his father had pinched her chin playfully and, leaning down, had kissed slowly each closed moist eyelid. "Good-by, Sweet," he had said, and released her quickly. On the verandah he had bent down to kiss his son and daughter and gently tweak their cheeks. Then he had pulled his wife's ear, given her a last quick kiss, and run down the steps. At the bending of the road two hundred yards south, he had turned in his saddle and waved and thrown them kisses. Nor could the son ever forget how at the instant the big woods had swallowed Eph and her husband, his mother had rushed, eyes streaming, into the parlor to fling herself upon her knees before the sofa, arms outstretched upon it, face pressed into a cushion, hands clenched and knuckles white, to sob out her desperate questioning: "Why, O God, did it have to be? Why couldn't they give us time to solve our problem, *our* problem, O God? Why? Why?"

Four years later Major Alexander Cardell had come riding home. But not astride the spirited roan mare nor at the reins behind the bays in his Rock Hill buggy. Well he remembered his father's homecoming. He and one of Eph's boys had been throwing rocks at a wasps' nest above the cream-bricked heart decoration centering the south end of the red-brick mansion when all of a sudden the sharp-eyed little colored fellow had seen the horse and the two men emerging from the woods bordering the road toward Hortonsville.

"Hit's my pappy, and yo'n, Claib! Hit's my pappy!"

They had raced screaming down the sandy road. And when they were still a hundred yards away he had seen his father's empty left sleeve, as he sat hunched forward on the poorest horse the boy had ever imagined, being led slowly along by an Eph so gaunt and ashen-faced and tattered that he hardly recognized him.

His father's life several times during the next few weeks had been despaired of; only his determination to live, old Dr. Mac told them afterward, had pulled the major through, and it was fall before he had recovered sufficiently to undertake the task of shaping even a bare existence for his beloved Holly Grove and its dependents. Nor did he ever overcome entirely the ravages of that spell of typhoid fever following four years of war's hardships, the kindly physician explained; but his family knew that it was the horror and heartbreak and hopelessness of the Reconstruction, more than the war and the fever, that had taken him off five years after Appomattox.

And three years later, the major's widow, unable longer to endure the weight of her accumulating burdens, had been laid beside him in the graveyard of Bethel Church. Violet had written to him in Philadelphia that their mother had succumbed to a short spell of illness following a stroke, but he had known that actually it was her distress over the woes of her suffering land added to her personal grief that had killed her. The funeral had been delayed so that he could get home for it, but it was his last year of medical school and he had been forced to hurry back to Philadelphia. There had been little time to talk with Violet about the situation at Holly Grove; actually he had been reluctant to hear about it; not knowing, he could hope at least that it was not as desperate as it had been in those tragic years immediately following the war's end.

Claiborne felt his right leg beginning to cramp; he shook it vigorously and shifted his position. The rectangle of light was bright on the wall of the carriage house, and the silhouetted shape of a woman was moving within it. He was hardly conscious of having noticed.

Less than two weeks ago in Philadelphia he had received a long and urgent letter from his sister. Come home, Claiborne, had been her plea. Holly Grove was in desperate need of a master; she herself was no longer able to see to the plantation's proper management. Unless he came home and took over Holly Grove, soon there might be no Holly Grove to take over.

Sitting in the light of the full moon, his feet propped on the balustrade's railing, he recalled Violet's enumeration of the mounting woes of their home place, which were but a localization, he suspected, of the troubles of Mecklenburg County and North Carolina and the destitute and despoiled Confederacy.

Much of what she reported he had known, because he had not left home until after his father's death midway of that tragic decade, but in her bitterness and fright she had recapitulated the wrongs endured, the sufferings and humiliations experienced since General Lee's surrender.

The full moon bathing the ancient bricks and the trees and fields of Holly Grove, the symphony of the cicadas and the crickets and the katydids should provide a respite from tonight's heavy thoughts. Tomorrow he would begin his examination of the problems of Holly Grove. After all, he had been home less than a week. Tonight he would leave those problems in Violet's letter on top of his bureau upstairs.

She hadn't been entirely pessimistic anyway. Times have begun to get better, she admitted. The Democrats have nominated our wonderful Zeb Vance for governor again and it does look like he has a good chance of beating the Republicans' Tom Settle in the November election; the white taxpaying citizens have voting privileges once more and are about to wrest political control from the shiftless freed Negroes and the sorry whites. And

Charlotte is certainly growing; there's talk of getting some cotton mills started.

And she would give up her position in Charlotte, where she had been teaching children of several of the old families, and come back to keep house for him. There were no carpetbaggers' brats sitting at her feet, she assured him, and he smiled as he envisioned her stamping her foot as she wrote that line.

But perhaps he was planning to marry Melissa Osborne and make her mistress of Holly Grove. If you do, Claiborne, that will be fine. I won't interfere, though I'll expect my share of the revenue from the plantation, if there's ever to be any revenue again. And until you do marry Melissa, Claiborne, you can have a cook and housekeeper, if you'd prefer it that way.

In fact, she had written him, she had arranged for the cook and housekeeper. The week before she had been out at Fair Meadows and talked with Eliza Allison about it. Eliza had told her about Sarah Gordon. Sarah was unmarried, had no children, and was a good cook; Eliza would vouch for her. And Sarah could live in the kitchen cottage. She was also a good housekeeper, and intelligent; doubtless she could keep up with the calls he got while he was away on other calls.

So Claiborne Cardell at twenty-four had come home. He had planned to return to Holly Grove in the early fall, when he would have completed his training. Two months less of residency in the University Hospital would make little difference in treating patients in North Carolina.

Between trams in Charlotte the other day he had talked with Violet a few minutes before he boarded the Atlantic, Tennessee, and Ohio coach for the seventeen-mile trip to Cardell Station; there he had borrowed a neighbor's horse for the short ride out to Holly Grove. One of the Negroes had returned the horse when he went over in the wagon for the doctor's trunk. Claiborne smiled at the pretentiousness of the little railroad's name. The area was fortunate though in having it restored to service; during the war its rails had been removed for use on a more vital line.

As he shifted his weight once more, his glance embraced for a moment the splotch of lamplight and the sharply outlined moving shadow of the woman. He jerked his feet from the railing and sat upright, his eyes fastened on the silhouette moving in and out of the light.

"Damn! She's naked as a jaybird! She's taking a bath!"

He leaned forward, his hands grasping the balustrade railing, and studied the moving shadow. The outline of her body, enlarged and at times grotesquely elongated as she bent over to scrub herself, was sharp and clear. Tomorrow he would tell her before she stripped off like that to pull her curtains together or turn down her lamp; people coming along the road might see her.

He walked to the end of the verandah from which he could look at her lighted window. But he was not able to see the woman. The kitchen cottage was to the rear of the mansion house and out to the left as one faced it. Her lamp must have been on her bureau against the wall toward him, and she stood bathing in a line between the lamp and the carriage house. But from the road most likely she could be seen.

From steps at that end of the verandah a path went through shoulder-high boxwood to the small front porch of the kitchen cottage. Just off the path not far from the lighted window a luxuriant English myrtle stood within the thick shadow of a large magnolia, screening the darkened pathway from the light streaming from the woman's bedroom.

He walked down the steps and along the path toward the protection of the myrtle. As he reached it he stepped on dried magnolia leaves and they crackled. He stood rigid.

But after a moment he ventured to peep between thick branches that noiselessly he had pulled apart. If the woman had heard, she gave no indication. She was standing to the right of the window, her left side and back toward it, so that the light from the lamp completely revealed her. Its soft warmth glowed in the drops of water clinging to her tapered shoulders and firm, rounded hips.

"Damn!" The expletive almost escaped him, and he was hardly twenty feet from the window. "You can hardly tell she's a nigger!"

The tin basin from which the woman was bathing was on the chair beside her. She dipped the washcloth into the water, squeezed it, and bending forward, legs apart, scrubbed her knees and lower legs; she lifted one foot, and then the other, to the chair and washed each carefully. When she finished her feet, she dropped the cloth into the basin and disappeared beyond the rectangle of the window.

He was about to turn away when she reappeared in front of the window and began vigorously to dry her body with the towel she had stepped aside to get. Her back was toward him; as she toweled herself he studied the contrast of the very light chocolate color of her neck, arms and lower legs with the rich-cream velvet smoothness of her body from shoulders to knees. He had seen many a tenant farmer's wife whose face and arms after a summer in the fields were as dark as Sarah's, and no doubt her unexposed parts were little lighter. Sarah was no darker than that Moroccan woman he had picked up at the Centennial Exposition a week or so before he left Philadelphia. What the hell, maybe the Moroccan was a nigger, too. Many mulattoes went north and called themselves Spanish or Portuguese or Algerian to cross the color line.

He stood behind the English myrtle in the deep shadow of the magnolia and watched as the woman methodically dried every inch of the firm, now glowing, light bronze of her body. Then she dropped the towel across the back of the chair and stepped quickly toward the bureau and out of his sight. But almost within the instant she was back and facing him, in her hand a shaker of talcum with which she began to powder herself. When she had sprinkled the powder liberally, she started rubbing it in, gently but firmly, until she had sheathed her body from forehead to toes in its clinging white softness. Then she stood back from the bureau and looked into the mirror as she began to comb her hair.

15

Long straight hair, he realized. He hadn't been observing her hair particularly. Nor had he given especial attention to it during the short time she had been at Holly Grove. He had hardly noticed her, in fact; he had been away much of the time. But now he was amazed at the length and straightness of the black hair that fell below her shoulders. No nigger hair. Not a kink. Old man Gordon's hair. And almost old man Gordon's skin. More Gordon by one hell of a sight than nigger.

When she appeared satisfied with her hair, she put the comb down and stepped back from the bureau, so that now the light flooded her. Approvingly, he surmised, she was studying herself in the mirror. Caressingly she ran her hands, fingers spread wide, along her thighs and around the outside of her legs to pat the rounded symmetry of her hips and smooth the almost imperceptible swell of her stomach. Then as she smiled at her image in the mirror, mischievously, he thought, she lifted brown fingers to fondle full firm breasts. A slight stirring of air brought to him a heady scent of the talcum.

Now she stepped to the bed, one corner of which was in the lighted area he was able to see, and picked up her white nightgown. As it dropped over her upthrust arms and head and fell into place, he saw that it was of a thinness that revealed her clearly even in the not-too searching light of the lamp. When she had tied in a loose bow the narrow ribbon threading the lace at the low neck, she observed herself again a moment. Then she walked to the bureau and, bending over the lamp chimney, blew out the yellow flame.

He heard the bed creak as she lay down. Already he had backed into the pathway and turned toward the cottage. The dead magnolia leaves crackled under his feet, but now he was not concerned. He felt himself moving along weightless, except for the not unpleasant tightening heaviness in his throat; a tingling, prickling sensation was mounting upward from the tips of his fingers. That night he had picked up the Moroccan woman he had felt the same upsurgings as he was letting her into the apartment and bolting the door behind them.

16

But within a step of where the bright moonlight broke around the magnolia to flood the path, he stopped precipitately.

What the hell! But he had not spoken the words aloud. Getting all stirred up over seeing a naked woman! And a nigger woman, at that.

Hadn't he seen scores, hundreds, of women in various stages of nakedness? In heaven's name, what could a woman have, any woman, that he didn't know more about than even she herself? That first year in med school at Penn hadn't he dissected a woman, a beautiful young white woman—the cadaver was that of a Philadelphia prostitute, they said—down to a pile of boiled bones and buckets of bloody hacked bits of skin and flesh?

Claiborne turned abruptly, went back up the pathway, and mounted the steps to the verandah. But he did not sit again in his father's chair. He crossed to the front door, entered the hall, and climbed the circling stairs. In his room he turned up the lamp on the bureau, picked up Violet's letter, slipped the sheets from the envelope, and scanned the second page; in putting the letter back into the envelope after he had read it in Philadelphia, he had got the second page on top.

"—of our Negro families have moved away, some through the beguilement of scoundrels in the Freedmen's Bureau, others driven through fear of mean Negroes led on by agitators from up North who seek the political and economic destruction of the Southern aristocracy. Some moved here to Charlotte to get jobs, thinking they could get along better than they could on the farm. Eph took his family and moved away; I wonder what poor Father would think of his faithful bodyguard if he could know that Eph had deserted Holly Grove. But they are children, Claiborne, as you well know; without a white man's leadership they won't be able much longer to make a living farming, and more and more they will be drifting away to the towns to find work."

He scanned the next sheet hurriedly.

"You remember how things were after the war, Claiborne, and while you were at Davidson College. You remember the humiliation we were forced to undergo, and the poverty,

17

the times we were actually hungry, the disfranchisement of the white citizenship and the enthronement of carpetbaggers and mean Negroes. You remember the Federal troops stationed in Charlotte, and how some of them instead of supporting order and providing protection went out of their way to insult and bedevil us, and thieved and pillaged. You remember how they stole horses from the plantation owners and put the vagrant Negroes to stealing and destroying and humiliating us; you remember how in Charlotte these freed blacks, some of them, would shove white women off the sidewalks and go unpunished by the Federal authorities. You remember, Claiborne—"

You remember, you remember. Of course. Who ever could forget? But what virtue is there in remembering? Hell, Violet, doesn't it just build up and build up and build up inside of you a hate that must some day burst? And in bursting, won't it destroy you?

Yes, Violet, I remember. I shall remember to my dying day, and I fear I will transmit in my blood and very bones a remembering that will live through my grandchildren's children. I wish I could forget, but I can never forget things burned into my soul. But I also remember the people in Philadelphia who knew nothing of what was going on in the South after the war had ended; they did not countenance those terrible things, Violet; they didn't know. And all over the North they didn't know and had they known, they would never have permitted such outrages upon defenseless people who are of the same blood and bone and mind and heart that they themselves are. I lived in Philadelphia, and I remember this, Violet. I remember this, too. And I'm no less loyal a Southerner in remembering.

He stuck the sheets back into the envelope, tossed it on the bureau top, and sat down on the side of the bed. He bent down, untied his shoes and pulled them off, and the socks, which he flung across the shoes. Then he stood up, unknotted his cravat, slipped the collar free of the buttons which held it to the neckband of the shirt, front and back. One of the collar buttons slipped from his grasp; he heard it hit the floor. But he didn't search for it; Sarah would find it in the morning when she swept. With his thumbs hooked in his suspenders, he slipped them off his shoulders, dropped his trousers, stepped from them, and tossed them over the chair back. Quickly he peeled off his undershirt, and unbuttoning his drawers, let them fall to the floor; he threw them on top of the undershirt and trousers.

But he did not walk over and open the closet door; it was too damnably warm for that long nightshirt. In front of the open window he raised himself on the balls of his feet and thrust his arms straight above his head in a long stretch. Then he blew out the light.

The sheet under him was crisp and faultlessly smooth. The top sheet had been folded at the foot, and he kicked it farther down so that not a thread would cover him. Eliza Allison had been right about Sarah. The meals she had prepared had been well cooked and properly served, and already in the short time she had been there she had transformed the appearance of the house inside.

He wondered if she were as efficient a bedfellow as she was a bedmaker.

Bob Allison knew, Claiborne would be willing to swear. And Jim, too, likely. Bob and his bachelor brother, it was generally talked, had been known to quarrel over nigger wenches at Fair Meadows, even black ones.

"What the hell's the difference in women anyway, in the dark?" Bob had asked the question, they said, one day at Bub Barkley's store when a group of loafers there were discussing nigger-wenching. "Don't they all have more or less the same equipment?"

Eliza suspected it, too, he was sure. She was bound to have known what the neighbors for years had been saying about her husband and her brother-in-law. "Hell"—the sudden thought amused him—"maybe Eliza caught old Bob with her." At any rate, the other day at Fair Meadows Eliza quite frankly had asked him to take the woman. It was the day after he got home, and he had gone over to the Allisons' to see if the offer as reported in Violet's letter was still good. Eliza had assured him it was, that she would be happy to let him employ Sarah.

"It's not because she isn't a good servant that I don't want to keep her, Claiborne," Eliza had said. "She's a wonderful cook, as I think Violet wrote you, and just as good a housekeeper. I'll have to confess that she could probably run Fair Meadows just as well as I. And she isn't uppity. She knows her place. I'm quite fond of Sarah." For a moment her face had clouded. "But you need her, and it would be better for us all if you took her over to Holly Grove. You see, Claiborne"—she had hesitated—"Father gave her to me when she was born, to be my body servant. I was then six or seven. Her mother, who died when Sarah was three or four years old, was the child of a nigra mother and a Catawba Indian from up around York. Father had bought the woman a year or so before Sarah was born."

She had paused again, the better to choose her words, he had thought. "Uncle Ben lived with us. Like Jim, he was a bachelor. Claiborne, I feel a certain responsibility for Sarah; I wouldn't want anything to happen to her like the thing that happened to her mother. I don't know it for sure, Claiborne, but I'm pretty certain that Sarah is my first cousin, or maybe even my half sister."

"And you are confident that she would be safer at Holly Grove?" He had smiled as he asked.

"Perhaps there *is* little difference in men." Her tone had been matter of fact. "But at Holly Grove she would not be on *my* conscience."

Claiborne stretched his legs along the wilting sheet and listened to the incessant small din of the insects which seemed to heighten the loneliness engulfing Holly Grove. He watched the parallelogram of moonlight dropping almost imperceptibly down the hallway door, inching toward him along the foot of the bed. Once again he was in the shadows, looking into a creeping panel of light as a few minutes ago from behind the English myrtle he had been looking through a bedroom window at a woman bathing.

He closed his eyes against the invading moonlight and his mind against problems sectional and personal, and he brought his eyes mentally to focus on the picture he had seen through the uncurtained window. Unrestrained, they traveled up and down the woman's body, examining, lingering here and there to explore and fancy, imagining, feeling, tasting.

All men perhaps are alike, Eliza had said, meaning alike when it came to women. She suspected Bob, and Jim, if indeed she hadn't caught one or the other or both of them with Sarah, and she took it for granted that the situation would be unchanged when the quadroon moved to Holly Grove. But on the Cardell plantation Sarah no longer would be Eliza's responsibility. Eliza would be washing her hands of her first cousin, her half sister more probably. For years he had heard stories of how old Colonel Gordon at the slave market in Charleston had ogled and pinched and felt young gingercake-colored wenches before making his purchases.

. sure. Old man Gordon's hair. With help maybe from her Indian grandfather. Hell, she isn't but a fourth nigger anyway. One-fourth nigger, one-fourth Indian, one-half old Colonel Gordon. . . .

His eyes clamped shut to envision more clearly the picture. Again he saw her standing before the mirror combing her long black hair, the light olive of her shapely body warmed and softened by the lamp's mellowing flame. Again he felt the tingling, racing now upward from his toes, inward from his fingertips. Once more, as it had out there on the box-bordered pathway to the kitchen cottage, his throat was tightening. He sat up, his eyes wide; the moonlight had crept up to engulf his feet.

He could go to the back window and call her; she'd hardly be asleep. He could ask her to bring him a glass of milk and a piece of that apple pie from supper. If anybody heard, what of it? But nobody would hear. Charlie Gunn's gone back to his father's in Cabarrus for a day or two, and old Uncle Stephen and Aunt Ca'line have been asleep in their cabin for hours and they're half deaf besides. The nearest other nigger shack is a quarter of a mile away, on the other side of the woods beyond the stables.

The tingling, prickling sensation had become a surge of hot blood, pounding, demanding. He twisted around and put his feet to the floor.

The rapping on his room door was subdued, hesitant.

"Doct' Claib," her voice was low and the tone apologetic, "awhile ago before you blew it out I saw your lamp turned up, and I thought maybe you were feelin' bad, sorter sicklike, and needed somethin'."

Quickly he lifted his feet to the bed; reaching down, he pulled the sheet up past his waist. Then he lay back on his pillow.

"Come in, Sarah," he called out. "I do need something."

2

She had picked up the lamp from the kitchen table and carried it into her bedroom, set it on the corner of the bureau. Then she walked out to the porch and dropped wearily into the straight-back rocker in front of the window.

It was a relief to get out of that steaming kitchen. She would sit a moment and catch a breath of air while the water for her bath was heating in the kettle. She wouldn't need to have the water very hot, just warm enough to keep off the chill, and in a few minutes it would be ready. She was sweaty and smelly from a hard day of cooking and cleaning the big house and just now finishing the supper dishes; the bath would refresh her.

Above the carriage house she saw the full moon floating cool-white beyond the black-green of the hollies and the elms and the thick magnolia guarding the path that curved from the verandah of Dr. Claib's house to her front steps. It looked down imperturbably on Holly Grove's loneliness and was reflected muddily in the carriage house's rusting sheet-iron roof. On the near wall, protected from the moon, the woman's shadow thrown by the lamp on the bureau rocked gently in the rectangle of light from her window. Were Dr. Claib sitting in the arm-chair at the end of the verandah, the novel thought suddenly came to her, he would be able to see the moving silhouette.

But he wasn't sitting there. He was upstairs in his bedroom, likely reading in one of those thick doctor books. Yesterday he had been away on a call and while cleaning his room she had peeked into two or three of them. The reading was hard, harder even than the Shakespeare book Eliza had given her, with all those long doctor words. Some of the pictures were frightening, those showing how to cut off arms and legs, and she had turned the pages quickly. But other pictures she had discovered, too, and this morning she had got down that big book and looked at them again. She wouldn't want the doctor to catch her look-ing at those pictures.

I'd rather, she thought, catch him looking at me. Bob Allison wasn't long seeing me around. And Jim. And they had to be careful because of Eliza. But here he's the only man and I'm the only woman. That Charlie Gunn's not even here tonight. And those niggers on the place are already sprawled out asleep in their shacks, their mouths wide open to the flies and the mos-quitoes, or laying up with their stinking women. Nobody here but just him and me.

A shadow crossed his lighted window, and then the light dimmed.

. . . he's going to bed. But why didn't he blow out his lamp? He told me to save every drop of oil I could. If he burns his lamp all night, even turned down low, it will take a lot of oil. . . .

She heard a door opened, and then it was closed, and along the upstairs hall someone was walking. She listened intently; the steps, she was sure, were descending the stairway. An excited, sudden eagerness seized her.

. . . he must be coming out here. But I've never seen him looking at me; not the way the Allisons looked when I was around and Miss Eliza wasn't. And maybe he's only coming to the back door to call for me to take him something to eat. But if he does come, he'll have to wait until I take my bath. . .

But he didn't come to the back hallway door, and presently she heard the front door open and close, and a chair at the end of the verandah being dragged across the floor. It creaked as he sat down, and he cleared his throat.

He had come down to catch a stirring of night air, she reasoned. He would sit awhile and watch the moon and listen to the crickets and the katydids. He hadn't given her a thought.

The water must be hot enough by now. She stood up, and with her, the shadow on the carriage house. She held out an arm; on the wall a shadowy arm moved with hers.

. . . damn him, he will give me a thought! He'll be sitting there looking at the moon, and he'll notice my shadow. And this time, he'll notice me. . .

She went into the kitchen, poured steaming water from the kettle into the wash basin, and tempered it with water from the wooden bucket on the shelf beside the door. Then she carried the basin into the bedroom and set it on a chair.

. here's the place to stand. . . .

Hurriedly she began taking her clothes off.

. . . he'll be able to tell by the shadow on the wall that I'm bathing. Then he'll want to see more. So he'll slip down the path. And I'll hear him. He'll step on a dead stick or something. And after he's peeped awhile, he'll come on in.

She stood naked beside the chair, and a toying, vagrant stir of air touched her teasingly; the image she had conjured of the white man spying upon her from the darkness added a strange exhilaration. She picked up the washcloth, dipped it into the hot water, and soaped it liberally. Then with the lathered cloth she scrubbed her face and arms, chest and stomach, and reaching over her shoulders and under her arms, her back and shoulder blades. She spread her legs apart and soaped her thighs, she turned sideways to the window, her chest thrust forward and head back, and washed again her upper body, this time with cloth squeezed out, and then rinsed away the soap below her waist; the silhouetted pantomime, she was determined, would show clearly that she was bathing.

24

. . . why doesn't he come down the path? He must still be on the verandah; I'd have heard him if he'd pushed back his chair to get up. Maybe he's asleep. Maybe he's already slipped out here without my hearing him and is watching me right now.

She was sure just then that she heard a crackle of dead leaves—crisp, dried, magnolia leaves stepped on—in the path beyond the myrtle bush. A crunching sound, and then silence except for the insects in the trees.

The woman moved a step to the left, so that she would be certain to be seen from the myrtle with the lamplight fully revealing her. But she stood with her left side and back to the window. Deliberately she dipped the washcloth into the water, squeezed it, and bending down, washed her knees and lower legs, and then one foot after the other as she rested it on the edge of the chair.

When she had finished washing she stepped aside for a towel, but momentarily was back in front of the window, her side to it as she dried her body with vigorous rubbing.

by now Bob Allison would have been in here. .

Without hesitation she turned to face the window, with the lamplight upon her, and began to dust herself with the talcum. The powdering from face to feet completed, she reached for a comb and stroked into lustrous smoothness her straight black hair. Then she stood back and appraised herself in the mirror.

why doesn't he come? .

From the foot of the bed she picked up the thin white nightgown, the little-used one that Eliza had given her the day she left Holly Grove, and arms held high, dropped it over her head and shoulders and tied the pale-blue ribbon in a bow.

. . . maybe he went back to the house without my hearing him. Maybe he hasn't even been out there. But I was sure I heard somebody. .

She blew out the lamp and lay down. The bedsprings squeaked, but she lay still. She heard it again, the crunching of footsteps on dry leaves. And the footsteps were coming toward her porch.

Tense, hardly breathing now, her legs thrust out from the pulled-up nightgown, in the room's dim closeness she waited.

But almost at the steps he paused and turned back toward his house. After awhile she heard him crossing the verandah, and then the front door opened; she heard the catch click as it closed.

. damn him, why did he go back? Did he remember that Melissa Osborne, and his conscience get him? It didn't bother him while he was peeping. Did it come to him all of a sudden that he was about to be going to bed with a nigger woman? While he was watching me take a bath I must have looked pretty good to him; he wasn't seeing nigger then. But when I turned out the light I guess he remembered. By hell, in the dark or the light I could make him forget again. Damn him, don't he know I'm more white than nigger? Don't he know me and 'Liza's got the same daddy? And couldn't he see I'm younger and better built than 'Liza? If it'd been Bob Allison out there peeping at me, he'd been in here before I got through drying myself. .

Angered, affronted, her steadily mounting desire the more intensified because of its sudden frustration, she lay sprawled on her back and surrendered herself to a frenzy of voluptuous imaginings.

But the sheet beneath her was warm and moist; she felt the perspiration beading on her flattened stomach under the crumpled nightgown, and it welled out and rolled down her steaming thighs. Back in the bed corner not a stirring of air reached her. And the night's swiftly matured demanding need, denied and even flouted at the threshold of fulfillment, forbade sleep.

She swung her legs around and stood up. The lace hem of the nightgown dropped past her waist to cover her ankles. On the porch it would be cooler; after awhile in the rocker she might be able to attune her senses to the lullaby of the crickets and the katydids and put away for another night her lascivious envisonings. She went outside and sat down.

His bedroom window stood out yellow in the darkened bricks of the big house's rear wall. He hadn't gone to bed yet anyway, she reasoned. Maybe he had sat down to calm himself by reading awhile in one of those doctor books. **Probably's** got on his long-tailed nightshirt, split up each side—she had seen it hanging in the closet—and sitting on the side of the bed.

A shadow across the lighted window momentarily dimmed the yellow glow. Suddenly tensing again, she watched. Then quickly she stepped off the low porch and strode barefooted into the protecting obscurity of the woodshed at the left of her cottage and directly behind his upstairs bedroom. Through the narrow slit between the jamb and the almost closed door she could see now straight into the room.

He was undressing. She stood back in the shadows and watched him remove his cravat and then his shirt. She presumed he hung the shirt on the back of a chair, though she could not see the chair because the line of her vision above the window sill revealed him only from his waist up. She saw him pick up the trousers he had stepped out of; she had a glimpse of them as he dropped them, doubtless across the same chair back. Then he stripped off his undershirt; his white skin, heavily hairy on his chest, shone in the light of the lamp.

Now, she said to herself, he'll be going to the closet for his nightshirt; he'll put it on, and then he'll blow out the lamp.

But he didn't. Instead, he came straight to the window. And standing there, completely revealed to her from his knees up, he lifted his arms above his head in a prolonged stretch. Then he bent down and blew out the light.

Back in the rocker, she kept her eyes on the darker splotch in the wall that a moment before had framed him in its yellow light; a surge of desire renewed swept over her and with tremulous excitement she examined in imagination the lithe white body of the man she had seen standing naked in that lighted rectangle. Maybe, she dared to hope, he was lying up there in the darkness thinking about what he had seen as he peeped from behind the bush into her window.

She could sit no longer. She went into her bedroom and put on the dark wrapper over her nightgown; she slipped her feet

27

into the worn but still frilly bedroom slippers Eliza had given her to go with the sheer nightgown.

The back door of the mansion house was unlocked. She walked boldly in and along the dark hallway to the foot of the stairs which she began noiselessly to climb. At his bedroom door she paused to knock, not too insistently, and as she heard a movement inside, called out to him.

A few minutes ago, she told him, she had seen him turn up his lamp and then pretty soon he blew it out; she wondered if he might be feeling bad, if he might like for her to get him something.

She heard the cords of his bed give as he moved on it. Would he dismiss her petulantly, tell her he wanted only to get to sleep?

Then he answered. "Come in, Sarah, I do need something."

She opened the door and stepped inside.

He was sitting up in bed. A wide swath of bright moonlight from the side window cut across his legs under the sheet. To his waist he had on nothing.

The moonlight likewise revealed her to him, she knew. He was staring at her, lips slightly apart, and then his eyes moved from her head to her feet, and looking down, quickly she pulled her wrapper together over the transparent gown as though inadvertently she had allowed it to fall open. She wondered if he could see that her lips were hot and drying, if he could sense that her whole aching body was struggling to keep from springing with delirious abandon into that widening band of moonlight across his bed. She wondered if she could longer speak matter of factly, as servant to employer, now that her hot blood was racing, pounding.

She ventured to try. "Dr. Claib, if there's anything you want— if I can get you something to eat." But there was no need pretending. She saw that he understood.

"It's nothing to eat I want now." His tone was neither gentle nor callous, and she thought it had a certain highly pitched intensity. Then suddenly he seemed visibly to relax. "Hell, Sarah," he said, laughing, "I'm not going to bite you. Shut the

28

door. Now throw your wrapper over there on the chair, and come sit on the bed beside me."

3

Dr. Cardell hadn't finished his breakfast when the man rode into the yard on a rawboned, foam-lathered horse.

"That fellow must be in a big hurry, Sarah." He peered through the window. "Meet him at the door and tell him to come on in here. He can tell me his trouble while I'm finishing my coffee."

The man was already at the front door when she reached it. "Good mawnin', Ma'am," he said, bowing as nervously he fingered a frayed straw hat. "Is yore husban' in?"

"Doct' Cardell's in the dinin' room. He saw you when you rode up, and he said for you to go right on in there. He's just finishin' his breakfast."

"Thank you, Ma'am; I'm in a right smart hurry to see him."

He followed her as she showed him into the dining room. She continued across the hall into the doctor's office; she foresaw that in a moment he would be calling for his bag.

Dr. Cardell looked up from his plate. "Good morning," he said pleasantly. "What can I do for you?"

"Good mawnin', Doct' Cardell. This here's Babe Atkins from over in the edge o' Cabarrus. I work one o' Colonel Osborne's places. I'll pay you, Doc; I'll be shore to pay you, and the colonel said tell you he'd stand fer it anyhow." He was fumbling with his hat.

"I remember you, Babe. And I'm not worried about the money. But what's your trouble?"

"I didn't think you'd mind me, Doc," he said, flattered. "It's my old 'oman, Doc. She's 'bout to have a young'un, and the old granny what looks after the wimmen in our part o' the country took sick and couldn't come, and I'm 'fraid she's gonna have trouble birthin' it, Doc."

"Is this one her first baby?"

"Oh no, sir. This here'll be—le' me see—hit'll be our seventh chap, I b'lieve."

"You look pretty young to have seven children. How old's the oldest?"

"Le' me see"—his leathery forehead crinkled—"hit's close on to twelve year old, if I rec'lect right." He grinned. "I got married pretty young, Doc, 'fore I had too much sense." Then the grin was gone and his expression was inquisitive. "But I didn't know you was married, Doc. Colonel Osborne didn't say nothin' 'bout you havin' no wife. You ain't been married long, is you?"

Across the hall the listening Sarah heard. She eased into the hall to hear more.

"I'm not married, Babe." Dr. Cardell set down his cup, wiped his lips, folded the napkin, and slid it back into the silver napkin ring.

"But I didn't know you had no sister neither. I knowed yo' pappy when I was a chap, Doc, but I didn't know the rest o' yo' fambly."

Sarah could see that the doctor was a trifle annoyed.

"She isn't my sister, either," he said. "Sarah's my cook and housekeeper."

"Well, I do declare. When I seen her at the door I said to myself, 'this here must be Mis' Cardell.'" His expression betrayed a swiftly mounting curiosity bordering on astonishment. "But you don't mean, Doc, that that 'ere woman"—he lowered his voice as he nodded his head toward the hallway—"is a nigger?"

"Not entirely one," the doctor observed tartly, "as you doubtless saw yourself." He shoved his chair back, stood up. "We'd better be starting for your house, Babe. I don't have any of the hands around this morning. If you'll run out there and hitch up the bays to the buggy while I'm getting my bag and things, we'll get started. The horses are in the stable and the harness and buggy you'll find under the shed. You can tie your horse behind the buggy and ride with me; yours looks pretty well tuckered out." He stepped to the hall door. "Sarah, will you be getting my bag ready, and the instruments? We're in sort of a hurry."

30

When she nodded, he faced the farmer again. "How was your wife doing when you left, Babe? Were her pains getting closer together?"

"Pretty close, Doc. She was gruntin' consid'able. And her water'd done broke."

4

When the two men had driven away in the doctor's buggy she collected the breakfast dishes and carried them out to the kitchen. She ate, washed the dishes, made her bed and swept. Then she went back to the mansion house to put it in order.

Dr. Cardell had told her he probably wouldn't be home until supper time; from Babe Atkins' house he would go on calls that would take the rest of the day, and he might even be after dark getting back to Holly Grove.

... but likely as not as soon as he's fetched that white trash's brat he'll strike out for Colonel Osborne's to see that Melissa. ...

In the parlor she raised the shades and windows and opened the curtains to let in the sunshine and air while she was cleaning. Generations of stern-visaged Cardells from the haughty seclusion of their gold-leaf frames watched her, disapprovingly, she was sure, for she had the feeling that last night they had been peering through their ancestral walls. When she had finished sweeping and dusting, she closed the windows and darkened the room, and moved with her broom and dustpan and waxed cloth out into the hall. Later she would sweep the circular stairway from the third-floor landing downward and at the foot catch the accumulated debris in the dustpan.

Returning to the dining room, she brushed the table clear of crumbs, laid out clean silver, straightened the rolled napkin in the ring beside his place, swept the floor and dusted the chairs, the sideboard and the outside of the china closet. Then she removed the wilting flowers from the vases; she would replace them with fresh zinnias and bachelor's-buttons from the garden at the north end of the house.

With the exception of his own, the upstairs bedrooms had not

31

been disturbed. She would clean his room before starting on the upstairs hall and stairway.

She knew that the bottom sheet would have to be changed, though she had slipped from his bed before daylight. She had feared that one of the Negro hands would be coming to the house early, and even Charlie Gunn might get back before sunrise; it wouldn't do to be caught in the mansion house, or leaving it, with nothing on but a nightgown and wrapper.

A renewed excitement, a certain elation possessed her as she examined the sheet. Then she stripped the two sheets off and dropped them to the floor. He wouldn't see the offending sheet again until it was clean and crisp. She would take them out to the kitchen, wash and starch them and hang them on the line to dry. Before he got home she would iron them and put them away in the linen closet.

She struggled with the heavy mattress until she had turned it. Then from the hall closet she brought fresh sheets and a counterpane and made the bed.

. . his bed will be as clean and inviting tonight as it was when he lay down last night. And I will, too. I'll get my bath before he comes home. All he'll have to do tonight is to come to his back window and call. If he wants me; if today he hasn't got stuck on that Melissa. . . .

As she was straightening the scarf and brushing off the bureau top she saw the letter from Violet. She picked it up, held it a moment, debating, and then she pulled out the sheets and began to read them.

"But perhaps you are planning soon to marry Melissa Osborne and make her mistress of Holly Grove." Her eyes narrowed, her forehead crinkled. "If you do, Claiborne, that will be fine." She read on. "—until you do marry Melissa, Claiborne, you can have a cook and housekeeper. Last week I was out at Fair Meadows and Eliza told me about Sarah Gordon. Sarah is unmarried and has no children"—Sarah frowned—"and Eliza says she is a good cook and an excellent housekeeper. Eliza says she's an intelligent Negro; she would be able to keep up with calls you'd have

32

while you were away from home. Claiborne, she could live in the kitchen cottage; she could stay with you until you married Melissa, and then it would be up to her whether Sarah stayed on or left. I think it would be a good arrangement, for the time being, anyway."

She replaced the sheets in the envelope and threw it down on the bureau. She bundled up the bedclothes and took them out to her house; she filled the kettle and replenished the fire. With only two sheets to do, there'd be no need for using the iron pot in the yard.

. it would be up to her whether I stayed or not. Well, she'd send me kitin'. Claib wouldn't be able to keep it from her any more than Bob was able to keep it from 'Liza. Wonder if she knows that my skin's damn nigh white as hers and my hair's as straight. What if that white trash Babe Atkins hints things to Colonel Osborne? What if Charlie Gunn starts carrying stories over there . . . ?

She slid open the kettle top, with middle finger tested the water. In nother minute or two it would be hot enough. She reached for the dish of lye soap on the shelf beside the wooden water bucket.

. . . to hell with Melissa Osborne. She hasn't got him yet. And maybe she won't get him. What has that bitch got that I haven't got? She can't cook any better, she can't keep house any better. And I'm damned sure she ain't as good in bed with him. She can call her daddy's name, but hers is no whiter than mine, and he's not near as rich. . .

She lifted the steaming kettle from the fire and poured a stream of boiling water on the hunk of soft soap in the tub of crumpled bedclothes. The strong alkaline odor of the soap enveloped her.

let that clodhopper Atkins go to Colonel Osborne with his grinning and hinting. And what if Charlie Gunn should see me early of a morning leaving the big house in my nightgown? Hell fire, let 'em! It'll get to Melissa, and likely she's proud and stubborn and bossy, and she'll give Claib hell, and maybe he'll be just as stubborn. .

Furiously she grasped the sheet and with clenched brown fists began to scrub it, one fistful against the other. In the hot water around the edges of her closed hands the palms peered out deeply pink.

5

Melissa stood back from the marble-topped walnut bureau and calmly inspected the image in her mirror. The perfection of her figure, she saw pleasurably, was revealed in the faithfulness with which her new princesse gown clung to it. From swelling bosom past hourglass waist over symmetrical rounded hips it fell in not too-full lines to the floor.

A deft brush of her palms smoothed the reddish-brown hair parted carefully in the middle and a swift twirling of thumb and forefinger adjusted a recalcitrant curl behind her right ear.

Turning sideways to the mirror, she twisted her head to appraise herself from that angle. The forward thrust of her bosom was emphasized more when seen from the side, she realized, because of the rearward pull of the bustle and the bowknot on the hipline.

The bustle, Melissa thought mischievously, must have been invented by a woman whose behind was either too big or too little. How in the world would a man ever be able to know, until she took it off, where her behind ended and the bustle began? A bustle, she would insist, was more deceiving even than the bosom pad.

She smiled into her mirror, pleased at the naughtiness of her reasoning, but pleased all the more in the assurance that nature had so endowed her that she would need to practice deception neither in front nor behind.

Facing the mirror again, she studied with concentration the deep V-cleft of rounded white bosom centering the new-style, square décolletage that left her neck and much of her shoulders bare.

How can I, she wondered, wear the neck low enough to excite Claiborne without at the same time irritating Papa? If I wear it this way Papa will surely think that I am shamelessly flaunting myself, which I most assuredly will be. Right before Claiborne he might even suggest that I go to my room and fix it; he still thinks I'm a child, even if I have finished Salem College.

But she smiled nevertheless at what she saw in the mirror. And then a sudden dreadful thought possessed her: maybe it won't stir Claiborne any if I do wear it low like this. He's probably used to seeing those Philadelphia girls showing their bosoms. He may not even notice that this gown is stylish, that it would be stylish even in Philadelphia. Certainly he won't appreciate what effort it has required in times like these to find the material and have it made into such a dress as this.

Melissa was pleased that the material of the princesse and the grenadine of the overskirt complemented each other happily. She examined with mounting pleasure the workmanship; the sewing lady in Charlotte had done excellent work, both in the fitting and the stitching. The dark green of the gown accented the red in her hair, and the pale yellow grenadine with the tiny black-and-white figures, pulled tight to the green silk in front but behind generously fluffed to the floor, contrasted harmoniously with the green; the big bowknot in the grenadine softened the precipitate rounding of the bustle, and the two small bows that bound her hair in the back, fashioned from a bit of the green silk left over, gave just the proper touch.

But she had not been able to manage all the buttons in the back; the silk gaped at her shoulder blades. She would call her mother to finish the buttoning, but first she would pull the dress down a little behind, thereby lifting the venturesome collar an inch in front, and anchor it in safer position with a pin through the corset cover.

That will be Claiborne's chore after we are married, to button and unbutton those pesky, evading, down-the-middle buttons.

He'll pretend to fume, she had no doubt, but he'll like it; particularly the unbuttoning, I hope.

Claiborne had been home for days and days and he hadn't been to see her yet, she pouted into her mirror. Of course he had been busy getting Holly Grove into some semblance of order and doubtless as soon as the word got out that he was at home he had been urged to start making professional calls. His place must be run-down, she reasoned; Charlie Gunn has hardly had time to effect many improvements, because Violet didn't hire him until whatever crops they put in over there were up, and ready, in fact, for the second plowing, Charlie said.

Claiborne had written her just before he left Philadelphia and had said that he wanted to visit her the first opportunity he had. And during the years he was in medical school and interning and working in the hospital he had written intermittently, sometimes in what she had considered impassioned words.

But she hadn't seen him since his mother's funeral three years ago. Maybe they had both just been assuming that some day they would be married to each other; because our families have always been friends we have been expected to marry, she admitted, an old southern custom.

. . . maybe when I see him tonight I'll discover *I* don't want him. Maybe when he sees me, bosom covered or bosom flaunted, *he* may decide he doesn't want me. . . .

She called her mother from the kitchen to do the buttons and once more confronted her mirror. The lifted square neckline was not too low now; even her mother offered no comment about it. And it would not trouble her father. But if after supper, in the parlor with the light turned low to conserve the lamp oil or out on the verandah with the moonlight sifting through the elms, she might stealthily remove the pin, what of it? By then she would have learned more definitely of her feelings toward him and of his toward her. Too, Papa would be in bed.

From a drawer in one of the small stands on the bureau she took a zealously hoarded small vial of French perfume and holding it upside down with the ball of her forefinger to its mouth, she moistened her fingertip and with quick darting motions dabbed it to her hair, the lobes of her ears, and the now less-revealed cleft. Then with a final peek in the mirror, she went out to the porch and sat in a chair from which she had an unobstructed view along the cedar lane from the house down to the big road.

She wondered if Claiborne would stay for supper. All Babe had reported was that after the baby was delivered, the doctor had left to visit a typhoid fever case, saying that before he returned to Holly Grove he would ride over for a visit with the Osbornes. Babe had come to beg an old white shirt or a strip of sheet to make bellybands for the baby. Melissa had heard the tenant telling her mother about the Negro woman he had seen at Holly Grove. "She's so white, Mis' Osborne," Babe had declared, "that I thought Doct' Claib had done got married, and I come mighty nigh callin' her Mis' Cardell."

she's the one Charlie was telling Papa about. Charlie said Claiborne had hired a nigra cook and housekeeper who'd been working at Fair Meadows. But Charlie didn't say she was a white nigra. . . .

6

They sat beside each other on the joggling-board. He slumped his spine against the cool bricks of the wall and pushed his feet out into the dapple of moonlight on the verandah floor.

"It was a wonderful supper your mother set out, and I was hungry. Hadn't eaten since breakfast; don't relish eating in the homes of some of my patients."

"I can see how you wouldn't—especially at Babe's."

"I would have to be mighty hungry to eat at Babe's." Gingerly he patted his stomach. "Gosh, I'm stuffed. I can hardly bend in the middle, I'm so full. Did you cook it, Melissa, or help?"

"I helped some. But Mother planned it and Aunt Nancy did most of the cooking; she's one of the best cooks anywhere around." She paused, and then she was deliberately casual. "Do you have a good cook, Claiborne?"

"Yes, she's all right. I can't complain."

"They say she could easily pass for a white woman."

He sat up. "Who said it—Charlie Gunn?"

"No, it was Babe Atkins; he told Mother that when your cook opened the door he thought she was your wife. But why'd you think Charlie Gunn said it?"

"I didn't know Babe had been over here today. I thought maybe Charlie had been carrying stories from one plantation to another"

"Has he carried any to Holly Grove from here?"

"I don't believe so. But I've hardly seen him; I've been pretty busy with sick people." His tone was quizzical. "Were there any he might have?"

She was not certain whether he was teasing or half-serious. "I don't know any that would have interested you, or"—she added indifferently—"any he could have brought from Holly Grove that would have concerned or interested me."

He shrugged his shoulders, grinned. "Well, you put that pretty plain." He leaned back against the wall.

"The other day Charlie did tell Papa you had a nigra woman cooking for you, but he didn't say she was a white nigra. And he didn't say anything to me about her."

"I wouldn't have expected Charlie Gunn to be talking with you about a nigra woman—or about anything."

"Because he's a tenant?" Her question evidenced irritation.

"I just wouldn't expect you to be having conversations with a fellow like him."

"Charlie's not just another tenant farmer or ordinary overseer. He's ambitious and he's intelligent, and some day he'll amount to something, I can promise you. I wouldn't be surprised if before long you'd be losing him."

"I suspect Holly Grove will get along."

She pursued the subject no further. Nor did she refer again to Claiborne's quadroon cook. They talked awhile about other things, the chances of the Democratic Party's upsetting in November the nauseating rule of the carpetbagger-dominated illiterate blacks and scalawag whites; the great tragedy for the South of Lincoln's assassination; the unconscionable treatment, through the instigation of a few unprincipled northern congressmen, of Jefferson Davis; the kindness and charity of the common man and woman in the North toward the southern people and the willingness to forgive and forget, and the reciprocation in the South of that attitude, and how the northern people, the good people, understood little of the ways in which the bitterly contriving politicians had been taunting and torturing their southern brothers.

They sat and talked, but it was of things impersonal. To Melissa he seemed little interested in talking at all. Had her defense of Charlie Gunn, coupled with her perhaps patently prying references to his cook and her plainly hypocritical profession of lack of interest in the quadroon, served to raise this invisible wall between them? Or had he already begun to lose interest? Could there be a girl in Philadelphia? Whatever the cause, the wall was there, and for her the afternoon's thrill of anticipation was gone, the spell of the before-supper dreaming ended. She did not protest when he said he would have to be going, that he was tired and needed to be getting to bed.

At the door he took her in his arms and kissed her. But he held her lightly and did not linger, and his kiss stirred in her no fires. He waited to descend the stone steps until she had closed the door behind her.

The moon lighted her bedchamber so that she needed no lamp to undress by. She went to the closet, took her gown from the hook, and laid it across the foot of the spool bed. Standing back in the shadows away from the broad beam of moonlight, she took off her clothes. A sudden small stirring of air between the front and side windows refreshed her, and she stood a moment exulting in the sensuous embrace. Then she heard the pounding of his horses' hoofs on the gravel of the driveway, and braving the moonlight, she darted to the window to watch his buggy disappear around the turn of the gate.

. . . after three years of waiting for him to come, and I let him leave this early. But he was tired; he had had a hard day, delivering Babe's baby and treating a lot of patients. He hadn't appreciated Babe's telling about the white nigra cook Eliza had let him have. And heavens, is Claiborne Cardell jealous of Charlie Gunn? But Charlie will amount to something, I'm sure he will. I could have told him that some day Charlie will be making cloth from cotton rather than bossing nigras working it. I could have told him he'd been over to Alamance to see how Mr. Holt's cotton mill operates, and that he brought me enough Alamance plaid to make a dress. But that would only have offended him. It's really none of Claiborne's business whether I talk with Charlie.

. . he'll be back, and he'll want to stay longer. Maybe it was my fault he didn't tonight. I didn't offer him any excitement, I had no fire. Good heavens, I didn't even once think of slipping the pin out. But he probably wouldn't have noticed it tonight if I had slipped my dress off.

She stood naked in front of the window and looked out beyond fields lying silvered in the moonlight and along a twisting dirt road that had swallowed all of him but the waning rhythmical clomp-clomp clomp-clomp of his horses' hoofs.

. . . he was in a hurry to get home and to bed, all right. Yes, damn him, he couldn't wait to get home and to bed with his white-nigra bitch!

Sarah had lighted his bedroom lamp and turned the wick low. Little oil had been consumed, he saw, because the bowl was almost full; the lamp had not been burning long.

He turned it up.

The bed beckoned invitingly; he was tempted to fall across it without undressing.

He was tired to the bone; the day had been a hard one. This long driving over roads of every description, but generally wretched, to treat patients of every class and type, but preponderantly the illiterate and shiftless and penniless recently freed Negroes, was far more exhausting than serving as resident physician in an efficiently operated general hospital.

Nor had the evening at the Osbornes' relaxed him, despite the excellent supper of which he had eaten too much. And the hour after supper with Melissa on the verandah had dragged.

     she must have thought I was a slow one. . .

He had hung his coat on the back of a straight chair. He sat on the side of the bed, took off his shoes and socks, stood up and untied his cravat and unbuttoned and removed his collar.

    . she popped us down on that damnable joggling-board so we'd be close together and I'd love her up. Thinks she's already got the hooks in me. Thinks she can tell me how to run Holly Grove. What business is it of hers if I've got a quadroon for a cook? What business is it of hers what goes on between me and my cook? Even Eliza Allison never had the temerity to tell old Bob what not to do with his nigger wenches; if she did raise hell, he paid her no mind. . . . .

He threw his undershirt on the chair seat and stepped out of his drawers. He walked over to the window, bent down to touch the floor with the ends of his fingers, stood upright, hands straight above his head, and took a long deep breath of the cooling air; slowly he exhaled, and raising himself on the balls of his feet, fingers stiffened, stretched his lean frame. Then he leaned over and blew out the light.

    . . . that damned Charlie Gunn. Could she possibly be interested in that clodhopper? Telling me he's going to be a big man some day, too big for Holly Grove. Let him go. I don't have to have him. And I don't have to have her either. Sarah can look after me. .

He peered out the window. Her house was dark. She's probably been asleep a long time, he thought. She must have worked hard all day; she's bound to be tired.

    . and, man, am I bushed.

Stretched his length on the bed, he blessed her for the clean-smelling, starched sheets. And in two minutes he was snoring.

She watched him doing his exercise. Then suddenly his window was dark. A moment longer she sat looking at the shadowed wall. She stood up, took off the wrapper, and turned toward her bed.

he must be too tired tonight. . . .

7

The next morning, refreshed after a night's sound sleep, he came down to the breakfast awaiting him.

"I could've kept breakfast hot till you were ready to get up," Sarah said. "Thought maybe you'd want to rest a little longer this morning." But she didn't ask why he had been so late getting home.

After he'd had his second cup of coffee he walked down to the stables. Someone had fed the horses; he didn't know whether it was Charlie or one of the Negroes. He hadn't asked Sarah whether she had seen the overseer. "Maybe he's off somewhere planning his cotton mill." Immediately he reproved himself for his unspoken petulance.

He had turned to go back to the house when a small Negro boy came around the corner of the feed house. His friendly black face broke into a broad grin. "Doct' Claib, Unc' Stephen he say will you please sir come down to he house?"

"What's wrong with Uncle Stephen, son? Is he sick?"

"Naw sir, I don't think he much sick. He maybe a little sick."

"Well, listen." He pointed toward the mansion house. "You run up there and tell Sarah to give you my bag, and you bring it down to Uncle Stephen's. I'll go on down there now."

"Yo' doctor-bag, Doct' Claib? That 'ere black doctor-bag?"

"Yes. Tell Sarah to give you my doctor-bag. And hurry."

He walked along the path to the old Negro couple's cabin and stepped up on the small ramshackle porch.

"He right in here, Marse Claib," he heard Aunt Ca'line call out to him. "He settin' up in he ch'ir. Jes' come right in."

Uncle Stephen had on a white, long-sleeved undershirt, and one frayed suspender held up clean work pants. He was bare-footed. As the doctor walked in, the old man gave him an almost toothless grin. "I knowed yo'd come, little Marse. Bless God, I knowed yo'd be here."

Claiborne went up to him, put his palm on the wizened black forehead, under his chin, caught up his wrist. "What's wrong, Uncle Stephen? Where're you hurting?"

The old fellow puckered up his forehead and frowned solemnly. "I ain't 'zackly knows, Marse Claib. I ain't r'ally hurtin', you might say, nowheres. I reck'n I's jes' sick—jes' a sick old man."

The child, beaming with importance, had come in with the doctor's kit. Claiborne opened it. "I'll give you a pill, but there's nothing wrong with you, Uncle Stephen. You got no fever, your pulse is good." He paused. "Stick out your tongue." The old fellow did. "No coating on your tongue." He looked his patient in the eyes. "You're putting on, Uncle Stephen. You're just an old fraud." He affected stern dignity. "You can't fool me, old man. You're playing off sick right here before cotton-picking time so you can get out of work. You're afraid these young niggers will show you up." He sat in the chair Aunt Ca'line had pushed up for him.

Uncle Stephen raised his hand, sat up in the chair, and his white-grizzled black face mirrored painfully injured and calumniated innocence. " 'Fore God, Marse Claib," he protested, "you done 'scused me wrong. I ain't tryin' t'git out o' no pickin' cotton. You fotch any o' them young niggers to the field you wants, and le' me pick agin 'em and if'n I don't put more cotton in my bag than they puts in they bag, then you don't have to pay me for none what I do pick. If'n I don't pick out two hund'ed pound in one day, Marse Claib—"

"No, you're just wanting to lay out this fall, old man—"

Aunt Ca'line, who had been hovering about the little room,

stuck rheumatic twisted fingers beneath her snowy white ker-
chief with which her silvered kinked hair was tightly bound,
and scratched her gnarled cranium.

"You jokin' wit' Stephen, Marse Claib," she said solemnly,
"but you done come pretty close to hit, talkin' 'bout pickin'
cotton."

"What you mean, Aunt Ca'line?"

"Stephen he ain't sick; he skeered. He so skeered he 'most
sick." She marched up to the doctor, whom many a day she had
held on her lap as a nursing infant and for whom her wide
skirts and imperious looks had often provided protection when
his young mother, breathing threats for his having run away,
had come to the cabin to switch him home. "You can't take him,
Missy," Aunt Ca'line would say, her challenging eyes stern, "on-
til you's done cooled off. The chile ain't done nothin' nohow but
come to see Aunt Ca'line to git some cookies. You ain't gonna
lay nair cut on him!"

His mother invariably would be unrelenting for a moment,
and then she would smile, and in the next instant she would
burst out laughing. "I do know, Ca'line," she would say, "you'll
be the ruination of my children!" And she would surrender to
the reaching hand of Aunt Ca'line the freshly broken off peach-
tree switch.

It all came back in a flooding of sweet memories as Aunt
Ca'line strode up and waved her twisted old fingers before his
face in emphatic gesturing. "Yist'day Stephen hear dem young
niggers tellin' Mist' Charlie say 'gin dey gits all de cotton picked
out he gwine run 'way all de old slavery-time niggers on de
place. Dat's all what's wrong wid Stephen; he skeered he gonna
have to leave Holly Grove."

Claiborne confronted the old man. "You heard what Aunt
Ca'line said," he declared sternly. "Is that what's wrong with
you?"

"Dey did say Mist' Charlie he tell he gwine run off all de old'-
uns."

"Aren't you ashamed of yourself, Uncle Stephen?" His tone

44

was scolding. "Don't you know that isn't so? I doubt if Charlie was fool enough to say it, but don't you know that whoever runs you and Aunt Ca'line away from your house here will have to run me away first?"

" 'Fore God, little Marse," the old fellow's eyes were watering and a tear trickled along his cheek. He wiped it away with the back of his hand. " 'Fore God, you is jes' lack yo' daddy, and he was jes' lack his daddy, and dey was de bes' men ever put dey foot to de groun'! But I ain't seen you in a long time, ain't seen you much, Marse Claib, and you been living up dere in Philadelphy wid dem Yankee peoples, and I warn't certain you might not got yo'self changed—"

"But they have good people up there, Uncle Stephen." He was amused. "They're just like us down here—there're good ones and bad ones up there, too."

"I s'pose they is, but seems like they sont a mighty lot o' no-count 'uns down here on us'uns. But you been up dere; you ain't seen how it 'twuz down here, Marse Claib." He shook his head solemnly. "Maybe good thing you ain't; mighta got yo'self kilt if'n you'da been home them times." He nodded his head toward his wife. "Ain't hit so, Ca'line?"

"Might be," she agreed. "Hit was bad times, and dey say it was wo'se some places than hit was 'roun' here." She shook her head sadly. "Free niggers runnin' 'bout de country stealin' de hosses and breakin' in de houses, and de white mens from up nawth puttin' de niggers up to hit." Her scowl was heavy and she gestured with balled fist. "Some o' yo' pa's niggers rid off holle'in' 'bout bein' free, but 'twon't long till some o' dem back mighty nigh starved and beggin' fer somethin' t'eat." Her mood changed suddenly, as she laughed. "Dey told 'bout goin' to Charlotte to see de Bureau mens 'bout gittin' dey forty acres o' land and dey mule—"

"They didn't get the forty acres and the mule, did they?" Claiborne asked, so that he could hear Aunt Ca'line's version of what they did get when they applied to the agent at the Freedmen's Bureau.

"Did dey git hit?" Her expression was dramatically solemn. "Little Marster, dey didn't git nothin', dey didn't, and sarved 'em right. All dey got was tricked outer whatever dey had when dey went dere. Sarved 'em right fer b'lievin' dem lyin' mens."

"Tildy got her fill o' dem lyin' Yankees," Uncle Stephen commandeered his wife's theme. "She was down to de Bureau one day whar she had no business bein' nohow and she got to talkin' wid a man what was hangin' 'round dere—one o' dem cyarpetbagger fellers, I 'spect—and she say she 'bout dyin' to git one mo' sight o' her boy what went off up to Wa'hin'ton right a'ter de war over and she ain't never seed since.

" 'What kind o' lookin' man yo' son be?' the Yankee feller he ax her.

" 'You reck'n you ever seed him, Mister?' Tildy ax him.

" 'I 'spect I did,' de man say. 'I knowed a passel o' colored gent'emens up dere in Wa'hin'ton. What he look lack?'

" 'Cicero he a kinda dark kinky-haid, slue-foot nigger what had on a dark-blue suit what Mr. Bub Barkley's pappy done give him a'ter he 'bout wore hit out.'

" 'I shore done see dat colored gent'eman,' de man he tell Tildy. 'I see him in front of a store one day and he say he shore lack to come home and see his mammy in No'th Ca'lina; if'n he had de money he shore come, but he ain't got de money for de ticket on de cyars.'

Uncle Stephen's old white eyes were rolling as he warmed to his story. He reached over and grasped Claiborne's knee. "And Marse Claib, you know what dat Tildy done do?"

"What'd she do?"

"She told dat cyarpetbagger man do he reck'n he ever see dat Cicero again when he go back to Wa'hin'ton, and de man he say, 'Yes, ma'am, lady, I be shore to see dat colored gent'eman when I goes back and I'm 'spectin' to go back tomorrow or next day.'

"Well, dat Tildy she come home and she didn't tell nobody what she goin' to do, but she had a five-dollar gold piece her old marster give her to save fer her old age and she took'n got hit and took'n it to Charlotte and give hit to de cyarpetbagger man fer to give her Cicero to buy a ticket on de railroad cyars."

"And she hasn't seen Cicero or the man since?" Claiborne laughed

"And her five-dollar gold piece neither." Uncle Stephen rolled his eyes dramatically. "God knows, Marse Claib, she ain't never gonna see dat money no more neither."

"A lot of that kind of stuff went on, I know, Uncle Stephen, but you mustn't blame everybody up north for it. The good people didn't know what was going on down here; they had no way of knowing. It was the sorry politicians and the human buzzards who were trying to enrich themselves; they caused the trouble."

"And the fool niggers who listened to dem 'stead o' they own white folks. But dem niggers is l'arnin' who to listen to, Marse Claib; dey'd better." He slapped his palm against his leg. "Don't, dey git mighty hongry."

The old man, the doctor saw, had entirely forgot his morning's ills, and his spirits had lifted as his story of the carpetbagger sharper had progressed.

"I'd like to stay longer and hear you tell about what went on around here while I was gone, Uncle Stephen," Claiborne told him as he stood up to go, "but I expect Sarah's already got a call waiting for me, some sick people to go to see."

A sudden troubled expression clouded the old Negro's face. "Dat Sarah, Marse Claib—she mighty white. Be keerful, boy, be keerful." And he shook his head sadly.

Sarah did have a message to give him. A man on the way to Hortonsville had stopped by to summon the doctor for a neighbor up beyond Bethel Church whose wife was expecting a baby. Please tell him to go as soon as he can, the man said; he thought the woman's time was getting short.

The messenger's forecast had been accurate; he delivered the baby within less than an hour after his arrival. From there he rode over to Beatty's Ford to visit a patient who was beginning to recuperate from a stubborn case of typhoid fever.

47

He was back at Holly Grove in time for a bath before supper. He ate leisurely, and Sarah had prepared an excellent meal. When he finished, he walked about the place for half an hour to stretch his legs from the day's horseback riding. By the time he got back to the house it was dark, and the moon, now fast retreating from its rounded fullness, had risen. He sat in his father's chair on the verandah, cooling from his walk, until the moon was beginning to peek above the carriage house.

No rectangle of light on the wall, tonight. Sarah must still be in the kitchen; her bedroom was dark, but she surely wouldn't be in bed this early.

He lifted his legs from the balustrade and stood up, stretching. There was an article in one of the medical journals he had brought from Philadelphia that he had been planning to read; he might do it tonight. So he went upstairs, undressed, and lay down on the bed, his head braced on an elbow, to read.

But soon his arm was numb and he sat up, shaking it to restore the circulation, and finished the article. Then he tossed the magazine over on the seat of the chair and leaned over to blow out the light. But he reconsidered and turned the wick lower instead.

He strode over to the window. Sarah's bedroom was lighted. He leaned out his window and called. "Sarah! Could you bring me a glass of milk and a piece of that cake?"

He went back to the bed, stretched his length on it, and pulled up the sheet to his waist.

"Excuse me, Doct' Claib," she said, when she came with the milk and cake and set the tray on the bedstand; "I was undressed when you called me, and I didn't take time to dress before I brought it."

She was wearing the thin nightgown and wrapper.

8

Out of a darkly shadowed bottomless deep Sarah felt her weightless body lifting. As she ascended toward the level of thin light and returning consciousness, instinct, or perhaps caution born of generations of inherited fears, held her silent and tense, awaiting the clearing and focalizing of her senses.

Some noise, maybe a sound for which her subconscious mind had been listening, must have signaled the start of her waking. It was not Dr. Cardell's snoring. Emotionally released and physically spent, he had dropped off quickly to sleep and begun almost immediately to snore, but it had not disturbed her and soon she, too, was asleep.

She was turned slightly on her side, facing him, so that when she ventured to open her eyes she saw him lying stretched out on his back, his long body coolly white in the brightening dawn, the hairy chest lifting and falling in cadence with his rhythmical snoring. Wide-awake now, she lay still, her ears closed to the chattering of the birds and the shrill raspings of the July-flies but listening intently for a recurrence of the sound that must have awakened her.

Presently she heard it, the harsh grating of rusted hinges on a door down at the stables. That was the discordant noise that a moment ago had roused her; she was sure of it. Someone had opened the door, perhaps to the feed house, and gone in, and just now he had come out.

And in another few minutes he'll be coming up to the mansion house to get his orders from Dr. Cardell, she realized suddenly, or he might go by her house first to ask if the doctor had arisen. Either way, if she wasn't careful, he would catch her. And she wasn't ready yet to be caught.

Noiselessly she lifted her feet from the bed, swung them around to the floor, and stood up. Her crumpled, twisted nightgown straightened itself as it fell. She picked up the bedroom slippers under the edge of the bed and grabbed the wrapper from a chair as she scurried from the room.

But the bedroom door closing behind her awakened him, and he heard her padding along the hall and down the stairs. The back door opened, and then he heard a commotion on the

49

back porch. She must have bumped against something, he thought, as he sprang from the bed and ran to the window.

Her shoes and wrapper bundled under an arm, she was bolting toward the kitchen cottage, the lacy tail of her nightgown whipping her knees.

"Must have thought she'd overslept," he conjectured. "Hell, there was no need of her being in such a hurry to get my breakfast."

He was turning away from the window when he happened to glance down toward the stables. In the barnyard, Charlie Gunn, hands on hips and head hunched forward, was staring, mouth open, at the running woman.

9

Dr. Cardell was unfastening the reins when the farmer whose wife he had been treating appeared suddenly in the doorway and held up his hand commandingly.

"Hold on a minute, Doc!" He stepped briskly across the yard. "Doc, I was 'bout not to 'member, and then when it come to me, I says to myself, 'I'll jes' tell Doc 'fore he gets gone.' I thought whilst you're over on this side 'twouldn't be much out'n yo' way to ride by Rock Springs camp meetin' ground and take a look at yo' tent. Camp meetin's startin' in 'bout three weeks and might want to fix up yo' tent 'fore it starts. I was over there t'other day lookin' 'bout mine and I seen yours needed some work done on it mighty bad. Some boards has been pulled off, for firewood, more'n likely, and I've a notion the roof leaks pretty bad, too. Ain't nothin' been done to yo' folk's tent in a long time, since a good while 'fore yo' ma died, I've a notion."

"I'd almost forgot about that tent, Aaron. Haven't been over there since I was a boy. I wouldn't have been much surprised if you'd told me the tent had rotted down."

"Oh, no, Doc, 'tain't that bad. But it do need some fixin' up. Ain't nobody tented in it in a long time, 'ceptin' maybe now and again when some stray folks jes' took up in it, I guess. Miss Vi'let I don't think has been in it in a long time."

Some day, Claiborne resolved lightly, he would try to discover why all these years those little cabins, some of logs and the others of rough, unpainted boards, and clustered about the weather-beaten frame preaching arbor, had been called tents. Perhaps his father would have been able to tell him. But Aaron wouldn't know. He recalled with a tinge of nostalgia early childhood summers at Rock Springs.

"Is camp meèting still running the same way it used to, Aaron—preaching and singing in the morning and after dinner and again after supper, and cooking and eating and swapping lies and drinking a little liquor?"

Aaron's wide grin revealed almost toothless gums. He slapped an overalled hip with the palm of his hand and simultaneously let fly a stream of amber tobacco juice in a quick sideways twist of his head. "Dang my skin, Doc, you do 'member 'bout camp meetin', and that's a fack!" Then quickly his expression was deadly serious; he leaned forward, spoke in lowered tone. "But look here, Doc, ain't you fergittin' the best part o' camp meetin' week ever' year in August—leastways fer the young folks anyhow?"

"Maybe so, Aaron." The doctor lifted the rein over the roan's head. "You wouldn't be referring to horizontal refreshment in the bushes?"

The farmer bent double, slapped his legs, and roared with such sudden vehemence that the horse threatened to bolt. "Law', Doc, I've heared it called many a name"—he straightened up and in an instant he was serious again— "but I ain't never heared it called that before. That must be what they calls it up there in Philadelphy!" Slapping his thighs again, he burst into a paroxysm of guffawing and began jigging. "Doc, dang my skin if'n you ain't learned a heap whilst you was up there, and 'tweren't all 'bout doctorin' neither." He straightened again, calmed. "But it's a fack, Doc. I'll bet you a lot o' folks can mind more 'bout such doin's than they does 'bout the preachin', and I ain't meanin' no disrespeck to the preachers; they bound to done a lot o' good. But the way I figure it, Doc, they's more little bastards been got in them bushes 'round Rock Springs meetin' ground, and not more'n a couple hund'ed yards from the arbor, too, than has been got in all the rest o' the surrounding country put together."

Aaron paused, obviously impressed with the accuracy and importance of his observation. "And meanin' no disrespeck, Doc, but they's been a lot o' young'uns got at camp meetin' in them there tents, got lawful, I mean. You take me, Doc; I was borned in May. I al'ays figured after I got old enough to do such figurin' that my Paw musta got me on a August night after preachin' at the arbor had let out."

"A pretty sound deduction, Aaron," the doctor agreed, amused. He lifted a foot to the stirrup, swung into the saddle. "I've got to be going. Look after your wife; she's a pretty sick woman, Aaron. I'll be back to see her pretty soon."

"I'll do it, Doc. I wouldn't want nothin' to happen to my old 'oman. If'n anything happened to her, I jes' don't know what me and the chaps would do." He reached out, caught the horse's bridle. "Jes' one more minute, Doc. Meanin' no disrespeck, but you ought to git yo'self a wife and do yo' honeymoonin' at camp meetin'. And speakin' o' chaps, if'n you soon don't git married, Doc, when you do start to gittin' 'em, you'll be old enough to be they granddaddy 'stead 'o they daddy." His wizened, leathery face was solemnly inquisitive. "I sorter thought that one o' them Yankee gals in Philadelphy woulda had a stout plowline wropped 'round you 'fore now."

"No; too busy studying medicine to do any courting."

"Holly Grove's a mighty big place not to have no woman on it, Doc. If'n I had to do the cookin' and keepin' that big house, I know pretty soon it would look like the hawgs been livin' in it."

"I don't have to do that." He was beginning to get impatient. "I've got a cook and housekeeper; she looks after me."

"A white old lady or a nigger woman?"

"She's a nigra, but she takes care of me pretty good."

"She don't take care of you too good, eh, Doc?" There was the hint of a sparkle in the farmer's faded blue eyes.

"What do you mean, Aaron?"

"Is she a plumb black nigger, or is she got some white blood?"

"She's a light-skinned nigra. But what business is it of yours?"

Aaron held up a calming hand. "Hold on, Doc, don't get het up. You know I'm yo' friend; yo' paw and maw was my friends, too. Never two finer folks in the world. And I'm mighty nigh old enough to be yo' daddy." He lowered his voice. "I heared you had a high-yaller nigger cookin' fer you, Doc. Meanin' no disrespeck, but no young white feller's got no business havin' a white nigger woman doin' his cookin' and housekeepin', and her the only woman around the house. It's dange'ous, Doc; 'twon't lead to no good." He paused, and a wry grin softened his preachment. "What it leads to gene'ally is a passel o' mulatto bastards." He raised his hand again against the protest he was anticipating. "Now I ain't sayin' that it will happen at Holly Grove, Doc, but it has happened at a lot o' other places, and 'mongst the high-falutin'est folks, too. In fack, I've noticed that gene'ally it's the highest-falutin'est folks that gits mulatto bastards. Look at Bob Allison, and Jim. They been bad after nigger women ever since they been growed. And I tell you somethin' else too, Doc"—he had released the bridle, but now he caught it again, for the doctor was threatening to ride off and leave him talking—"I don't blame the nigger wimmen, neither. Pretty nigh ever' time you see a mulatto nigger you can put it down that it was a white man's fault. And I tell you, Doc, it may sound funny, but I feels sorry for these mulattoes; they don't have much of a chanct; the white folks looks down on 'em and the niggers is kinda suspicious of 'em. Gene'ally a yaller nigger's mean, too, and I wouldn't say it's all they fault. Crossbreeds is likely to be mean. Now you take a mule. A mule's 'bout the orner'est thing they is, and he's a crossbreed; he's a plump freak o' nature which wasn't meant to be nohow and weren't till men got to mixin' hosses and jackasses. It's the same way with mulattoes; they's named for mules, more'n likely; anyhow, they's gene'ally 'bout as ornery; they's a mixtry o' a nigger woman and a jackass white man."

"I've never heard it put just that way, Aaron; it's an interesting theory you've got. Hmmm—mules and mulattoes. But let me go, man; I've got a lot of other sick people to see today. I'll be back in a day or two. Look after the missus."

"I will, Doc." He started to turn toward the house, wheeled and caught the bridle. "Oh, Doc, just one more thing. Now, Doc, 'bout the pay—"

"You can pay me when you sell your cotton, Aaron."

"I'll shore do it, Doc. I'll pay you out'n the first bale I sell. And, Doc, you figure on gittin' to camp meetin' this time." He let go his grip on the mare's bridle. "I've a notion this here one's goin' to be a good'un."

But Dr. Cardell did not ride by Rock Springs. He would send Charlie Gunn and one of the Negroes with a wagonload of pine boards and split shingles to make the needed repairs.

10

On pleasant summer days at Fair Meadows the Allisons often had their meals on the terrace in the shade of a giant oak. The rainy, rather cool spell in August had ended now and it was warm again and beginning to get dry. Soon the hot days and cool evenings of September would mark the coming of another fall.

Dr. Claiborne Cardell was eating with the Allisons. During the forenoon he had been treating a patient on the plantation, and Eliza had left word for him to come by and have the midday meal with them. His back was to the mansion house, which crowned a knob that fell away gently on three sides and somewhat precipitately on the fourth to bottom lands that extended for at least a mile, level and fertile with countless years' rich deposits of washed-down soil, along meandering Allison's Creek.

"I can easily see how this place got its name," the doctor said, pointing. "This must be one of the finest meadows in upper Mecklenburg. And your grandfather knew how to pick a site for his house, too. It's a wonderful view you have from every side, but I believe the view from right here is the best."

"You'd better take a good look now, Claib," Bob Allison said, as he put down his fork. "You'll probably never see it looking this good again. In another few years, or a generation at best, it may be covered with scrub pines and elderberry bushes thick along the creek banks, a regular jungle."

"I know what you mean, Bob." Claiborne solemnly buttered a triangle of hot cornbread. "I wish I felt justified in arguing with you, but I don't." He put the cornbread on the corner of the plate. "How many hands you got now?"

"Counting Eliza and Jim and myself—" he paused, reflecting. "Counting us, we've got probably twenty—and we're the hardest working ones on the whole place."

"Bob's right, Claib. They've freed the slaves and enslaved the free. I can never be sure now when I'll have enough help to keep the house going, and half the time I'm doing the cooking myself." She laughed, and there was a hint of bitterness in the tone. "I couldn't boil an egg when I was married, and well, I cooked dinner today." She shrugged.

"You've certainly learned, Eliza. This is a wonderful dinner."

"I wasn't asking for a compliment, Claib," she replied. "I was just supporting Bob's statement. Of course, that's not entirely right. Southern-plantation white people have always worked, and the Yankees can't seem to understand that. They think all we used to do was sit around under magnolias in hoopskirts and recite poetry or make love, while the men were either drinking mint juleps or cowhiding nigras. They should have watched our mothers and fathers, Claib, for just one day and night, and they'd have got a different picture of plantation life in the South. Many a time my poor mother sat up with a sick nigra baby or old woman or old man, sometimes till daylight—well, why tell you, Claib? You know yours did the same thing."

"And it wasn't because they were property either," Jim Allison joined in; "it was because they were people—our dependents, our friends, our children, you could even call 'em."

"But to get back to what I was saying," Bob spoke up. "Father had more than a hundred slaves when he died. Probably half of them were working hands. He treated them well, but they worked. And he made a sight of stuff on this place, and it was self-sustaining. Father hardly bought anything outside of coffee and cane sugar and now and then some fancy knickknacks, broadcloth, and the like. And everybody, white and black, lived well. He kept up the place."

"But you can't do it with twenty hands, Bob."

"No—and half of the twenty not half working." He pointed toward the creek bottom. "Give it three or four years, if things don't change quick, Claib—and they're more likely to change for the worse than the better—and it'll be grown up in scrub pine and honeysuckle, and most all our nigras will be gone—most of them are already gone, in fact, as I said—and God knows what we'll be doing or where we'll be."

"You aren't thinking about leaving Fair Meadows, Bob?"

"We've talked about it, some. A lot of folks are going west, you know."

"But you couldn't leave all this, man. And if you wanted to, likely you couldn't sell it to advantage."

"All this—" Bob Allison swept his hand around "—is a skeleton, a shadow, a ghost of other days, days gone forever, Claib. This house, expensive to keep up, impossible to keep up without lots of help, three-thousand acres of land and a lot of it rundown from being overworked, and every day getting less productive," he threw out his hands, palms up, in a gesture of hopelessness, "and not half-a-dozen nigras I can depend on to work. And taxes, Claib! Lord'lmighty, taxes, taxes, taxes!"

"The thing about it, Claib," Jim Allison spoke out, "is that our people, many of them, don't realize that we've gone through a revolution that has turned us upside down, inside out. And I wonder if we can stand up under it. It's like blowing out an oil lamp. There's light and then, pouff! and there's darkness. I just wonder if we can stick it out long enough to get the lamp lighted again."

"Yes, it's been about that sudden," Bob took up the discussion. "All at once with Lee's surrender we had nothing, you might say, when four years before we thought we had a secure future. And by *we* I don't mean just the aristocracy. I mean the nigras and the poor-buckram. Nigras were slaves, but they had homes, they had food and care and medicine and affection, with mighty few exceptions, Claib. They worked, but mighty few of them were exploited. Then the war was over, the slaves were free, and now today thousands, millions of them are virtually homeless and hungry and sick and preyed upon by sorry white vultures who pose as their friends and protectors; they won't work, many of them, and thousands have no place to work; they're shifting from one place to another, becoming vagrants and some of them criminals, and there are none to whom they can go for help. The freed nigras, Claib, are generally in one hell of a fix—excuse me, Eliza—and so are we."

Eliza faced her guest, smiling. "I hope you don't think Bob and Jim and I are entirely pessimistic, Claiborne. We aren't. We think eventually things will work out for the better. Isn't that what the Bible teaches? And we aren't defending completely, either, the institution of slavery. It's just that right now things look mighty blue."

"No, Claib, we aren't defending slavery. My father used to say that slavery would be the ruination of the South and that it should be done away with gradually until there wasn't a slave left anywhere. He even said that the invention of the cotton gin was a bad thing for the South because it put everybody to raising cotton, which meant that they had to buy more and more slaves to work the crops. He used to cuss out those old New England slavers who brought the nigras over and sold them to us when it became unprofitable for them to own them up there. Did you know, he even manumitted a bunch of his nigras, though few if any of them left the plantation?"

"I'm not surprised," the doctor told him. "My father manumitted Uncle Stephen and Aunt Ca'line years before the war started and they used to wear their papers in little oilcloth sacks around their necks, but they refused to leave Holly Grove. I remember once Aunt Ca'line came up to the house breathing fire and brimstone, and when Mother asked her what was wrong, she said, 'Some man come to my house and he say, "You ain't got no marster no more, lady," and I tell him, "Go 'long, mister, you don't know what you talkin' 'bout; I is got a marster; he up to de big house and I can take you up dar and show him to you if'n I wanted to; you jes' go long, sayin' I ain't got no marster, and I got de best marster in dis whole country!" ' And Mother never could make Aunt Ca'line understand that the carpetbagging visitor was right; she even resented very plainly Mother's laughing about it."

Eliza was busily peeling her baked sweet potato. She cut a slab of butter, pushed it with her knife down into the slit she had opened in the steaming tuber, and looked up. "If the hotheads on both sides could have been silenced and the war prevented for four or five years longer, I do believe," she declared, "plans could have been developed and put into operation for the gradual elimination of slavery. And look what a tragedy would have been prevented—not just the tragedy of the war years and the Reconstruction period but also the tragedy of bitterness and tears that is likely to endure for generations."

"She's right," Jim agreed with his sister-in-law. "Slavery was on its way out, because it was becoming economically unsound. Every day the slaves were getting the better end of the deal. And had we been able to work out the problem gradually, we would have avoided what this sudden revolution in our way of life has brought us and our children and their children's children." He crossed his knife and fork, wiped his lips, and shrugged. "Now we're going to pay hell for it for many a year, South and North."

"Listen, boys," Eliza held her forkful of sweet potato poised in mid-air, "for heaven's sake, let's talk about something cheerful. Things are difficult enough without conducting an autopsy on them. Say, Claiborne, had you heard about the picnic and tournament they're having at Hortonsville Saturday, and the rally for Governor Vance that night?"

"Hell, Claib," Bob Allison spoke up before the doctor could reply, "you ought to ride that tournament. You used to be one of the best in this whole country."

"You know, it's a funny thing, but the other day I was snooping about in the harness house and I came across the lance I used to use. I wondered if they were still having tournaments."

"Do they? Man, they're getting more popular all the time. And the one Saturday will draw a big crowd, what with the picnic and the political speaking. Say, Claib, if you'll ride Saturday, I will."

"Bob, I haven't ridden a tournament since the summer I finished Davidson. I bet I couldn't spear three barrel hoops in a row."

"The devil you say. You can't tell me you've lost your sleight this soon."

"But where'd I get a horse? You know the horse counts as much as the rider, maybe more."

"That roan mare you've been riding ever since you got home is one of the best tournament horses in Mecklenburg. Violet got her from McCoy Nisbet—you remember McCoy—and the only reason he let her go was because Violet gave too much for her, and McCoy had a sorrel he figured he could train for tournament riding anyway."

"Why don't you do it, Claiborne?" Eliza added her urging. "You could have picnic lunch with us. And I've a notion Melissa and her parents will come."

"The picnic part sounds mighty good; you're tempting me, especially after this dinner."

"By the way, Claiborne, is Sarah looking after you all right?"

"I don't see why you ask him that, Eliza," Bob commented. "He's getting fat. I'd say she was looking after him quite properly."

"Maybe a little too well," Jim suggested. The two Allisons

snickered and Eliza reddened perceptibly. The doctor pretended not to understand.

"I suppose she does feed me too well. I eat too much, anyway."

Eliza had recovered quickly. "And if you win the tournament, Claiborne, you can crown Melissa the Queen of Love and Beauty"—now she was smiling beatifically—"and if Bob wins, he can crown me."

"If I should win and crown some other woman, my love," her husband observed wryly, "I would certainly get crowned, and good."

Before he rode off for Holly Grove, Claiborne promised he would attend the picnic and ride in the tournament.

When he hung up his saddle and bridle in the harness room, he picked up the lance and carried it to the house. After supper he took it into his office and with a broken bit of window pane carefully smoothed away the accumulated dirt and roughness. When he had removed the tiny ring nicks from the last tournament in which he had used it, he rubbed a thin coating of beeswax into the hard pine of the long thin shaft and with an old wool sock shined it until it glistened in the soft lamplight.

11

Colonel Osborne saw Dr. Cardell dismount and tie his horse at the edge of the Academy grove where they were having the picnic and tournament. He strode over to the young physician, his pink round face and white mustache beaming competition with the gay cravat and striped waistcoat. The cravat and waistcoat, Claiborne observed, were laundered and starched and appeared newly bought, but he remembered having seen them in the years before he went off to medical school.

"How've you been, young man?" The colonel shook hands cordially. "Haven't seen you since you had supper with us. Didn't even hear you when you left that night. Don't know whether it was early or late." He smiled broadly, winked.

"It was early, Colonel. I was pretty tired; didn't stay as long as I would have liked to."

"Well, come back, Claiborne, any time you can. Always glad to have you, if you're not doctoring on us, I mean. And look here, we missed you at Rock Springs."

"I just couldn't get over, Colonel. There's been a lot of sickness around; August's a bad month for the fevers."

"Yes, I know; the miasmas seem to have been heavier than usual this summer." He took the doctor's arm, brightened. "Claiborne, we want you to eat with us today. The missus and Melissa have brought plenty. In fact," he grinned, "we'd sorta expected you would, if you got the chance to come."

"I'd like to, Colonel, thank you. But the other day I was over at Fair Meadows and the Allisons asked me to eat with them today."

"Well, hell's bells, Claiborne, we can fix that. We'll just set out our stuff together, and you can eat with them and us, too. I want you to stick your teeth into some of that boiled ham we fetched, boy; I believe it's as good as any I've ever cured; it's been killed two years and it's got white specks. You know when a ham has white specks in it, it's getting right. You can eat Eliza's fried chicken, but I want you to grease your gums on my ham."

At that moment the colonel spied his wife and daughter in a group of women and girls some fifty paces away, and he called out to them. When they spotted him, he beckoned with his hand and a jerk of his head, and they came over to join him and the doctor. The colonel told them he had invited Claiborne to eat with them, that they could put out their food with the Allisons'.

"Yes, do, Claiborne," Mrs. Osborne insisted. "I'll find Eliza and we'll make the arrangements."

"It would be fun, eating with the Allisons," Melissa added. "Then we could get all the news from Fair Meadows."

He wondered suddenly if Charlie Gunn had told the girl what he had seen that early morning at Holly Grove. He couldn't escape the impression that she was telling him, though not in so many words, that she knew more than he suspected. But she looked charming nevertheless, as stylish, he was sure, as any girl he might have seen in the throngs visiting the Philadelphia Centennial earlier in the summer. He wondered how she could have managed to achieve such a smart and expensive appearing costume; he had wondered the same thing the night they had sat for an hour on the joggling-board.

Her close-fitting bodice was of a green-and-brown plaid cotton, with long, tight sleeves, lace-trimmed at the cuffed wrists. It had a narrow, turned-over white collar that went up high on the sides and back of her neck and was cut rather daringly low in front. The skirt was of darker brown; it dropped straight down at the front but in the back was gathered in a generous fullness over the bustle. A perky little bonnet of the plaid of the bodice sat jauntily on the front of her head.

But he was denied time to admire in further detail Melissa's costume, for the colonel caught his arm and started steering him toward a clump of trees where a crowd of men had gathered. "Girls, holler when you're ready and we'll go to the buggy and get the baskets," he called back. "Bub Barkley bought some stuff the other day from a Wilkes County fellow who came through here in a covered wagon," he confided to Claiborne. "I've already had a little nip. I want you to try it; it's the best apple brandy I've had in many a day. Damned if it ain't as good in its way as my ham; in fact, I don't know any two things that go together better."

The scraggly bearded young storekeeper's ostensible purpose in being there was to sell the wagonload of watermelons he had brought from his own patch. Bub Barkley was known throughout the northern end of the county for his ability to grow choice melons of two delectable varieties, the dark green, almost round Stone Mountains and the long, light green, striped Georgia Rattlesnakes.

Bub was standing in front of an up-ended large wooden drygoods box that he had brought from his store manifestly to serve as a counter for merchandising the melons. They had been piled behind him and already the two piles were diminishing.

But the storekeeper's sales were not limited to Stone Mountains and Georgia Rattlesnakes, for the big box provided a not too public place for setting several jugs of Wilkes County's widely heralded product, and from time to time with the approach of some thirsty citizen, Bub would thrust hands into the box and from the improvised shelf bring out a filled tin cup which he would hand to his customer.

They watched as a bearded and mustached Mecklenburger reached for the cup and downed the contents in one tremendous gurgling gulp. Then with a grimace of having swallowed molten lead, he whacked the cup down on the box, licked his lips, smacked them loudly and wiped them on his sleeve and the back of his hand.

"Whew-w-w!" he exclaimed, grinning, as he flipped open a grimy leather snap purse. "Lawd'lmighty, Bub, that 'ere stuff's good, but it kicks like a damn mule!"

Claiborne and the colonel pushed up to the box. "Bub, I want Dr. Cardell to have a taste o' that Wilkes County brandy," Colonel Osborne said. "You got a clean cup or glass you can pour him a shot in?"

"Yes, sir, Colonel, I shore has. Step right up, Doc, and 'twon't cost nair one o' you a cent neither." Bub's hands were busy beneath the box top, and presently he handed the doctor a new tin cup. "I've a notion you ain't never wet yo' whistle on no better brandy'n this stuff, Doc. How 'bout you, Colonel? You want another drink? 'Twon't cost you nair penny."

"Not just yet, Bub. I may get another after the picnic. I just wanted Claiborne to try it." He turned to the doctor, still holding the cup. "Go ahead, Claiborne. It's good stuff."

Dr. Cardell sipped, grimaced, and then swallowed the brandy without taking the tin from his lips. He set the cup down, licked his lips, took out his handkerchief, wiped them. "You're right, Colonel, it's good; but it's got a powerful wallop. That stuff must be a hundred proof."

"Maybe more," Bub commented. "Have another, Doc?"

"No more now. If I had another shot of that stuff I probably couldn't stay on my horse in the tournament."

"You riding today, Claiborne?" The colonel's interest was evident. "Hadn't heard about it."

"I'll probably get eliminated after the first run. I'm pretty rusty."

Bub caught his arm. "Come by just 'fore it starts, Doc. A little shot'll steady yo' nerves. 'Twon't cost you nothin' neither." The storekeeper motioned with his head, and Colonel Osborne edged nearer. "I ain't talkin' it too loud, but if you'uns wants some brandy to take home, I got some jugs in the wagon, hid down under the straw. The wagon hit's over there in the ai'ge o' the woods behint the boys' backhouse. I'm keepin' hit sorter special for my friends. Step down there if you want some later on and tell that nigger boy I said to let you have whatever you want. You can pay the nigger or you can jes' pay me later at the store."

"I may get a jug, Bub," the colonel responded. "This mountain stuff's about the smoothest apple brandy I've ever tried."

They eased away from Bub's improvised stand and sauntered toward the trees under which the rough-board picnic tables had been put up. The colonel caught the doctor's arm. "I'm glad you're going to ride, Claiborne. Reckon you still got your sleight?"

"I doubt it, Colonel. But Bob Allison bantered me into riding, and I guess pretty soon now I'll find out if I can still pick off those little rings."

"Bob going to ride too? I'll bet he'll be too drunk. A few more nips of Bub's brandy and he won't be able to stay in the saddle—or even get on his horse."

They were sidling around a knot of guffawing farmers when Colonel Osborne pointed. "There's Eliza and my folks stretching their necks like turkeys, trying to find us. They're probably ready for the baskets. And I'm certainly ready to eat. Bub's brandy sorter calls for some of those ham biscuits, eh, Claiborne?"

12

Tournaments invariably attracted participants from among the more daring young bloods, and throngs of excited partisans cheered and shrieked for their favorite riders. Though he had given little thought to how they had originated, Claiborne Cardell had supposed them to be a survival or renewal in greatly modified form of the old English jousts in which knights competed in virile, often bloody and sometimes mortal struggles for the winner's reward of being permitted to crown as queen of the day his lady fair.

In Mecklenburg much of the virility of the ancient sport had been lost, and no longer was there likelihood of the spectators seeing blood spilled. Sometimes a clumsy or inebriated contestant fell from his horse, or was thrown off, but not often, and no longer did men on horseback lunge at each other with long pikes while fair ladies alternately tittered or swooned. The old game had survived, however, to the extent that the champion was privileged to place the glittering crown—no longer of diamonds and emeralds and rubies but more likely of pasteboard covered with gilt or silvered paper—upon the blushing, proud head of his lady love.

The modern sport pitted the contestant not against an adversary on a horse but against three iron rings, each two inches in diameter, wrapped in red flannel to make them the more easily visible to the charging rider, and suspended beneath braced crossbars extended from two-by-four posts set thirty yards apart along the tournament course. The rider's purpose was to spear all three rings on the point of his nine-foot, slender lance as his horse sped beneath the crossbars; this he had to do within a specified time, usually eight seconds, from the beginning line thirty yards in advance of the first post, so that the timed run was over a distance of ninety yards.

Each contestant made three runs. A judge with a stop watch recorded his time; if his horse made the run within the prescribed time, the run counted and the number of rings speared was added to his total. Nine rings and he had made a perfect score. But sometimes two or more contestants would score perfectly. So to break the tie they were called back to make runs with smaller rings set up—rings of but one-inch diameter.

Melissa had professed surprise when she learned that Claiborne was going to ride tournament. But she had seemed pleased and wished him luck.

"I'll need it," he told her. "I'm rusty at it, and they say some of the best riders in the county will be in it. But I'd like to win, Melissa," he had paused with a ham-biscuit half way to his mouth, grinning, "so I could crown you queen."

She had laughed, and she seemed pleased. But she hadn't said, he noticed, whether she would be happy to be his queen. Nor had he pressed her. But he wondered agam if Charlie Gunn had told her anything.

Not until the chief judge read out to the assembled throng the names of the day's contestants did Claiborne know that Charlie was riding. Charlie had said nothing to him about the tournament or the picnic, and he did not recall having contested in any previous tournament with any farm overseer.

After the names had been called, they were placed in a hat and drawn out one at a time by a small child; the order in which they were drawn would be the order in which they would compete.

McCoy Nisbet's was the first name drawn.

"He'll be a tough one to beat," Colonel Osborne ventured. "But maybe being first will put him at a disadvantage."

Brevard Alexander was in second place and Marshall Puckett third. Both men, Claiborne remembered, were skilled riders. Three other names were read, and then the little girl pulled another slip from the hat and the judge called out the doctor's name. Three more names were quickly called: Albert Nantz, Bob Allison, Charlie Gunn.

Charlie, he reasoned, and not without considerable satisfaction, would have pressure on him all the way; he would be riding against the field.

The horses were not lavishly caparisoned as were steeds in the days when knighthood flowered, but that permitted them to run the faster and keep more closely to the course. And the modern knights, freed of cumbersome armor, could compete with more skill than their medieval forebears had been able to employ in their joustings. But a bit of the pageantry had survived in the crowning of the queen, and sometimes the riders stuck feathers in their hats and wore bright-colored shirts.

Today several of the men were wearing their Confederate uniforms, either newly tailored to be worn on such special occasions or brought out from closests where they had been carefully preserved during the decade since they had been worn in battle. McCoy Nisbet was wearing the gaily plumed hat he had worn in many a charge with Jeb Stuart. Around Brevard Alexander's waist was a red sash, the same one that had girded him when he had ridden at the head of his company.

McCoy Nisbet was called. He cantered his horse back some fifty yards behind the starting line and adjusted his lance in position just above his right shoulder and almost parallel with the ground. The horse stood motionless; when the rider lifted the reins, the animal was off on a smooth, level dash down the course. As the horse crossed the starting line, the timing judge thumbed his watch, and the tournament officially had started.

"That's a great tournament mare!" exclaimed Colonel Osborne. "I believe she'd rather be in it than McCoy. Look how level she runs!"

Nisbet's steady hand picked off the first ring and the second; but then his mare momentarily seemed to falter. "He's reined her in a little," the colonel observed. "If he doesn't mind, his time may be too slow."

But the long lance in the firm hand speared the last ring, and as the horse crossed beneath the gallowslike upright, the judge thumbed his watch again. Nisbet reined his horse about and came back, and the crowd waited the judge's announcement. "The time," the official said, "seven and three-tenths seconds."

Nisbet had made it, and three points were recorded for him.

A judge called Brevard Alexander's name. Alexander took his place, signaled his horse, and the eager animal was off down the track. When the rider had made the run and circled back, he too had three rings speared.

The left sleeve of Marshall Puckett's bright blue shirt was tucked into red silk and he wore a big plume stuck into the brim of his army campaign hat; his trousers were of Confederate gray. As he took his position the crowd cheered; the people remembered that Marshall had lost his arm on that memorable day of Pickett's charge at Gettysburg.

Marshall missed one ring, the next rider scored a three, the fifth man speared only one, and the sixth contestant picked off all three.

The judge called for Dr. Cardell to take his position.

"Good luck, Claiborne," Colonel Osborne said, as the doctor swung into the saddle; "I'm pulling for you, and," he winked, "so's Melissa."

When the starting judge signaled, Claiborne gave his roan's bridle rein a mild jerk, and he was off on a fast and straight run down the course. Beyond the third post, the doctor turned her and came back.

"It was just good luck, Colonel," Claiborne said as the judge slipped off the three rings. "Good luck and a good horse."

Albert Nantz missed the second ring, and Bob Allison speared only his second.

Colonel Osborne nudged Claiborne who had dismounted to give his horse a breather. "I told you Bob would be too drunk to ride. I'll bet he falls off his horse the next run."

When Charlie Gunn was called to get into place, Claiborne ventured a glance toward Melissa. The girl, he sensed, was engrossed in Charlie; as the overseer cantered over to the starting point, she kept her eyes on him, and when Charlie sped down the course and neatly speared all three rings, she seemed to Claiborne to be unduly excited and happy. She applauded and even yelled, considerably beyond the bounds of mere politeness, the doctor convinced himself. But maybe she had applauded that way every time a rider had made a perfect score, he conceded; maybe she had yelled when he had made the run without a miss. He hadn't noticed her particularly until Charlie's turn to ride had been announced.

But Dr. Cardell had time to conjecture no longer, for McCoy Nisbet was getting ready for his second run. And this time his luck failed him; he missed the third ring.

"Pressure's on him," suggested Colonel Osborne. "Or maybe he was overconfident."

Brevard Alexander missed a ring too, but Marshall Puckett speared three to even his two-run score with Nisbet and Alexander. The next two riders, one of whom had scored three in the first, missed a ring each, and the one just ahead of Dr. Cardell missed two.

"Don't be thinking about anything but riding the same course you did the first time," Colonel Osborne counseled. "And good luck, boy."

His good luck or his skill or his horse's skill held. He picked off the three rings.

"Fine!" the colonel was beaming. "Nobody else but Charlie has a chance of having a six at the end of this run, and I doubt if he can do it again."

Albert Nantz made a perfect score to bring his total to five points and a tie with the first four riders. And Bob Allison surprised everybody by getting two rings on his lance. Bob had an explanation for his better showing on the second run.

"I always said a man could do anything better with some good liquor inside him," he declared pontifically as they helped him from his horse. "It gets a man limbered up to where he can perform better. I reckon I ought to know; a few swigs o' Bub's brandy made me do just twice as good as I did before I got oiled up." He spotted Dr. Cardell. "Claib, before you make your last run you better take a good stiff swig o' that mountain stuff."

Once more Melissa was eying Charlie, the doctor noticed, as the overseer prepared to make his second try at the rings. She certainly seemed interested in Charlie, he thought. He wondered if her parents had ever suspected such a preposterous thing.

But he turned to watch Charlie as he took his place, then sped across the starting line. The first ring flashed along the shaft of the overseer's lance, the second, the third.

"You'll get him next time, Claiborne." Colonel Osborne was smiling reassuringly. "Who'd have ever thought Charlie could ride tournament like that? But his luck can't hold out for another run."

"You mean maybe mine won't hold out, Colonel "

Preparations were quickly finished for the final test. McCoy Nisbet took his place, his horse raced down the course, which by now had been pounded into a fine dust on the surface, and came cantering back to the judges with the three rings safely pinioned. Brevard Alexander speared the rings, but he was overcautious and slowed his horse just enough to fail to do the distance in the required time and added nothing to his score. Marshall Puckett followed with a perfect score, and once more the crowd roared its delight. But the next man missed a ring, which eliminated him, and since perfect scores on their final tries would have advanced them to totals of but seven points each, the next two did not compete. Then the judge called Dr. Cardell to take his place at the starting point.

Once more the doctor ventured a glance toward Melissa. About the same time she looked his way and waved in what he hoped was an encouraging gesture. But he wondered whom she wanted to win.

He cantered to the beginning point, jerked gently on the mare's rein, and she was off. The first ring slid down the lance, but just then a child standing against the restraining plowlines suddenly screamed his delight, and the roan momentarily shied, throwing him off balance. Barely in time he righted himself and as the horse flashed under the crossarm he aimed the lance at the small red-bordered circle. He felt the lance touch the ring, but whether its point was inside the circle or the shaft had merely knocked the ring from its trigger catch he was not sure. Before he had time to conjecture he was almost under the third ring. But this time he saw it slip along the shaft. Quickly he reined the mare around and headed for the judges.

They pulled three rings from his lance.

"Perfect score, Doct' Cardell," one of them said. "Nine points. Everybody ahead of you's out. The next two would be out even if they made their three points. Nobody left agin you but Charlie Gunn." He called out to the overseer. "Get ready, Charlie. It's you agin the doctor."

"He'll never do it this time," said Colonel Osborne. "He couldn't do it three times in a row."

"You've already said twice he couldn't do it," Claiborne reminded him.

Charlie was at the starting line, ready. The judge nodded, Charlie lifted the rein; the horse darted toward the timing line, crossed it, in an instant was under the crossbar, and Charlie's first ring was on his lance. And before the excited crowd's applause could gather volume, he speared the second ring.

Then his horse stumbled and almost went to her knees.

"You got him now," Colonel Osborne said, not too loudly.

But Charlie kept to his saddle and held his lance level; the sleek animal clambered to her feet and headed toward the crossbar of the third post. Deftly Charlie impaled the third ring, and the throng roared. Out beyond the last post he turned his horse and trotted back.

The timing judge was shaking his head.

"You got the rings all right, Charlie, but you took too long—eight and eight-tenths seconds. The last three rings don't count. Doct' Cardell wins the tournament, nine to six." He scratched his head, crinkled his forehead. "I guess by rights some of those other fellows gets second place."

By then Dr. Cardell had reached the timing judge. "No, Charlie would have been under the time limit if his horse hadn't stumbled. I refuse to accept first place. Charlie got his last three rings too. It's a draw."

"Well-l-l, now—" the judge began. But the shouts of the crowd drowned him out.

Charlie faced Claiborne. "But, accordin' to the rules, Doc, you beat me anyhow."

"Let 'em run it off!" a long-necked leathery fellow yelled. "Put up the little rings and let 'em run it off with them. Ain't that all right, Doct' Claib?"

The doctor, calmly eying the overseer, nodded. "I'd be willing."

"Well," the judge spoke up, "if that's agreeable to everybody, let's get the little rings put up."

Someone located the small rings, only an inch in diameter, and hastily wrapped the red flannel about them. "It'll take a good man to hook three in a row of these here," he observed. "It's just room enough for the point of the lance to get in; there's no room to spare."

His words were prophetic. On the doctor's initial attempt, he speared the first two rings, but knocked the third one to the ground. And Charlie hooked only one.

"I told you, Claiborne," the colonel whispered as he nudged up to the doctor while the rings were being replaced in the triggers.

But on the next try the scoring was reversed. The doctor had only one ring when he came back, Charlie Gunn had two. The chief judge held up his hand for silence. "It's tied now, three rings to three. Now, Doct' Cardell, take your place for the runoff. And all you folks stand back from the ropes and give 'em plenty room!"

Dr. Cardell knocked down the first ring; it fell to the ground instead of circling his lance point. The next two he caught.

"Five out of nine for these one-inch rings is a good score," the colonel declared, still optimistic about Claiborne's chance. "I believe you've got Charlie beat now."

But Charlie promptly speared his first two rings, and with the possibility of victory but seconds away headed for the suspended third ring. Once more, though, the tensely excited animal missed her footing and stumbled. Charlie's lance dipped and the two rings slid toward the point. But in the instant he righted

the lance, and as the animal regained its stride and headed toward the third post, Charlie aligned it with the tiny ring, and
in the next second the ring swept along the polished shaft.

The crowd yelled and applauded, and as Charlie Gunn, grinning happily, rode back to the judges' place, the chief judge
held up his hand for silence. "Charlie Gunn has three rings, and
he made his run inside o' eight seconds. The tournament
champeen is Charlie Gunn, with Dr. Cardell second."

When the applause had subsided, the judge once more motioned for silence. "Now, ladies and gent'emen," he announced,
"it is the privilege of the champeen to choose his Queen of Love
and Beauty and place the crown on her head, and later"—
he paused, grinning—"if she's of a willin' mind, escort her to her
home in his buggy." He turned to Charlie Gunn. "Now, Charlie, choose your queen."

Meanwhile, Claiborne had tied his horse to a small tree and
walked over with Colonel Osborne to join the Osborne ladies
and the Allisons. It was immediately evident to them that Bob
had revisited, perhaps several times, Bub Barkley's stand. He
advanced to meet Claiborne, a bit unsteadily, and held out his
hand. "Shorry, old man, shorry, 's shame, 's plumb shame that
oversheer feller beat cher, damn 'f 'tain't." He turned ponder-
ously to address Melissa. "If Claib'd won," he stabbed a fat forefinger toward the girl, "you'd been Queen o' Love and Beauty;
you'd got that shiny crown on those red tresses, those flaming,"
suddenly he seemed to lose interest in further describing her
hair, turned again to the doctor, "now wouldn't she, Claib? Now
wouldn't she?"

"I most certainly would have been honored to crown her
queen, if I'd won," Claiborne agreed, looking her levelly in the
eyes, "if she'd have allowed me. For that reason, I'm sorry I lost.
You'd have made a beautiful queen, Melissa."

"You're right, Doctor. Miss Melissa will make a beautiful
queen."

Claiborne whirled around to confront Charlie Gunn. The
overseer sat calmly in the saddle, his feather-decked hat held at

his chest in his left hand; in his right hand he clutched the lance, the three rings still encircling it, the lowered point extended toward the girl.

"And Miss Melissa will be my Queen of Love and Beauty if she will do me the honor of allowing me to crown her, and then later will permit me to escort her home."

Claiborne felt his hands suddenly aching to drag the fellow from the horse and knock his teeth down his throat, but he stood rigid and clamped his jaws together. Until Melissa had spoken he would deny himself the pleasure of flattening the presumptuous bumpkin. He faced Melissa, waiting.

"Oh, Charlie," she was smiling prettily as she stepped forward and with thumb and two fingers slipped a ring from the lance in token of acceptance of the role of tournament queen, "I will be most honored and happy to be your Queen of Love and Beauty and accept the crown at your hands, and—" Claiborne thought he saw the trace of a blush, "—have you escort me home."

13

He struggled to push upward through tepid dark waters, to gain the surface and the sunlight; but his heavy head, sodden, huge, swinging around and down, battled his every effort to rise from the black depths. For ages and aeons he seemed to be struggling, but his arms and legs were tired and heavy, and his eyelids, weighted with iron rings wrapped in red flannel, pressed down upon eyeballs raw and unseeing.

He labored to lift himself toward the light he sensed but could not see. If he could but spear upon the point of his lance the heavy rings, he might lift them from his eyelids and open his eyes; but the lance was heavy and his right arm was tiring fast. If by exerting all the power of will he possessed he could force his imprisoned eyes to see through the eyelids into the ʳᵉd circled rings, he might gain for each eyeball a pinpoint of light. But he was too tired to try longer. He relaxed, the lance slipped from his hand, his head lightened and slowly righted itself, and the rings fell from his eyelids; almost imperceptibly at first he began to float upward, and now a little faster, and faster, faster.

Dr. Cardell opened his eyes. Pain stabbed at each eyeball, and he clamped the eyelids shut. He held them tightly clamped; his feet lifted level with his head as it sank heavily to the pillow. He ventured to open his eyes again and squinted through narrowed slits, and windows floated into position and the bedroom squared itself.

Sarah was standing by the bed. On the nightstand he saw a cup and saucer and steaming pot. By the delectable odor he knew that the pot held coffee.

"Good morning, Sarah," he said, blinking.

"Good morning, Doct' Claib." She was smiling; her tone was cheerful. "I've brought you some hot coffee. It'll help straighten you up."

He struggled to raise himself upright, but his leaden head pulled him back to his pillow, and he groaned.

"Here, let me help you." She grasped him at the armpits and raised him to a sitting position, then patted out the pillow and pushed it snugly against his back. She poured coffee and handed him the cup. "It's pretty strong, but that'll be better."

He drank the coffee, sipping it slowly at first, then finishing the cup with a gulp."

"Any more?"

"No, that's enough, thank you. I feel better now." He wiped his lips with the napkin and motioned toward the chair near the bed. "Sit down, Sarah, and tell me about it." He blinked his eyes and essayed a grin. "Tell it all; don't leave out anything."

"Your mare fetched you home last night 'bout dark. I helped you off and put you to bed."

"I was past going, eh?"

"You were pretty drunk. You had a jug of brandy tied to the saddle, and it was 'bout half empty. I set it in your office."

"I bought it from Bub Barkley after the tournament. But I didn't drink all that brandy, Sarah. I can remember giving drinks to several other men, some of them maybe on the way home. Have you heard about the tournament? Charlie tell you anything?"

"He hasn't been here today." She smiled. "This is Sunday afternoon, Doct' Claib. But I did hear them say Mist' Charlie beat you ridin'."

"But that wasn't why I got drunk."

"They said Mist' Charlie crowned Miss Melissa the queen. That the reason, wasn't it?"

"Because she let him, I guess."

Sarah nodded. "I can see how that would upset a body." But quickly she dismissed the subject and stood up, smiling. "Do you feel like you could eat some dinner now, Doct' Claib? I cooked you some chicken, and hot biscuits, and "

"Not yet, Sarah," he interrupted, frowning. "Maybe after awhile. But don't you wait for me; you go ahead and eat your dinner."

"I don't want none either, Doct' Claib. I just sorter got filled up frying the chicken, the smell, I mean."

"What's wrong, Sarah, sick at your stomach? Go downstairs and get a couple of those brown pills out of my bag—"

" 'Twon't no pills help none, Doct' Claib. 'Twon't nothin' like that help now."

"But they'll settle your stomach, Sarah."

"No, sir, not now, they won't. 'Twon't nothin' settle it." She picked up the coffee tray and turned with a wry smile to confront him. "I'm in a fam'ly way."

14

It was cotton-picking time and to anyone of suspicious eye Sarah Gordon's pregnancy was apparent when late one afternoon in October, Violet Cardell drove up in the Fair Meadows carriage.

"Eliza had Uncle Zeke drive me over," she told Claiborne, who had just returned to Holly Grove from a strenuous day of visiting patients. "I came up to Fair Meadows day before yesterday with Abigail Davidson who was on her way to Rural Hill.

She spent the night with Eliza and yesterday went on over to the Davidsons' ''.

"And I presume you three women settled Mecklenburg's, if not the world's, problems?"

She laughed. "We went into some of them rather fully."

But he did not pursue the subject, and when he had carried her valise up to her room and she had freshened up from the ride, Sarah called them to supper.

"Your meal tonight brings back memories when Claiborne and I were children, Sarah," Violet said, as they were finishing eating. "Your cooking reminds me of Aunt Tilda's. But I'm afraid you will be getting my brother so fat he won't be able to get around to see his patients." She turned to the doctor, smiling. "And, Claiborne, if she keeps on looking after you so well, I'm afraid you'll continue to put off getting married."

He shrugged. "Sarah feeds me all right. But as you know, practically everything's raised here on the place; we don't buy much. Can't afford to; not much money in practicing medicine; folks put off paying the doctor, and mighty few have any money to pay if they wanted to."

Out on the verandah, when they were settled in their chairs and he had his feet comfortably on the balustrade, she remarked that he had said nothing when at the supper table she had chided him for not having already got himself involved in matrimony. "Just what is your suituation in that respect?" She laughed, but he had the feeling that the inquisition was beginning.

"You're talking about Melissa and me, of course," he replied. "I can't say that I've made much progress."

"Well, what's the trouble, Claiborne?" Then she added: "If it's any of my business."

"I've been mighty busy ever since I've been back. There's been a lot of typhoid, and babies to deliver, ailments of one sort and another; and I've got a lot of country to look after, Violet. It keeps me riding day and night. And lately I've had the place to look after, seeing to getting the cotton in."

"Eliza told me you'd turned Charlie off."

"Eliza must have given you a lot of news. Did she say why?"

"She said Charlie beat you in the tournament, and crowned Melissa, and you were pretty mad about it and got drunk. Pretty soon afterward she heard you'd turned him off."

"I suppose she said I was jealous of him." He was palpably nettled.

"No, Claiborne, Eliza didn't say that. I got the impression from what she did say that you were madder at Melissa than you were at Charlie."

"I suppose I was."

"I can't say that I blame you too much. Eliza told me how it was. But maybe Melissa did it just for a lark, on the spur of the moment. I'm sure it was a thoughtless thing she did, Claiborne; she couldn't have been purposely offending you, and you know she couldn't possibly have been interested in Charlie Gunn. Hasn't she told you so?"

"I haven't seen her since the tournament."

Violet's tone evidenced mounting concern. "But you do expect to continue seeing her?"

"I'm in no hurry to."

"But, Claiborne, you don't really believe she's interested in Charlie Gunn?"

"I don't suppose so. But I don't know. I haven't asked her, that's for sure." He pulled his feet down, sat up in the chair. "That's not why I fired Charlie, not altogether the reason, anyway. I didn't particularly need him after the crop was laid by, and I didn't have the money to hire him. Times are improving, but money's still scarce, Violet, as you know. And I think Charlie figured anyway that he was getting too important to be a farm overseer. I let him go so he could start being the big man Melissa told me he would be before long."

"*She* told you?"

"Yes, the night I had supper at Colonel Osborne's."

"What in the world did she say Charlie Gunn was going to do?"

"She didn't say. But I've found out that he's got his head set on getting into the cotton-mill business. He's even been to a meeting they had at Davidson to promote interest in building a cotton mill there."

"Well." Her tone was incredulous. "That's one thing Eliza didn't tell me. I suppose she hadn't heard it. But ever since the surrender there is no use being surprised at anything you hear. The nigras freed and shiftless, and voting, the white men doing the manual labor, and disfranchised, until right lately at any rate, and now Charlie Gunn fancying himself a powerful textile industrialist. The bottom layer's getting on top, all right. If it weren't so tragic, Claiborne, it would be downright ludicrous." She sat silent a moment, musing. "I must admit that I'm surprised at Melissa's attitude," she said after awhile. "Do you suppose she's encouraging Charlie in his ambition? Claiborne, why don't you go to see her and ask her just what she does have in mind? Why don't you just have it out with her?"

"I suppose I will—when I go. But I'm in no rush to go. In fact, I'm in no hurry to get married, Violet. Sarah's looking after me all right." Instantly he knew that he had said the wrong thing.

"Somebody's been looking after her, too, I noticed. Eliza admitted one of the reasons she let you have her was to get her out of reach of Bob and Jim. Has Bob been slipping over here, or Jim?"

He wondered how he could fend off her probing. "What do you mean?"

"You know perfectly well what I mean. Anybody can see for himself she's going to have a baby."

"If Bob or Jim has been slipping over here, I don't know about it."

"Eliza told me she'd told you that Sarah was her first cousin, or maybe even her half sister—something I'd certainly never have done if the shoe had been on my foot. And I'm thankful I can say that none of our forebears ever stooped to such a thing as having a nigra child. Claiborne, you know," she was deliberately choosing her words he felt, "if I'd seen Sarah before Eliza and I talked about her coming over to Holly Grove, I'd never in the world have agreed to it. I didn't have the least idea that she was so fair-skinned. I would never have sent such a temptation."

"I thought you had convicted either Bob or Jim Allison of being the daddy of her baby—if she's going to have a baby."

"I haven't convicted anybody, Claiborne. I certainly hope that you haven't so disgraced the family. But whether you have or haven't, if she stays here much longer the whole community will be saying you are responsible for her delicate condition. I think it would be wise for you to send her away as quickly as you can arrange it, maybe to where she was in South Carolina before she came up to Fair Meadows. It would kill me, Claiborne, if such a report got out on you; I'd feel personally disgraced. A nigra niece or nephew at Holly Grove—God forbid!" She sat forward imperiously. "If such a disgrace should come upon this house, I'd never set foot in it again as long as that woman and her child were here!"

He had the feeling that the best defense was in a determined offense. "You say she's pregnant, and you suspect me. Yet you were very friendly to the woman, you said her cooking reminded you of Aunt Tilda's—"

"Whether you or Bob or Jim or some other man is responsible, I'm not blaming the nigra. I don't blame any nigra woman for a mulatto child; I blame the white man, Claiborne. In slavery times a nigra woman, as you well know, had to submit to her white owner, whether she wanted .) or not. And though they are freed now, they're little more than children in responsibility. And any mixing of the races is the white man's fault, and I have no patience with the white man that does it, Claiborne, none whatsoever!"

15

Bub Barkley's store, one might have pointed out with no violation of the truth, was the community's social center, loafers' congregating place, and gossip exchange. Here of a summer afternoon three or four once wealthy and aristocratic, and now only aristocratic, ladies might happen upon each other and while fingering delightedly a newly arrived bolt of Alamance gingham divest themselves of, and encumber themselves with, choice tidbits of neighborhood news. On summer days when the land was too wet to be worked and in the fall and winter when the weather was too raw for hauling up wood or clearing the ditches, the farmers congregated at Bub's to swap crop news, argue religion or politics, and tell stories of varying degrees of ribaldry. On almost any such day at different times and sometimes simultaneously a not even sensitive nose might readily detect the addition to that peculiarly delightful smell of the country store an admixture of soiled, wet clothing, talcum powder, Negro sweat, perspiring feet, scented soap, and, in winter, tobacco juice expectorated on the red-hot pot-bellied stove centering the spittle-drenched, tobacco-cud-bespattered sandbox.

Today no ladies graced Bub's sprawling emporium, but several white men were lounging about the stove when a Negro man, of strong build, very black, and looking to be in his middle thirties, entered the front door and sidled over to the counter at the left behind which the proprietor stood.

"Mist' Bub, I'd like to buy 'bout two pounds o' them 'ere cheese," he said, pointing.

"W'y, howdy, Eph, how you?" Bub greeted him. "Where you been, boy? I ain't seen you in more'n a year, I know. You still workin' down at Charlotte?"

"Yes, sir. Still down 'ere."

"Where you workin' at down 'ere, Eph?"

"Still fi'in' the boilers at the flour mill, same place I been all the time I been gone from home."

"Well, I swarn." Bub lifted the knife, attached to the frame of the metal turntable on which the round cheese sat. "How you doin' down 'ere, Eph? Gettin' on all right?"

"Yes, sir, Mist' Bub, gittin' on pretty good, I reck'n."

"Waal-l, howdy, Eph; what you doin' back here, boy?"

The Negro turned his head, nodded. "How you, Mist' Babe." Another white man spoke to him, and he nodded. "How you, Mist' Aaron?"

"D'you say two pounds, Eph?" Bub inquired, the knife poised above the cheese.

"Yes, sir, two pound."

The knife came down with a thud and the segment fell over. "You want it wropped up, Eph, or you gonna eat it now?"

"Yes, sir, wrop it up, please, sir. I wants to take it home." He grinned, showing an expanse of white teeth. "I wants it fo' my paw and maw."

"How's they?" The white man's tone was solicitous. "Ain't seen Uncle Stephen and Aunt Ca'line in a mighty long time."

"They's pretty well, Mist' Babe," Eph replied. "But they's gittin' mighty old. I jes' got off two or three days and come home to see 'em."

"I reck'n you seen Doct' Cardell, Eph?"

"Yes, sir, Mist' Babe, jes' long 'nough to speak, though; he had to go off on a call 'bout time I got up to the house."

Babe Atkins laughed. "I seen him t'other day when I had to git him to pull a tooth fer me." He turned to face the white men at the stove. "You know, he dang nigh kilt me too. And he'd a never got hit out if it hadn't been fer that woman th'owin' her arms 'round me and the ch'ir and holdin' me down whilst he snatched hit out with them pl'ars." He guffawed. "But with her pinnin' me down, he got hit out." Then he confronted the Negro again, grinning crookedly. "Look here, Eph," he said, turning his head to spit in the direction of the sandbox, "'twouldn't be yo' young'un that woman's carryin', would hit?"

"Naw, sir! Naw, sir, Mist' Babe! I don't know nothin' 'bout that woman. I ain't never seen her till yest'id'y!" He paid for the cheese and started for the door. "Naw, sir, 'twon't me."

"I had no notion 'twus Eph," Babe said, laughing, as the door closed behind the Negro. "I got a purtty good idea, though, who it is. And, my opinion, it ain't no nigger nowhow. But I ain't callin' no name."

Aaron was listening, mouth open, a strained, suddenly pained look on his thin, leathery face. But he made no comment.

Bub came around from behind the counter, held out his palms to the stove, and rubbed his hands together. "Speakin' o' wimmen carryin' young'uns, Babe," he said, "how many kids you got now?"

"Le' me see," the tenant answered, and paused a moment. " 'Bout seven now and one on the way."

"Hell fire," Bub said, incredulous. "Doct' Claib jes' fetched you one in July or August, didn't he?"

"Well, yeh, he did. But this here's November, ain't it?"

Bub turned around and warmed his back. "I guess with Babe it's like what old man Clem Hager told my pappy one time." He hesitated, for effect. "Old man Clem he said, 'Boys,' he, said, 'the only way to keep yo' old lady contented and at home,' he said, 'is to keep her bigged and barefooted.' "

Babe slapped his thighs, guffawed. "Old man Clem he was shore right 'bout that, he shore was. I done found that out."

16

Weary after an exhausting, distressing day that had brought the death of one of his several pneumonia patients, a young mother of two small children, Dr. Cardell settled himself on the sofa and stared abstractedly at the blazing hickory logs. Almost without a respite since this morning when he had slowly lifted the sheet over the still form, he had been carrying before him the tragic, agonized expression on the face of the husband at the moment the young man first seemed to realize that his wife was dead. Though he had been trying desperately, Dr. Cardell could not put out of mind the look of utter terror possessing the man while he held his motherless babies pressed in iron grip to his anguished heart as though he would protect them fiercely against a world suddenly grown empty and heartless and without meaning.

He sat with long legs stretched toward the comforting warmth and watched the flames dancing a ballet of infinite variety and intricacy in flowing and shimmering reds and oranges and lavenders and yellow-whites. And as he watched the stricken face in the leaping blaze, he felt that he was seeing courage and strength and a man's consuming strong love for his own, beginning to overcome and overleap fear and fright and doubt and loneliness and despair.

"Why not? He still has his children to protect, to live for, to enjoy."

He had said the words aloud, so vivid had been the face in the fire, so persistent the vision that the day's tragedy had evoked.

. I, too, will have a child. In the spring, come April, six thousand years, according to some stiff-necked theologians, after Adam and Eve, more likely seventy-five thousand, seventy-five million years, God only knows how many years and how many people down the long avenue of time, will have brought to fruition their efforts, their prayers, and their spermatozoa in order that I might become the father of a nigra baby. . . .

Claiborne raised his eyes to study the canvassed likenesses of two of the most recently engaged artisans of that Herculean task. According to a family tradition that he had never been able to substantiate and in recent years had come more strongly to doubt, the portraits of his grandfather and grandmother Cardell had been done at Philadelphia by Gilbert Stuart shortly before the artist painted the most celebrated of his oils of General Washington. Another story was that it was not Stuart but one of his pupils who had left to their venerating posterity the oil likenesses, in their later years, of the founders of Holly Grove. More likely, thought Claiborne, the portraits had been done by some itinerant painter to earn a summer's board and lodging at Holly Grove and a small stipend in cash.

Claiborne had never known either of his grandparents on the Cardell side. Grandmother Cardell, like the pneumonia victim today, had died when her children were young. To Claiborne, since his earliest childhood, she had been little more than preserved piety hanging sedately to the left of the parlor's pedimented mantel. And tonight Grandmother Cardell was returning his gaze, he felt, with an expression that was an admixture of hauteur, embarrassment, and sad resignation.

His eyes crossed the graceful plastered decorations of the pedimental to settle upon the fierce visage of Grandpa Cardell, whose luxuriant black whiskers seemed to bristle while silently, but with stern disapproval, he regarded his errant offspring.
. . I wonder how many nigra bastards you sired, Colonel. I'll bet you had some. But *they* weren't recorded against *you*. You had a legitimate family; their names were written in the big family Bible—their births, marriages, deaths. They got painted for posterity. Violet can spiel them off, all the vital statistics. She can climb the Cardell family tree and disport herself from limb to limb like a monkey. And never encounter even one small pickaninny. You knew how to hide 'em, Colonel. You knew. . . .

Above the blazing logs once more he saw the face of the young man. But he saw also the little boy and girl, their father's consolation in adversity, his continuing joy, his support and security in old age. Beautiful, promising children.

Sarah's child should be beautiful. It won't be but one-eighth nigra. And one-eighth Indian. Three-fourths white. The nigra blood may hardly show. The white blood may drown out the nigra and Indian. .

But he'll still be a nigra. Preponderantly white, but still nigra and barred inexorably from the white man's world, barred from his father's bed, barred even from his father's table. A beautiful child, but promising? Oh God, promising what?

He closed his eyes against the brightness of the weaving, darting flames, but he could not close his mind to the weighing of his problem. For weeks now he had thought of little else. He stood up and walked to the fireplace, turned his back to the comforting blaze, and stretched. Then he sat down again, thrust out his legs, and contemplated the logs being consumed.

. . . Violet wants me to send Sarah away, perhaps to South Carolina, down in old man Gordon's country where she came from; she wants me to send the woman back to the nigras, her and her baby, *my* baby, my little bastard baby. Send him into the world of the nigra, to live with them, grow to manhood with them, marry one of them, sire nigra babies. . . .

But what the hell else can he do, here or in South Carolina, or anywhere? A drop of nigra blood, a *known* drop, and he's nigra, he stays nigra.

. . . if they remain at Holly Grove, they are forever and unalterably nigras. And I? God knows what the people will think of me, a white man of the gentility, with a nigra family. I could go away with them, give up everything, take Sarah north, let her pass for a Spaniard or something, maybe marry her. But hell, I don't want to marry her. I will not marry her.   Even if I were not in love with Melissa, I'd never marry Sarah. . . .

In the north she might pass for a dark-skinned Caucasian. In Philadelphia he had seen many women darker than Sarah who were accepted as white.

I'll send her to Philadelphia after I have found a job for her, perhaps in the hospital. She can be a widow, and soon she will be able to marry a white man. She can raise her child as white. He can *be* white. And he can grow up and marry a white girl.

Suddenly it was clear to him that he would follow that course. It would give his son a chance, he assured himself. That is the solution. Heaven knows it had been troubling him, trying to decide what to do.

He would send Sarah money, he would see to it that she and the child did not suffer. Nor would Melissa have to know. And time would provide the ultimate solution. Within a few generations inexorable time would thin out that nigra blood until not a drop, not one *known* drop, remained.

And he would have his legitimate family. It would carry proudly the tradition of Holly Grove, it would see the Cardell line safely and handsomely through another generation. Melissa

86

Osborne would share his name, his mansion house, his bed.

Tomorrow he would go to see Melissa. If it should become necessary, he would confess freely to her his indiscretion, his sinning, if she insisted on so labeling it. He would reveal the plans he was making for Sarah, at any rate to the extent that he had decided to send her away. Then he would tell Melissa how much he loved her, how much he had always hoped that some day she would be his wife, and he would ask her to marry him. And before another summer Holly Grove would have a mistress.

. . . Grandpa, you'll have to move over; you'll have to make room, Grandma. You all will have to make room for Melissa and me. . . .

He lowered his eyes from his forebears Cardell and stood up. Tonight he would be able to sleep easily. From beside the mantel he picked up the brass-handled shovel and began to douse the fire with hot ashes.

17

Sarah Gordon straightened up from the steaming tub, with wet fingers pushed out of her eyes a straying wisp of black hair. It was beginning to be uncomfortable, bending over the tub, stomach pushed hard against the washboard to hold it steady as she scrubbed. With the baby developing so rapidly now, it was becoming more difficult every day for her to keep on her feet long at a time; she noticed herself tiring more quickly.

She dried her hands on a dish towel and went out to the porch and sat in the rocker, for although it was not long now until Christmas, the sun was high in a cloudless sky and the sunshine on the porch flooring and against the wall was warming and comforting.

if I was his wife and carryin' his child, he wouldn't have me bendin' over a washtub; he'd have one o' those cornfield nigger women doin' the washin'. But I'm not his wife; I'm just his woman. And pretty soon I won't even be his woman. I'll be sent off, so he can be respectable, and then he'll fetch that Osborne woman here as his wife

He was whistling this morning when he drove off in his buggy, she recalled. He had told her he might be gone all day, even into the night; he had said he had a lot of patients over in Cabarrus, some of them with bad cases of grippe. "Look for me when you see me," he had told her, and he had gone off whistling, the first time she had heard him whistling since the day she had told him she was in a family way.

he's on his way to that Melissa's house, or I'm a suck-egg mule. . . .

Dr. Cardell's mood at breakfast and her womanly intuition, coupled with his announcement that he was spending the day in the Cabarrus community, satisfied Sarah that he had decided to marry Melissa Osborne. And that could mean but one thing: she would have to leave Holly Grove before Melissa came, and likely as quickly as he could arrange it.

She wondered what he might be planning for her and the child. Where would he send them? Back to Fair Meadows? With her white baby that everybody would be thinking was Bob's or Jim's? Eliza would never agree to her returning.

Nor did she wish to go back there. It would be just as well if she never saw any of the Allisons again.

He may try to marry me off to some nigger, she said to herself.

. in bed with a smelly nigger. A houseful of little naked-belly niggers, their navels sticking out half an inch, their noses running. I couldn't stand it. My white blood just couldn't stand it. If I was a nigger, or mostly nigger, it would be different. . . .

What if Dr. Cardell should try to marry her off to Zeke? Zeke's gone to Charlotte; that would get her and the child safely away from Holly Grove and scandal talk.

. . . I'd rather be dead. I'm not going to shack up with no nigger. . . .

If he should arrange for them to go north somewhere, maybe Washington, maybe New York, somewhere up there, maybe Philadelphia where he went to study to be a doctor, somewhere up north, she might be able to get away from her Negro blood, certainly the child might. She might marry a white man even; surely the child could marry white.

I don't want to marry anybody. I can't marry Doct' Claib and I don't want nobody else. I don't want to go to Fair Meadows or back down to South Carolina or to Washington or New York or anywhere; I just want to stay here, Lord, I want to stay right here with him!

But in her heart she knew that Dr. Cardell had gone to Cabarrus to ask Melissa Osborne to marry him; she knew any day now he would be coming to her to tell her, politely, graciously, even a little sadly perhaps, that her days at Holly Grove were ending.

. . . O Lord, why? Why, why, O Lord? Why did I have to be part white, part black? Why, O Lord, couldn't I be one or the other?

18

The bays turning in at the gate must have waked her. She heard them as they came along the drive almost even with her porch, and then they stopped. But she did not hear any sound of the doctor's getting out.

She slipped from her bed, went to the window, and peered out. He was still in the buggy, slumped over. The bays were standing quietly. She ran back to the bed, slid her feet into her shoes, and grabbed her wrapper. As she stepped off the porch she heard him vomiting.

"Sarah, I'm—I'm sick. I'm so sick-k-k!" He leaned forward, retching, and would have pitched headlong from the buggy had she not stayed him. Sickened by the stench of the raw corn whisky arising from the vomit in the foot of the buggy and smearing his clothing, she almost lifted him from the vehicle and supported him, her left arm holding his arm about her shoulders and her right arm about his waist, until she got him into his office, where he sagged to his chair. She had left his office lamp burning low. She turned it up.

"I'll be right back, Doct' Claib. I'm afraid the horses might get hurt or break up the buggy tryin' to get in their stables. You just sit there and don't move till I get back!"

She hurried out to the bays, unhitched them, and led them to the stables; she slid the harness off their backs, turned them in, and closed and bolted the doors. Then she hurried back to the mansion house.

Dr. Cardell's chin was sunk into his befouled waistcoat, his inert arms hung almost to the floor; he was snoring heavily.

The woman found a towel, wiped her reeking, slimy hands, and went out to the kitchen. The fire had not gone out entirely; she put some small sticks on the coals and blew on them until the wood blazed. Then with water from the wooden bucket she filled the kettle. Next she poured a dipper of water into the tin basin and washed her hands.

Returning to the mansion house, she went upstairs and from the hall closet procured soap, a washcloth, and a towel; from the doctor's bedroom closet she got his nightshirt. She brought them downstairs and left them in his office; he was still snoring. Then she ran back out to the kitchen and brought the kettle of hot water and the basin, which she set on his desk and filled. While it was cooling she would get his clothes off.

Her struggling with his coat aroused him, and he tried to help. "I'm so sick, Sarah," he said, his eyes rolling, "I'm so sick, so bad sick-k-k," and his heavy head fell forward.

"You'll be all right in a little while," she said, "soon's I get you washed and put to bed."

When at length she had succeeded in peeling off his be-smeared coat and waistcoat, she took off his shoes, unbuckled his belt, and grabbing his trousers at his ankles, pulled them straight down and off. Then she unbuttoned his shirt, un-knotted his bespattered cravat, and detached his collar. When she had removed them all, she bathed his face and hands with the washcloth.

"I've fetched your nightshirt," she said. "Now you can wash all over. Then you'll feel better, and you can put on your night-shirt and I'll help you get in your bed."

"Sarah, oh, I'm sick." He fell back in the chair, and his head lolled. "I'm just too sick to do it—yet. Just let me rest awhile. Just let me—Oh, hell, Sarah—"

She caught his woollen undershirt at the waist, pulled the tail out from his long heavy drawers, and skinned it wrong-side out over his head. Then she unbuttoned the drawers, pulled them from under him, and peeled them down over his long legs. Having freed him completely of his clothes, she scrubbed the washcloth on the soap, squeezed it above the basin, and proceeded to give him a head-to-foot washing.

Not until she had got him in·his bed with the covers up under his chin did she venture to question him.

"You been over to Colonel Osborne's?"

"Yes."

"Charlie Gunn?"

"Yes." He nodded, his head heavy. "One reason."

"I reckon I know the other one." She said it laconically, paused. "Now you better go to sleep, Doct' Claib."

"I got to have a little to taper off on, Sarah. There's a half-gallon jar in the buggy—"

"I saw it when I went to hitch out the horses. You drunk mighty nigh all of it. It's a wonder—"

"I know. If I hadn't vomited most of it, it might have killed me, I guess. But I need a little now, Sarah. I'm not drunk, but I'm sick."

She made no comment but turned and left the room. In a few minutes she was back with two glasses. She held one, about a third filled, in front of him. "There wasn't much left."

"That's enough to settle me down."

She handed him the glass, and he drank the whisky gluttonously, frowned, and held out his other hand for the glass of water.

"You're good to me, Sarah," he said, when he had gulped the water. "You are always helping me out. She—" But he said no more. Nor did she offer to press him.

"Now you better try to get to sleep," she said. "If you need

91

me, holler out the window." She smiled grimly. "But like as not, you'll be sleeping a pretty good while. Good night, Doct' Claib."

On light feet, despite her growing heaviness, she went down the circling stairs and out to her kitchen cottage.

19

The first week in December Dr. Cardell wrote to his sister Violet in Charlotte and invited her to come up to Holly Grove for Christmas. "We'll try to make believe that it's the old Christmases come back," he added at the end of the note.

Several days before Christmas he had a letter from her saying that she would not be able to come home. She had promised Abigail Davidson that she would spend Christmas with her at Rural Hill. She was sorry, she said; she so wished that she might wave a magic wand and find herself back at Holly Grove for one of the Christmases of years gone by.

"But that can never be, Claiborne," he read. "Too much has been lost for Holly Grove ever to be the same again."

He understood what she meant. He opened the package she had sent: a black cravat and two white handkerchiefs.

Claiborne slept late Christmas morning, ate a light breakfast, and went into the parlor where Uncle Stephen's little great-grandson with Sarah's prompting had built a cheering fire. Sarah had meant for it to be cheering, at any rate, he knew. But he was finding it difficult to be cheerful; on this most significant of all anniversaries he knew he would be weighing today's every hour against those joyous memories of other Christmases. He realized that all anniversaries have overtones of sadness, especially to persons of mature years, and Christmas most of all.

Sitting here alone except for the presence on canvas of austere forebears staring sternly upon him, Claiborne remembered Christmas mornings of his childhood. Fires burning brightly in this parlor, in the dining room, the bedrooms; two bulging stockings hanging from the mantel in his parents' bedroom; gifts piled under a Christmas cedar in the front hall, with lighted tiny candles in little holders attached to the cedar's branches—remembering, he wondered why the house hadn't been burned down—and now in his loneliness perhaps most vividly of all he recalled the jollity and warmth of family feeling at the Christmas-morning breakfasts before daylight, with the flickering light of candles heightening the festival mood. And those breakfasts! Country ham and sausage, scrambled eggs, grits and ham gravy, hot biscuits with butter, jellies and jams, sourwood honey, steaming coffee, even some diluted with milk for Violet and himself.

And after breakfast, as dawn was breaking, the slaves assembling in the front hall, scrubbed and in their Sunday clothes, men, women, and little pickaninnies, laughing and calling out in the excited, quick joy of children, "Chris'mus gif'! Chris'mus gif'!" and answering, white eyeballs rolling, "Gi' hit here, den! Gi' hit right here!" And under the tree a gift for each of the slaves, shawls and scarves and bright trinkets for the women, socks and plug tobacco and maybe a wool hat for the men, candy and simple playthings for the children. He remembered, too, how early on Christmas mornings his father would give each of the men a stiff drink of whisky and the merriment it provoked; but the major never permitted drunkenness.

Looking through the doorway into the silent and deserted front hall, Claiborne recalled with a sharp nostalgia the Negroes singing. Throughout the year they sang, the women in the mansion house, the men and women in the fields, in their quarters at night, on Sunday afternoons when his mother taught them Bible stories; but best of all they sang on Christmas mornings out there around the gay Christmas tree.

This Christmas morning he had sat alone at that same breakfast table; it was ten o'clock and the sun was high in a leaden sky when he had eaten. No Christmas tree stood out there at the curving of the stairs, no gifts, no Negroes singing, no holly decorating the halls and parlor and dining room, no mistletoe hanging beneath the hall chandelier with pretty girl cousins and neighbors daring, quite happily, to venture under it.

Claiborne wondered what had become of those Christmas-happy persons who less than two decades ago had peopled the front hallway of Holly Grove. His parents and the older slaves dead, Violet spending Christmas at a neighboring plantation, disappointed, humiliated, no doubt angry with him, and the young slaves, the jubilant pickaninnies, where are they this Christmas Day? Only God knows where they are. Throughout the slowly, painfully recovering southland only God knows the whereabouts of the suddenly freed, suddenly lost slaves. To how many of them at this moment does Christmas have any meaning?

. . . Heaven knows I'm not defending slavery. People are not property; the ownership of one human being by another is an abomination. But is the sociological advancement of any people best served through the sudden and violent overthrowing of a region's very way of life? Was the ultimate welfare of the Negro assured and hastened by the action of hotheads North and South who refused to consider in tolerance and work out in patience and mutual understanding the solution of a problem of such vast intricacy and import? O God, why couldn't the fuzzy headed do-gooders, North and South, have given the plain, honest, quietly good people in both sections, preponderantly in the majority, time to effect a real and lasting solution? The nigras are free, sure; but on this Christmas Day where are they? Where will they be fifty years from now, seventy-five, a hundred?

And where was he himself? the doctor wondered. He couldn't blame the war for the situation in which he found himself. Nor anyone else. Nor Melissa even. Nor Sarah.

Sarah was now out in the kitchen preparing his Christmas dinner. In other days that kitchen had been filled with cooks bustling over pots and pans, skillets, ovens, bandannaed and aproned, and chattering and laughing women excited over Christmas and Christmas guests in the big house. But today Christmas at Holly Grove was reduced to one cook and one diner. Claiborne had thought that the Allisons might invite him to have Christmas dinner at Fair Meadows. When they hadn't, he was relieved; his presence at their table might have caused strained conversation, embarrassing silences. He had heard nothing from the Allisons, as a matter of fact, he remembered, for weeks. Eliza must have heard the news, perhaps from Melissa. But he had sworn to leave Melissa out of it.

. . . I wonder if Charlie Gunn is having Christmas dinner with the Osbornes, sitting smugly beside Melissa or grinning loutishly across the table from her. But surely the aristocratic Osbornes haven't invited that brash overseer to eat with them. And surely, too, despite what she said that night, Melissa cannot seriously be thinking of marrying the oaf. We both said things we shouldn't have. Both of us lost our tempers and unbridled our tongues. I shouldn't have said what I did about the fellow, nor should I have told her it was none of her affair whether I had a baby by Sarah or not. But that hardly gave her a right to castigate me in the bitter manner she did. Even then I had no excuse for coming home as drunk as a fiddler's bitch. . . .

He heard a horse's hoofbeats and, looking out, saw a man dismounting at the hitching post. He walked to the front door and out on the verandah. The man was coming up the walk between the boxwoods. Claiborne saw who he was.

"Come in, Aaron," he called out. "Merry Christmas!"

"Howdy, Doc! Merry Christmas to you, too. How's things goin'?"

Claiborne took him into the parlor and seated him in front of the fireplace. "What can I do for you, Aaron? Hope your folks have no bad sickness."

"Nothin' real bad, Doc. I been over at Hortonsville and on my way back thought I'd stop by and git some more o' that medicine you give my old 'oman. What you give her before is done run out. And hit done her so much good I thought mebbe I ought to stop by and let you give her some more."

"I'll do it, Aaron. I got some here at the house. How is your missus getting on?"

"She's doin' pretty well, Doc. Can't work like she used to, but she's gittin' 'long pretty good." He stood up. "Well, I 'spect I better be gittin' on. If you'll jest git me that medicine—"

"Sit down, Aaron. You don't have to be going yet. Stay and have dinner with me. Sarah'll have it ready before long. I'll be mighty glad to have you."

The farmer, embarrassed but pleased, sought to excuse himself, but the doctor insisted, and Aaron sat down. They talked— of illnesses in the community; the plight of farmers now that most of the Negroes had gone to Charlotte, or, little more than vagrants, were shifting from place to place; the price of cotton; continuing bad times in the aftermath of the frightful Reconstruction.

Aaron nodded to Sarah when she came to announce that dinner was ready. After they were seated at the table she entered the dining room several times in the course of serving, but the visitor made no mention of her to Dr. Cardell, and when they had finished the meal, bountiful enough but hardly comparable with past Christmas dinners at Holly Grove, they returned to the parlor. Even then Aaron did not refer to her, except to praise the dinner and thank the doctor warmly for his hospitality. Soon afterward, with the medicine for his perennially ailing wife, Aaron left.

No other caller, even to seek professional service, appeared at Holly Grove. Late in the afternoon Claiborne went for a brisk walk in the chill air. Returning, he was coming through the gateway when the sun, momentarily breaking through the sodden clouds, suddenly gilded the large heart in cream brick high in the south end. He wondered again why the heart had been built into the red-brick wall of the house. Family tradition, or maybe he had heard his father say it, held that Grandfather Cardell in building his family seat as a young man years ago had ordered the masons to put in the unusual decoration to make sure that through the generations Holly Grove would always be a place possessed of a great heart. A nice fancy, a pretty fiction, he told himself, for already the sun had retreated behind the clouds.

He went into the house and drank a glass of milk and ate a small slab of pound cake Sarah had left for him on the sideboard. He sat for awhile in the continuing loneliness of the parlor. Then he covered the fire, blew out the lamp, and climbed the stairs to his bedroom. For a few minutes an article in his current journal held his interest, but before he had finished it he tossed the periodical aside and stood up. Quickly he undressed, took his nightshirt from the chilly closet, slipped it over his head, and shivered as it dropped to his ankles. Bending over the lamp chimney, he extinguished the light and slid between the icy sheets.

20

As the plodding, heavy Sarah paused on the second-floor hall landing to catch her breath before going in to clean his room, she felt suddenly a sharp small pain clawing at the pit of her bulging lower abdomen. She clutched the stair well's baluster railing.

It can't be coming yet, she thought, bracing against panic. He had figured it wouldn't be until the second week in May. But babies often come two weeks ahead, she'd always heard, and how could a doctor—even when he was also the prospective father—know to the day?

But the pain had gone and with it her sudden fright. Maybe it was just a touch of indigestion anyway, something she had eaten, maybe that boiled cabbage. She went into the bedroom and began making the bed. Even if the sharply stabbing, quickly gone pain were signaling the beginning of labor, it should be hours before the baby came, and by then Doctor Claib would be home.

He hadn't told her where he was going, except that he had several calls to make, enough to keep him away until the middle of the afternoon. She certainly shouldn't need him within four or five hours. Why hadn't he told her where he was going today, where he might be located in case of an emergency, not her emergency but maybe that of someone fearfully hurt, somebody shot while hunting or cut in a sawmill accident or something?

Surely he hasn't gone to Colonel Osborne's, she thought despairingly. Surely she is through with him, even if he should be willing to go crawling back to her. That Melissa must have refused him or he wouldn't have come home in such a shape. And he hadn't mentioned her since, and that was back around Thanksgiving. But has he entirely given up hope of marrying her? She still wondered. Certainly he hasn't been able to forget her, else why has he been for days at a time moody and depressed, why has he been drinking much more than he used to? And could it be that that Melissa has had enough of that Charlie Gunn's big talk and is willing to take Doctor Claib back?

and her knowing I'm carrying his baby? Not much of a chance of that. I hope not much of a chance. . . .

She had forgotten to bring the broom. She went downstairs to get it, taking care to hold to the railing of the stairs. She was so heavy in front and overbalanced that she was afraid of falling, and she shuddered at what a fall on the stairway might mean.

Climbing the stairs with dustpan and broom, she paused midway and rested a moment, and on the second-floor landing she stopped again to get a long breath. The pain did not return, and she went on into the bedroom, raised the windows, and began sweeping. She swept toward the fireplace and on the hearth brushed the sweepings into the dustpan. With the pan in one hand and the broom in the other she started for the door.

She had set the broom against the door frame and was reaching for the knob, when suddenly a rude hand with white-hot fingers reached deep into her insides and squeezed and twisted. So intense and unexpected was the pain that she almost dropped the dustpan. But she managed to set it down without spilling it, and she bent double and clutched her cramping belly as she managed to hobble to the bed and fall across it. She lay on her side, knees drawn up, groaning, and perspiration popped from her forehead.

. . . Oh, Lord, am I gonna have it on his bed? He wouldn't

like that. I've got to get back to my bed. He wouldn't want it born on his bed even if he got it here. I've got to get back to my room. I've got to hurry, too. It's not gonna be long now. Climbing up and down those stairs, raising those windows and lettin' 'em down, that's makin' it come. . .

She lay in the grip of the squeezing, twisting, hot hand and pressed her wet face into the counterpane to smother her muffled screaming, and she prayed frantically for the doctor to get home in time. When after a few moments the pain eased, she dragged herself from the bed and moved slowly and clumsily to the door and out into the hallway. At the head of the stairs she caught the railing and slid her hand along it until she had reached the first floor. Then she went out the back door and down the back-porch steps to the gravel path leading to her kitchen house.

Oh Lawd, fetch him home! Fetch him home quick, Lawd! .

She heard a noise down toward the stables. Eph's grandson, who had been staying with Uncle Stephen and Aunt Ca'line, was coming toward the big house, swinging a stick with which he was knocking at pebbles.

"Jimbo!" she yelled to the little boy. "Jimbo!" She saw that he had heard. "Run get Aunt Ca'line! Hurry, boy! Tell her to come quick as she can. To my house, Jimbo, to the kitchen! Tell her, please ma'am hurry!"

Jimbo threw up his hand, wheeled about, and disappeared behind the stables, running.

21

It was after four o'clock when Dr. Cardell turned in at Holly Grove and drove on to the stables. He was unhitching the bays when Jimbo, a wide grin on his round black face, sidled up.

"Doct' Claib," he said, looking down to consider solemnly his bare toes, recently freed of shoes for the summer despite the fact that May and dependably warm weather were still a week away, "Gran'ma Ca'line say, please sir will you come up to Miss Sa'ah's house jes' as soon as you can git dere?"

"Anything wrong up there, Jimbo?"

"Naw sir, don't think nothin' wrong, but she say, please sir will you come up to Miss Sa'ah's quick's you can."

"All right, Jimbo, soon's I get these horses in the stable, I'll go. You can feed 'em for me. Give 'em some oats and throw 'em some roughage down from the loft."

"Yes sir, Doct' Claib; I'll feed 'em good."

Claiborne turned the horses into their stalls and started up the path toward the mansion house. Where the path forked he took the one to the kitchen. Aunt Ca'line must have heard his footsteps on the gravel. She was waiting on the porch.

"Marse Claib, hit look like you wasn't never comin' home," she said, a tone of mild reproof in her voice. "Hit was a good thing I got here in time for the birthin', else I don't know what dat po' Sa'ah'd done. But as 'twus, she got 'long all right. I had Stephen helpin', though 'tweren't much he could do 'cep' keep plenty hot water." Suddenly her wizened old forehead doubled its wrinkles and she was staring imperiously at him as she had stared on many an occasion when as a child he had been forced to endure her stern lecturing. "And now, little Marster, how comes you stands out here listenin' me runnin' my mouf 'stead o' goin' in dere seein' 'bout dat po' chile?"

Claiborne, smiling, shook his head, said nothing, and walked into the kitchen house and Sarah's bedroom. "How're you feeling, Sarah?" he asked the pale woman on the bed in the corner.

She ventured a wan smile. "Pretty good, Doct' Claib, I reckon, considerin'."

"That's good. Let me have a look and see how good a job Aunt Ca'line did." Quickly he examined her. "Clean as a whistle," he said after awhile. "I couldn't have done a bit better myself. But I suspect she's delivered about as many babies as I have—she started a long time before I did." He looked toward the old woman, who was standing in the doorway. "Didn't you, Aunt Ca'line?"

"Go 'long wid you, little Marster," she said, beaming. "Sa'ah, he's here now and I'm goin' back home. I'll tell Jimbo to stay 'round to wait on you, and I'll be back a'ter while. Pretty soon now you go to sleep, you hear me, chile?"

"Yes'm, and thank you for what you done for me."

"Go 'long, chile; I ain't done nothin'. And I'll be back 'fore long." She disappeared into the hall, and a moment later Dr. Cardell heard her step down from the porch.

"Aunt Ca'line was right, Sarah; try to go to sleep now; you're all right, but a long nap will do you good." He pulled the sheet up toward her chin, smoothed it. But she lifted her head from the pillow, wearily, pointed. "Ain't you goin' to go over and look—" She settled back on the pillow.

"Oh, of course."

From a bureau drawer Aunt Ca'line had improvised a baby bed; it sat on two straight chairs placed to face each other against the wall, and in it she had folded quilts and a blanket to make a soft resting place for Sarah's first-born.

He walked over and looked down into the drawer-bed.

"Twins! Damn! Sarah, you didn't tell me you had twins!" But he was smiling. . . . My babies. Bastards, yes, but mine!

"Do you think they are pretty babies, Doct' Claib?"

"Why, yes," he answered, as he studied the sleeping tiny infants, "they're handsome babies, Sarah." He saw that they were almost white. Only a faint shading of brown in their coloring and widened nostrils betrayed their one-eighth of Negro blood; their hair was straight and black. "What are they?" He turned to face her.

"A boy and a girl, Aunt Ca'line said."

"Have you named them, Sarah?" He came over and stood beside her bed.

"I been readin' in my Shakespeare book," she answered, hesitantly, "and when I got so big I thought maybe it would be twins. So I thought, if it suits you, I'd call 'em Romeo and Juliet."

"Romeo and Juliet." He was thoughtful an instant, and then

he smiled. "Sarah," he said, "I think Romeo and Juliet would be nice names for *your babies.*"

22

Early in June a season of rainfall forced the farmers of the Cardell Station community from their fields and sent them stamping their soggy feet and shaking coats and slapping dripping wool hats into the fellowship of Bub Barkley's store. Such occasions of interrupted work afforded welcomed opportunities for the interchange of bits of neighborhood news and the indiscriminate scattering of unique pearls of philosophy.

This afternoon's subject of the moment had developed from a consideration of the birth some six weeks ago of Negro twins to Dr. Claiborne Cardell into an arguably tangential discussion of the profound problem of whether or not a Negro has a soul.

It was Bub Barkley's opinion, he had just declared, that the Negro, having been consigned by the Almighty to the position of hewer of wood and drawer of water, was a servant of the white man in somewhat the same category as the horse and mule and therefore was unpossessed of a soul. But one man promptly disputed the proprietor's reasoning.

"And how come, Aaron, do you think a nigger's got a soul like a white man has got?" Bub challenged.

"But don't the Good Book say that the Lord He made Adam and Eve? They was bound to be white people, Bub, and they had child'en and it come on down after a long time to Noah and he had three sons, and when Noah he got drunk and laid 'round naked one o' them sons, Ham he was, looked at his daddy, but Shem and Japheth took a coat and wropped it 'round the old man, and when Noah sobered up and found out what Ham done, he cussed him and said his child'en would be servants o' the other boys' child'en?"

"Maybe so, Aaron," Bub agreed, "but what's all that got to do with hit?"

"Well, the Good Book it says Ham was the first nigger, don't it, and I don't reckon Noah's son didn't have no soul, do you?"

"But how come if Noah was a white man his son Ham was a nigger?"

" 'Cause the Good Book says so, and ever'thing in the Good Book is so, hain't it?" Aaron smiled at the knowledge that his logic was unassailable. "Course, Bub, I see yo' point. But if the Lord wanted to make a white man's son the first nigger, I guess He could do it, couldn't He?"

"I don't say He couldn't. But seems to me if his daddy was a white man, he'd have to be a mulatto, at least, and if his mama was a white woman, I can't see how he'd even be a mulatto."

Aaron spit into the sandbox at the cold and now defenseless stove. "Because the Lord jes' made him the first nigger, I reckon, Bub." His little eyes sharpened. "Now I'll grant you, Bub, that it may be that a mulatto nigger don't have no soul. I ain't never found nowheres in the Good Book where it speaks 'bout no mulattoes, but my 'pinion ever'body what the Good Book speaks about's got a soul."

A thin-shanked fellow who lived a mile beyond Bethel Church spoke up. "Well, then, Aaron, do you figure as maybe them little bastards o' Doc Cardell ain't got no souls? I hears they's not much nigger blood in 'em. They mama, I hear tell, ain't but one-fourth nigger, and that makes them jes' one-eighth. Do you claim that a one-eighth nigger ain't got no soul?"

Aaron started to reply, swallowed, and for a moment his Adam's apple chased up and down his long gullet like a cork bobbing. "Now I didn't say a mulatto nigger didn't have no soul. I said it might be he don't. But I believe a black nigger, a real out-and-out nigger, jes' like a white man, does have one."

But the Bethel man was not relenting. "But what I'd like to get yo' 'pinion on, Aaron, is jes' how far out a mulatto has to go 'fore he gits his soul back. When these little bastards o' Doc Cardell grows up and gits child'en with a white daddy or mammy, will those child'en have souls or won't they? Or how many mo' generations will hit take 'fore they gits to havin' souls?"

From the other side of the stove another farmer offered his

contribution of wisdom. "Once a nigger, always a nigger, I says. Jes' one drap, one drap o' nigger blood, and he's a nigger."

The Bethel citizen grinned. "How 'bout one-hund'eth part o' a drap, 'Fonso? He'd be lookin' mighty white by then, eh?" He rubbed his back up and down against the corner of the dry-goods box on which he was leaning and held out his thumb and forefinger barely separated. "Have all but 'bout this much of his soul, wouldn't he?"

Fonso shrugged. "I ain't no nigger-lover. Far as I'm concerned, he'd still be a nigger, and I wouldn't give a damn whether he'd have no soul or not."

"I guess if he went up to New Yawk or Philadelphy or Wa'-hin'ton he'd be a white man and have a soul," the Bethelite observed casually, "but if he stayed down here he'd be a nigger and wouldn't have no soul, eh, 'Fonso?"

Aaron burst into a loud guffaw and slapped his hips. "He's got you cornered, 'Fonso. He'd have a soul up there and not have a soul down here!"

"He ain't got me cornered," 'Fonso protested. He stuck a lean forefinger in his needler's direction. "He can go up there or stay down here, and you and him can both go to hell!"

"Now, 'Fonso," the Bethel man stood out from the drygoods box, drawled, "if'n he ain't got no soul, how could he go to hell? He'd jes' be like a horse or a dog or cat or 'possum, and you don't claim they goes to hell, do you?"

But he was spared 'Fonso's answer and a further philosophical exploration, for at that moment Dr. Cardell came through the front door. He nodded to the men around the cold stove, and singled out several whose families he had been treating in recent months, to inquire about the state of their health.

"How's your missus getting on, Aaron? You aren't letting her work too much?"

"Doin' very well, Doc. And not to give you no disrespeck, she ain't hardly working a-tall." He laughed coarsely and spat toward the stove. "I'm a notion you done ruint her for good 'bout workin'."

The doctor turned to 'Fonso. "How's Mis' Lizzie and the rest of your folks, 'Fonso?"

"They's all gettin' on pretty good, Doc," 'Fonso replied. "How's your folks?"

Dr. Cardell leveled his eyes at the farmer. "My sister Violet's quite well, thank you, as far as I know. She's living in Charlotte and I haven't heard from her for some time." Then he stepped over to the counter. "Bub, I need a few things for the house," he said. "Thought I'd stop by and get 'em while I was over this way on a call."

The proprietor beamed. "Yes, sir, Doc, glad to fix you up. Now jes' le' me know what you needs "

Under the doctor's directions he was busily engaged in filling the order when a lean, leathery fellow came in.

"Howdy, boys," he said as he approached the group. Then he saw Dr. Cardell. "Howdy, Doc."

"Well, Babe," spoke up 'Fonso. "How's things over yo' way? Been havin' plenty o' rain, I guess."

"Dang nigh all the frogs is done drownded," Babe Atkins answered. "If'n hit don't dry up pretty soon, the cane grass'll have us et up in no time."

Bub was assembling the doctor's purchases at one end of the counter. "Now would there be anything else, Doc?"

"I don't believe so, Bub."

Bub removed a short, blunt pencil from above his ear and stuck the lead end into his mouth. "Well, I'll just run this up, Doc."

At the stove Aaron was grinning, his sharp eyes bright. "Babe, are you over here lookin' for Doct' Cardell to fetch you another young'un? Is that how come you're over on this side?"

Babe took off his hat, scratched his head, replaced the hat. "Hell, you boys must figure I keep the old 'oman bigged all the time. No, I ain't lookin' for Doc today. I had to come over to Fair Meadows on a little business for Colonel Osborne. He sent me on account the wimmen folks's keepin' him so busy gittin' ready for the weddin'."

"The weddin'?" 'Fonso's mouth was open.

"Yeh. Miss M'lissy and Charlie Gunn they's gonna git married week a'ter next."

"You mean that M'lissy Osborne's gonna marry that *overseer* feller?" 'Fonso's tone was incredulous. "And the Osbornes, they's willin'?"

"I reckon they got to be long as Miss M'lissy's bent on hit." He grinned. "I think mebbe the colonel and the old lady th'owed a fit when she told 'em she was. But, hell, 'Fonso, my opinion she ain't lowerin' herself none nohow. Charlie ain't no ord'nary overseer. He's done bought in to a cotton mill they's gittin' started over our way. I got a idea time Charlie he's as old as the colonel he'll have a sight more money than the colonel he's got now."

Aaron glanced furtively toward Dr. Cardell, but the doctor appeared not to have heard. He was paying Babe. "I'll carry this out to the buggy," he said to the storekeeper. "You can bring the rest."

They set the purchases in the back of the buggy. "Sure there wouldn't be something else, Doc?" Bub asked.

The doctor's countenance was grim. "You got any real good corn liquor, Bub?"

"Got some o' the best, Doc. Been aged a good while; smooth as a whistle but got a kick like a mule."

"Fetch me out a jug."

23

August came in hot and dry, and Holly Grove drowsed under a heavy sun. In the big water oak near the road a cicada blasted the drooping stillness with cadenced rasping. From the kitchen house in the back yard a baby's shrill high wail of hunger answered.

Claiborne Cardell stood up and with his legs pushed back his father's chair in which he had been lolling. A buggy pulled by a chestnut mare was turning in through the gateway. He recognized Bob Allison and threw up his hand in greeting. Then he walked down the steps and out to the driveway.

" 'Light, Bob, and come in," he said. "Had your dinner yet? I've just finished, but I think Sarah could scare you up a bite."

"Ate just before I left home, Claib, much obliged."

"Well, get out anyway and come in. We'll sit on the verandah; too hot to stay out here long. Just pull your mare over there in the shade. I'll get somebody to lead her down to the trough; she looks hot." He motioned toward the magnolia.

"No, I don't reckon I got time, Claib. I—"

"You got nobody sick at home, have you?"

"Oh, no, Claib. I didn't come for you to do any doctoring. I just thought I'd ride over and see you. I'll tell you why: two reasons, I guess. I wanted to see if I could give you any help with the crop, case you might need some. And I wanted to take you over to have a look at my bottom-land corn. Just got it laid by yesterday."

"Well, Bob, to tell the truth, I don't know just what shape my crop's in. Haven't been in the fields much lately. I been pretty much—"

"Yeh, I know, I understand." His neighbor nodded his head slowly. "I've been hearing 'bout it. That's the reason I thought maybe you'd got behind with your crop, and I could send some hands over and give you a lift. Mine haven't got much to do till cotton-picking time anyway; they could get yours laid by pretty soon."

"It's good of you to offer to, Bob. But I don't know just what shape they're in. Sarah's been saying they were doing pretty well; she's been trying to see after the hands—" a baby's sudden crying caused him to pause, and he shrugged, "but she's had her hands pretty full otherwise, and I'm afraid I haven't been much help."

"Yeh, I understand, Claib; I know about it. But say, hop in and let's run over to the bottom lands this side o' the place. Get your hat. I won't keep you long."

The doctor turned toward the verandah, hesitated. "I might get a call."

"Oh, hell, we won't be gone long, Claib. Tell Sarah; she can watch out for you."

"Well, I reckon so." He walked down beyond the magnolia, called to the woman, and told her he would be gone a short while with Mr. Allison. Then he went into the house and came out with his hat.

"Bob," he asked, as he got into the buggy, "what all you been hearing about me lately?"

"Well, I know you been on a drunk off and on since back in June, ever since—"

"That's right," Claiborne confirmed the time, "ever since I heard that day at Bub Barkley's store that Melissa was going to marry Charlie Gunn. I got on a hell of drunk that night and I haven't been really cold sober since."

"Really, Claib, that's how come I drove over here: to talk to you about that. But I wanted you to see the corn, too."

"Hell, Bob, you going to lecture me on the evils of alcohol, or having babies by nigger women, or getting on a big drunk when the girl you thought you were going to marry, marries some other fellow, or all of 'em?"

Bob Allison laughed. "None of 'em, Claib. I wouldn't have the nerve to lecture anybody on the first two, you well know. And the last, well, I guess a fellow's got a right to a good reason, anyhow. But still, it don't get you anywhere."

"Yeh; I reckon I was just a damned fool all the way round."

"I wouldn't say that, Claib. Not so far. But from here on out, you could be, you know."

They rode along in silence a moment and presently Bob pointed. "That corn just did make it 'fore it turned off dry," he said. "If it'd been planted a week later it wouldn't made half a crop." The doctor nodded his agreement but said nothing. "I must have got mine in a couple weeks ahead of this," Bob went on. "I don't think the dry weather will hurt mine now."

They passed Bub Barkley's store and, a quarter of a mile

beyond it, turned left and drove along a narrow farm road that led into the back side of Fair Meadows. Half a mile on this road and they turned right and came out on a flat bit of land that looked off to Allison's Creek two-hundred yards west. Bob swept his arm in an arc. "How you like that meadow corn, Claib? Got anything'll match it?"

"I got some good bottom land, you know," he replied. "But I haven't seen it since June. Haven't seen much of any of my crops you couldn't see from the house, in fact." He shook his head. "Pretty nearly wasted the whole summer, Bob."

"Yeh, reckon you did, Claib. You didn't get much practicing done, either, did you?"

"Couldn't answer all my calls, that's for certain. Guess it's been pretty hard on Dr. Horton, with all the typhoid there's been this summer."

"Yeh, no doubt it has, Claib. And that's another thing I wanted to talk with you about, the main reason, in fact. You been sorter down in the dumps lately, eh?"

"I guess so, Bob. A lot of things have combined to get me down, I reckon."

"I understand. But you don't have to stay down, Claib. There's no sense in taking it the way you have. Melissa isn't the only woman in the world. There're plenty left, you know."

"Sure. I know that. I wasn't so anxious maybe to marry her anyway. I guess it was a combination of things. Her marrying that damned Charlie Gunn, for one thing. And, well, you know the rest."

"That's what I wanted to talk about, Claib, and straight from the shoulder, man to man." He looked the doctor in the face. "You mind?"

"No. But I don't think it'll do any good, Bob. I don't see any way out of this mess."

"The hell there ain't! There's a good way out; all you got to do is make up your mind, and then take it, Claib." He hooked the reins over the dashboard. "It's too crowded in here. Let's sit over there on that log."

109

They climbed from the buggy and seated themselves astride the log, facing each other, their legs outstretched.

"Claib, you been home a year now, thirteen months or more, in fact," the master of Fair Meadows began. "And in that time you haven't made much headway for the chance you had, I'm bound to say. I ain't aiming to hurt your feelings, but I'm going to give it to you straight, boy. You're a good doctor, Claib, one of the best in this whole country. You ought to be; you've had the advantage of the best training in the latest methods in medicine in one of the best schools in the country, and on top of that you've had a lot of hospital experience; and that's something few young doctors in the South have had a chance at, you know. You could have had the biggest and best practice in this part of the country by now; in fact, if you'd had a mind to, you could have hung out your shingle in Charlotte and been right in the lead down there." He kicked at a pebble and looked up to face the doctor again. "But you haven't, Claib. And you know why. And I'll say, too, that you could have married Melissa if you'd wanted to, really wanted to, back when you came home." He paused. "And, hell, it ain't all your fault, either." He laughed grimly. "I guess I'd have done just what you did if I'd been in your shoes, Claib. Eliza figured I would anyway; that's why she wished Sarah off on you." He lifted a finger, punctuated his words. "But this is where I'd have done it different, Claib. That woman would have been long gone from my house before she had those babies; she'd never have birthed 'em there, even if they were mine."

He pulled his knife from his pocket, opened it, and pecked with the long blade at the bark between them. But Claiborne made no comment, and Bob Allison, his knife poised in mid-air, eyed him again. "You've got to get rid of her, Claib. You can't keep her at Holly Grove, even if she's living in the back yard and eating at the kitchen table, and continue to be accepted as a Mecklenburg blueblood. You know that, boy. And if you begin to slip socially, you'll soon be slipping fast in your profession. First thing you know, won't anybody be having you but the poor whites and nigras."

Allison stabbed viciously at the log's bark, pulled out the knife, closed the blade, pocketed it. "You know, Claib, down here folks don't hold it too much against a white man of the aristocracy if he has a baby by a nigra woman so long as it's birthed in her shack and it's not too openly known to be his; so that it's a little mysterious, you know, something the women can titter over and whisper about when the men aren't around. But when he brings the woman to his house, gets the baby there, has it born there, and continues to keep the woman and the baby there, when he lives with her almost as if she were his wife," he paused, shook his head, shrugged, "hell, Claib, that's going too far, that's going farther than custom, or whatever you call it, will sanction; that's considered by the women, I reckon, a pretty direct slap at them, and I guess it is. They don't mind too much maybe—I'm not so sure of that, but tradition has permitted it, let's say—they don't mind a little denting of the marriage vows, even, so long as it's just sex and nothing more. But, damn it, Claib, you've gone 'way past that, boy, and it just comes down to this: you got to back up pretty soon or it'll be too late for you to even try to." He threw a leg over the log and stood up. "Listen, man, you been pretty drunk most of the time since those babies came, certainly since Melissa got married, and maybe you haven't noticed. But I've a notion that if you'd been sober all that time and going on with your practicing, you'd have found out that already some of the high-born sisters have checked you off their lists, even for doctoring on 'em. They'd say they smelled nigger every time you handed 'em a pill!"

Dr. Cardell sat silent, looking across the lush corn toward the creek. Then he raised his eyes to his neighbor. "You still haven't said what I could do about it.

"I said you could send her away, Claib, get rid of her, make a new start, you might say."

The doctor turned to confront him, his face beginning to

111

flush. "You mean, throw her and her babies out! And they not four months old! What the hell, Bob!"

"I didn't say throw them out. I said send 'em away. There's a hell of a lot of difference." He paused, hands on hips. "Damn it, Claib, do you love that woman?"

"I didn't say anything about loving her. I was talking about throwing her and the babies out, with no place to go."

"I heard what you said. And you know I didn't mean for you to throw her out, Claib. And I'm asking you again, as a friend, do you love that woman? If you do, that knocks everything I'm saying and planning in the head. That ends it; I'll take you home and we'll forget the whole deal. But you're bound to know this, Claib: you can't keep on like you are now, you can't keep having children by her," he shrugged, gestured with his hands, palms up, "You can't keep it just the way it is now, boy, and have the respect of the community, or a medical practice. And you know you can't marry her in North Carolina, and if you could, you still wouldn't be accepted. So, Claib, if you love Sarah Gordon enough to want to marry her, then you'll have to leave Holly Grove, you'll have to get to hell out of the South and go north somewhere and start out under the guise of her being white. Go to Washington or New York or somewhere up there—I wouldn't think you'd want to go to Philadelphia—and tell 'em she's the daughter of a Brazilian cattleman or a Portuguese count or something. But if you don't love her, damn it, Claib, you got to send her away if you plan to keep on living at Holly Grove. And I know it ain't none of my business, but somebody had to make it their business to have it out with you, boy, and I figured I was elected. So I took the chance, and you may hate me for it. But—well, what d'you say?"

For a moment Claiborne continued to stare out over the twisting tops of the corn. When he faced his Fair Meadows neighbor his countenance was grim, pained. "You know I don't really love her, Bob," he said, "although sometimes," he paused, as if searching for words, "oh, hell, I don't know how to say it. There are too many, well, complications, and still—" He got up from the log. "Of course, I don't want to marry her, and I wouldn't if I could. But, damn, Bob, they're my babies, and how can I get rid of 'em, and her, just—just like that?" His gesture expressed his feeling of futility.

"You won't be drowning 'em like a litter of kittens." Allison smiled. Then he was serious again. "Actually, Claib, it'll be better for them; you'll be doing Sarah and the babies a favor. I'm sure you'll realize it when you face the situation squarely. Here's the way it is now, I'll bet, and you can tell me if I'm not right. Sarah's living in that house in the back yard, sleeping there, except when she's in bed with you up in your room, eating in the kitchen, keeping the babies in her room and feeding them there. In other words, Claib, to put it bluntly, the only time she's fully a wife to you is when she slips over and gets in bed with you. And the babies aren't yours any way except biologically. You don't play with them, change their diapers ever, walk the floor with them at night."

"No, but they're—"

"Just hold until I'm through. And when they get older, it'll be worse, more awkward, more embarrassing to you and to them, and to Sarah. They'll be living back there in that little house while you live by yourself in the big one; they'll be eating in the kitchen, while you, their father, eat by yourself in the dining room. If they go to church, they won't go to Bethel with you, Claib—you 'bout stopped going anyway, haven't you? But they'll go with their mammy to some little nigra church, because with the nigras free, they'll more and more be having their own churches, which they should. Well, that's the way it will be, Claib, and you know it. You can't be proud to show them off, introduce them as your children, of course you can't. And think how they'll feel. Eating in the kitchen, with their daddy too good to eat with them out there and them not good enough to eat in the mansion house. And a thousand other things, discriminations right and left separating you and them. You riding in one coach on the train and your children, Claib, riding in another. Hell, there's no end to it. And the thing about it, there's no solution, as far as you are concerned, if you keep them with you at Holly Grove. Now isn't that right, boy?"

"I guess I've never looked at it that way, Bob—about the children growing up, I mean. I've never considered that it could be against them, that it might get to be embarrassing from their standpoint. That does put a different face on it, at that." He gazed for a moment across the wide field, then turned back, intent of countenance, to confront Bob Allison. "But you still haven't suggested any solution except just getting rid of them. Have you got any plan?"

"Yes, I have. And Eliza thinks it's the thing to do, too, I can tell you that." He lifted a foot to the log and braced an arm on his knee as he bent over and with the other hand peeled off a strip of bark. "She told you about Sarah, didn't she?"

Claiborne nodded. "That Sarah was her cousin, or maybe half sister. Yes, she told me that."

"Well, let's sit down a minute, Claib, and I'll tell you what Eliza and I have in mind. As I said, it will suit her, and you can see that the way things are now with you and Sarah couldn't be pleasing to Eliza."

The doctor agreed. "Eliza must be pretty sore with me."

"Well, she's not too happy, let's put it that way. But for the moment, forget about Eliza. I'm sorter slow about getting to the point, I reckon, but here's why I really came to see you today. Eliza's got another kinsman that lives down in Chester County—she did have; he's dead now—but he got mixed up with a nigra slave woman and had this boy by her. I guess you think all of Eliza's menfolks had nigra babies, eh? Well, not all of 'em, of course, but this one did, and now that boy's living down there—he's a year or two older than Sarah—and he's a good mulatto boy, Claib. And he's not married. Somebody told Eliza that he used to like Sarah, too, and Eliza's got the notion that it wouldn't take much arranging to get him to marry Sarah. He might like to anyway, and if he didn't hanker to, very likely a little money to help take care of the babies, your babies, Claib, would fix everything all right." He was silent a moment, and so

114

was Claiborne. "And there's something else about it," he resumed his role, "and that's probably the most important of all, Claib. It's this. If this fellow marries Sarah, it'll mean that those babies will have a home, and they'll be brought up as nigras." He eyed the doctor sternly, as though he expected to be challenged by him. "And, hell, that's what they are, even if they are only one-eighth nigra. They can never be accepted in this part of the country, at any rate, as anything else. And if they are brought up in this mulatto's house rather than yours, Claib, they'll have status. They'll be accepted as nigras, they'll grow up and marry nigras. You see," he hesitated a moment, "they'll be moving toward their nigra side instead of their white side, and down here there's no other way for them to move." He snatched off another strip of the dead bark. "And everybody— you, Sarah, the babies, Eliza, me, all your friends, Claib—will be a damn sight happier." He clapped the younger man on the shoulder, stood up. "Think it over, boy, think it over. And if it's got any sense to it, if it appeals to you after you have considered it, then let me know. I'm pretty damn certain it can be worked out, and so's Eliza." He reached down and caught Claiborne's arm. "Now, let's go. I'll take you home, and then I'll get on over to Fair Meadows. I imagine Eliza's already wondering what's keeping me so long. She didn't know I was going over to Holly Grove today."

When they reached Dr. Cardell's home, Bob didn't get out of the buggy.

"I really got to be getting home," he insisted. "I got some things I got to do before supper time. But think over what I said, Claib. And excuse me, boy, if I was a little blunt. I'm your friend; you know that."

"You probably said what I needed to hear, Bob. And I'm much obliged. Maybe you got me set straight. I'll be getting in touch with you pretty soon, anyway."

That night as Sarah served his supper she seemed strangely silent. He wondered if somehow she had sensed the import of Bob Allison's visit; he had told her only that the master of Fair

Meadows had driven him over to look at some of his bottom-land corn of which he was particularly proud. She had offered little comment.

Afterward, in his bed he lay long awake. Holly Grove was still, outwardly tranquil except for the sleepy din of the insects in the trees and the occasional wail of one of the babies demanding to be nursed or changed. As objectively as he could, he weighed Bob Allison's visit; he wondered if Sarah, likely sleepless also, were pondering it, too.

This afternoon Bob had certainly been unabashed in offering his unsought opinions and determined in urging his scheme for solving Holly Grove's problems, and as Claiborne examined his neighbor's observations and proffered plan for resolving the situation, he felt a resentment developing, even though when Bob left this afternoon he had thanked him. But after all, why had Bob Allison had the temerity to come to his house and tell him what he should do? What business was it of his or his wife's? Hadn't Eliza brought about his involvement with Sarah? Wasn't she trying then to wash her hands of her dark-blooded cousin or half sister or whatever the hell she is?

Claiborne lay still in the warm darkness and forced himself to consider what Bob Allison had said, and he knew that in his observations, his deductions, his projections, yes, in his sug-gested solution, his Fair Meadows neighbor had been right. He should send Sarah and her babies away. It would be best for them to go back to their own race, for although the preponder-ance of their blood was white, they could never, like Bob had said, in the South certainly be anything but Negroes. And for himself, Claiborne knew, the continued residence of Sarah and her babies at Holly Grove could be nothing but disastrous. Bob's reasoning was unassailable.

Tomorrow he would find some way, as pleasantly and as kindly as he could manage it, to tell Sarah. And then with Bob's help he would make the arrangements. Sarah might even agree it was for the best; no doubt she has begun already to realize that this situation is not good. And she might not object to

116

marrying, indeed, she might welcome the chance of marrying a man like herself half-white. Soon her twins would come to be considered her husband's children and the children she would have by him would be legitimate. Yes, Sarah, after she thinks it over certainly will want it that way, too.

In the morning, maybe tomorrow afternoon, the first good opportunity he had, he would tell Sarah. They would talk it over calmly, and she would understand and agree. Then he would see Bob, they would go together to South Carolina, talk with the mulatto, make all the necessary arrangements. And in another month or two, by fall certainly, the man would come, he and Sarah would be married—or maybe it would be best for them to wait until they got back to South Carolina—and the man would drive off for Cardell Station and the train with her and the babies.

"With her and *my* babies, my little flat-nosed, pink-cheeked boy and girl, to start a nigra home in South Carolina, with *my* babies." The words had come aloud, wrenched from him suddenly to disturb the quiet darkness.

yes, and with *my* wife. Not legally, of course, with a marriage license and words said in front of a preacher, but my wife except for that. My woman, my warm-blooded, affectionate, understanding, agreeable, always pleasant woman. My indispensable companion starting up a new home with my babies miles away, and a yellow-skinned nigra getting babies by her. I don't want her sleeping with any nigger! I don't want her sleeping with any man, any man but me! My babies and my Sarah gone, gone to South Carolina, for good. How can I let 'em? How can I send 'em away?

But it will be for the best. The best for them certainly. And I'll look after them; I'll send Sarah money; they won't suffer.

He struggled to dispel the image that had troubled him by evoking another. With Sarah and her children gone and provided for, he would find a Negro couple and move the two into one of his cabins. The man could work on the farm, maybe he could get one capable of managing it, and the woman could do his cooking and housekeeping. She would be black, as black as Sarah's washpot in the back yard, and fat and nigger-smelling.

When things were settled and running smoothly and his medical practice was being regained and once more he was being welcomed to such places as Fair Meadows and Rural Hill and the plantations along the Catawba River, when his sins of the flesh—and more particularly his carelessness in not concealing them—were being forgiven or smilingly winked at, he would begin looking around again. In Charlotte or down at Hopewell or across the river in Lincoln he would find a girl who would adorn Holly Grove, inspire and entertain him, and provide an adequate array of beautiful, handsome, intelligent, legitimate heirs. So, consoled and cheered by his hastily conjured new family, Claiborne stretched his long legs, clutched his pillow in the bend of his elbow, and head snuggled into it, fell off quickly to sleep.

When he awakened, a boisterous mocking bird was chattering in the tree near the side window, and sunlight streamed across his bed. He sat up in bed, swung his legs around to put his feet on the floor, stood up, and stretched. Amazing, he thought, what a difference sunshine makes. Last night's problems, his heavy pondering of them, returned clearly, sharply, completely in an instant of memory's prodding. But, how strangely, he felt, had this morning's cheering sunshine, the bird's noisy, brash bickering, lessened the problems, proportioned them for solution.

He dressed quickly. A cup of coffee would start the day well for him. After breakfast, while he was still in the mood, before the heat of the morning began to build toward a sultry and steaming midday, he would talk with Sarah, get the matter over, have the thing settled. The business finished with Sarah, he might ride over and see Bob, make plans. Clever, that Bob. Decent of him, too, to come to see me, to talk the way he did, even if he did let me have it right between the eyes. He saw the business right, too, in the proper perspective, past, present, future, especially future. He did me a good turn by beating my brains into getting a look at the future, a damned good turn,

Bob. One of these days I'll tell you just what a good turn you did me.

He walked into the dining room. No coffee on the table lifting up its curling fragrance. No food. No sign that Sarah had been here this morning.

Maybe she overslept, he told himself. Those babies wake often in the nights; it's a task keeping them fed, changing diapers every time one of them wets, and between the two, one is wet all the time, and hungry. Sarah's having it pretty tough, with two babies, and the house, and the cooking.

He crossed the back porch, went down the high steps, walked quickly the path to the kitchen house. As he stepped up on Sarah's porch, both babies began to cry. Too late doing so, he tiptoed along the passageway between the front rooms. Then he heard Sarah vomiting.

She was on the back porch, leaning over the railing beside the water-bucket shelf.

"Sarah!" He started toward her. "What's the trouble?"

She straightened, and with hand behind her back motioned for him to stay where he was. Then she poured a dipper of water into the tin basin beside the bucket, caught up the end of the towel hanging on a nail by the basin, wet it and mopped her face. With water from a glass she filled with the dipper she rinsed out her mouth carefully.

"I'm sorry I ain't got your breakfast ready," she said, turning then to face him. "I didn't wake up when I oughta; the babies kept me up 'bout all night; they musta been sorter sick. Maybe my milk's got 'em a little upset. But 'twon't take me long to get your coffee and—and—"

She cupped her hand over her mouth, whirled around to the water shelf and leaned out over the railing, barely in time. Claiborne strode over to her, grasped her right arm with his left hand, with his right palm on her forehead supported her until she was relieved. Then he took down the towel, dipped it in the basin, squeezed it, and sponged her face.

"Now you go in and lie down, while I run over to the office

and get you something to settle your stomach," he said. "I can't understand, though."

"It ain't no use, Doct' Claib. Ain't nothin' do no good." She smiled wanly. "It's just like I was before. I've done got in a fam'ly way again."

<h1 style="text-align:center">24</h1>

After he married Melissa, Charlie Gunn, at Colonel Osborne's insistence, came to live with his wife's parents. During the remainder of the summer he helped the colonel direct his farming operations, but when the crops had been laid by, Charlie went to Alamance and arranged with the Holts for employment as a cotton-mill operative. He promised he would work hard and faithfully, accept cheerfully any tasks to which they might assign him, and endeavor to advance the mill's interests. He would start work, they agreed, as soon as he had helped his father-in-law get the crops gathered.

Charlie did not mention, however, that he had acquired stock, even though a small amount, in a cotton-manufacturing enterprise being started in Cabarrus, and that as quickly as he had learned the fundamentals of the textile-manufacturing process he would leave their employment and become actively associated with the Cabarrus cotton mill.

"The way I see it, Colonel," he said when he returned from the interview with the Alamance people, "that's the coming thing in this country, manufacturing. We got the advantage over the North; we got the cotton down here, and if we make the cloth close to where we grow the cotton, look how much we can save on freight charges. The way it is now, we have to pay the freight on the cotton going to the mills up north and on the cloth coming back, too. But if we make that cloth down here, look at the advantage we'll have over them mills up there."

"Yes, Charlie, you're right. If our folks can make cloth to compete with theirs, we should have a big advantage."

"We can do it, Colonel. We're already doing it, in fact; the only thing is that we just don't have enough mills; we got to have a lot more, and I'm aiming to see that we have at least one more 'round here." He paused, his eyes bright, and then he spoke again, his voice eager, intent: "And look at the good labor we can get, Colonel, and cheap. These farm boys will be glad to get jobs in the mills; farming's going down all the time, getting worse instead o' better. Whatever's made on the farm, generally speaking, is owed to the merchant before the crop's picked, for carrying you. Ain't that right, Colonel?"

Regretfully, Colonel Osborne had to agree. "Yes, with the South down like it is, Charlie, it looks like we won't be able to make it if we stick to the old pattern, when farming was the backbone. The war took our slaves and ruined us; but if we hadn't got into the war, the slaves in time would have ruined us, too, so we would have had to free them within a few years— by now, I'd say—or they'd have eaten us up. So any way you figure it, it looks like farming as we used to do it is not going. to save us. And of course the Reconstruction made everything ten times worse; I doubt if there's ever been rottener politics perpetrated on any people than the politics we've had to live under in the South, Charlie." He sighed, shrugged. "But with the Federal troops being withdrawn by President Hayes," he added, hopefully, "I guess we'll soon be able to run our affairs without too much interference from the radicals."

"Yes, sir, I hope so," his son-in-law agreed. "But the way I see it, we got to do more than straighten out politics. We've got to get to making money and we won't do it with this one-crop system. We got to diversify our farming, but the main thing we got to do is get started manufacturing, and on a big scale, a lot bigger than we were doing when the war started and knocked out what we had. I was pretty young then for noticing such things, Colonel, but lately I been studying all I can 'bout what the South was doing then. And the only way I can figure it is that we got to get back to manufacturing and in a lot bigger way, and I aim to get in on it as quick as I can."

Melissa's parents were distressed when their daughter moved

out with her new husband to live a hundred miles away, but they were all the more excited and delighted when Melissa returned in the late spring to await the arrival of her baby.

Claiborne Cardell heard about it one day at the blacksmith's shop at Cardell Station, where he had gone to have his mare shod. The blacksmith had finished and the doctor had paid him and was preparing to leave when the man, innocently enough but with a wry grin, inquired: "Doc, you been over to Colonel Osborne's any time lately?"

"No. Why? Any of them been sick?"

"Not that I've heared of. But you'll be havin' a job over there 'fore too long, I hear tell. I hear Melissy's home to be with her ma to have her baby." He gave the doctor a quizzical stare.

"I hadn't heard about it," Claiborne revealed. "I haven't been consulted in the case."

"Well, I guess you will be," the blacksmith observed, wiping his forehead with his forearm. "They say it won't be long 'fore she'll be havin' it. I ain't seen her myself." He glanced about and lowered his voice though no one else was near them. "You know, Doc, my opinion that gal played hell marryin' that Charlie Gunn 'stead o' you." He held up his hand, as if to forestall the doctor's protesting. "Hold on, now, Doc; I ain't sayin' she coulda married you, but I heared tell more'n a year ago, I guess it were, you and her was doin' some courtin' and I'm a notion if she'd carried her end o' the stick, you two mighta made it."

"Well, Ab, I wouldn't say that," Claiborne commented. "But anyway, she married Charlie. What you got against him?"

"I ain't got nothin' agin him, Doc. He jest ain't in the Osbornes' class, if you know what I mean, and you was—and still is, far as I'm concerned," he hastened to add.

Claiborne did not invite further comment and the blacksmith did not volunteer it. They hitched the mare to the buggy and the doctor drove home. As he turned into the Holly Grove driveway, he saw Aunt Ca'line duck into the kitchen house. She had come out to the porch, he surmised, to see if the buggy she had heard coming along the big road might be his.

122

Sarah's baby had not arrived. Claiborne had come in time to deliver it, with Aunt Ca'line's solicitous help and at times, he was amused to notice, directions. The birth was not difficult.

The baby was a boy.

"Have you decided on a name for him, Sarah?" Claiborne asked, after Aunt Ca'line had taken the infant into the kitchen to bathe and dress it, and Sarah was resting from her ordeal.

"If it suits you," she said, "we'll call him Caesar."

"Caesar. I see you been reading some more in your Shakespeare book, eh? Well, Caesar was a mighty man. I guess maybe he'll be, too. Yes, Caesar suits fine."

The twins lacked three weeks of being a year old when Caesar was born. They were a year and one week old when Melissa's son arrived. She named her son Charles Gunn, Junior. Claiborne heard that news a day or two later from a Cabarrus man who happened to be at Bub Barkley's store when the doctor stopped in to buy some plowpoints.

HOUSE OF THE CRACK

Dr. Claib Cardell, shirtless and in his socks, sat in his father's verandah chair with his feet on the baluster railing. On the little square pine table within easy reach of his hand was a whisky glass, now hardly a third filled. With the whisky and his pocket handkerchief he had been fighting the night's sodden heat, which had been so unbearable in his bedroom that he had pulled on his trousers and come down to sit in the open air; he had taken the precaution of fortifying himself with the glass.

The heat on this last night in August, it seemed to him, had served to give energy to the cicadas and other summer insects; they were raising a terrific din in the magnolia above the path to the kitchen house and in the hollies and oaks out front, and their harsh grating calls tonight were disturbing rather than soothing. And the moon, shining through a gap in the water oak's thick foliage where a large dead limb provided no leaves, seemed to make the night hotter.

He raised his eyes to study the moon, and beneath it he saw shadows moving on the carriage-house wall.

"Ten years ago—ten years ago last month," he said to himself, watching the dancing shadows. "Ten damned long years, ten damned years I'll never get back."

He remembered, clearly now despite the whisky tonight and the whisky of those ten gone years, that first shadow he had seen on the wall. But these shadows were not of a disrobed Sarah. The shadows and the noises that broke now and then with shattering discordance on his ears were the silhouetted images of

Sarah's children playing and shrieking and quarreling back there in the kitchen house.

"If that night I hadn't seen her damned shadow on that wall there," he said aloud. "But, what the hell, if I hadn't seen the shadow that night, I'd have seen her the next day or the next, or some time—" he shrugged his shoulders, "I'd have looked at her straight, and it'd been all the same. Hell, yes."

The shadows were jumping and dodging and darting on the carriage-house wall, now almost completely denuded of paint, as was the woodwork of the mansion house itself. Six shadows maybe—he made no effort to count or distinguish them—six children in ten years, and a five-month miscarriage six months ago. But there'll be no more; getting Sarah fixed up after that miscarriage had seen to that.

He put his feet on the floor, sat up in the chair, leaned out over the balusters' railing, and studied the radiant, hot moon. "What a hell of a difference ten years have made." He struggled with the heat of the night, the prying brilliance of the moon, the insects' incessant noise, the befuddling of the alcohol, the raucous din of the children playing. "It's time their mother was getting them to bed," he observed aloud—and objectively as he could he tried to review the decade he had been back at Holly Grove.

After that night, he asked himself, could there ever have been a turning place? Could he have sent Sarah away as soon as her pregnancy was discovered? And what if he had?

He recalled, and vividly, the afternoon with Bob Allison in his bottom-land cornfield. It had seemed easy, resolving his situation, as that night he lay in bed and made his plans for sending Sarah and the twins to South Carolina. But the next morning— Oh, hell, that had been the end. The balloon had burst there at the water shelf on the back porch, the dam had gone out, the house had burned down, the dream vanished.

Six babies, six Negro babies. The twins, past nine now, and Cleo, almost four. And in between, Caesar, Ophelia, and Macbeth, a Shakespearean dramatis personnae. Desdemona or Hamlet or Mark Antony, or whatever the hell Sarah would have named that one, didn't get born.

He had added two small rooms at the back of the kitchen house. The children lived there with their mother. Never had he sat down to a meal with them, never had one of the children slept in his bed. Bob Allison had been right. They were Negroes. His own children, his flesh and blood, living in his back yard, were regarded by everybody, even themselves, as Negroes, and could never be anything else, certainly as long as they lived at Holly Grove or anywhere in the South where it was known that they possessed that drop of Negro blood.

Among their schoolmates they were accepted without reservation as Negro children even though their faces were as white and their features as Caucasian as some of the children who went to the white school, Claiborne had observed in driving by the two schools from time to time as he went on calls or returned from them. The four older children were doing well in their books, the teacher had told Sarah last winter, and secretly Claiborne was pleased; brains should help them overcome the handicap of mixed blood. The two younger, Macbeth and Cleopatra, would be starting in another year. The schools, white and Negro, ran four months a year, two months in the summer time —from the laying by of the crops to the cotton-picking season— and two months in the dead of winter. And Sarah was always reading to them, every opportunity she had, from the Bible and that book of Shakespeare's plays. And now and then he himself had asked the twins to read for him and had called out their spelling words for Caesar and Ophelia. Feelie, he believed, would be the best scholar in the whole bunch. He might send Feelie off to school if she showed enough interest. He'd likely send her to Scotia Seminary over at Concord; it was a good school for Negro girls. For Negro girls—for his daughter.

Claiborne's hand sought the glass, and he swallowed the whisky that remained, and wiped his lips.

How would it have been with him now, he suddenly considered, had he married Melissa and had children to go to the little white school and then perhaps to the academy at Hortonsville and afterwards to college, likely at Davidson or Chapel Hill, or if they were girls, to Salem maybe, their mother's college? And what of that damned Charlie Gunn, if he *hadn't* married Melissa? He had to confess that she had been right about Charlie. The farm overseer had escaped from farming; he was a cotton-mill man now, and doing well, according to reports the doctor had been getting occasionally. Since Colonel Osborne's death, Charlie had taken over as master of the Osborne plantation. He was being accepted now as one of them by some of the best people of the community; he was fast becoming an aristocrat of the pocketbook, a blueblood of the bank account.

. and I?

The comparison pained him. He hadn't seen Melissa since her boy was born, and that was eight years ago. She and Charlie had been back from Alamance and his mill apprenticeship some six years; they must have had illnesses in that period surely, but they had never called on him for professional services. Dr. Horton or that new doctor at Davidson had been doing the doctoring for the Osborne plantation, Claiborne had been told; some people were now calling that place the Gunn plantation.

Claiborne Cardell sat back in his chair and lifted his feet again to the railing. The hell of it, the Gunns aren't the only family that has cut me off, he told himself. Bob Allison and Eliza never send for me any more, even to doctor the Negro farm hands, nor the Davidsons at Rural Hill.

. and none of the old families, Father's friends, ever asks me to dinner... Today he had been busy making his calls, but only among the poor buckras and Negroes. And his pocketbook was little the heavier for it.

He studied the unblinking face of the moon, remembering vividly that night on the colonel's piazza when he had sat on the joggling-board with Melissa . . I could have married her. That damned Charlie wouldn't have had a chance. And if I had sent Sarah away and married Melissa— He reached for the glass and drank.

. . . if I had married Melissa, by now I would have been the most prominent citizen in north Mecklenburg, in this whole section. But, what the hell, I didn't marry her, and that bastard Charlie Gunn did. I shacked up with a nigra woman, had a houseful of young'uns by her. There's no way out now. Charlie Gunn'll get rich and still richer and I'll keep getting poorer, and pretty soon nobody but the tenants and the nigras will call on me to do their doctoring, fetching their squalling brats and treating their fevers and erysipelas. And Holly Grove will keep on deteriorating and finally rot and fall down. Ten years gone, ten years gone to hell. And what now, what the next ten?

"Damn! It's hot!"

He mopped his face with his handkerchief and stood up. The air seemed so utterly still, tense, foreboding even. But, hell, what else can happen to me? Maybe it's just the liquor. Maybe I can sleep now. . . . He climbed the stairs, in his bedroom slipped out of his pants, kicked off his socks, lay down naked on the hot bed. If only there were a stirring of air. Why does Sarah pull the curtains together in the summertime? Just like a nigra. .

Claiborne got up, went to the back window, and drew the curtains apart. The lamp was low in Sarah's room; the children were in bed. He'd have to speak to her in the morning about getting them into bed earlier. He crossed the room, sprawled on the bed, turned on his back, straightened his legs.

2

He sprang from the lurching bed and before he was fully awake was standing beside it. He felt for the matches in the little Centennial souvenir saucer by the lamp on his bedside table, found one, struck it hurriedly, and with frantic fingers lighted the lamp. In the same instant the room swayed, and all hell descended with a deafening roar on the roof directly above his room.

Claiborne knew then that the bed actually had quivered beneath him; it had not been a nightmare that had snatched him to his feet. The shaking house and that thunderous avalanche above him were no dreamed-up violence. He pulled on his pants and raced to the back window.

"Lawd Gawd! Gawd a'mercy! O Lawd!" The dim light in Sarah's bedroom flamed up as he heard her high, frightened voice calling out desperately; and then, screaming for their mother, the children came surging from the back of the house into Sarah's room. Claiborne could see their shadows as they sped past the window opening on the front porch.

He ran back to the bed, slipped into his shoes, and grabbing up the lamp rushed with it out into the hallway and down the stairs, which seemed now to be quivering beneath his tread as though they had been fastened onto rope supports. He heard Sarah and the children running across the back yard and as he reached the bottom of the stairway, they burst into the hall, wailing and moaning in utter hysteria.

"Go into the office," he commanded sternly, his voice calm though he was hardly composed himself, "and get 'em quieted, Sarah. It's nothing to be afraid of, just a big windstorm. Light the lamp in there. I'll leave this one out here in the hall and come in there with you. As soon as the wind calms down, you can all go back to bed. Nothing's going to hurt you."

Sarah's eyes were wide with fright. "There ain't no wind blowin', Doct' Claib, not one breath. This ain't no storm; it's the Devil rockin' Holly Grove! Didn't you hear the rocks fallin' on the house and limbs crashin' down from the trees, Doct' Claib!"

"Nonsense, Sarah! You're talking like a superstitious, cotton-field—" He had started to say "nigra," but patently as a quick revision, he said "woman."

"I may be a superstitious nigger, Doct' Claib," she raised her voice, "but I heard rocks fallin' and I felt the kitchen house shakin' and I know it's the Devil after Holly Grove. I jus' know it's the Devil."

Abruptly she stopped, clutched at the medicine shelf beside

132

which she was standing, for a new tremor, beginning almost imperceptibly, was agitating the old house with increasing violence. Bottles rattled together on the shelf, and on the back porch a tin bucket, teetering on the edge of a table, fell to the floor with a clatter. Speechless with fear, Sarah was pointing to the lamp dancing crazily on the doctor's table, its yellow flame leaping and dipping like a ballerina. "He's in there!" she screamed, suddenly recovering her voice. "The Devil's got in the lamp!"

"Sarah! Stop it! You're scaring the children to death!"

But before he could get to her to attempt to calm her, to push her down into his big armchair and speak soothingly to her, they heard a tearing, ripping, awesome sound toward the south end of the house, the floor heaved and fell back, and the lamp, blazing high, swung in an eerie, flaming yellow arc to plunge to the floor.

Dr. Cardell sprang for it, grabbed it up; the glass bowl had not broken, but the light went out, fortunately before it could ignite the oil spilled in a widening circle. He set the lamp in the center of the table. And suddenly, almost unnaturally now, it seemed, the house was still.

The children, screaming in terror, were clutching at their mother's skirt. And now all at once Sarah was the calm one. "Hush, now! You all hush! Ain't nothin' goin' to hurt you. Romeo, you go out there in the hall and fetch that lamp in here. And be careful; don't you drop it. And you, Julie, pick up Cleopatra and get her quiet. It ain't nothin', like Doct' Claib says, but a storm. Hush, now! You all get quiet!"

Romeo came in with the lighted lamp. Sarah took it and set it beside the one that had gone out. "Now, I guess we can light that one, can't we, Doct' Claib? Didn't much oil spill out. Then we can put this one back in the hall."

Claiborne nodded. He knew he would never understand Sarah. Or any other woman likely. But certainly not Sarah.

After they had quieted the children and the house appeared to have settled again into undisturbed peace, Sarah led her brood back to their house, with Claiborne trailing them to examine it. The earthquake—for he was convinced that it had been an earthquake—had done no damage to the kitchen house as far as he and Sarah could determine in the nighttime, and he returned to his room and bed.

In the first light of morning he awakened quickly; he got up, strode to the side window, and looked out. Tree branches littered the ground. Craning his neck, he saw the dead limb had tumbled from the water oak; it doubtless would have fallen soon of its own weight, he conjectured. And down at the base of the chimney, almost beneath his window, lay a jumble of bricks. "I thought that's what happened," he said aloud. "The top of the chimney fell off."

When Sarah came in to serve his breakfast, she was serene, unruffled. "It was pretty bad," she agreed, when he referred to the startling events of last night. "I guess I did act crazylike. But I was scared, Doct' Claib. I ain't never been in no earthquake before. And I'm jus' thankful we didn't get hurt none."

"The devil you heard on the roof, I reckon you saw, was the top of the west chimney on the south side." He smiled as he remembered her dramatic pronouncement. "I saw bricks on the ground when I looked out the window this morning."

"There's some lodged on the roof, too," she said.

When he had finished eating, he went out on the front verandah and down along the box-bordered path. He looked up to the tops of the twin chimneys. A few bricks were missing from the east one; from the other more than a foot of the stack's top, down almost to the decorative iron grill that braced the chimney to the hipped roof, had tumbled to the ground or lay scattered along the steep slope.

"Before wintertime I'll have to get Harry Gilbert to fix it," he charged himself. "It looks bad, and it might be dangerous."

But then his eyes, startled, were riveted on a more alarming discovery. From the gutter, at the very top of the brick wall and extending in a jagged line through the great cream-brick heart midway between the chimneys, ran a torn crack, in places more than an inch wide.

"Hell's fire! The Devil must have been up there last night, sure enough!"

Two days later Dr. Cardell stopped at Bub Barkley's on his way home from a call. Everybody at the store was talking about the earthquake. "Fellow come through here this mornin' from Charlotte," the merchant told him. "Said hit was bad down there, too, but nothin' like hit wuz down at Charleston, South Ca'lina. Said down there half the town got shook down."

3

On a Tuesday morning early in the April following the great Charleston earthquake, Uncle Stephen died. He was dead before Claiborne could get down to the little cabin beyond the stables. The old man had been sitting in his rocker on the porch in the sunshine, talking with Romeo about old slavery times. Romeo said he had just stopped talking, and his head had dropped on his chest. His rugged old heart had simply run down, as a spent watch, Claiborne thought.

The doctor at once sent word to Eph in Charlotte and asked him to notify Violet; his sister had not been out to Holly Grove since the October Sarah was pregnant with Romeo. He had seen her a few times in the intervening years and had some letters from her, business letters concerning the operation of the farm, with which she had not been pleased; but Violet evidently had been utterly truthful when she had told him she would never visit Holly Grove as long as the quadroon remained there. But Claiborne felt that his sister would wish to attend Uncle Stephen's funeral; he was beloved by them both almost as a flesh-and-blood member of the family.

Eph came that night and he and Aunt Ca'line decided to keep Uncle Stephen until Sunday; the weather was still reasonably cool, the long years had withered and dried the old darkey until he was little more than a mass of leathered skin over bones, and anyway it would hardly be considered decent to bury him until his friends could hold for him a proper wake.

The wake began simply enough the night of his death and grew in numbers attending, fervor, and intensity as the evenings went by and more and more Negroes learned of the old man's passing. By Saturday night the mourning, praying, shouting, the feasting and drinking had attained a climax that left the participants nearing physical and emotional exhaustion.

Dr. Cardell and Sarah attended the two-hour funeral at Beulah Land Church, though they did not go there together. Sarah rode in the Cardell surrey with Aunt Ca'line, Eph and Eph's wife. Claiborne followed later in his buggy. Nor did he and Sarah sit together during the service. Sarah entered and sat with the mourning relatives. The doctor was ostentatiously escorted to a section at the front, across from the relatives of Uncle Stephen, which had been reserved for white friends.

Violet was there, several places away and seated beside one of the Charlotte Alexanders, who evidently had brought her. The two nodded to him as he sat down.

Beulah Land Church had been organized early in the Reconstruction period when Negroes left the white churches to organize congregations of their own. Until he joined that body, Uncle Stephen all his life had belonged with the Cardells to Bethel Church; Claiborne could remember, though he was quite young then, the slaves sitting in the balcony, in their Sunday clothes, their ebony faces scrubbed and shining, their eager countenances radiant as they joined in the singing of psalms and hymns. He recalled it in paying tribute to Uncle Stephen, at the request of the preacher when he had finished his grandiloquent eulogy. "Many a Sunday my parents and Uncle Stephen and Aunt Ca'·line went to church together," he said. "We all belonge\ to the same church, we were friends; we were more than friends; we loved each other with a devotion that nothing could destroy. Uncle Stephen was a good Christian, a fine gentleman, a wise counselor; he was indeed a great man. He and Aunt Ca'line taught me as a child what was the right and what was the wrong road to travel; they taught me by words but more by example. I only wish I were more worthy of them."

When he sat down his eyes were wet, and so were the eyes of many of the blacks. He ventured a glance toward Violet; she was staring straight ahead.

At the burying ground, when the grave had been filled and the flowers spread out on the red mound and the Negro preacher's committal service concluded, Claiborne walked over to Violet. "Won't you come by Holly Grove, Sister," he said, "and have supper and spend the night?"

"No, thank you, Claiborne," she answered pleasantly. "I came with Lucretia and we've already planned to spend the night at Fair Meadows." She asked him about his health and chatted a moment; but she made no mention of Sarah, and in a few minutes she climbed in the buggy with Lucretia Alexander and drove away.

The doctor went over to Aunt Ca'line, put his arm around the old woman's stooped shoulders, and helped her to the surrey. Then he and Eph tenderly lifted her into it. He patted the tired, worn black hands. "I'm losing him, too, Aunt Ca'line, you know. And you'll never suffer for anything as long as I'm here." Then he turn to her son. "Eph, soon's you get a chance tonight after supper, come up to the mansion house; I want to talk to you."

"Yes, sir, Marse Claib; yes, sir; I'll be right t'ere."

He was at the back steps before Claiborne had finished his supper.

"Tell him to have a seat in the office; I'll be in there in a minute or two," he told Sarah.

Eph stood up when he walked in.

"Sit down, Eph," he said. "I want to talk to you." He sat in his chair, facing his father's bodyguard of the war days. "Eph, your mammy's old, and now your daddy's gone and she's by herself."

The colored man was nodding solemnly.

"How old you reckon Aunt Ca'line is, Eph?" the doctor went on.

"I don't 'zackly know, Marse Claib," Eph replied. "But way I figure it, she must be past eighty. I must be past sixty myself."

"Well, all your ages are down in the book; I could look 'em up. But that don't matter; we're all getting old, Eph, and your mammy's all by herself, and that's bad."

"Yes, sir, Marse Claib, I been thinkin' 'bout it."

"Eph, she can't live by herself, that's for sure. And if you take her down to Charlotte, she won't live long. She's been on this plantation all her life; she'd grieve herself to death if you took her away."

"It's the tru'f, Marse Claib; she shore would."

"Well, now," Claiborne leaned forward, tapped the colored man on the knee, "that gets me right down to what I wanted to say, and that's this: Eph, why don't you come back to Holly Grove? Your children are all grown and married off and there's just you and Lizzie left; you and Lizzie could move back and go right in with Aunt Ca'line." He held up his hand, for Eph seemed on the point of answering the question he had asked, "It would make her happy, and I don't see why it wouldn't be a good thing for you and Lizzie, too; you'd be getting back home, Eph, and you won't ever feel at home anywhere else but here. Ain't that right?"

Eph's round black face widened in a broad smile. "You right, Marse Claib. I ain't never been feel like I's at home since I lef' Holly Grove; that's the tru'f. And I sorter always wanted to git back here to stay." His smile vanished. "And here lately I ain't been doin' too good in town. Things is gittin' sorter tightlike and I'm gittin' old, Marse Claib; I ain't so good no mo' for public work, and times ain't too good noway. D'you reck'n I could make a livin' farmin'? Or is that what you figured for me to do up here?"

Dr. Cardell leaned toward Eph again, his countenance serious. "Eph, you know 'bout things up here since—since I came home from Philadelphia. You know 'bout Sarah and her children?"

"Yes, sir, I have heared things 'bout 'em, course. But, Marse

Claib," his eyes rolled in solemn affirmation, " 'fore Gawd, I don't know nothin'."

"Well, what you likely been hearing is the truth, Eph. And I'm not blaming Sarah, either. I'm just as responsible—more so, I reckon—than she is." He shrugged. "And nothin' can be done 'bout it now, Eph. But you went to the war with my daddy; you risked your neck for him. Now I want you to help me out. I want you to come back up here, look after Aunt Ca'line as long as she lives, and run the farm for me, Eph. That's what I want you to do."

"But, Marse Claib, how 'bout Sa'ah and her child'en? Now I don't know wheder I could git 'long wit' Sa'ah and them child'en or—"

"Of course, you can get along with them. That's what I want you for, Eph, mainly. I want you to sort of take charge of those boys. Romeo and Caesar are plenty old enough to work, and won't be long till Mac can, too, and you're the one to teach 'em. Sarah can look after her girls, but I want those boys to learn how to work, Eph. If they don't learn how now, while they're young, I don't know what'll become of them when they get a little older."

"But I tell you, Marse Claib," Eph paused and he looked about the doctor's office and then his perplexed eyes fastened again on the younger man, "the way it is, with them boys not bein'—" He stopped again.

"Not being nigras, you mean, Eph? But that's just it. They are nigras and they'll always be nigras, Eph, even if they're three-fourths white and one-eighth Indian. That nigra blood makes them nigras and ain't nothing they can do about it but be nigras. And I want you to teach them not only to work, Eph, but to realize always that the world takes them as nigras and that the only way for them to be happy is to accept the situation. Sarah understands that, I'm sure, and appreciates it."

"You right shore she do, Marse Claib?"

"Well, I think she understands, Eph. She's got sense; she knows they can never be anything but nigras—and live round

139

here, or anywhere else in the South where it's known who they are—regardless of how white they may look to be."

"It's shore the tru'f what you jes' say, Marse Claib. That's what I been tellin' some them big-talkin' niggers down'n Charlotte."

"What they saying, Eph?"

"Some say 'fore long the white chil'en and the nigger chil'en be goin' to school together and first thing you know niggers and white folks be marryin' each other." He paused, the whites of his eyes rolling, "Some o' them niggers shore been sayin' it, Marse Claib, I ain't goin' tell you no lie. They says them cyarpetbagger mens changed the law to make white chil'en and nigger chil'en go to school together, Marse Claib; but I says 'twon't never work if it's the law or ain't. Nigger chil'en and white chil'en git to goin' to school together, first thing you know'll be little brown babies, and that ain't no good, Marse Claib." Suddenly he stopped, as if aghast at what he had just said. "I warn't speakin' 'bout you, Marse Claib; I'm talkin' 'bout gene'ally speakin'."

"You were right, Eph," he said. "What do most of the colored people think about it?"

"Most of 'em thinks the way I do," he answered. "If you'd as' any of 'em, they'd say that, Marse Claib, talkin' to you. But wouldn't all of 'em mean it. Some of 'em talks one way to a white man and 'nother way to a nigger. That's the way it 'pears to me." He grinned. "It's mostly them town niggers talks that way. Us country niggers don't want no mixin', Marse Claib, mostly. And that's why I'd shore like to move back up here and git to farmin'. A nigger what was raised in slavery times on a plantation ain't rightly got no business tryin' to make he livin' in no town." He was serious again. "But I don't know 'bout comin' back to Holly Grove, Marse Claib. I jes' wonder 'bout what Sa'ah say 'bout it."

"It'll suit Sarah, Eph. But, after all, I'm running Holly Grove, you know."

"Yes, sir, that's right, you is."

"But I'll talk to her. And I can pay you day wages, Eph, but it would be better for us to work it on a sharecropper basis, I expect. And you can boss the other nigras, Eph, sort of manage things for me, as far as the crop goes; and I believe it'll be a good move for you."

"Me and Lizzie'd have a roof over our heads and plenty to eat if we jes' raised it," Eph agreed. "And long as we been in Charlotte we ain't never been right shore o' either one."

Before he went back to Aunt Ca'line's cabin Eph had agreed to return to Holly Grove and start a crop; since it was only April now, he would have time to get a crop in. He would have general oversight of the farming operations, sadly deteriorated in the last several years, and direct the training of Sarah's boys in practical farm work.

4

Sarah Gordon sat barefoot in her rocker and looked out beyond the big road to cotton fields baking in the still heat of an early July afternoon. She had come out from the stifling heat of the kitchen after having finished washing the dinner dishes. Ordinarily Julie and Feelie did the dishes, but Eph was trying to get the cotton and corn laid by and the girls were helping this week in the fields. They were chopping suckers in the bottomland corn, and Romeo and Mac were side-harrowing the cotton.

She had brought her shoes out to the porch; they were within reach on the floor beside the chair so that she could put them on quickly should Dr. Cardell or anyone else turn into the driveway. Never had the doctor caught her on the porch or in the mansion house shoeless; she had not forgotten the time years ago he had told her—he was drinking, but just enough to be speaking in complete frankness—that the most slatternly creature he could imagine was a grown woman with all her clothes on and barefoot.

She wondered, though, as she looked out upon the gentle decadence of Holly Grove, if the doctor would remonstrate should he come upon her barefoot even on the verandah of the mansion house; perhaps, and the thought even now was disquieting, he wouldn't notice.

. like the house and the plantation, he has been going downhill, too. And he's not old. He must be only about forty, but he looks fifty already. I reckon he's just sorter give up. He goes on the same way, day after day, treating sick folks, fetching babies, mostly babies and sick folks among the nigras and the white-tenant farmers; don't many of the quality folks ever have him if they can get any other doctor. .

Sarah's eyes wandered over the drying lawn of Holly Grove, once velvet smooth but now for years little tended, the grass in spots entirely gone, in some places choked with weeds and unpruned rose bushes and spiraea and crepe myrtle. A jungle of periwinkle all but covered a heap of bricks at the base of the mansion-house chimney nearest her. Her eyes lifted along the chimney to its ragged top and the bricks still scattered on the roof. Then they focused on the crack between the chimneys.

Five years after the earthquake, the crack was still there, cleaving the great cream-brick heart, unmended, untouched, a haven for flying squirrels, mice, lizards. The first several months following the shock that split the brick wall, Dr. Claib had spoken a dozen times of his determination to have the brickmason repair the chimney tops and the crack. He would have all the broken bricks pulled out and others of the same age and color put in so that it would be impossible to tell exactly where the crack had been. But that fall he hadn't been able to get Mr. Gilbert to do it, and in the spring Uncle Stephen had died, and the next fall Dr. Claib had said he reckoned it would serve just as well if they had the crack filled with cement mortar. That would be a lot easier to do; even if they didn't make it look so well, it would keep out the weather.

. . it won't ever get fixed. Dr. Claib ain't even mentioned the crack in the last three years. Maybe he doesn't think about it any more; maybe he's just failed to notice it. Maybe, too, he's just stopped thinking. Sometimes it's better just not to think. Thinking ain't good for me. Maybe thinking, for him, remembering, thinking back, maybe that's just too painful. Anyway, it ain't so worrisome if you just don't think, if you don't resist, just float downstream, just go along day to day and don't think much about what's going to happen to you, to the children, those little white-skinned nigra children just floating along helpless in the downstream current.

That's why Dr. Claib's been stopping by Bub Barkley's store more and more, she reasoned, to get whisky with which to provide himself a respite from thinking. And the whisky has combined with other things to speed his journey downstream.

he'll likely come home drunk this afternoon or tonight. He won't know whether I've got on shoes or am barefooted. And if he ain't drunk when he gets home, he'll be drunk 'fore he goes to bed. He can sleep better if he's drunk. . .

Suddenly Sarah reached down, pulled the shoes in front of her and stuck her feet into them. Someone was turning from the big road into the driveway. It wasn't Dr. Cardell; she didn't recognize the buggy and horses; they were spirited sorrels, and the buggy in sharp contrast to the doctor's, appeared newly painted. A colored man was driving, and a white man, well dressed and prosperous looking, sat beside him. Evidently they had seen her; they drove up to the kitchen-house porch. As Sarah stood up, the white man alighted, came up to the steps.

"Sarah, don't you know me?"

"Mist' Charlie! I sure didn't know you till you got up close. But I ain't seen you in a long time."

"It has been a long time, Sarah. I don't get over this way very often any more. Been keepin' pretty close over 'round Concord, workin' hard."

"Looks like work 'grees with you, Mist' Charlie."

"Well, I been gettin' on pretty good, I reckon. How's things been servin' you, Sarah?"

"I reckon pretty good, Mist' Charlie, considerin' "

Charlie Gunn smiled understandingly, and then his countenance quickly was serious. "Is Doctor Claib home, Sarah?"

"No, sir; he's gone off on some calls; typhoid cases over on the river, I think he said."

"When you lookin' for him back, Sarah? Got any idea when he'll be home?"

She told him that Dr. Cardell had gone that morning and expected to be away until late afternoon; she explained that fever cases had been keeping him away from home day and night since the weather had turned so warm. "He might be home most any time now, though," she added. "Won't you go up on the porch or sit in the parlor and wait awhile, Mist' Charlie, or can I tell him anything for you if you ain't got time to wait?"

"It's 'bout my son, Sarah. He's got typhoid fever and he's mighty sick; he's mighty nigh dead, I'm afraid." He turned to look out toward the big road and faced her again. "I wanted to talk to Doctor Claib and ask him if he would come to see my boy. I—I don't know just how he'd feel about it, after all that's happened. You know what I mean, Sarah; you understand—" He paused, and his face revealed plainly his worry and fright. "Tell him to please come, Sarah; tell him Melissa is praying he'll come and save her boy's life." He started to step from the porch, turned back. "Sarah, you do all you can to get him to come soon's he gets home."

"I will, Mist' Charlie."

"I reckon I better get back to Melissa; she's 'most scared to death." He stepped down, faced her again. "Sarah, please tell Doctor Claib to hurry fast as he can."

An hour after Charlie Gunn left, Dr. Cardell drove in. Sarah, watching from her hallway, saw as he got out of the buggy that he had been drinking. But he walked steadily enough along the boxwood path to the verandah and she heard him open and close the front door.

He was in his office when she got to the mansion house. He heard her steps on the back porch and came to the doorway. "Sarah, I'm tired as a dog and half sick," he said wearily. "I been going all day, and if you'll give me just a little supper—some thing light; a bowl of milk and some cold cornbread to crumble in it will be all I want—I'll take a bath and go to bed." He grinned sheepishly. "I came by Bub's and got a little drink, but I didn't take much, Sarah, and I needed it; I needed it bad. And it'll help me sleep."

"Mist' Charlie Gunn was here 'bout an hour ago and he wants you to go see his boy; said he was mighty nigh dead with the fever; said Mis' Melissa was praying for you to save her boy's life."

"Charlie Gunn?" His tone was suddenly hard, cold. "That bastard came to ask me to help him, eh? And *she's praying* for me to get her boy well."

Sarah made no comment. The doctor sank wearily into his big office chair. For a full minute he stared stonily ahead, his arms outflung along the arms of the chair. Then quickly he stood up, resolute, his weariness gone. "Sarah, I wish you'd heat your iron and press out my Sunday pants and the Prince Albert and get me a clean shirt and socks and underclothes. I'll take a bath and then I'll have that bowl of milk and cornbread, and get started. I've a notion that boy's needing me pretty bad." He opened his bag, began removing bottles and putting in others from the shelf.

"Yes, sir, Doct' Claib." She was beaming. "You didn't fool me none. I knew all the time you'd go."

5

Dr. Claiborne Cardell stepped through the doorway of the darkened bedroom, softly closing the door behind him. The lamp on the walnut commode against the wall near the door lighted his bearded, haggard face, heightened the dark circles under his eyes, emphasized the wrinkles in his trousers and Prince Albert coat.

Because the lamp was between him and Melissa Gunn, and a stack of folded sheets and pillow cases on the commode caused that end of the hall to be in the shadows, he did not see her as she arose from a chair near her bedroom door and advanced toward him.

"Oh, Claiborne—"

He whirled about, surprised.

"I didn't mean to startle you. I thought you saw me,"

"No. Coming out into the light from his darkened room—"

"Claiborne—" she held out her hands to him as if for support. "How is he?" Suddenly she blanched and seemed ready to collapse. "It can't be that he's—"

Claiborne caught her hands firmly. "No. Of course not," he said. "His fever's broken, Melissa. He's past the crisis. He's on the mend now."

"Thank God! Thank God, Claiborne, for you!"

"He's been a mighty sick boy, Melissa; he could have died; there wasn't a hair's difference between dying and living, it looked like for a couple of days." He stopped, his expression puzzled. "How long have I been here anyway, Melissa?"

"It'll be four days this afternoon, Claiborne, and you've hardly been away from him. You must be dead yourself."

"Not quite. But I need a little sleep, some clean clothes," he felt his whiskers, "and a shave and bath," his drawn face relaxed a bit, "—and a stiff drink. I'm going home, but I'll be back tomorrow. Don't worry about the boy," he patted with his left hand the back of hers in his right, "because he'll be all right now." He nodded his head toward the bedroom he had just left. "That nigra's a good nurse; she's been a tremendous help. I've told her just what to do, Melissa, what to give him to eat, and to put on fresh bed linen every day, and she understands. Be sure to keep the room darkened but let him have plenty of ventilation—no drafts though, I warned her—and keep it quiet." He pointed toward the window at the end of the hall. "Sun's about up. I'll be going now, Melissa. You'd better get back to bed."

"But I'll call Charlie and he can get someone to hitch up your buggy—"

"No. Don't wake him. A little stirring around outside will do me good." He turned toward the stairway. "I'll be back some time tomorrow to see how he's doing, likely in the afternoon."

"Wait, Claiborne!" She came up to him, caught his hands in hers. "Claiborne, he's the only one I have, and you saved his life. I know you did. God bless you. And—" she was looking him in the eyes, and an entreatingly fragile smile lighted her tired / face, "forgive me, Claiborne!" Raising herself on tiptoe, she kissed him full on the lips, and then, turning quickly, she darted along the hall to disappear into her bedroom.

6

Strange, thought Claiborne, how that old cicada, like an impossibly fast Negro-bones clapper, seems purposely to be keeping time with the fiddles and the banjo back there in Sarah's house.

. . . interesting, these July-flies or dog-day cicadas or locusts or whatever they are. Some time I'm going to look them up and find out more about them. Some locusts, the encyclopedias say, live in the ground seventeen years, come out as adults to live only a few weeks. Seems hardly fair, or an overpreparation, or something or other. I wonder if cicadas return from year to year. If they don't, how is it that every summer there's a cicada at that exact spot in the water oak and another one on that very same limb of the magnolia? Or do I just forget from year to year where they were when they did their love-calling the summer before? Do I just forget?

Her warm lips were moist and luscious and tantalizing. For the thousandth time since that morning in her house he ran the end of his tongue along the circuit of his lips to taste again her kiss; for the thousandth time he conjectured, he pondered, he wondered.

She had kissed him quickly and fled into her bedroom; he had stood immobile a moment, and then he had gone down to hitch his horses to the buggy and drive back to Holly Grove. Several times he had returned to the Osborne place to examine the boy and give further directions toward speeding his convalescence. On each occasion Melissa had been friendly and courteous and appreciative, but never had she been willing, Claiborne assured himself, to risk being alone with him, even for a moment; always she had contrived to stay in the company of her husband or the Negro nurse or one of the maids or the cook, or someone. And yet, for the thousandth time he remembered the feel of her warm hands as she caught his that morning, and the taste of her lips, hot, delectable, enticing.

He pulled his feet from the baluster railing and sat up straight.

. I'm a damned fool. She was just grateful, that's all. I had just pulled her only child through a dangerous illness; she was relieved, excited, almost deliriously happy; she hardly knew what she was doing. Of course her lips were hot; she was excited, her heart was beating fast. .

But why then did she say "Forgive me, Claiborne" and why did she scurry back into her bedroom? Was she afraid to stay longer with me, alone, after she had kissed me that way? And if she was, why?

blood calls to blood, water seeks its level. Sure. And I'm still Claiborne Cardell, doctor, son of Holly Grove, son of a major in the Confederate Army, scion of oil portraits hung on the parlor wall; and she's Melissa Osborne, to the manner and manor born. I have a nigra common-law wife and six nigra children and Melissa has a poor buckram farm overseer for a husband. Sure. But blood calls out to blood; quality searches out quality. If I could catch her by herself some day—while that damn husband of hers was at his cotton mill, lint all over his britches, and her son was at school. If I should go by ostensibly to check on the boy's condition—

He leaned back in the chair and gave himself to a warm September evening's daydreaming. But the cicada's insistent rasping after a while demanded his attention and the fiddles and the banjo in their singsong rhythm brought to him again an awareness of the square dance under way in the kitchen house.

The music and the shuffling stopped, and he heard the high, gay chatter of Negro voices, and after a moment above the voices he recognized the commanding instructions of Willie Graham, the figure-caller:

"All right now. Everybody git yo' places. What tune you want fer this one?"

There was a chorus of suggestions.

" 'Had a Little Dog, Wouldn't Bite Me.' All right, balance all. Boy step right of girl. Slight yo' love and swing yo' left-hand corner; now swing yo' own and move on right, and promenade! Alligator back. Stand still. Give yo' right hand—" Claiborne listened to the rhythmical calling of the Negro man. "We gonna dance 'Lady 'Round the Lady.' Now git yo' partners and le's go! Lady 'round the lady and the gent go slow; lady 'round the lady and the gent don't go." And they were off on another set.

Claiborne got to his feet, walked to the end of the verandah and down the steps to go along the box-bordered path. When he stepped up on the porch the music had stopped for the ending of that set, and momentarily there was a lull. At the end of the little porch he heard a sound and, looking that way, caught sight of a movement.

"Who's over there?" he called out, somewhat sternly.

"It's us, Doct' Claib—me and Dan; this here's Julie. We ain't doin' nothin'. Jes' came out here on account it was so hot in there where they's square-dancin'."

"Dan who, Julie?"

"Dan Henderson, Doct' Claib. You know Dan."

"Yeh, sure. That you, Dan? How you, boy?"

"Pretty good, Doct' Claib. Gittin' 'long all right, I reckon, sir."

"Well, Julie, don't you reckon you and Dan ought to get back inside? May need you to do the next figure."

"Yes, sir, 'spect so. We's comin' right now, Doct' Claib."

He stood back in the shadows of the hallway and watched the young people dancing—his children and their friends, their Negro friends. Julie and Dan had come in behind him and rejoined the figure. From this hardly noticed position he studied

149

the dancers as they swept by the doorway, their faces lighted by the lamp on the wall stand.

"Lady 'round the lady and the gent go slow." Willie's shrill voice was calling out, "Lady 'round the lady and the gent don't go." Julie's face, white in the glow of the lamp, cheeks flushed from the exertion of dancing—or was it from her nearness to Dan?—indicated not a care in the world; she seemed interested in nothing beyond the loose-limbed, grinning, flat-nosed dark boy dancing with born ease and grace in perfect rhythm with the whining fiddles and the whanging banjo. On the other side of the ring, her twin, broad-shouldered, straight-nosed, blue-eyed Romeo was going through the steps methodically with the dark, squat daughter of Eph's son Lem. Romeo seemed happy enough, but he was a quiet one, serious, hard-working, anything but loquacious. But Caesar, his driver for the last year or two, happy, talkative, whistling, singing Caesar, was dancing with the natural ease and abandon of a jungle monkey. Caesar had light skin and blue eyes and a white man's features, but Caesar was a Negro.

He turned his attention to Feelie. Feelie was the student. She was still doing well in her books, and that's where her interests were. She would be a schoolteacher, or maybe a nurse. Feelie was ambitious; she had shown little interest in boys. But she was hardly old enough yet, he realized.

Sarah was in the kitchen fixing some cookies and pies. They would be hungry by the time the fiddlers and the banjo-picker had run out of steam; the refreshments would be quickly devoured. He paused in the kitchen doorway.

"They seem to be having a good time," he said.

Sarah looked up, her face flushed from the cooking. "I reckon they are. They makin' a big enough racket." She smiled, but not happily, he sensed. "Some of 'em in there's mighty black." She bent to open the oven door.

"There's no need going over that any more, Sarah. You know there's no other way. And they seem happy enough."

She had lifted the cookies from the oven. She set the pan on the table to cool and straightened up to confront him, eye to eye. "Sometimes you have to seem happy just to keep on livin'."

He said nothing but stepped out on the back porch. In a few minutes he came back into the kitchen. "If you'll give me a glass of milk and let me try a couple of those cookies," he said, "I believe I'll go to bed, Sarah. I'm pretty well tuckered out. You can send that bunch home when you think it's time for 'em to go."

She got him the glass of milk; he stood and drank it, and ate a cookie. When he finished, he told her good night and returned to the mansion house.

Without turning up his lamp, he undressed and went to bed. Through his windows came the crying of the fiddles and the plinkity-plink-plinking of the banjo, the swishing and thumping of the circling and weaving dancers.

He lay still and tried to close his ears and his thoughts to the sounds from the kitchen house. He sought to conjure up once more the look in Melissa's eyes that morning she had come to him outside her ill son's room, the pulsing pressure of her fingers, the heat and taste of her lips; but as he summoned them, they fled even before they came. All he could see were his white sons and daughters happily whirling and weaving in and out in a figure of the square dance, their arms encircling the waists, their fair fingers clasping the dark hands of black boys and girls with flat, flaring noses and drooping thick ashen lips.

"Some of 'em's mighty black," he could hear Sarah saying.

And his replying: "You know there's no other way. And they seem happy enough."

"Sometimes you have to seem happy just to keep on livin' " His eyelids clenched, he could see how Sarah had looked as she said it.

7

It was stifling hot in the kitchen; the blazing sunshine streamed through the west window and the wood stove on which the blackberries were cooking poured forth a steady volume of heat.

Sarah wiped her steaming forehead with the back of her hand.

"While this batch is cookin', let's go out on the porch and catch a breath o' air," she said to Julie. "I'm mighty nigh ready to faint, it's so hot."

They walked through the hallway and sat down on the porch. Sarah slipped her feet from her shoes, fanned herself with the palm of her hand. "I'll be glad when we're through. Hope Feelie and the children don't pick very many this time, and hope they come in pretty soon. It's too hot for 'em to stay out too long. They'll be havin' a sunstroke."

A cicada in the magnolia burst forth in a loud, ascending staccato.

"Hush! Hush yo'self!" Sarah commanded the raucous insect, without success.

"Ma, why don't you like to hear that dry-fly?" her daughter asked.

"I don't know, I reckon, except it makes so much fuss," the mother said. "I reckon I'm gettin' old enough to want as much peace and quiet as I can get."

"You ain't had much, have you, Ma?"

"I guess so. Much as I deserve, I reckon. He's been good to me."

"But he ain't been yo' husband, and you—"

"Hush, Julie." Sarah sat up in her rocker. "He's yo' pa, you know. Don't talk 'bout him none."

"I know. I been knowin' that. But what I mean is even if he's my pa—and the rest of us' pa—he ain't yo' husband, and that musta worried—"

"Don't you know he couldn'ta married me," she was scowling grimly, "if he'd wanted to," she added, less sternly. "And he mighta sent me off soon as—" She stopped.

"Soon as he found out you was 'spectin' me and Romeo?"

"He mighta. A many a white man's done that, but he didn't. And he's looked after us."

"But he ain't never been like a husband, and he ain't never

seemed like he was our pa. He livin' over there—" she pointed, "—and us over here."

"I know it, Julie. But the way things is, he couldn't do no other way."

"Yes'm, I know it. 'Twon't no other way neither one o' you could do, I reckon." She sat silent a long moment, her legs stretched out, her still flushed face solemn, her forehead furrowed. "Ma," she looked around suddenly, a thin smile lighting the grimness of her expression, "you don't like Dan much, do you?"

"Yes, I like him all right, Julie; in his place, he's "

"In his place? That sounds like a white person talkin', Ma. Why do white people talk about keepin' nigras in their place?"

"They mean keepin' them to their own race, I reckon, one race not havin' much to do with the other except workin' and such, I guess."

"But they don't never say nothin' 'bout a white man knowin' his place. Ain't he supposed to keep his place the same as a nigra is?"

"I guess he is. But back in slavery times, and now too, they don't all do it, Julie. Colonel Gordon didn't, or I wouldn'ta been here."

"He was my grandpa?"

"Yes."

She sat silent another long moment. Then she pulled her feet up, sat straight. "Ma, ain't Dan's place with nigras?"

"Sure it is. Why?"

"Wouldn't his place, then, be with me if he wants to be and I want him to be?"

Sarah's expression showed pain. "But you're so—so white, Julie, and he's so black." She hesitated momentarily. "You don't look like no nigra."

"But I am, Ma. I'm put with 'em. I go to school with 'em. I go to church with 'em. I have to." She leaned toward her mother. "But, Ma, I want to. I just wish I was blacker than what I am. Then maybe you'd think more o' Dan, because—" a sly grin softened her serious look, "—'fore much longer me and Dan aims to get married." She waited for her mother to say something, but Sarah remained silent, her eyes on the magnolia out beyond the box-bordered path. The girl got up, went over and stood beside the woman; she laid her hand lightly on her mother's shoulder. "It'll be all right, Ma. Me and Dan'll get along good, and—and 'twon't be nothin' for none of us to worry about."

Sarah reached up and patted the white hand on her shoulder, stood up quickly, slipped her shoes on her feet. "We better go see 'bout them blackberries," she said. "Wouldn't want 'em to scorch. I'm plumb wore out cannin' blackberries."

8

Dr. Cardell picked up the poison in one hand and the lamp from the dresser in the other. At the landing he turned to mount the circular stairway to the third floor, crossed to the door on the right, and turned the big iron key in the lock. The hinges squeaked as he pushed open the door and entered.

The lamplight on the spindle-legged Marie Antoinette mahogany chairs threw out grotesque, curving long shadows on the dust-covered floor, and nets of long undisturbed cobwebs—hanging like festoons from pilasters supporting the cathedral-like ceiling—heightened the eeriness of the great chamber.

He hadn't been up here since the fall after he had come home from Philadelphia, nor apparently had anyone else. Sarah had had no occasion to visit the room and the children very likely would have been afraid to stir the sleeping ghosts. That November day he had come up with hammer and tacks and sheets of canvas to weatherproof the narrow dormer windows; the canvas would help keep out the chilling winds of winter and the searing heat of summer.

He set the lamp down in the center of the floor and as he moved about the room placing pellets of poison on the chairs and near the windows, his shadow spurted out from him along the floor and in strange distortions leaped high up the wall and the curve of the ceiling.

Bub Barkley had seemed a little curious that afternoon when he had asked the storekeeper for the poison, even reluctant to sell it to him, the doctor felt. "This is high-powered stuff, Doc," he had warned. "Be careful and don't leave it lyin' round nowheres where it shouldn't ought to be." And then he had looked at him out of his little red pig eyes in the manner of a district attorney cross-examining a defendant. "You said you wanted this here poison for rats or maybe flying squirrels, didn't you, Doc?"

"Maybe so," he had answered, deliberately evasive. "That's what I told you I wanted it for." And he had offered no further information. But Bub evidently had sensed that the doctor believed he was suspicious. "Thought maybe you wanted to poison some o' these here nigger-lovin' Republicans or Populists that's raisin' so much hell," he had added, snickering.

"Might be a good thing for the state," Claibórne had retorted. "And you might include some of the Democrats, too. They been sittin' back holdin' office and lettin' us go to hell the last fifteen or twenty years." He had paid for the poison and left the store.

The rats, or maybe flying squirrels or ordinary gray squirrels, had been disturbing him for the last several weeks. They sounded like horses chasing each other above him as he lay in bed trying to get to sleep. He wondered how they had got into the abandoned ballroom. Perhaps a small pane in one of the dormer windows had fallen out and they had entered there; no doubt the canvas had rotted or been gnawed through; he had never thought when he was outside to look up to see if a pane might be out."

He went to each window and examined it carefully. There was no hole in the canvas sheets, and every pane seemed secure. Maybe the invaders had come in a second-story window and found their way up through an inside partition, located a knothole in the ballroom floor, and come out at night to play.

With the lamp held to one side so that he could see his way

better, he returned to the second floor and entered the large front bedroom, which had been his father's and mother's. He examined the front and side windows, but no panes were missing and the sashes were securely closed.

Then Claiborne noticed the crack in the plastering to the right of the fireplace. Of course. This was the crack that went down through the cream-brick heart, the tear in the wall suffered the night of the Charleston earthquake. He went over to the wall and, shading his eyes from the lamplight, sought to peer out through the breach. He saw the moonlight dappling the magnolia.

"Here's where the ballroom visitors have been getting in," he said aloud. The crack, he saw, was wide enough in several places to admit a squirrel sailing down from the magnolia or a rat scampering up the wall on the ivy overrunning it.

He went back to the third floor, retrieved some of the poison pellets to put on the floor near the crack. "I've really got to have that crack sealed," he said, and to him his voice sounded frighteningly loud in the great chamber's sepulchral silence.

Claiborne held the lamp high; the yellow light thrust the shadows farther into the corners, and the chamber thus more fully illumined brought to him a thronging of vanished figures out of his early childhood, men and women who on gay evenings in the years before the lost war happily had peopled this place.

He looked about him. One night, he recalled particularly, the Osbornes had been among those who had come to dance and feast at Holly Grove, and they had brought Melissa. She must have been about five then and he was six or seven. He and Violet had a tutor, a young man who was preparing to be a minister and was earning money to see himself through the seminary, and he taught them in the downstairs schoolroom that was now the doctor's office. That night the tutor was keeping the three children, reading them stories; but when the youngsters pleaded to be taken up to the third-floor ballroom to watch the dancing, he had done so, although he had insisted that they could stay only a few minutes.

Claiborne recalled that they had stood just inside the doorway over there, watching with wide eyes as their parents and the guests from nearby plantations had danced the intricate, graceful figures; they had watched wide-eyed the Negro musicians, too, intrigued not so much with the rhythmic singsong of the fiddles and the banjos as they were with the brass-buttoned red coats that the grinning, sweating Negro musicians were wearing.

It was a wonderful world that long-ago night, and other nights he recalled now that the drawers in the filing cabinet of his memory were springing open. The tremendous room—it was much larger then than it is now, he remembered—had been brilliantly lighted and lavishly decorated, and the gowns of the ladies and the clothes of the men were smartly fashionable; he remembered particularly old Mr. Allison's swallow-tails and his father's gaily checked waistcoat. His father, the young Claiborne knew, was the richest man in the world, and Holly Grove mansion house was the biggest and the most wonderfully furnished, and all the world was a glorious place except during those long hours he and Violet had to spend in the downstairs classroom with that persistent tutor.

That night, and doubtless on other nights when his father and mother were having dances up here, in the hall outside, against the wall opposite the door to the ballroom, an improvised bar had been set up; it was presided over by a grinning slave, white-coated. As they had stood there watching the dancing and the musicians, his father with Colonel Osborne and one of the Graham men from across the river in Lincoln County had come through the doorway, and he had seen them go up to the table. He remembered that as they went by Colonel Osborne had seemed already a little unsteady on his feet.

With the lamp still held high, Claiborne went out through the doorway as the three gentlemen had gone that night, and as the three children and the tutor had followed a moment later. At the head of the stairs, beside the walnut balustrade that circled the stair well, he paused; and now, almost as vividly as he had seen the terrifying incident that long-ago night, he saw it again in still frightening imagination.

The tutor had just led the three children from the ballroom when the men were turning away from the table to return to the dancing. Colonel Osborne was walking beside the balustrade and his father was beside the colonel. Suddenly Colonel Osborne lurched against the balustrade with such force that he was overbalanced, and as the children watched, horrified, was going over it; Alex Cardell grasped his flung-up arm and held on grimly. But the colonel, a heavy man, over the railing now except for his legs, was pulling Major Cardell after him; seeing it, the children screamed. And in that instant Mr. Graham and the tutor clutched at Claiborne's father. Miraculously, it seemed to Claiborne now, the balustrade did not collapse and send the four men crashing to the first floor twenty-five feet below. And Major Cardell held on to Colonel Osborne and the other two men held on to the major, and in another moment Colonel Osborne had been pulled back over the balustrade and the four were safe. And Colonel Osborne, he was satisfied now, was quite sober.

Claiborne looked down the circle of the stair well. They would most certainly have been killed had they fallen. And what if his father and Colonel Osborne had been killed? What would have been the affect upon Claiborne Cardell? Or Melissa Osborne? Or Violet?

He shrugged his shoulders, went down the stairs to the second floor, entered his bedroom, and set the lamp on the bedside table.

The flannel nightshirt would feel good tonight. He went into the closet, brought it out, dropped it across the bed. Quickly in the cold room he undressed, put on the nightshirt, crawled between the icy sheets. Then he leaned over and blew out the light.

As cautiously he eased his long legs toward the foot of the bed, he thought suddenly of Bub Barkley, wondered what Bub had thought he might be planning to do with that poison. When the sheets had warmed a bit, he turned on his side, and cradled the pillow in the crook of his right arm.

If they'd just stop those infernal fiddles and banjos. How can they expect me to concentrate with all that racket going? And this is a good article, a sound discussion, in the new journal just come in the mail this morning—if I could only put my mind to it. But with all that commotion up there in the old ballroom. Who in hell's up there anyway?

He picked up the lamp, climbed the circular stairs, around and around until he was dizzy with climbing. At the ballroom door he set the lamp on the old marble-topped washstand—wondered why his mother ever put it way up there—and opened the door, to a gush of music and chatter, the swishing of crinolines, and restrained stamping of feet.

"Lady 'round the lady and the gent go slow!" Willie Graham was shouting the figure, his eyes blazing, his big teeth shining. He looked closer; Willie was wearing a swallow-tail coat and a riotously checked waistcoat. But more amazing, beside Willie sat Bob Allison in a red coat with brass buttons, sawing away on a fiddle and patting his feet in time to the rhythm. But before he could scan the assemblage, Eliza Allison broke away from the square of which she was a part and came rushing up to him. Catching him by the arm, she pulled him into the ballroom. "Claiborne, I do want you to meet my half sister. Here she is. This is Sarah Gordon, Claiborne Cardell. Isn't she the most ravishing thing you ever saw, Claiborne? I'm so envious of her complexion; she gets that gorgeous olive-cream skin from her mother, who was half-Indian, half-nigra. Here, Jim, let Claiborne have your place and you dance with Sarah, Claiborne." And he was swinging through the steps of "Lady 'Round the Lady." But what the hell? Dancing with a nigra, in Major Alexander Cardell's ballroom? "You needn't act so damned pious-like," Bob Allison was saying to him, for now they were in touching distance of Bob's bow, "haven't you had six young'uns by her?" Bob pointed with his fiddle bow, and there they were,

Julie swinging on light feet with laughing, knee-fanning, foot-stamping, scuttle-black Dan Henderson; taciturn Romeo moving solemnly in time to the music, his arm about the waist of Lem's fat, dark daughter; little Feelie, taller, studious, ready to go off to Scotia to school, dancing absent-mindedly with the loose-jointed son of one of Bob Allison's Fair Meadows share-croppers; even Cleo, as fair as any woman in the ballroom, dancing, wide-eyed and ecstatic, with one of Lem's boys.

But they were in front of one of the pilasters now, and suddenly from behind it stepped Melissa Osborne, her beautiful face livid. "Get gone, nigger!" she screamed, as she gave Sarah a terrific shove. "Back to the kitchen house! He's mine! He's always been mine!" And grabbing him, she jerked him into the shadows of the pilaster, and hungrily she pulled his face down to hers and ground her hot lips into his. "Oh, Claiborne!" She had dragged her lips away long enough to whisper desperately in his ear, "let's go away from all this! Let's start over! Oh, Claiborne, let's—"

But the crying of the fiddles and the plinking of the banjos suddenly had ceased, and there was a knocking on the ballroom door. "My father's come to put an end to these bewitched, terrible doings in his ballroom," he told himself happily, as the insistent knocking swelled into a belaboring that threatened to shatter the door panels—

Dr. Cardell sat up in the bed, the dream vanished in the reality of someone's heavy pounding on his hallway door.

"Well!" he shouted. "I'm not dead. What—"

"Marse Claib! Lawd, wake up, Marse Claib. Git on yo' clothes! Hit's—"

"Open the door, Eph, and come in!"

Instantly the door swung open and his farm manager entered.

"What in the devil's the trouble, Eph?" The doctor was on his feet, skinning the nightshirt over his head.

"Hit's Mist' Bob, Marse Claib. He done—"

"What the hell, Eph!" He slung the nightshirt on the bed, reached for his drawers. "What's wrong with Bob?"

160

"Hit ain't Mist' Bob; hit's one o' those niggers on his place was workin' at the sawmill "

"He fall into the saw?" He was pulling his undershirt over his head.

"Naw, sir. Not that bad. Jes' his arm. But he's bleedin' mighty bad."

"Hell, Eph, didn't they put a tourniquet on it? If they didn't, he'll be bled to death before I can get to him. Where is he?"

"Yes, sir, they wrop a cloth 'round hit real tight, and they took him up to the big house. It warn't so far 'way. But he's mighty bad, Marse Claib. Mist' Bob say will you please come, and hurry fast as you can?"

"I reckon he tried to get Dr. Horton and couldn't, didn't he?"

"Naw, sir, don't think so. I jes' happen to be over there seein' 'bout borrowin' some o' his hands, when hit happen. I helped git him to the big house and Mist' Bob and Mis' 'Liza both said would I come a'ter you and as' you if you wouldn't please sir come right away."

He found the victim of the sawmill accident in critical condition; he wondered, as he worked desperately to repair the damage, if the man would live. He had lost much blood and the shock had been severe.

"I don't know whether he'll make it or not, Bob," he told his Fair Meadows neighbor. "He's lost a lot of blood, but it's lucky that the arm wasn't completely tied off with that tourniquet; if you hadn't kept a little circulation in it he'd have certainly lost it; gangrene would have set in sooner or later for sure. He may lose it yet, and he may die, in fact; the full effect of the shock hasn't hit him. Get some of the women to watch after him closely. I'll be back tomorrow to check on him."

"I'll do it, Claib; I'll see that he gets good attention." They were walking away from the small house, in former times a part of the slave quarters behind the mansion house to which they had brought the man from the sawmill. "And you don't know, boy, how much I appreciate your coming; he'd have died, sure as hell, if you hadn't got to him pretty soon."

"He was in a pretty bad shape," Claiborne agreed. "And he may die yet, like I said. Infection might set in, or his heart might kick out. But he's got a good chance."

"I surely hope he makes it. He's a good nigger, Claib, and a hard worker. And that combination's getting scarcer every day, ain't that right?"

"Yes, nigras—and whites—are getting sorrier all the time, seems to me."

They were at the point in the path where it divided; one fork went out toward the hitching rack at the driveway and the other led to the back door of the mansion house. Bob Allison caught the doctor by the arm.

"Claib, I'll bet you ain't had your breakfast."

"Well, I did sleep a little late this morning and—"

"Hell, I knew you hadn't. Come on up to the house and Eliza'll rustle us up some scrambled eggs and coffee."

"But, Eliza won't be looking—"

"That don't make any difference, Claib," Bob interrupted. "Eliza'll be glad to see you. It's been a helluva time since you were over here anyway."

Eliza welcomed him graciously. "How are you, Claiborne?" she asked.

"I stay pretty well, thank you," he said. "I guess I don't have time to get sick."

"There is a lot of sickness over the country, I reckon," she said. "We've had a good deal here on the plantation."

"You have? I haven't heard," he said casually. "I'm sorry." He saw that she realized she had spoken hastily. But she made no effort to retreat.

"Claiborne," she asked evenly, "how is Sarah?"

Her question surprised him as much as his observation had taken her unawares, but he took care not to show it. "Sarah keeps remarkably well, and so do her children."

She replenished his coffee cup but made no further comment, and quickly Bob took up the conversation. "You know, Claib," he said, "I remember one summer pretty soon after you started to practice—I reckon it was the summer you came home from Philadelphia—we sat out there on the terrace, you and Eliza and me, and talked about things in general and specially the situation the country was in. You mind how you were looking up the meadow and talking about what wonderful bottom land it was and the crops it had been producing, and I told you that you'd better get a good look because in a few years it might be grown up in scrub pines and elderberry bushes along the creek bank?"

"Yes, I do, Bob. It was early in September, I believe."

' Bob Allison nodded his head toward the window opening out on the meadow. "Well, take a look. Half of it's gone already—scrub pines, honeysuckles, plum bushes." He shrugged. "If things don't improve pretty soon, Claib, instead o' getting that stuff cleared out, I'll just have to let it all go. Can't get the labor, that's all." He laid down his fork. "And what I can get usually ain't worth' a damn. And now Milt's probably ruined himself, if he don't die. And he was the best field hand I had."

"I know what you mean. I'm in the same shape at Holly Grove. Of course, I'm practicing medicine, but what the hell—excuse me, Eliza—with our cotton only five cents a pound, how's anybody going to pay his doctor? And the doctor generally is the last fellow that gets paid, you know."

Eliza set down the plate of hot biscuits. " 'With five-cent cotton and ten-cent meat, how in hell can a poor man eat?' You've heard that jingle, I guess, Claiborne?"

"Yes. I saw it in the Charlotte paper one day, too. And it's a pretty pertinent question."

"I don't know what's coming of the South, Claib." The master of Fair Meadows was scowling darkly. "The politicians promise everything and do nothing except put more taxes on us. And what are we getting? The new state constitution set up a pretty fair school system, I thought—four months' schooling a year for both white and nigra schools—but the county commissioners can't seem to find the money, or don't want to, to finance them, and what schools we have, around here anyway, are sort

of a crazy patchwork business. And farming is gone to the devil."
He held the half of a biscuit midway to his mouth. "What's
coming of the country, Claib?"

"I don't know, Bob. I can't figure it. The Reconstruction
knocked us down so far that I don't know when we'll come out
of it, if we ever do. And when we do, I've a notion, our way of
living will be different. Could be better, of course. But it might
be worse. I'm afraid we'll be a long time getting over those ten
years after the war."

"Yeh, I agree. But," he chewed, swallowed, "it goes back
farther than that, Claib, I figure." He leaned forward and
stabbed his fork in the doctor's direction to give emphasis to
what he was going to say. "I couldn't say this to just anybody,
but," he smiled, "over at Bub Barkley's store, for instance.
I can to you. And you understand, I'm as strong a Southerner as you'll find anywhere, and I'd fight again at the drop
of a hat—and hell, we may have to—but we can't blame all our
troubles on Reconstruction." He lowered the fork and speared a
bite of Eliza's crisp bacon. "Claib, we won't move with the times.
That's one of our faults. And another is that we've been figuring
that we were either all of the United States or not any part of it.
You see what I mean? I guess we've been a sort of island. And
back before the War Between the States started, years before it,
we could see that slavery's days were limited. Slavery had been
abolished, I guess, pretty much over the whole western hemi-
sphere. Of course, the Yankees abolished it and sold us their
slaves, or maybe the other way around, when they saw that
slavery was economically no longer profitable. Some of those
abolitionists hollered and cried over the abomination of slavery,
but the reason they had got rid of theirs was because the slaves
cost them more than they were getting out of them.

"But the point is, Claib, we knew slavery was going out. Some
of us did something about it; some folks began freeing their
slaves. But we were too slow doing it, Claib, and then when they
started putting the pressure on us, we hollered states' rights.
You know, we claim we didn't fight to defend slavery; we claim

164

we were fighting for states' rights. And we were. But the thing got all mixed up. What I'm saying is that however that was, we'd never have had the war if we'd have got rid of slavery before 'sixty-one. Ain't that right?"

"I have an idea you're right, Bob. But our faults don't excuse the damned Yankees—excuse me, Eliza."

Allison smote the palm of his left hand with the outer edge of his right. "Exactly, Claib! I'm not defending those bastards— excuse me, Eliza. We're conservative, slow to move, but they're impatient fools. Like we were saying out there on the terrace that day, we were moving along toward freeing the slaves and would have done it in another ten years or even less, I'm vinced; but we should have done it already. On the othe if the Yankee politicians had had a little patience anc situation work itself out in the South, which it was doing   l you, if those damned politicians in the North had forget   lay their contemptible politics—and that's what they wei ing, Claib, trying to advance their own personal political interests by pointing to our errors and lambasting us—well, if we hadn't been so slow to move and they hadn't been such pushing, needling, interfering damn fools, there'd never have been any war. What do you think?"

"I think you've about sized up the situation," the doctor agreed.

Eliza set down her cup, and her eyes were flaming. "And I wonder if we'll change in the South—I'm not sure that I want us to," she observed. "And I wonder if the Yankees will ever learn to mind their own business and let us mind ours."

"It'll likely take another hundred years to change us or them," her husband said. "We'll keep on moving along slowly, doing things our own way, letting the situation, whatever it is, work itself out as it's bound to do, and the Yankees will keep on nudging and pestering and playing God and telling us what we got to do and when we got to do it."

9

Although the clock on her mantel minutes ago had struck two, Sarah Gordon lay wide-awake in the blackness of her front bedroom, staring unseeing at the ceiling.

Perhaps it was the excitement of Julie's wedding that was keeping her from sleeping, maybe it was because she was so tired from the preparations for the wedding supper, perhaps it was a mother's hopes struggling with a mother's forebodings on her daughter's wedding night. Anyway, for more than an hour she had been lying sleepless.

It had been a nice wedding. Squire Hubbard had even dressed up and put on his Prince Albert coat, and his wife had worn her dark-red silk dress and come into the parlor for the ceremony, which was considerably more than either of them usually did for Negro weddings, Sarah reflected.

Dr. Claib, of course, had not given his daughter away; he hadn't even attended the wedding; a woman about to have a baby demanded his presence, he had told Sarah, and she had made no comment. Romeo had served in his father's stead, and Feelie had stood up with the bride. And Caesar had been the grinning Dan Henderson's best man. But Dr. Claib had insisted that they use the surrey and the new iron-grays.

After the wedding, when they had all come back to Holly Grove and the supper in the kitchen house, where one bedroom had been cleared of furniture to provide a place for the festivities, Dr. Claib had come over from the mansion house to watch them dance and to eat a piece of Julie's wedding cake and have a cup of coffee. But he had gone back to his room and to bed before Dan and Julie and the other guests, all Negroes, had left. And now her other children doubtless had long been asleep.

But it could have been a gorgeous wedding. Sarah shut her eyes to seal off the night's blackness and saw in imagination her stately white daughter on her father's arm coming slowly down the ivy-entwined circular stairway to meet a handsome tall white youth standing with his best man and the preacher before an improvised altar of greenery lighted by tiers of long white candles in seven-branched holders. Julie's long train streamed up the stairs behind her, and its shimmering whiteness was heightened by the sombre blackness of Dr. Claib's cutaway. And as they took their positions in front of the altar and the preacher's intoned "Who gives this woman?" was answered by her father's "I do," the smiling tall white youth and her beautiful white daughter moved together and she took his arm and—

"No! I can't even be thinkin' 'bout that! No!" She was afraid her outspoken dismissal of the vision had awakened Cleo in the bed across the room, and she lay quiet. But there was no stirring in the other bed.

. . it does look like, though, he could have let his daughter get married in the mansion house and have her wedding supper in the dining room. Just once wouldn't hurt, looks like. And looks like he could have gone to Squire Hubbard's for the wedding. .

No, Dr. Claib was right, she reasoned. Julie's a Negro girl, even if she is only one-eighth Negro. That one-eighth makes her Negro, and she can never be white. So why lead her a little bit of the way to being white and then make her have to go farther back along the road to being Negro?

And Julie was happy being a Negro, her mother felt. Certainly no worries about race had seemed to disturb her wedding night. She's happy with her black all-Negro Dan. Sarah clenched her eyes shut again, and saw, all too clearly; in the cabin beyond the west woods, fixed up for them by old Eph after a sharecropper family moving away had made it available, her white daughter, happily spent now, lay asleep in the embrace of black arms.

Sarah shook her head to clear it of the vision.

. . . but she's happy, and it's the only way she can be happy. Does she want to pattern her life upon her mother's? Oh God, no. God forbid.

Her wedding day was Julie's and Romeo's nineteenth birthday. In three months Sarah, she suddenly realized, would have lived twenty years at Holly Grove. Twenty years, six children, one miscarriage, and soon—not long after Christmas, in all probability—a grandchild. It'll be—she figured the blood mixture—not quite half-white. And it'll be better for the blood to go toward the black. It'll be better for him. She considered her own case.

Twenty years living in a white man's back yard, all the time cleaning his house, cooking his food, yielding, and not unwillingly, to his demands of the flesh, birthing and raising his children. But never being his wife, never bearing his name, never being seen with him in public, never even sitting with him at table.

but Doct' Claib's been good to me. He mighta sent me off any time, but he didn't. I've always had a home and plenty to eat and clothes to wear and a place to live—a place to sleep even when it wasn't in his bed, which ain't very often any more. And he's been good to the chaps, too. They ain't wanted for nothin'. The girls have always got nice clothes and he's told Mist' Bub and Mist' Keller over at Hortonsville to always let 'em have anything they wanted and charge it to him. He's always give 'em everything they needed and a lot they didn't, I reckon. And he's goin' to send Feelie over to Scotia this fall. I reckon he's done all he could for me and the chaps, considerin'. . . .

Maybe Dr. Claib is the one who has had it rough, Sarah told herself.

. . . maybe it's been harder on him than us; most likely it has. He's mighty nigh an outcast 'mongst the white folks—his kind of white folks. His sister don't have nothin' more to do with him except take her part of the crop every fall, and that's gettin' smaller and smaller all the time. 'Liza and Bob Allison and Jim don't have much to do with him any more. And Melissa sure don't either

The remembrance of Melissa Osborne gave her a certain sense of elation. She didn't get him, like I said she wouldn't. And I guess she's glad, too. Mist' Charlie's a big cotton mill man and gettin' rich like she said he would, and Doct' Claib and Holly Grove both's goin' down the hill fast now. Both of 'em lookin' pretty run-down. .

When Sarah awakened to the sun's shining and the birds' singing and the reality of an April morning, the visions of the night had faded but not entirely vanished. And quickly the succeeding days and weeks carried her, busy and often wearied with the routine of heavy daily chores, into the stillness and drowsing heat of summer's listless dog days.

10

Bub Barkley saw the girl when she stepped from the path where it emerged from a clump of woods into the dusty road two-hundred yards east of the store. In the enervating warmth of the summer afternoon he sprawled in the decrepit, whittled-on straight chair tilted back against the dirty weatherboarding and from beneath the brim of his wool hat squinted bloodshot eyes at her as she approached.

The storekeeper shifted his weight forward, so that the chair came down on its four legs, and glanced one way and then the other along the road. The store sat on the outside of a gentle curve and from the porch one could see a half mile in either direction. Not another soul was in sight.

She came up the steps and paused in front of the door. "Good evenin', Mist' Bub," she said pleasantly.

"Good evenin', Feelie." He got slowly to his feet. "Anything I can do for you?"

"Yes, sir, Mist' Bub. Ma sent me to get a spool o' white thread and a spool o' light blue, Number two. And she said for me to look and see what kind o' cloth you got for dresses. Ma and me gettin' ready for me to go to school over at Scotia in September," she explained. "We makin' me some clothes."

"Well, I swarn, Feelie, I'd a never thought you was old enough to go off to school. Seems like no time since you was borned. 'Bout how old you now, Feelie?"

"I'll be seventeen in November, Mist' Bub."

"I can see you ain't no kid no more, Feelie." The storekeeper was measuring with quickening eyes her maturing body. "You done already shaped up good." He grinned, motioned toward the door. "Well, go right on in; I'll get yo' thread and you can be lookin' at the bolt cloth to see what kind you want. I got some mighty purty stuff, Feelie."

Bub followed the girl inside, went across to the spool cabinet, pulled open a drawer, and selected two spools. Then he came over to the counter beside which she stood, fingering one of the bolts. "This here's purty stuff, and hit's good and hit's cheap, too. I can let you have hit mighty reas'nable, bein' hit's you and bein's you're goin' off to school, Feelie."

"Ma sent the money for the thread and the cloth, Mist' Bub, if I find some like what I want. Course, I don't have to get it today. I can get it another time when I'm over here; I just come over today while things was sorter slack at home, and Ma needed the thread, too."

"What you mean, things slack at yo' house, Feelie?"

"Well, Mist' Bub, the menfolks is all gone and Ma's done got what supper we goin' to have ready 'gainst they get home, and we was mostly just settin' 'round. Juliet's been over there today helpin' Ma and me."

"Where's the menfolks at?"

"Caesar's drivin' Doct' Claib some'eres over in Cabarrus and Romeo him and Mac's gone to the river seinin' and won't none of 'em be home likely 'fore dark. And Juliet her and Cleo laid down awhile."

"Then ain't none o' yo' menfolks close 'round?"

"No, sir, they's all went off."

The girl meanwhile had been examining the various patterns and textures of the cloth. The storekeeper strolled back toward the front, from the doorway looked up and down the road. Then he called to her. "I'as 'bout to fergit, Feelie. Hit's some more cloth here; hit's jes' come t'other day. Hit's back there in the back room. I ain't had time to put it out here with this-here stuff. But hit's some mighty purty cloth back there, though. You can go back there and look at hit, if you want to, whilst I stay out here and mind the front part in case anybody comes in."

For a moment she was hesitant about going into the cluttered, dark back room. The storekeeper sensed her caution. "Hit's over there on the left side, Feelie," he pointed, "but you'll have to find hit yo'self. I'll have to stay out here. You just hunt 'round back there and you'll come acrost hit."

"I would like to look at it, Mist' Bub. I 'spect I can find it." She threaded her way between piled-up plowpoints, kegs of nails, coils of plowline rope and assorted sundries until she disappeared through the doorway into the rear storeroom. He could hear her walking around among the piled boxes, sacks of flour, and stacked slabs of fatback. Presently she reappeared at the door.

"Mist' Bub, where'd you say the cloth was at? I can't find it."

"Jest a minute, Feelie. I'll show you where hit's at." He strode past her into the gloom of the smelly storeroom. "Come right over here, Feelie," he called out obligingly. "This here's what I was talkin' 'bout."

Through narrow, twisting aisles between drygoods boxes, past the molasses barrel with the quart tin can on the floor beneath the spigot, and the tank containing lamp oil, she followed him. "But, Mist' Bub," she said, her tone betraying suspicion, "I don't see no cloth nowhere."

Bub Barkley pointed. "Hit's in that 'ere drygoods box, Feelie. I forgot I hadn't opened hit yit. But I'll open hit in a minute, and you can have all the cloth out'n hit you want and hit won't cost you nair cent if'n you'll jest be good to me and don't make no fuss, and 'twon't take long and 'twon't hurt you none—" he was talking faster, and as he caught the girl's wrist in a bony, viselike grip and twisted her roughly toward him she saw a scum of yellow saliva oozing in tiny bubbles between his reddening lips, "—and 'twon't nobody know nothin' 'bout hit but me and you."

"No, Mist' Bub! No, sir, no sir, Mist' Bub!" She was strug-

171

gling to break away from his grasp. "I didn't come here to do nothin' like that! Ma'll pay you for the cloth! No, sir, I ain't never done nothin' like that! Don't, Mist' Bub! Please don't! No, sir, Mist' Bub!" She was fighting to free herself, but he had the girl pressed hard against a heavy packing case, and her struggling was only intensifying his desire.

" 'Tain't no need o' makin' such a commotion 'bout hit," he taunted, as his spittle sprayed her face and he forced down her pinioned wrists. " 'Tain't nobody can hear you. I jest looked up and down the road an 'tain't nobody comin'. And ain't nobody goin' to know nothin' 'bout hit. Whyn't you jest lay down and don't make no fuss? 'Twon't hurt you none." He pushed his reddened, whiskered face close to hers and leered. "You know doin' hit don't hurt none. And I'll give you all the cloth you want, and yo' maw won't know how you paid fer hit, and you can keep the money which she gives you to pay me, and—"

But she was lunging again, twisting and kicking, trying to push him back, to break away from his gripping, cutting, jagged-nail fingers. "No, sir, Mist' Bub, I ain't never done nothin' like that! Don't, don't—" she kicked at his shin, but her bare feet could have little effect; she tried to claw him, but she could not get her pinioned hands in position to use her nails. And the more she fought, the less strength she had to fight, and the more he taunted and the harder he shoved her against the heavy box.

"Damn you, if'n you ain't a little wildcat!" He said it half laughing, half angry. "Why don't you stop makin' such a fuss, actin' like you'as a high-toned white gal, Feelie? Makin' such a commotion, and you a nigger gal, even if you don't look much like one and don't smell like one neither. Why don't you lay down quietlike? I ain't gonna hurt you none."

But she kicked at him again, and this time, infuriated, he jerked her to him and swung around so that now his back was against the packing case, and straightening his arms, forced her backward and down. She felt the edge of his bed against the bend of her knees, and out of the corners of desperately frightened eyes she caught a glimpse of the bedraggled faded checks of a dirty quilt. She had known that the bachelor storekeeper slept in the rear room of his store and she had heard her brothers speaking of his keeping batch, but in her eagerness to see the promised new bolts of cloth she had forgotten about the bed. Now it was pushing against the backs of her legs, and over-balanced, she was being forced relentlessly down on it.

"No, Mist' Bub!" she screamed. "For God's sake, don't, Mist' Bub! Turn me loose! Let me go home! Let me go!" But she felt her frantic protests, her frightened pleadings being smothered in the scratching bush of his tobacco-spittled mustache and beard; his hot, foul breath in her face was sickening her; his dirty broken teeth were fastening upon her neck beneath her ear; her feet were being pushed from under her. She went down, screaming and kicking; she felt the soiled, grease-slick quilt against her back, engulfing her; his eager weight was crushing her into the filthy quilt's loathsome softness, his talonlike, de-termined fingers, unrestrained now, were lifting, tearing, search-ing, finding.

11

"I do wonder what's keepin' Feelie so long. First thing you know, Doct' Claib and the boys'll be home before she is." Sarah closed the lid on the pot, into which she had just put fresh coffee, and set it on one of the stove eyes. Then she stepped out on the porch, from which she could scan a stretch of the road. "Come here, Julie, quick!"

Julie rushed out. Her mother was pointing. "It's something wrong with Feelie! I can tell the way she's walkin' with her head down." She craned her neck forward, squinted. "I do believe the child's cryin'. Hurry, Julie, run meet her and see what's wrong!"

Sarah followed as far as the gateway, and as the two girls neared her, Feelie came running, weeping hysterically, and clutched her mother around the waist. "Ma! Oh, Ma! Ma!" she wailed, and her slender body shook. "Oh, Ma! Oh, Ma!" She

173

held on desperately, as though she thought her mother might attempt to escape her.

"Feelie! What in the world, honey—what's happened?" Sarah put a restraining arm about the girl's shaking shoulders, with the other hand stroked her hair. "Don't be scared. I'm here, baby." She lifted puzzled, frightened eyes toward her other daughter. "Bub Barkley?"

The solemn-faced Juliet nodded. "Yes'm, it was him," she said. "He done it." She pointed. "It's blood on her clothes."

"Here, honey"—Sarah was trying to keep her voice calm—"let me catch you under the arm. Now, Julie, you catch her on the other side. You must be wore out, honey, walking all the way from the store, too."

"I run—soon's I got away from him—till I was out o' sight o' the store. I—Oh, Ma! Ma!"

"Don't cry no more, baby; you're home now; ain't nothin' goin' to hurt you, honey. Julie and me'll help you to the house and then we'll see."

Supporting her, for the girl was on the point of collapsing, they helped her into the kitchen house and she lay down on her bed.

"Fill up the kittle full and light the fire under it," Sarah instructed the older daughter. "Then run over and see if you can find some of Doct' Claib's whisky. He'll have some 'round somewhere—in the office or in his room upstairs. And don't be long, Julie!" She turned reassuringly to Feelie. "It'll settle your nerves, honey. Now just lay still and try to get quiet, and rest. Won't be long till Doct' Claib'll be here, I'm a notion, and he'll know what to do, baby." She gave the pillow a few deft pats, straightened the girl's head, smoothed back her hair with the ends of her fingers. "Feelin' better now, honey? You ain't hurtin' very bad nowhere?"

"I'm not hurtin' bad, Ma—not so bad—and it ain't bleedin' no more, but—but— Oh, Ma! Ma! Oh, oh!" She burst out crying again, and she whirled over and buried her face in her pillow.

Her mother sat on the bed beside her, patted her shoulder, massaged gently the back of her neck.

Juliet came in with the whisky. "Get some water. Fill a glass about a fourth full and put a little sugar in it," Sarah instructed. The girl went into the kitchen and returned with the water, into which Sarah poured an equal amount of whisky.

"Here, honey," she said, "drink all this you can. It'll help settle you down. Ain't nothin' better for that than a good strong toddy." She lifted the girl's head and held out the glass to her. Feelie took several swallows, handed it back, grimaced. "It burns." She dropped to the pillow again, pushed her face down into it, crossed her hands behind her neck; Sarah could see the fingernails and the skin of the girl's neck beneath them lighten as the nails dug into the flesh.

Cleo, awakened, came to the door. "Ma, what's the matter with Feelie?" she asked. "She took sick?"

"She ain't feelin' so well, Cleo."

"But what's wrong with her, Ma?"

"She had a little trouble over at the store. But you better go lay down awhile till it's nearer time for supper."

"Mist' Bub do somethin' to Feelie?"

"I'll talk to you 'bout it later, Cleo. But now you can sit on the porch and watch out for Doct' Claib."

The little girl's face was sober. "I know what you're talkin' 'bout, Ma. I know what old man Bub done to Feelie. Is she hurt bad, Ma?"

"Oh, no, Cleo—just not feelin' too good. Now you go out and watch for Doct' Claib."

Already Juliet had stepped out to the front porch. Sarah heard a sound at the door and looked up. Dr. Cardell stood in the doorway, his expression grim, and behind him in the hall were Juliet and Caesar.

"Juliet told me," he said to Sarah, as he came over to the bed and studied the girl lying face down on it. "Was she injured? Is she suffering?"

"She said she wasn't hurtin' bad. She told me she wasn't

bleedin' now. But she has been; it's blood on her underclothes, though I ain't looked close."

The doctor shook his head, but said nothing. Then he bent over the girl, put his hand gently on her shoulder. "Ophelia, you feeling better now?"

She nodded in the pillow, without turning to look up. "The blood's stopped? You're sure?"

Once more she nodded but said nothing. Dr. Cardell turned to Sarah. "I'll give her a sedative, and then I'll go for Dr. Horton. Under the circumstances, it'll be best for him to examine her before I do. And I'll get Neal Riley." Riley was the deputy sheriff living at Hortonsville. The doctor looked around for Caesar, saw him standing rigidly at the door. "Caesar, fetch me my bag from the buggy."

"I done give her some whisky from your bottle," Sarah said.

"Oh, you have? That's good. It'll do better. Never mind, Caesar." He took a step away from the bed, turned back again. "Before I go though, Ophelia, I ought to hear a little more about this, and from you. Turn over now, so you can talk." He said it gently, and the girl turned her tear-wet face toward him. "It was Bub Barkley that did this?"

"Yes, sir, it was Mist' Bub. He was the onliest one was there 'cept me."

"And you were never willing, you never gave him any reason to think that you—"

"Oh, no, sir, Doct' Claib, no, sir!" The girl's expression was a protest, a horrified denial. "He tried to give me some cloth but I wouldn't take it; I told Ma'd pay for it. When he grabbed me, I hollered and tried to get loose, but he—he—"

Dr. Cardell held up his hand. "It's all right, child." He patted her cheek. "I just had to have the story from you. Now you go to sleep; don't worry; everything will be all right." He walked to the door, turned and motioned to Sarah to come outside with him. Sarah spoke to the youngest daughter. "Cleo, you go out to the kitchen and start seein' 'bout supper." Then she followed the doctor from the room.

"Just try to keep her quiet, Sarah," he said. "And leave her like she is. Don't change her clothes. I want her to stay just like she is until the doctor and the sheriff get here; it'll be evidence against Bub Barkley; I want to see that scoundrel hung!" He started for the steps, stopped. "The boys haven't got back from the river yet, have they?"

"Not yet."

"Well, when they come, try to keep them from getting worked up. And keep them here. You know Romeo's pretty hot-headed."

12

When Romeo stepped from the path through the woods and turned to go westward along the road, he saw a dim light through the small window at the back of the store. Bub Barkley, he surmised, was getting his supper.

He shifted Dr. Claib's shotgun from the cradle of his right arm to his left, and as he walked he studied the weather-beaten frame structure and the grounds around it. With relief he saw that not a single horse or mule was tied at the hitching rack in front. Nor, as he drew nearer, could he hear any voices. With darkness fast approaching, customers would have gone home to their suppers and for another hour or so the loafers would not be returning to sit and spit until bedtime.

But Romeo did not continue along the road as far as the front door. Caution led him to slip aside some fifty yards from the store and ease his way noiselessly to a position behind an outhouse toward the rear from which he could watch for awhile and listen. In a moment he noticed a shadow move across the murky window panes, and, peering more intently, he recognized the lank and unkempt figure of the storekeeper. Still no voices disturbed the twilight quiet; the only noises were those being made by Bub Barkley with his pots and pans.

Romeo considered calmly which would be the better way to get into the store. He could go to the side door, hardly a dozen steps from him, which opened into the back room, and burst in,

177

or he could go around to the front, step up on the front porch, and slip stealthily through the store. If he were careful, he might even get to the door between the front part and the back room before Bub heard him. He thought of the possibility of making a commotion that would draw the storekeeper outside. But if he should do that, he reasoned, Bub likely would come out armed. And he didn't want that. Nor did he wish to encounter the man outside; witnesses might show up, and he wanted no witness.

Clutching the shotgun in his right hand and steadying it—muzzle toward the ground—with his left hand, as he had carried it many a time hunting partridges and rabbits, he slipped from behind the small building and stalked on light feet toward the front of the store. As he came around the end of the ungainly structure, he saw that the front door was open. Cautiously he mounted the steps and crossed the porch. Through the door he could see the lighted rectangle of the opening between the front section and the back room.

Quietly he entered the store, holding the shotgun at the alert, and made his way between piled-high counters toward the connecting doorway. Ten feet from it, his foot banged against a tin bucket which went clattering along the aisle to crash into a counter leg.

"Hey! Who's that?" The storekeeper came striding toward the door, wiping his greasy lips with the back of his hand, a heavy scowl creasing his forehead. But when he spied the shotgun, he swallowed quickly, licked his lips, and the scowl became an obsequious smile. "Romeo! Boy, you scared me when you kicked that bucket on the floor out there. I meant to set hit back on the counter but I plumb fergot 'bout hit. Serves me right, gittin' a scare like that." He came boldly toward the youth, beaming. "What can I do fer you, Romeo? First thing, though, I better go out and light them lamps in the front part."

"Stand back, Bub Barkley!" Romeo raised the shotgun menacingly. "You ain't goin' nowheres."

The merchant halted, stepped backward a pace; he opened his

mouth as if to say something but swallowed instead. Romeo, eying him intently, saw the man's Adam's apple bobbing up and down along the stem of his leathery neck.

"Wha—what's the trouble, Romeo?"

"You damn well know what's the trouble, Bub Barkley!"

The storekeeper tried to laugh nonchalantly, but even by the lamplight Romeo saw chilling fear in the man's eyes. "Feelie been tellin' 'bout me and her this evenin'?" He affected a shrug of his stooped shoulders. "Well, I mighta knowed it'd git out. But 'fore Gawd, Romeo—" he raised his hand aloft— "—'twouldn't never got out if'n it was left to me to tell hit, like I told Feelie. But I ain't blamin' Feelie none. I guess maybe yo' maw seen a drop o' blood on Feelie's clothes—" He paused, his words cut short by the look in Romeo's eyes, the way the youth's hands seemed to fondle the weapon.

"You're talkin', Bub Barkley," the octoroon said evenly. "What else you got to say?"

"Ain't nothin' to say, I reckin, Romeo, 'cept I'm sorry hit got out on us, and I guess we oughtn't to done hit." He paused again, but only for an instant. "But I'll make it right with Feelie. I shore will. I give her some cloth fer some clothes to go off to school with, but when she left she plumb fergot to take hit with her." He pointed. "Hit's out there—and the thread fer yo' maw too. I can git hit in a minute. I know right where " He made a move toward the door.

"Stay where you at!" Romeo lifted the gun again. "Feelie ain't forgot nothin'. And I ain't forgot nothin' neither." He advanced a step toward Barkley, and the storekeeper stepped back. "Don't you move!" Romeo commanded. "I'm gonna whup the plumb livin' hell outa you, Bub Barkley! I'm gonna whup you till I'm plumb wore out, and I'm gonna stomp you maybe plumb to death!" The store man's fast swallowing and his ashen face only heightened the octoroon's fury. "And I ain't 'preciatin' you standin' here lyin' 'bout my sister. You done ruint her, and now you low down enough to try to put her in it, you dirty yellow-bellied son of a bitch!" The boy smiled, though grimly, as if

179

satisfied with having unburdened himself of this supreme insult to a Southern man.

Barkley swallowed and started to say something, but Romeo silenced him before he could utter a sound. "Just open yo' mouth or make one move and I'll blow you to hell!" His trigger finger was caressing the trigger guard. "You done yo' big talkin' and now listen to me do mine. And soon's I git through I'm gonna whup you damn nigh to death, and I don't care if I kill you! And don't you move one hair, you dirty stinkin' old bastard!" He laughed. "You hear what I'm callin' you, Bub Barkley? It's what you been callin' me all my life, and the rest o' Ma's young'uns too. I guess we is bastards, too, but we couldn't help it. But you—" he shook the weapon in emphasis to his words, "—you's a self-made bastard, and I ain't meanin' no disrespeck to yo' ma. Bub Barkley, you been makin' fun o' Doct' Claib and his back yard full o' young'uns him and Ma had, and laughin' 'bout him gittin' drunk, and you been makin' slurrin' talk 'bout Ma. I been hearin' 'bout it; you ain't kept it from me or Ma or Doct' Claib. Don't reckin that mattered to you, 'cause I was jest dirt under yo' white-man's feet, and so's Ma and the rest of us?" He was talking calmly, as though he were a judge pronouncing sentence. Now he moved a step toward the storekeeper, and Bub stepped backward. "Stand still!" Romeo shouted, his anger rising again. "I done told you don't you move!"

The merchant froze where he stood, his eyes watching fearfully the boy's hand at the trigger. "I ain't goin' nowheres, Romeo! I ain't doin' nothin' nor sayin' nothin' "

"You dad-blame right you ain't—till I git through talkin'. And you ain't never goin' to do no more talkin' 'bout Doct' Claib and my ma. He's a good man; you ain't even fit for him to walk on. And you ain't fit for my ma to wipe her foot on neither even if you do call her a nigger. Them two ain't done nobody no harm unless it was to theyselves. And you ain't fit to be in the same house with my sister, and now you done ruint her." His voice was rising again, he was talking faster. "Now,

Bub Barkley, it's yo' time to git to talkin', and you better git at it! You tell me what you done to her, and you damn well better tell it straight!"

" 'Tain't no need o' lyin' to you no more, Romeo." Barkley's voice was weak with fright. "She come in the store this evenin' to git yo' maw some thread, and she was lookin' at some bolt cloth to make her some dresses, and I told her there was some purty stuff back here, and when she come back here I follered her, and—"

"And what?" The youth's angry eyes were drilling him. "Go ahead!"

"Well, she hollered and kicked and tried to git loose, but I pushed her down on the bed over there, and—" he shrugged, gestured with his hands.

"So what you said about her a little while ago was jest a damned lie?"

"Yeh, Romeo, it were; hit weren't none o' her doin'. Whatever she told was the truth, I 'spect. Hit were all my fault. And I reckin I'll pay fer hit. Does Doct' Claib know 'bout hit?"

"Yeh. And he's done gone for Doct' Horton for Feelie and the sheriff to take you to jail. He told 'em he was gonna see that you got hung." He laughed bitterly. "But I don't think no jury'll have you hung. If you was a colored man and Feelie was a white gal, you'd git hung 'fore daylight. But t'other way 'round—" he shook his head. And then his eyes flamed, and he cocked the weapon. "But that don't make no difference."

"No! No!" the storekeeper screamed. "Don't shoot me, Romeo! I'll do anything to make it right. Fer Gawd's sake, Romeo! I—I—" He was trembling from panic.

"Hell, I ain't gonna shoot you—not right now nohow. Not till I plumb stomp yo' guts out first! And I got to do it 'fore the sheriff gits here!"

He was standing beside the packing case between him and the storekeeper's bed. Barkley faced him three steps away in the open space beside drygoods boxes and piled supplies; at the merchant's right the fatback was stacked against a low counter on which stood the scales for weighing the meat. Beside the scales, unseen in the shadows, lay the long heavy knife used in cutting the slabs.

Without taking his eyes from the merchant's terrified countenance, Romeo stepped forward, catlike, and laid his shotgun on the packing case. With his left hand he reached out to grasp Barkley. But in that instant the storekeeper darted to his right, fumbled a moment at the meat counter, and then his right hand came up clutching the gleaming blade.

"Now, you damn nigger!" he screamed, as he sprang toward Romeo, "I'll kill you!"

But he had been a split second too late finding the knife. The shotgun's blast caught him in the face, he spun around and crumpled to the floor on the blade fast reddening with his own blood.

13

Dr. Horton stepped from Sarah's bedroom into the hallway. The deputy sheriff motioned to him to come out to the porch, where he and Dr. Cardell had been waiting while the examination of the girl was being made.

"Well, Doc?"

The physician nodded solemnly. "I made a thorough examination, Sheriff. I would say without any reservation in my mind that the girl's story is correct. She was violated. Clothes torn and bloody, from being herself lacerated. Would never been that way if she'd been willing. And undoubtedly she was a virgin." He turned to Claiborne. "She'll be all right, Doctor. I took a few stitches, gave her a sedative. Her mother can clean her up now. Suggest you keep her under surveillance awhile; she's pretty nervous, of course. Terrible thing, terrible thing." He faced the deputy again. "Well, Sheriff, anything else?"

"No, sir, Doc. Don't reckon there is, not right now. Course, they'll have to have you for a witness when they try Bub."

The doctor picked up the bag he had set on a chair at the

door. "Yes, I understand. I'll tell the court what I found. Be glad to. Well, gentlemen—"

"Caesar will take you home, Doctor." Claiborne held out his hand. "And I'm deeply grateful. Mighty sorry I had to call on you for such a thing."

"Yes, yes. Terrible thing, Doctor. But I was glad to do what I could. Sheriff, let me know when you need me." He offered his hand to Riley. "Well, Caesar, if you're ready—"

When the two had driven away in Claiborne's buggy, the deputy took the physician by the arm. "We better go pick up Bub, Doc. I ain't lookin' for no trouble out o' him, but maybe you better get your gun. I'm deputizin' you to help me arrest him."

"I'll have to run over to the house and get it," Claiborne told him. "I'll get my shotgun."

He was gone longer than the deputy sheriff had expected, and when he returned he was carrying a pistol. "Haven't used that shotgun since last winter hunting birds," he explained. "Might have let Bob Allison borrow it. Guess this will serve; we won't have to use any guns on Bub anyway."

As they neared the store, Riley pointed. "He must be there; ain't run away nohow, I reckon; his light's still on in the back room. But we better stop before we get there and tie up this horse. Then, Doc, you go to the back door and stand there in case he tries to get away when I go in through the front. Call on him to halt, if he comes out, and if he don't halt, let him have it. But try not to kill him, Doc." He turned off the road toward a small tree. "Court might get the idea you meant to kill him all the time, you know." When they had dismounted from the sheriff's buggy, he pulled the bridle rein over the horse's head, tied it to the tree. "Now, let's go, Doc."

The deputy went in the front door of the store; Claiborne heard him a moment after he reached the back room. Immediately Riley called to him to come inside. As the doctor joined him at the door into the rear of the store, the deputy turned and pointed toward the floor. "Step in here, Doc."

The storekeeper lay sprawled on his back in a welter of blood that filled the small open space between the drygoods boxes and the stacked slabs of fatback. The light through the soiled, smoked lamp chimney revealed splotches of reddish-brown on the boxes and the greasy meat. But its most gruesome revelation was the slain man himself. Sheriff Riley pointed. "If I didn't know it was him, I couldn't identify him," he declared illogically. "Half his head's done been blowed off." He studied the mutilated corpse. "He's one won't nobody have to hang, all right."

Then he went over to Bub's bed, jerked off the top quilt, brought it over and covered the body. "Can't move him till I get the coroner," he explained. He picked up the lighted lamp. "Let's get out and lock up the store," he said, as he led the way into the front section. "We don't need nobody tramping around in here, and I'm damned sure Bub ain't going nowhere."

He set the lamp down on a counter near the front door. "Get out, Doc, while you can see good where to walk. Then I'll blow out the lamp and lock up this here store."

When he had closed the door and swung the hasp over the staple, he slipped the opened spring lock into the staple and snapped it shut. "Now let's be gettin' back to your house, Doc," he said. "Likely as not he'll be slippin' your shotgun back in 'bout now. I'm goin' to have to take Romeo to town and lock him up on the charge o' murderin' Bub Barkley."

14

Sarah Gordon leaned the broom against the door frame, looked over her shoulder at the Cardells eying her coldly from the parlor walls. "You can look all you want, but I ain't goin' to dust none today. It's too hot and I don't feel so good, and don't nobody ever come in here no more anyhow."

She walked out on the verandah and sat heavily in the doctor's big armchair. With the already hot morning sunshine cutting in a sharp line across the verandah, out here it was hotter than in the high-ceilinged gloom of the downstairs; but there seemed to be more air, and it didn't seem as hard to breathe—especially in there with those old-time folks lookin' down on you like they were so high and mighty at every little speck o' dust you ain't wiped off the tables or the mantelpiece or the chairs and sofa, and still begrudgin' you bein' here.

She leaned back in the chair, pulled her long skirt high to let the air to her legs. . . . seems like it's so hard to get enough air, maybe like a dog feels pantin' after he's been runnin' a long time   She closed her eyes . . . I reckon it's this August weather that keeps me drowsy most all the time, but this heat does feel good; makes you sleepy-like and helps you forget your troubles. . . .

The noise of a horse and buggy made her drop her skirt quickly and sit up in the chair; she recognized the horse, and as it came nearer she saw that the man was Bob Allison. When he was even with the opened iron gate he turned off the big road and came down the driveway. He saw her and stopped at the front hitching rack; he looped the horse's rein over the peg and came over to the verandah, as Sarah stood up.

"Good mornin', Sarah. Is Claib home?"

"Good mornin', Mist' Bob. No, sir, he went down to town this mornin' on the train. Said he reckon he'd be back on the evenin' train if he got through his business time enough to catch it."

"I see." He stood nodding his head solemnly. "I was afraid I'd miss him."

"Won't you come in anyhow though and rest yo'self awhile, Mist' Bob? And can't I get you a cool drink o' water?"

"Well, Sarah, I guess I better be gettin' on back to Fair Meadows. I reckon I can see Claib some other time." Quickly his mood changed, and he smiled. "But I do believe I'll have a drink. It's sure hot this mornin'."

"Jus' come in and sit down, while I go draw a fresh bucket."

He came up and sat in the big chair. A moment later he heard her turning the well windlass, and presently she came with the water. He emptied the glass. "That was good, Sarah. I was thirstier than I thought."

She asked him to have another glass.

"No, thank you; that was a plenty." He stood up. "I better go, I reckon." But he hesitated, awkwardly.

She sensed that he wanted to say something else. "You better sit back down and rest awhile. It's mighty hot out on the road, I bet."

"Well—yes, I will, Sarah." He sat down, motioned to a chair near his. "You sit down. I just as well tell you what I was goin' to tell Claib. It's just as much your business as it is his." He looked out across the parched yard to the big road, searching, she thought, for a way to begin. "Sarah—" he turned to face her, his expression serious, "we were mighty distressed, Eliza and I, and Jim too, when we heard about your trouble. I been meanin' to come over before now, but I just, seems like, couldn't figure what I'd say. But this mornin' we just decided not to wait any longer. We thought maybe we might be able to help out some way. I guess that's what Claib's doin' in Charlotte, tryin' to help out the boy." He paused. "I reckon he's got him a lawyer."

"Yes, Mist' Bob. He got Mist' Plummer Smith. And he's down there talkin' to him now, I guess." She shook her head. "But it ain't goin' to do no good. Romeo's bound to get hung."

"Well, I wouldn't give up hope, Sarah. The boy had provocation, that's a fact. It was a terrible thing old Bub did—"

Tears were in the woman's eyes. "It was terrible," she agreed. "But Romeo took Doct' Claib's shotgun and went on a hunt o' him and shot him down in his own store. Course Romeo claims the storekeeper come at him with the big knife, and I believe Romeo. But he went after him with the shotgun, to kill him, the jury's bound to figure it—" She paused, the tears coming freely now. "Ain't nothin' can save that boy, Mist' Bob."

"I don't know, Sarah; don't give up yet. Maybe the court'll take into account what Bub did to cause Romeo to go after him. How's Claib takin' it?"

"Pretty hard, Mist' Bob. He ain't doin' no good."

"Still drinkin' a lot?"

"More'n ever. Been drunk mighty nigh all the time since it happened—after he got the lawyer for Romeo—till last night. He got sobered up enough to go to town this mornin'. But goin' down there ain't goin' to do no good." She turned to face him squarely, eyes dry now but heavy with sorrow long endured. "Everything here's in bad shape, Mist' Bob—the folks and the place. Feelie's so shamed and put out she won't show herself to nobody, and she's got the idea it's her fault Romeo's layin' up down there in jail. And Caesar's took to drinkin' bad lately and I'm 'fraid he'll be gettin' into bad trouble some time when he's drunk."

"I'm sorry, Sarah. And Eliza's put out—"

"And you can just look 'round and see how this place's been goin' down ever since"—she paused, went on—"well, you know all 'bout everything, Mist' Bob."

"Yes, sure." He nodded. "But two or three years of good farmin' and some paint and a little brick work on that south end," he motioned with his head, "will get Holly Grove back in pretty good shape."

She shook her head. " 'Twon't no paint and new bricks fix our trouble. Won't nothin', Mist' Bob. And I ain't expectin' to see Holly Grove lookin' no better; it won't in our time, I'm a notion. Things has got too far gone now. But I ain't blamin' him; it ain't all his fault. I reckon he ain't had much of a chance since he come back from Philadelphia. And the children ain't had much neither, and I don't think Romeo's got none. Folks got a notion nigras with white blood's mean, you know." She shrugged resignedly. "And ain't nothin' nobody can do 'bout it now."

15

Romeo Gordon's trial was docketed for the fall term of Superior Court, scheduled to convene on the first Monday in October. Early in September Sarah caught the train at Cardell's

Station and went down to the jail to visit her son; she carried him some food, including two pies and a cake, and she tried to talk cheerfully during the time she was allowed with him. She promised him she would come down to the courthouse for the trial.

When the fall term convened, Sarah was there, sitting quietly with Feelie in the section reserved for Negroes. Impassively she listened as the judge charged the new grand jury and sent it out to deliberate; in the same way she followed the proceedings as the court gave its attention to the trial of defendants, most of them Negroes, charged with the commission of relatively minor offenses, in the main fighting and stealing. She and Feelie followed in the motley stream emptying the courtroom for the noon recess and sat on a bench on the courthouse lawn to eat their lunch, and they were in their seats again when the sheriff's sonorous "Oyez! oyez, oyez!" reconvened the court's sitting as the judge entered and took his place on the bench.

With the same apparent indifference Sarah followed the proceedings as the grand jury came in with a bill of indictment against her son charging him with the murder of one Bub Barkley of the county and state aforesaid; she listened as Romeo was brought in, led by a deputy sheriff, and as he stood for formal indictment; not once did a sudden change of expression or a rolling tear betray to her neighbors the violence of her inner conflict. And when after conferring with the state's solicitor and Attorney Plummer Smith, the judge announced that the trial of Romeo Gordon for the murder of Bub Barkley would be called as the first case on tomorrow's docket, that all witnesses in that case were dismissed until then, and that witnesses in other cases need not report until the following morning, Sarah and Feelie stood up and edged their way toward the door. There Sarah turned and lifted her hand in quick reassurance to her son, whose eyes had found her in the Negro section and had followed her as she crossed the courtroom. Calmly she watched as the deputy led Romeo out through the doorway on the other side of the judge's bench, and then she and Feelie went quickly from the courtroom.

Dr. Cardell was waiting for them. He had been most of the day with the lawyer. "You all go on home on the train," he told the two. "I'll spend the night in town." His countenance was grim. "We're working—Smith and I—and we'll be up late. Be sure to get to the station in the morning in plenty time to catch the train."

Sarah nodded. "He looked so pale," she said, almost as though she had not heard the doctor. But Claiborne understood.

"He hasn't been out in the sun since August."

The next morning she and Feelie seated themselves just inside the bar immediately behind the defense counsel's table in the area reserved for witnesses and for relatives of defendants coming to trial. When the deputy sheriff brought Romeo into the courtroom, in the moment before court was convened for the day, she stepped over and spoke cheerily to him and squeezed his hand, and Feelie smiled timidly. Then the sheriff ordered everyone to rise, and as the judge entered, convened the court.

A jury of white men, was quickly selected and empaneled, and the state solicitor called the coroner to the stand. He testified that he had examined the body of the deceased. Death had resulted from a shotgun discharge that had struck the man on the side of the face; he found several of the shots lodged in the victim's skull.

The defense attorney did not cross-examine the coroner, and he was excused. The solicitor next called Neal Riley. The deputy sheriff told how he had discovered the slain merchant and subsequently had arrested Romeo Gordon. In lurid detail he described the gruesome scene in the back room of the store, his return to Dr. Cardell's home, and the arrest of the youth. Dr. Cardell's shotgun, he swore, still smelled of discharged gunpowder. Confronted with the evidence, Gordon had readily admitted firing the shot that killed Barkley, said the deputy sheriff, but had insisted that he fired as the merchant was advancing on him with the meat knife.

The solicitor in his direct examination of Riley sought to emphasize the defendant's confession that he had taken Dr. Cardell's shotgun to Bub Barkley's store, that he had been violently angered at Barkley's alleged mistreatment of Feelie; the defense attorney in the cross-examination grilled the deputy sheriff in developing the self-defense evidence.

When the cross-examination was completed, Riley was excused and the state rested. The solicitor smiled confidently. Certainly the state had shown by the evidence that the defendant had taken the shotgun and gone to the merchant's place of business, entered it on an unlawful mission, and slain Barkley. How could the jury fail to find that Gordon had premeditated the murder of the storekeeper? And premeditated murder is murder in the first degree, a capital offense.

The defense lawyer sent Ophelia to the stand and as he prompted her gently, she told her story, in low voice and with eyes averted. Several times the judge kindly admonished her to speak more loudly so that the court and the jurors could follow her testimony.

She had known nothing of Romeo's actions that evening; she had been asleep when he came home from the river, her mother had told her later. When Attorney Smith finished examining her, he tendered the witness to the state.

"The jurors have heard the witness, Your Honor," the solicitor said. "It is their prerogative to believe or disbelieve her testimony. I do not care to question her."

So Feelie was excused and the defense sent Dr. Horton to the stand. He tesified that he had examined the girl after the alleged rape; he gave it as his opinion that she had been violated, by whom he did not know, though she had declared in his presence that the man was Bub Barkley.

"But, Doctor," the solicitor asked, when the witness was turned over to the state, "can you swear that you know unequivocally, as a result of your examination of this witness, that the witness, at the moment this clandestine act was begun rather than at the moment it was consummated, was unwilling?"

"No, I couldn't swear that, of course."

"Then come down, Doctor."

There was a stir in the courtroom as Lawyer Smith sent Romeo to the stand. Spectators craned their necks and in the Negro section there was a titter of whisperings. The judge gaveled sternly. "Mr. Sheriff, I'll have no disorder in this court. I'll jail the first person who disturbs this trial." Immediately the courtroom was as silent as a graveyard at midnight, and the judge nodded to the defense attorney to begin the examination of his witness.

Romeo calmly related what had happened from the time of his arrival home from the river and his discovery of Barkley's assault upon his sister until his return from the store and his arrest a few minutes later.

"Did you kill Bub Barkley?" his lawyer asked.

"I shot him, and he was layin' there when I left. I reckon I killed him," he replied.

"Why did you shoot him?"

"He was comin' on me with that big meat knife; I shot him just as he was fixin' to chop me. I figured if I didn't shoot him he'd kill me."

The defense attorney smiled. "The witness is yours," he said, turning to the solicitor.

"Romeo, how come did you decide to go to Bub Barkley's store that night?"

"I wanted to see him a little bit."

"Why'd you want to see him?"

" 'Bout what he'd done to my sister."

"You just wanted to talk with him? Do you expect the jury to believe that?"

"I had a notion to give him a good beatin'."

"A beating? Then why did you take that shotgun?"

"I knowed what he'd done already. I figured he wasn't wantin' to see me."

"You went there to kill Bub Barkley, didn't you, Romeo? That's why you took the shotgun?"

"I went there to give him a beatin'. I don't reckon I'd cared if I had beat him to death."

"You were mad, Romeo, weren't you? You were mighty mad at Bub?"

"Yes, sir, I was."

He continued to grill the defendant, seeking to drill into the minds of the jurors his contention that the defendant had gone to the store with the purpose from the beginning of killing the storekeeper. Romeo answered calmly, admitted without reluctance that he would not have been particularly disturbed if he had killed the man, but maintained that he had shot to save his own life.

His examination and the cross-examination were completed by the noon recess, and Sarah spoke a moment with her son just before they led him from the courtroom. She and Feelie went out to the bench on the lawn and ate their lunch. Dr. Cardell had gone with the lawyer to the latter's office; during the forenoon session he had sat on one of the front benches in the white spectators' section.

When the court was reconvened for the afternoon session the arguments of counsel to the jury began immediately, with the defense having the first speech. Attorney Smith reviewed the evidence, with flourishes of dramatic oratory pictured the heinous nature of the merchant's crime against the girl and the natural reaction of a brother to such treatment of his sister.

"Just turn this case around, gentlemen of the jury," he proposed. "Suppose Bub Barkley, a white man, were on trial here for the murder of this nigra boy who had raped the white man's sister. Why, gentlemen of the jury, you well know," his voice was rising, "that if it had happened that way, this Bub Barkley would never have been brought to trial, would never have been arrested, would never have—"

The solicitor sprang to his feet. "I object, Your Honor!" he shouted. "I object to this line of reasoning! The defense counsel knows it is highly improper, prejudicial—"

"Objection sustained!" The judge banged his gavel and

turned to the jury. "The jurors will disregard the remarks of the defense counsel. The deceased Bub Barkley is not on trial. He stands before the Bar of a Higher Court, gentlemen. The defense counsel knows that the matter of race should not be injected into this trial. Race should not and in my court shall not have any bearing on trials of defendants."

Attorney Smith was back on his feet. "Thank you, Your Honor. That was all I was seeking. I thank you for thus instructing the jury." He smiled and turned to the jury.

But the judge smote the bench with the gavel and leveled it at the lawyer. "Mr. Smith, you put yourself dangerously near being in contempt of this court, sir. And now, will you proceed with your proper argument to the jury?" He laid down the gavel.

The lawyer turned back to face the judge squarely. "I beg Your Honor's pardon. I had no thought of holding this court or this jury in contempt. On the contrary, I hold them both in highest respect. I meant, Your Honor, to be speaking rather of the prevailing views and conditions of our times in our troubled Southland—"

"Yes," the judge interrupted, but this time he was smiling faintly. "I well understood the counsel's purpose. And now, sir, I admonish you to get on with your argument in this case."

The lawyer developed his client's testimony relating to what happened at Barkley's store the night of the slaying, reviewed in considerable detail Romeo's story of how the storekeeper suddenly had procured the meat knife and was advancing on him when he shot. He argued that the testimony showed clearly that Gordon had not gone to the store to kill Barkley but instead to give him a sound beating, and that therefore the charge of premeditated murder could not be sustained.

The solicitor's argument was brief. "This is an unfortunate affair we have reviewed today, gentlemen of the jury. All murders are unfortunate. And it is most unfortunate for society, for the victim, for the perpetrator, when a man takes unto himself the authority of being court, jury, and executioner to try, convict,

193

and execute any person, regardless of the enormity of the crime that person has committed against him. Such authority, gentlemen, is given only to corporate society, what we call the state; when it is taken by an individual, we call that murder. And the case before us is that simple. That young man," he turned to point to the defendant, "took upon himself the authority of the state. He tried Bub Barkley—and on incomplete evidence—and he, and we, will never know how truthful was that testimony on which he acted; he convicted him; he premeditated his execution; he obtained a shotgun and walked the long way to that store, and he proceeded to execute the man he had convicted. It is a simple case, gentlemen of the jury, even though an unfortunate one, because all the evidence indicates clearly that this defendant premeditated the slaying, and a premeditated killing, His Honor will tell you, is first-degree murder."

He swung about to point to Feelie, sitting by her mother. "The state did not elect to cross-examine the defendant's sister," he said. "We wish not to add to her burdens that already must be heavy. Only two persons knew what happened that afternoon in Bub Barkley's store. You gentlemen have heard her version. You will never hear the other, this side of the Pearly Gates. Bub Barkley cannot give his testimony, gentlemen of the jury. Bub Barkley is not in this courtroom. He had been tried, convicted, and executed by that defendant there!"

Summarizing, the solicitor argued that the defendant in premeditating the slaying of Barkley and then in slaying him had been guilty of first-degree murder, whether or not he had shot the storekeeper as the man was advancing on him with a knife. Barkley, he insisted, was acting within the law in defending himself, even should the jury believe Gordon's testimony at that point. In fact, he argued, Gordon was guilty of premeditated murder on his own testimony.

The judge's charge was impartial. He reviewed the evidence carefully and then instructed the jury on the degrees of murder, told the twelve men they might bring in one of four verdicts:

guilty of first-degree murder, guilty of second-degree murder, guilty of manslaughter, or not guilty.

"And, gentlemen of the jury," he concluded his charge, "this court instructs you that in considering the evidence in this case you will give no consideration to the fact that the deceased was of a different race from the defendant." He looked sternly over the upper rims of his spectacles. "Now, gentlemen of the jury, take the case."

As the jury members filed into their room to deliberate on Romeo Gordon's fate, the judge retired into his chamber immediately behind the bench and the deputy sheriff led the defendant out for a short recess. Sarah smiled reassuringly as her eyes met her son's, but as soon as he was gone she sat back in her chair, stolid and apparently indifferent, to stare unseeing at the stack of law books on the now-vacated defense counsel's table.

An hour later there was a light rap on the inside of the jury room door. The sheriff walked over and opened it, and slowly and solemnly the twelve men filed out and took their places in the jury box. The judge came in, sat down, and nodded to the sheriff. "Mr. Sheriff, have the defendant brought into the courtroom." In that same instant Romeo came through the doorway at the right; the deputy had a firm grasp on the defendant's belt. He led him to the chair behind his lawyer.

"Mr. Clerk," the judge commanded, "take the verdict."

The clerk stood up at his small desk across the bar from the jury box. "Please stand, gentlemen," he said to the jurors, and they arose. He turned to face Romeo. "The defendant, stand up." Romeo stood. The clerk turned again to the twelve.

"Gentlemen of the jury, have you agreed upon a verdict?"

A tall, beak-nosed weather-beaten farmer, whose leathered face contrasted strangely with the pallid countenance of the octoroon, cleared his throat, swallowed. "We have," he said.

"Jurors, look upon the prisoner. Prisoner, look upon the jurors. What is your verdict?"

The foreman's eyelids flickered; he licked his lips.

"Guilty of murder in the first degree."

"So say you all?" the clerk intoned the question, and the jurors nodded. The clerk motioned to them to sit down.

Feelie screamed, a shrill, high, anguished wail. Instantly her mother grasped her arm. "Hush, child! Hush!"

Romeo, still eying the foreman as if he had not comprehended, turned to face his sister; his pain was for her, it seemed, and not himself. The judge, watching, spoke to the condemned youth, not unkindly. "The defendant will take his seat." Romeo sat down.

In a moment his lawyer arose, addressed the bench, offered a motion that the verdict be set aside. The motion was denied. The attorney followed with the customary defense legal maneuvering. When all his efforts were of no avail, he sat down. The judge gaveled the courtroom to rise as the defendant was ordered to stand.

In the solemn hush, broken only by the muffled sobbing of Feelie, the judge sentenced Romeo Gordon to be hanged in the county jailyard on the first Friday in December.

Lawyer Smith promptly served notice of appeal to the state supreme court, and the dates for the completion of the appeal papers and the state's answer were set. When the formalities were finished, the judge gaveled. "This court is about ready to adjourn. The prisoner is in your custody, Mr. Sheriff. And now, Mr. Sheriff, adjourn court."

"Everybody rise!" the sheriff commanded. "Oyez! Oyez! This honorable court is now adjourned. God save the state and this honorable court!"

Before the deputy sheriff led Romeo away, Sarah stood a moment with her arm about his shoulders. She stretched on her toes as he bent down, calm and dry-eyed, to kiss her, while Feelie pushed against him, weeping. "It ain't over with yet, son," said Sarah, as she surrendered him to the deputy sheriff. "Don't you be worryin' none."

At the railway station Dr. Cardell bought three tickets and handed two of them to Sarah. "Don't get in the dumps now," he said. "This is the first go-round. We haven't given up yet." But his tone lacked conviction, and in his thin smile she read pain and fear. But she said nothing.

Sarah and Feelie sat up front in the coach for colored passengers. Stonily the woman watched the lengthening shadow of the train sweeping like the relentless unfolding of fate across drying, dead fields, some with spilling cotton still unpicked, some with corn bursting the husks and fodder burnt and twisted.

Behind them in the coach for whites rode Dr. Cardell.

16

Bareheaded, Claiborne Cardell stood at the head of the grave and studied the newly placed stone. The marble man had done well, he had carried out Claiborne's instructions faithfully; the stone was large enough but not pretentious; it was not ornate but neither was it too severe.

Carefully he examined the lettering:

VIOLET BREVARD CARDELL

Aug. 12, 1849
May 13, 1898

The names were spelled correctly and the dates were right, he saw with satisfaction. Many names in old Bethel graveyard, even prominent family names, had been misspelled by careless or illiterate monument makers in generations past.

He was glad he had decided against having put on the stone some quotation from the Bible, with book and verse, as the marble man had suggested. It was better the way he'd had it done. Violet wouldn't have wanted any sanctimonious words, any pious-sounding phrases. She was an aristocrat, a true daughter of those Cardells on the parlor walls, plain, direct, a little austere even. No hypocrisy about Violet. Firm, unrelenting.

There was no carrying-on when she was living and none when she died. When her time came, she departed this world.

197

No unctuous words, no dramatic exit, the people with whom she lived in Charlotte had told him. A heart attack, it must have been, and she was gone. And now her monument seemed perfectly suited. The fellow did a good job, and his price was fair enough. Even then, with the casket and funeral, it took about all that Violet left, maybe a little more. There's little money in teaching, and heaven knows she never got much from the crops at Holly Grove.

The stone over Violet's grave—and that's another good thing—matches the other two on the Cardell plot, he reasoned. Simple stones, with only the names ALEXANDER CARDELL and ISABELLA CARDELL and the dates of their births and deaths. No tributes, no quotations, no ornamentation except the small Confederate flag carved above Major Cardell's name.

Yes, Violet would approve of the stone's being like her parents', and she would approve particularly of being placed to rest here with them rather than in the cemetery in Charlotte. He glanced at the one space remaining in the Cardell family plot and wondered if she would object to his lying down beside her in perhaps the not-too-distant future.

"Of course, she wouldn't," he reproved aloud his wondering, "not if—" But abruptly he cut short his observation; it seemed irreverent, if that was the word, like the gossiping of chattering women. Besides, it was pointless; he had acquired a sufficiently large plot in Beulah Land burying ground.

The shadows of his parents' stones were stretching eastward; that of his mother's was inching upward toward the bottom date on Violet's. He put on his hat and turned away quickly; he strode across the graveyard and out through the gateway in the rock wall. At the tree under which his parents had tied the horses and surrey when as a child he had come with them and Violet to the church—it seemed like a thousand years ago—he untied the rein and climbed into the buggy.

Caesar hadn't been driving for him much in recent months. That's why he wished to get back to Holly Grove before Lem came in from the fields; he could catch him at the stables and talk with him before he went to his cabin. Lem had taken over from his father the direction of the farming, what little direction it was having, because Eph was too old to handle the field hands. Claiborne wanted to talk with Lem about Caesar, to see if he thought it advisable to let the boy go to Charlotte and get a job in public work of some sort. Caesar was not interested in the farm; he was showing little interest in anything, in fact, and old Eph hadn't been able to do much with the boy. He was running around with a group of reckless Negro youths, drinking and carousing; maybe going to Charlotte and getting away from them would be good for Caesar. Certainly Lem's advice would be sound.

Claiborne had one stop to make. He wished to visit for a moment a sharecropper's wife near Beulah Land church; she had a new baby and was having a little trouble with her milk, and he feared milk fever was developing.

He was there longer than he expected he would be, and when he got into his buggy the shadows were long across the yard. He clucked his horse to a fast trot for a mile, but let her slow to a walk as he drew near the Negro church; there, although he had not planned to, he pulled over in the churchyard and got out.

The grass completely covered Romeo's grave now; it needed cutting, and in a glass fruit jar sunk into the earth at the head, the flowers—put there by Julie and Feelie on the boy's birthday —had withered and dried into a brown crispness; the girls had taken them out to the graveyard, he remembered, on the boy's birthday, the second since his death. He lifted the dead flowers from the jar and threw them away, and then he stood a moment, bareheaded, as he had stood at Violet's grave, and on the small stone read the inscription, beginning to gray now with fine lichens in the cuts of the lettering:

ROMEO GORDON

Born April 27, 1877
Died Dec. 4, 1896

He stood a long moment, and then, eyes wet, he put his hat on and walked back through the unkempt, ragged crab grass and weeds, past unmarked sunken graves of nameless and forgotten Negroes.

<h1 style="text-align:center">17</h1>

Cleo came up on the porch and sat down beside her mother. "Supper 'bout ready, Ma? After walkin' home from Julie's I'm mighty nigh starved."

"Everything's ready, except I'm waitin' till Doct' Claib gets here to put the biscuits in the oven. But you can eat now if you wanta and when he comes you can ca'y his supper over there."

"I reckon I can wait awhile." She lifted her feet to the porch railing. "Maybe I oughta cool off first anyhow."

"How's Julie? She look like it might be comin' pretty soon?"

"Yes'm, she sure does. And, Ma—" her eyes warmed and a sudden excitement edged her voice, "—she told me what she's goin' to name it. If it's a boy," quickly her manner was subdued, "she's goin' to name it for Romeo."

"That's nice. I'm glad she is."

"And if it's a girl—but I can't tell you, Ma; it's a secret. I told Julie I wouldn't tell you; you'll just have to wait and see."

"For me, I reckon. It'll be puttin' a burden on the child."

"Why, Ma? Well, anyway, if I ever have a girl I'm goin' to name it for you, that's for sure."

Sarah smiled. "You won't be doin' the poor young'un no favor, I'm 'fraid. But you didn't say how was little Claib."

"He was all right, runnin' all round, gettin' into ever'thing." Her forehead wrinkled and a frown darkened her expression. "Ma, ain't little Claib black? He's mighty nigh black as Dan. He don't look a bit like Juliet, does he? Or none of us."

"I guess wasn't nothin' but Dan come out, and Dan's pretty dark." She was silent a moment. "But it's better he went to Dan's side instead o' Julie's."

"But why, Ma?"

"Hush, child." She said it gently. "Don't be askin' questions I can't give no good answer to. But I just know it would be better that way for little Claib and Julie and the rest of us, I reckon." She studied the shadow of the kitchen house pushing out toward the iron gate. "Course it don't make no difference to me; I've 'bout had my time, I reckon, but it's you all I'm talkin' 'bout."

Cleo shook her head. "Not me, Ma. You ain't talkin' 'bout me. I ain't never goin' to have any black babies."

Sarah Gordon's expression revealed astonishment, apprehension.

"What you mean, honey? You ain't goin' to do like—like your ma?"

"No'm," the girl was smiling, "I just ain't goin' to have none unless I marry a white boy. I ain't goin' to marry no nigra. I just couldn't—" she was shaking her head solemnly, "—think of marryin' somebody like Dan, Ma."

"But they ain't all as black as Dan, honey." Sarah's laugh lightened the tension. But then she was serious again. "You know if you stay round here you can't marry no white boy—or anywhere else they find out about you, honey."

"Yes'm, but if I went off and nobody knew—if they didn't find out—I mean, if they didn't ever find out—"

"But they would. There's always some mouthin' people."

"But if I went way off and nobody from around here ever saw me."

Sarah shook her head sadly.

"It's always somebody shows up that knows a person and can't keep his mouth shut. Don't matter how far away you go, it's always somebody comes along that knows you and—" She broke off, shrugging her shoulders.

"Well, I ain't goin' to marry no colored boy, and that's a fact, Ma." She shuddered. "I couldn't stand it. I reckon I just don't feel like Julie did 'bout it. If I ever have any kids, Ma, they'll be white kids." She paused, and then her blue eyes suddenly were smiling. "And like I said, Ma, I'm goin' to name my first girl-baby for you, makes no difference whether Julie names hers for you or not."

18

Lem was feeding the stock when Claiborne Cardell drove down to the stables. He came out and unhitched the horse from the doctor's buggy.

"Where's Caesar, Lem? Been helpin' you any today?"

"Yes, sir, Doct' Claib. He didn't knock off till 'bout four 'clock, I reckon it was. Said he wanted to go to the house and take a bath and git dressed up a little 'fore he went to the fish fry."

"The fish fry. Where in the devil is it?"

"It's over at the colored folks new schoolhouse. It's the lodge havin' it to make up money. I 'spect it'll be a lot o' niggers over there, bein' it's Sat'day night."

"Hell, yes, and a lot of fighting. Tell me straight, Lem: Did Caesar have any liquor in him when he left?"

Lem hesitated, fidgeted. "Tell you the truth, Doct' Claib, I don't 'zackly know. But I sorter think he mighta had a little drink. Him and that Wilson nigger that come by in the buggy for him was both feelin' pretty good, look like, when they left here. That nigger mighta had some liquor."

"Yes, and Caesar might have had some too." Claiborne shook his head. "I don't know what to do about that boy, Lem. You know, I can't say much to him about drinking liquor; I'm no example, of course, except a bad example, you might say. But Caesar's going to get into bad trouble some time, I'm afraid; you know, a boy as white as he is out with a bunch of niggers at a fish fry, half of 'em drunk," He paused a moment. "I wanted to talk with you about him, Lem. Caesar's been after me about letting him go to town and get a job. He don't seem to be interested in the farm, and it might be a good thing if he went down there and got in some kind of public work. What you think, Lem?"

"It might be, Doct' Claib. Course, Caesar's a good hand when he works, and they is a lot o' saloons down there. But he can git liquor without goin' down there, seems like too. So it might be just as good if you let him try it out, anyhow."

"Well, I'll talk to him, and you do too, Lem. Sort of feel him out, and talk to him about drinking." He turned to go toward the mansion house, stopped, and faced Lem again. "And, Lem, soon's you've had your supper and washed up, why don't you hook up the buggy and drive over to the schoolhouse? I'd like for you to sorter look after Caesar and get him home tonight soon as you can."

He walked to the house where he found his supper ready, for Sarah had popped the biscuits into the oven when she saw his buggy come through the gateway. After he had eaten he sat on the front verandah a few minutes and then went up to his room. A new journal had come that day and he glanced through it. An item about the recent change in administrators at the hospital where he had interned and served as resident caught his attention.

"Hah! They put Alfredo in to take old Smith's place. Well, he'll probably be all right, though I would never have thought of him for the job." Alfredo Vicente had been one of his classmates in med school. "I'll have to write him a note and congratulate him. Old Alfredo, I'll be durned."

He read an article and started on another. But it was a dull, poorly presented paper, he thought, and he was tired; he'd been going all day. He dropped the journal on the stand beside the lamp, got up, and undressed. Then he bent over, blew out the light, and slid his legs between the cool sheets.

A moment later, it seemed, though it must have been several hours, the doctor was awakened by heavy pounding on his bedroom door.

"Doct' Claib! Doct' Claib!" Someone was shouting. Then furiously the pounding began again on the door.

Claiborne sat up in bed. "Who is it? What you want?"

"Doct' Claib! This here's Lem—"

"Come in, Lem! What in the world—"

The door was flung open. Lem was holding a lantern out at

arm's length. "Doct' Claib, Caesar's hurt! I just now fetched him home. I'm scared he's bad hurt! You better—"

But already the doctor was on his feet and fumbling for a match on the tray to light the lamp. Then he reached for his pants, stepped into them, and slid into his shoes.

"Where is he, Lem? What happened?" He was moving toward the door. "Come on; you can tell me while we're going."

"He's in the kitchen house on his bed, Doct' Claib. I just now got him home in the buggy. He's mighty bad, I'm scared."

"What happened, Lem? How'd he get hurt?" They were going down the circular stairs. Claiborne glanced at the grandfather's clock on the landing, its face lighted by Lem's lantern. "Damn! Past midnight." He turned to glare at the Negro. "You scared to tell me what happened?"

"No, sir! No, sir!" the overseer answered quickly. "He—he got shot, Doct' Claib. One o' those young niggers from over on the river—"

"Here, give me the lantern!" They were downstairs now at the door to the doctor's office. "I'll be getting some stuff while you light that lamp. I may need it, too, to see what I'm doing."

In two minutes he had his bag and was crossing the yard along the path to the kitchen house; the lamp was burning in Lem's room across the hall from Sarah's, and shadows moved on the window panes.

Sarah was standing beside the bed, her face pale and set with fear; beyond her, in the fringe of the gloom beyond, Claiborne caught a glimpse of Cleo and Mac, wide-eyed and frightened. He went quickly to the bed, caught up the still youth's inert wrist, with his other hand felt his forehead and under his chin.

"Get his clothes off!" he commanded. "Lem, you help. And be easy." He turned toward Cleo. "Get another lamp, Cleo; we've got to have more light. Get two more." His eyes had focused on a small dark spot rounded above the boy's belt some two inches left of his navel. "Easy now," he cautioned Sarah and Lem; "we don't want to start any bad hemorrhaging." Gently Lem lifted the wounded youth so that Sarah could pull off his trousers;

204

already they had eased his coat off, and his shoes. "Leave his socks on," the doctor said, "and pull up the sheet. We must keep him warm."

In a moment they had stripped him, and carefully Dr. Cardell began examining him. "How many shots were fired, Lem?" he looked up to ask.

"Three or four, I think, Doct' Claib. But didn't but one hit him, I'm pretty sure."

"Did you see it? How far away from Caesar was the fellow when he shot?"

"Yes, sir, I was right there; I was trying to git to him to git his pistol away from him; I was right at him, and so was Caesar. He coulda re'ch out and touch him."

"Hmmm," he felt gingerly of the now fully revealed wound, "that might be better; bullet maybe didn't get its full force, but that might make no difference, though." He looked up. "What was the pistol—thirty-two?"

"Yes, sir, I'm pretty nigh certain it was."

"Turn him—easy now—on his side so I can see if the bullet came through." He shook his head. "No."

"He's bad, ain't he, Doct' Claib?" It was the first thing Sarah had said to him; she had been following his instructions mechanically.

"Yes, real bad." He answered her gently. "You'll have to be ready, Sarah—for anything." He was bending above the boy. He reached up quickly and patted her hand. "How long has he been unconscious, Lem?"

" 'Bout the time I got him to the porch, Doct' Claib. First, I didn't think he was hurt bad. Thought maybe the bullet just grazed him. He walked to the buggy and I didn't have no trouble gittin' him in. And he talked some, comin' home. And he didn't 'pear to be bleedin' bad."

The doctor was shaking his head. "I'm afraid he has bled a lot internally. And he's in deep shock, I fear."

Cleo and Mac came into the room, each carrying a lighted lamp.

"Set 'em over there where the light will be on him, but get a card or something and shade them out of his eyes," the doctor said, "though I don't believe it will make much difference, he's in such deep shock, it looks like." The children set down the lamps as he had directed. "Now, Sarah, keep him warm. And Cleo, you and Mac, I think, had better go back to bed. I'll call you if I need you to do anything. Now, Lem, you come with me over to the office."

"I don't believe Caesar'll make it, Lem," he said, when they were crossing the yard in the band of light from the Negro's lantern. "I didn't want to say it, though, in Sarah's hearing. But she probably thinks the same thing; she's hard to fool." They walked on a few steps. "The only chance he's got is for me to operate on him, Lem, and I can't do that yet. And I'm afraid he's not going to come around enough for me to attempt it." In the office he confronted his overseer. "How come did the nigger shoot him, Lem? Was it Caesar's fault? Was he drunk?"

The Negro hesitated. "Well, now ''

"I smelled liquor on him, Lem. I know he was drinking. I just want you to tell me if it was Caesar's fault."

"Well, now, Doct' Claib, Caesar was pretty drunk, but 'twon't no need o' that nigger shootin' him. He didn't have to kill ''

"What had Caesar done, Lem? Tell me the truth. I got to know, and you said you saw it all."

"Caesar did have his knife out, and that nigger claim he was fixin' to cut him when he shot. But I don't believe Caesar was doin' nothin' but talkin' big, Doct' Claib." He reached in his pocket. "When Caesar fell over I got his knife and put it in my pocket, right quick-like 'fore anybody knowed what I was do-in'." He handed the knife to the doctor, who placed it on the shelf beside the medicine bottles.

"Why did Caesar have his knife out? Why was he advancing on that nigger?"

"I didn't hear it all, Doct' Claib, or I coulda got it stopped. They had been fussin' right smart though, somebody said, and I was tryin' to git Caesar to come on le's go home, but I couldn't, and so I stepped over to the stand and et me a feesh san'widge, and 'bout that time I heared this nigger cuss Caesar and call him a yallerskin," he hesitated, "you know what, Doct' Claib, and somebody hollers, 'Look out! He's got his knife out!' and I went runnin' over, but 'fore I could git to the nigger he pulled out his pistol and shot Caesar. I don't reckon nobody knowed he had a pistol on him."

"Did the nigger run, Lem?"

"I don't know, sir. I was tryin' to do somethin' for Caesar. I didn't think first he was bad hurt, not till I was helpin' him to the house when he started to fall and I thought he was dyin' maybe."

"Well, they'll catch the bastard, I reckon. And when they try him, Lem, you'll be a witness. And then you tell just what you told me. I wouldn't want you to lie, even if he did shoot Sarah's boy. I guess it was self-defense."

While he had been questioning Lem the doctor had been assembling his instruments. "Hand me that bottle of cocaine there, Lem—the blue bottle, that one," he pointed, "that's right. Now you go back over there and tell Sarah to get some old sheets and towels out, and tell Mac to make a fire in the stove and fill up the kettle. We'll need a lot of hot water. And tell Sarah you'll sit with Caesar. I want Sarah to get away, anyway. Doing something will be better for her than staying there watching the boy." He shook his head. "She's having a tough time, ain't she?"

"She sure is, Doct' Claib. But she ain't makin' no big to-do 'bout her trouble." He started toward the door, then paused. "You want me to tote any o' that stuff?"

"Well, yes." Dr. Cardell handed him the towel in which he had wrapped the instruments. "They'll have to be sterilized. Take 'em on, and I'll be right over soon's I fix up a little more stuff."

Lem had reached the hall when the doctor heard Sarah Gordon at the back steps screaming for him. He ran out to the porch.

"Hurry up, Doct' Claib! He's— Oh, hurry up, Doct' Claib, I'm 'fraid—"

The doctor ran down the steps and caught her arm. "Get in front of us and hold the lantern so we can see," he said to Lem. Then he spoke to Sarah calmly, reassuringly. "He's in deep shock, Sarah. People like that sometimes look like they're—past helping. Maybe he'll be coming out soon and I can—"

"No, it ain't that!" She was almost running. "He's so white and still. And I couldn't find no pulse."

Caesar lay motionless in the yellow light from the lamps. Dr. Cardell walked to the bed, lifted up the languid wrist, bent down to place his ear against the bare chest. To Sarah, watching, breathless, it seemed that he would never raise his head. When he did, he spoke to her and motioned to the chair beside her. "Sit down, Sarah," he said, his voice gentle, calm.

She sank to the chair. He stood looking down at the curling thick hairs, crow-black on the chest almost as white now as the sheet reaching to them. Then quickly he caught the sheet and pulled it up to cover the chest, the pallid still face.

Sarah cried out, in one piteous long hopeless wail as of the damned, and then, moaning, fell forward to press her face against the cover and fling out her arms, fingers clenched.

19

As Sarah Gordon turned from the stove and set the pound cake on the table, all of a sudden, it seemed, the fiery blast from the opened oven grabbed with flaming white-hot hands at her chest. She swayed, clutched the edge of the table with one hand, and with the spread palm of the other pushed hard against her heart.

She stood braced against the table edge as the kitchen walls dipped and soared and spun around her like an ocean-wave swing, and then she stretched her neck and shook her head to steady them. When they had settled again to immobility, with her hand still on her chest she walked out to the porch and sat in the rocker.

For several minutes with her mouth wide she laboriously inhaled deeply and with a sudden rush released the air thus briefly impounded. After a while the sharp edge of pain was gone, and she dropped her hand and sat back in the chair.

       that's the worst it's ever been. I guess I oughta tell him. But what good would it do? Maybe give me some pills or something. Maybe make me go to bed a few days, and it wouldn't do no good. Long's it ain't no worse than this, I'll just keep my mouth shut.

Dr. Claib might get down drunk while she was down sick, and who would look after things then? And they're bad enough as it is with both of them on their feet and going through their daily routines, she reasoned.

She looked out across the yard, dead again in the August heat, dead not only with the heat and dryness of the season but dead with neglect and slow decay. She lifted her eyes to the bricks still on the roof, the chimney tops still unrepaired, the jagged crack through the cream-brick heart green with moss and spreading ivy. That crack came in the wall the night of the great earthquake—could she ever forget that night?—when the children were hardly more than babies. The children—

    poor Romeo. The good Lord'll give him justice, if they didn't down there at the courthouse. And Caesar, poor Caesar, dead, too, since June last year. And Feelie married to Jimbo and give up on the notion o' going to school. Mac workin' down at a liv'ry stable in Charlotte. And Cleo finished one year at Scotia, and Doct' Claib got his head set on Cleo goin' back. She was smart, she did fine; but she ain't goin' back

Tonight she'd talk with the doctor about Cleo. After he'd had his supper and was in a good, easy frame of mind, she'd have a straight talk with him. Maybe in his office, or when he was out on the verandah cooling. She'd have it out with him. She just couldn't wait any longer to get it settled. Nobody could tell what might happen. She wanted it settled before something might.

When he had finished eating and she had carried the supper dishes out to the kitchen, she returned to the mansion house.

209

He was in the office, refilling some of his bottles with medicines from larger ones. "Doct' Claib," she said from the hall doorway, "I want to talk with you some about Cleo."

He looked up quickly, his forehead furrowing. "What in the world's happened to Cleo, Sarah? Don't tell me she's "

"Ain't nothin' wrong," she hastened to assure him. "But still I want to talk 'bout her—soon's it suits you."

"Well, we'll talk right now. Come sit down, Sarah." He motioned to a chair. "What's on your mind?"

"Cleo and me's been talkin', and I agree with her, I just as well say."

"What about?"

"You mind how you used to always say whenever it come up that anybody with even a little bit of nigra blood in him couldn't ever be nothin' but colored as long as anybody knew about it. You said it was best for my children to marry colored folks and let the blood go towards the colored."

"Yes. But that wasn't just my notion; that's the way the world looks at it. I can't change it. But why? What's that got to do with Cleo?"

"Cleo says she ain't never goin' to marry no colored man. She says she can't stand the idea of it even; she says she's three-fourths white and one-eighth nigra, and her white blood's pullin' stronger."

"But she can't marry any white man around here anywhere, Sarah, if he wanted to marry her." The doctor's expression was grim. "It's against the law; if she did marry one, the marriage would be annulled when it was found out, and they'd be forced to separate."

"Down here, that's so. But that ain't what Cleo's figurin' on. She's wantin' to go up north to live, Doct' Claib, not mainly to marry a white man, but to live like a white girl. She says she feels like one, she wants to be with white folks; she don't want to live with nigras no longer, and she says she'd die before she'd marry one."

"But I thought she wanted to finish Scotia; she's smart, and I was sorta hoping she would. I think maybe the cotton this fall will turn out enough to put her through another year."

Sarah shook her head. "She ain't wantin' to go to school no more, leastways to no colored school. She thinks she's learned enough to know how to get along all right by herself if she goes up north."

"But where would she go? What would she do?"

"She's got a notion she might get a job in a hospital, learnin how to nurse maybe." Sarah smiled wryly. "Cleo said maybe she got a likin' for such from you; you know she always did like to watch you workin' on folks that got cut up and such like, and handin' you your instruments, and all." She was hesitant. "She thought maybe you'd help her get a job."

"I don't know." His concern was evident. "What you think about it?"

"I'd miss her mighty bad. She's the only one left at home. But I know how she feels; I been feelin' the same way all my life," she looked him in the eyes, "and she ain't got but half as much colored blood as me. I wouldn't want to keep her from havin' a better life."

"I wouldn't either; you know that. But would it be better—"

"It ain't no question with Cleo; she's done decided, she told me. She said she couldn't never live like Julie and Feelie, and I see how she feels; I couldn't neither."

Claiborne walked to the back window and looked toward the stables and the big woods beyond; the red sun sinking fast thrust their shadows toward him like thin fingers reaching out to clutch the mansion house. He turned back to face her. "I think I understand, too, Sarah, how she feels, and how you've been feeling. Let me think about it awhile, and then we'll talk about it—you and I, and Cleo, too."

Sarah went out to her house. Cleo was finishing washing the supper dishes. Her mother scalded them, dried them, and put them away. Then she and Cleo went out to sit on the front porch and cool off. They were there an hour later when Dr. Cardell came to the mansion house back porch and called them to come over to the office.

"Sit down," he said, as they entered, "and see what you think of this." As they sat, he picked up a sheet of paper. "I've written this letter about you, Cleo. It's to Dr. Vicente in Philadelphia. He was a classmate of mine in school and he's head of the hospital where I interned. See how this sounds:

Dear Alfredo:

Last summer I saw a notice in the medical journal of your appointment as the hospital's administrator. I planned then to write you my congratulations, but I am still a procrastinator. I do wish to say, however, even though unpardonably late in doing so, how pleased I was, and I trust that you are having great success.

Recently I have been seeing in the journal that the hospitals are having difficulty in procuring qualified girls to begin training in the nursing field. Should this be true of your hospital, I can recommend a young lady who wishes to become a nurse and who in every way, I can assure you, is well qualified. I have long been on the friendliest of terms with her family. I might add that her grandfather in the days before our tragic Reconstruction era was a prominent and wealthy South Carolina planter.

I remain, Alfredo, with esteem and affection,

Respectfully yours,
James Claiborne Cardell, M.D.

Cleo's eyes were beaming as Claiborne laid the letter on the desk. He glanced toward Sarah. She, too, seemed pleased.

"How'd it sound?"

"And you'll let me go if he writes and says he needs somebody?" Cleo's delight was evident. "And you reckon he will, Doct' Claib?"

"I don't know." He smiled. "But he'll answer soon, I reckon, and then we'll know. And of course if he wants you, you can go." He turned to Sarah. "What you think of the way I worded it?"

"It said just enough, and not too much," she replied. "And everything you said's so."

20

About a week later Dr. Vicente's reply reached Holly Grove. He was happy to hear from his old classmate, and he appreciated the congratulations and well wishes. And particularly he appreciated Claiborne's telling him about the girl. The hospital was indeed finding it difficult to recruit a sufficient number of qualified girls of good background to begin its courses in nursing. Could Claiborne put him immediately in touch with the girl, or better still, could he arrange for her to come to Philadelphia in time to begin the new course starting early in September? "You can tell her, Claib, that she's already accepted; certainly I would take anyone on your recommendation sight unseen." Just be sure to let him know when the girl would be arriving in Philadelphia so that he could see to it that someone met her. "And again, Claib, my warmest thanks."

Dr. Cardell answered the letter that day. He would see that the girl got to Philadelphia in ample time to begin the course on its opening day, and he would telegraph him when she left so that he could send someone to the train to meet her. And he could assure Alfredo that the girl, when he informed her of her acceptance, would be most appreciative.

The next two weeks Sarah and Cleo were busy getting the girl ready to go north. "I won't need many everyday clothes, Ma, because I'll wear uniforms mostly, I reckon," Cleo suggested, her eyes bright with anticipation, "but I'd like to have two or three nice dresses and a pretty hat to wear when I'm off duty, and maybe when I might get to go out some times. You know, Ma, you never can tell what might happen, can you?"

Sarah sewed and Cleo sewed, and one day the two caught the train and went to town, where they got two dresses, a hat, and some underclothing. Sarah seemed as excited as the girl, and when all the preparations were made and the trunk packed, she stood over Lem and Jimbo and supervised its roping. "If 'tween't for that rope," she declared, "that trunk would shore bust, it's packed so tight."

The night before Cleo was to leave, Dr. Cardell handed her a slip of paper. "It's the telegram to Dr. Vicente that you're coming," he explained. "I've written everything except the time the train gets there. The man at the station can tell you that, and you just put that in." He hesitated. "I may be gone on a call when you get up in the morning, Cleo," he said. "So I'll tell you good-by just in case. Be good, and take care of yourself. And be careful how you talk." He put his arm about her slim shoulders. "God bless you, child. And write your mother as often as you can."

Cleo understood, and so did Sarah. And in the morning he was gone, whether on a call or not they did not know. Lem and Jimbo loaded the trunk on the one-horse wagon and Sarah and Cleo rode in the surrey, for Claiborne had taken the buggy. They sat silent, not knowing what to say, as they waited for the coming of the train, and each was glad when its whistling up the track broke the strain. They jumped up and sped out of the colored waiting room. Cleo would pay the conductor the passage to town, and there she would buy the ticket to Philadelphia and send the telegram Dr. Claib had written. At the track Lem and Jimbo waited with the trunk to lift it into the baggage car.

Sarah caught her daughter to her as the train ground to a stop, hissing steam and belching black smoke. "Good-by, honey." She kissed her, held to her, and then, laughing through misty eyes, pushed her away. "You 'bout to get left." The girl, lips tight, stepped up quickly to the platform. "Lawd 'a mercy! Honey!" Sarah yelled as she rushed to the steps and handed up a shoebox tied with a heavy cord, "You come mighty nigh leavin' your eatin's!" She stood back as the train began to move. "Write soon's you get there, and 'member, honey, be careful what you tell."

"I will, Ma. And—good-by!" Eyes streaming, she turned quickly and disappeared inside the colored coach.

The train was gathering speed now; Sarah stood beside the

track and waved, though she knew that her daughter was not seeing her. As it sped around a curve to disappear in the deep cut, she burst out crying. Jimbo ran over to her. "Come on, Mis' Sa'ah, I'll drive you home. Pa, he can take the waggin."

21

Claiborne stopped at the upper hitching rack, got out, and threw the mare's reins over the peg. He was tired after a busy day of doctoring; Jimbo could take the horse and buggy down to the stables and unhitch. He picked up his bag and was turning to go into the house when Sarah came running out on her porch, waving a sheet of paper. She ran up the box-bordered path to meet him at the big magnolia.

"I know what you've got," he said, "a letter from Cleo."

"How'd you know?"

"Nothing else would make you so excited. I haven't seen you acting that spry in years." He took the letter she handed him. "Must be good news, the way you're grinning. I don't know when you've looked so happy."

"It is, Doct' Claib. She's getting 'long fine, she says, and likin' it mighty well up there." She was beaming, radiant. "But go ahead and read it yourself."

"Let me wait till I get inside and sit down. I'm pretty well worn out. What else did she say?"

"Didn't write much this time, but she says things are goin' to be fine, she thinks, and everybody's good to her. Ain't that nice, Doct' Claib?"

He took the letter into his office and read it. Sarah had reported faithfully what Cleo had said. But the doctor was interested in one bit of news Sarah had failed to mention. He read the sentence again:

And Mother, Dr. Vicente has been treating me just fine, and he even sent his son, who is studying to be a doctor, too, to the train to meet me and take me to the place where the student nurses live.

That night when she had gone to bed, Sarah held the letter under the bedside lamp's yellow glow and read it again. And when she dropped off to sleep she dreamed happily a crazy-quilt dream at the center of which were her little white Cleo and the son of the Philadelphia doctor with the funny-sounding name.

Cleo wrote to them faithfully. Her letters were never more than two weeks apart, and they were interesting and detailed; Sarah, Claiborne shortly came to realize, lived from one letter to the next, and any small progress the girl reported was for her mother a reason for further rejoicing. Early in November Cleo wrote that although the nursing-school girls would not be dismissed for Thanksgiving Day, some might have the day off; she was hoping she might be among the lucky ones. "I've got something nice planned to do, if I am," she explained without explaining much. But the letter written the day after Thanksgiving revealed what Cleo had meant. "Mother, I was one of the girls who got Thanksgiving Day off, and it was just wonderful. Alfred took me out to supper—they call it dinner up here—and after that we went to a theater and saw a play. Oh, Mother, you can understand how wonderful it was! Sometimes I get scared just thinking about things."

Sarah cried a little when she read the letter, and Claiborne reading it experienced a strange lifting and inner tugging, as if for the first time, now that she was six-hundred-miles away, he were really seeing Cleo, as if he were appraising her through the admiring eyes of old Alfredo Vicente's boy.

The letter that came the second week in December informed them that she would not be able to come home for Christmas. Only those girls who lived in Philadelphia or nearby would be able to go home, because the ones relieved of Christmas duties would have only two days off. "But, oh, Mother, they posted the list of the student nurses getting off, and my name was on it. I think maybe Dr. Vicente had something to do with it. And—don't faint, Mother!—Dr. Vicente and his wife have invited me to have Christmas dinner with them! And I think Alfred had something to do with that! ! ! "

Sarah's gratification, her elation, she knew not how to measure or express, but Claiborne understood when, with eyes hardly able to contain her happiness, she spoke to him. "I'm going to make the child a nice big pound cake and send her, and don't you reckon you could send her enough money to buy her a new little dress to wear when she goes to the doctor's house?"

Laughing, Claiborne promised. "I think we can scrape up enough for a new dress."

When he left to go on a call she went to the kitchen and started the cake. And after she had mixed it and stirred the batter and poured it into the cake pan and placed it in the oven, she read the letter again, while the cake baked. When it was done, she set it on a fresh dish towel on the kitchen table to cool. Then she cleaned her room, made her bed, and swept the hallway and front porch.

"I feel so good," she said to herself, "I believe I'll just go over and start on the Christmas cleaning. I'll open up the parlor and let it get a little sun; maybe Doct' Claib might have some company this Christmas."

She tucked the letter into her bosom and crossed the yard to the mansion house. First she swept the downstairs hallway, and then she entered the parlor; she pulled back the curtains and raised the south windows. As she crossed the room for the broom she had left beside the hallway door frame, she glanced up at the austere Cardells and smiled. Then she stopped and studied the portraits. "I do believe," she said aloud, "you all don't look as sour this mornin' as you been lookin' all these years." She picked up the broom. "Maybe you all been readin' Cleo's letter too."

When she had finished the parlor, she went up to the doctor's bedroom. "I just as well put fresh sheets on the bed 'fore I clean the room and sweep the hall and stairs," she told herself. "I can lie down and rest awhile after dinner, 'fore time to start supper."

She pulled the bedcovers off. She saw that the mattress needed turning. "He always sleeps in the same place. Looks like he's been sleepin' in a bowl, it's so mashed down."

At the head of the bed she caught the mattress and tugged.

It seemed so heavy, so much heavier than usual. It's not really so heavy, she reasoned, but it's just so awkward to handle. She walked the head of the mattress to the foot of the bed, and then, panting heavily, caught the underside of the bend and lifting and tugging, pulled it to the head. The mattress was turned over now, but it was still a little catercornered on the bed. She bent over again, clutched it midway at the foot and, bracing with both hands, jerked.

A white-hot fist smote her in the chest, and fiery sharp fingers clawed beneath her ribs; under her eyes the mattress lifted and curled above the spinning, reeling bed. She clutched the bed post, shook her head to steady the bed and the swaying room. As they slowed, she sat down, lay back. If she could just lie still a few minutes, the dizziness and the pain would go away; it always had. But the pain—

Sarah lifted her right hand—strangely heavy now—to push, fingers spread wide, against her chest. She felt the letter in her bosom; her fingers closed about it, and in her clenched fist she pressed it hard to her heart.

22

The shadows were pushing out long from Aaron's hitching rack when Claiborne untied his horse's rein. Aaron's wife was dead now; his married son was living with the old man, the son's wife had just had her first baby.

. . . right here old Aaron gave me that lecture on miscegenation. Strange how well I remember it after almost a quarter of a century. Mules and mulattoes.

Claiborne thought about it as he drove away from Aaron's. He thought of the truism he had heard all his life, had often stated himself, had never doubted. But is it actually true that a drop of Negro blood, an eighth part, even a fourth, must consign a person to the Negro race? A boy, a girl, with fair skin, blue eyes, long straight hair?

It hasn't consigned Cleo, not in Philadelphia.

. . . what if I had taken Sarah to Boston or New York or New Orleans, and we had brought up the children where nobody knew about that black blood? How would the other five have turned out?

But he knew there was no need of conjecturing. Nothing, nobody, could roll back the years. Still, what has happened to Cleo up there makes a fellow wonder.

. what about that little gal! Eating Christmas dinner at old Alfredo Vicente's table! And I, her father, have never sat down to a meal with the child. Nor with her mother. A strange world, this.

He rode toward Holly Grove, the lap robe tucked under his knees, his collar drawn close around his throat. He would be glad to get home, toast his feet before the fire, sit down to Sarah's good supper, see Sarah happy again, happy about Cleo.

"I'll make her sit down and eat with me! I'll do it. She won't want to; she'll be embarrassed at first, but what the hell, I'll make her."

The mare, thinking the doctor had called out to her, speeded her jogging; she, too, was anxious to get back to Holly Grove.

. . . and Christmas we will have our dinner together and we'll talk about Cleo eating her Christmas dinner at the Vicentes', and Sarah will be happier than she's been in a long time. .

He'd give Sarah a nice present this Christmas, maybe a dress. Beyond a living, she has never had much, the Lord knows.

Claiborne turned in at the gateway and drove to the stables and unhitched. He saw no light in the kitchen; by now without the lamp it would be too dark to see how to cook. Nor was there any light in the mansion house, he discovered as he went along the hallway, and in the parlor no fire had been lighted Maybe Sarah took a nap and overslept. .

But she wasn't in her room. He thought then that she might have gone over to Julie's. But it wasn't like her to stay away this late.

He went back to the mansion house, peeked into his office, the dining room, the library. . . . Maybe she went upstairs to clean my room and sat down a moment to catch her breath and fell asleep. . . . He bounded up the stairs, two steps at a time despite his weariness, and went into his room.

Sarah lay on her back. One foot was on the uncovered mattress, the other was on the floor beside rumpled bedclothes; her right arm was partially over the side of the bed.

He ran over to her as a sudden fearful heaviness clawed upward into his tightening throat. In the thickening gloom he studied her an instant, and then gently he shook her shoulder. When she did not stir, he bent down, put his ear to her chest. For a moment he listened. Then, straightening again, he grasped her right arm to lift it to the bed so that he might feel for the pulse.

Sarah's arm came up unbending at the elbow, as rigid as a bowed dead tree limb. The bluing, clenched fingers, Claiborne saw, held a crumpled white envelope.

CANYON OF THE YEARS

Cleo Vicente adjusted the wicker carriage top so that the sun would not be shining in little Gordon's eyes and, facing him an arm's length away, sat down on the small ornamental iron bench. Stout Rosemary Toomey, the baby's doting Irish nurse, had wrapped him well for his mother to take him rolling, and already Cleo had had him out an hour or longer. She had not planned to keep Gordon outdoors so long, but he had been enjoying his ride, his mother was sure; and, too, so many men and women and even small children had paused in the park and on the sidewalk to peek at the child and speak admiringly of his warmly pink complexion that she had dallied purposely.

As she had pushed the carriage along the park walks she had been careful to see that little Gordon's face was shielded from the direct rays of the sun. Even a short exposure might damage his eyes or cause him to be sunburned, and she shuddered at the thought of seeing those fair, rose-petaled cheeks darkened even by a shade. Studying the sleeping baby's face now, she recalled how fearful she had been in the months she was carrying him that the newborn infant might betray in some way the terrible secret of his ancestry; she remembered vividly how relieved she had been when she had had the first sleepy glimpse of her son. Later, while nursing him for the first time, gently she had pinched the tiny flat nose between thumb and forefinger, and the nurse had seen her.

"But his nose seems so flat," she had attempted to explain, laughing shyly.

The nurse had come over to the bed and looked down upon

her. "Silly," she had said, laughing too, "don't you know that all babies when they're born have little button noses?"

Cleo lifted her eyes above the baby-carriage top to study the house of the Vicentes, which with the deaths of Alfred's parents, within little more than a year of each other, had come to him. Along with the property, including the Oldsmobile touring car the elder Dr. Vicente had bought only a few months before his death, Alfred had inherited Rosemary and her equally Irish husband Terence.

From the garden side where she was sitting, the narrow three-storied red-brick house with the brownstone quoins and window sills seemed less stern, Cleo thought, and more able to breathe and relax in the sunshine. Looking at it from the side-walk on which it fronted, she had the urge to thrust away from it the nondescript row house that seemed to lean against it on the right. Alfred's grandfather, the first Alfredo Vicente to come to the United States—Alfred had dropped the o of his grand-father and father—had built the house even with the property line of what was probably a seventy-five foot lot that went through the short block; later someone had built this two-story structure almost touching Dr. Vicente's.

But from the garden's bench just inside the iron fence the house reminded Cleo vaguely of Holly Grove, though the two were similar in few ways. Stately, gracious, elegant Holly Grove's natural bricks had weathered to a lovely brownish-pink, hidden in many places beneath a luxuriant growth of darkly green ivy; the brick of the Vicente house bore many coats of thick, very dark red paint and the lines of the mortar joints between the bricks had been emphasized by white stripings.

The wall of the Vicente house on the garden side ran straight and without ornamentation to the square corner at the rear, and it rose above the roof to be capped by a severely plain brownstone crown. It lacked the grace and style of the chimney ends of the Holly Grove house, particularly the south end with the great heart in cream brick.

. . . wonder if Doct' Claib has ever had that crack in the heart fixed. Wonder if he's ever had the doors and the windows and the rest of the woodwork of the mansion house painted, or the kitchen house, which already was needing it mighty bad when I left home. I wonder if Mother's dying didn't knock him off his feet completely. Maybe he's staying drunk most of the time. Likely Julie can't do anything with him. If she's even trying. . . .

For the millionth time since she had received Dr. Cardell's letter more than four years ago she saw it spread open before her mind's eye, its neatly inked words running line upon straight line across the white pages and becoming blurred with the tremor in her hands and the welling tears in her eyes as she read. For the millionth time the frightening thought of being alone and lost and without protection in a strange and alien world possessed her, though since her marriage, two years ago last spring, the feeling of being unprotected and friendless had dulled rather into a dimming remembrance of the pain the letter had brought her.

Her mother was dead and buried before the letter came. Dr. Cardell had been too shaken to write at once, he had explained, and he had thought it not advisable to telegraph. He had known that Cleo would not be able to come home for the funeral. "You have crossed the bridge, child." She remembered every word of that letter, though in accordance with his strict injunction, she had burned it, after holding it one frightfully long night and reading it again and again. "And now the bridge must be burned behind you. You have started on a great journey that I pray will see you safe into a land of great happiness for you. Remember, Cleo, the past is completely behind. Never think of turning back, never, my child,"—that was as near as he had come to claiming her as his daughter—"even look back. And may God lead you and keep you."

He had explained that from time to time he would send her money until she had received her portion of the Holly Grove inheritance, and this he had been doing until she wrote him a few weeks before her marriage that she would no longer need aid. "You have already been mighty generous," she had written in that letter, whose main purpose was to tell him that she was going to marry his old medical-school-friend's son. "In view of everything, it might be best anyway not to be sending me money after I'm married. If you had expected to send me any more, please give it to the others." His letter of congratulations, enclosing some money to be used in completing her wedding preparations, had come quickly. And it had been his last one to her. He had burned his end of the bridge.

Her eyes were on her son again. He slept soundly, all but his round pink face buried in the soft blue blankets.

. I wonder what Doct' Claib would think of his grandson, *this* grandson, this *white* grandson. He has other grandchildren, I wonder how many now, but they went toward the black blood. This one, thank God, was born beyond the other end of the bridge, and the bridge is gone. There's no way back, no bridge any more. Only a tremendous gully, a chasm, a deep canyon, unbridgeable, never to be crossed. There's no Holly Grove back there in the darkness of the black blood; there never was any Holly Grove or any kitchen house. There is only Philadelphia, only the stern house of the Vicentes, sturdy and solid in its red-painted, brownstone-trimmed bricks, only the bright sunshine and the white blood going back and back and back. . . .

She was thankful that the Vicentes had never seemed particularly curious about her background. They had appeared quite content to accept her on Dr. Cardell's recommendation and her own behavior and had never sought to pry into her ancestry. It had been accepted without question that she came of an aristocratic Low Country, South Carolina family impoverished in the Reconstruction era, and quickly she had come to be considered an orphan girl left to her own resources.

A distant noon whistle blew. Soon Alfred would be coming home for dinner, she realized, unless he goes by that automobile dealer's place to have another look at that runabout he has been threatening to buy.

I hope he doesn't buy it. Now, anyway. That's a lot of money to pay for an automobile, $750, a full hundred dollars more than the Oldsmobile cost Father Vicente. And with such an abominable name, too. Why would anybody name an automobile for a dead Frenchman by the name of Cadillac? But I wouldn't be surprised any day to see him come riding up in the new runabout. Besides, a touring car would be better. There'd be no room for Terence to drive us in a one-seat car. And maybe in another few years there'd be a little girl. . . . Cleo studied her sleeping son. . . . Maybe even twins. Ma had 'em. I have an idea Alfred is thinking about keeping the Oldsmobile, too, so we can all ride. Heavens! Two automobiles in one family, as expensive as they are!

A stentorian honk of a horn behind her caused her to jump almost against the baby's carriage. Turning about quickly, she saw that her husband was the culprit; he was just straightening in his seat from having leaned over Terence to give the bulb a sudden crushing squeeze.

Terence drew up to the curb and Dr. Vicente stepped through the front seat opening to the sidewalk and strode toward the gate.

"You almost made your son jump out of his skin," she said, as he bent over to kiss her."

"So I see."

She turned to glance toward the baby. He was sleeping soundly. They both laughed. "But you really did 'most make me," she protested.

He wheeled the carriage through the gate and toward the marble steps leading up to the front door.

"I thought maybe you'd go by that automobile place," she said.

He grinned. "I did. I finished the last operation a little earlier than I had expected I would. So I had Terence drive me by. Cleo," his eyes were shining, "you just ought to see that new black touring car they got in just a couple of days ago. It's a beauty!"

"But I thought you had about decided on a runabout."

"No," he was shaking his head, "too few can ride in a runabout. I had been looking at one, but—well, when you pay that much for a car you must think of keeping it several years, and," his slow grin lighted his youthful face, "you can hardly seat three in a runabout comfortably, and sometimes we may want to sit back in style and let Terence do the driving."

He helped her get the baby carriage up the steps; they hardly disturbed their son; he opened his eyes, yawned, and promptly went back to sleep. Alfred hung his coat on the hat tree, and stretched himself on the sofa. But only for a moment; Rosemary was calling them to the noon meal.

"You can lie down after dinner and get a short nap," Cleo said, as they started to the dining room.

"No, I've got a pretty heavy schedule, I'm afraid. And I'd like to get away from the hospital in time maybe to take you to see that car. The man said he'd allow us four hundred on the Olds; maybe I can push him a little higher."

After they had eaten and he was as far as the front door he called back. "Oh, say, Cleo, the new medical journal came to the office this morning and I glanced through it hurriedly. What do you know? That doctor down in North Carolina, the friend of your family who wrote Father to recommend you—well, he's dead. There's a note about his death in the obituary column. Seeing it sort of made me sad. I know nothing about him, of course, except that he was responsible for your coming up here. I thought maybe you'd like to read it, and I brought the journal home. It's here on the hat tree."

"I will, Alfred. Thank you."

She had tried desperately to answer matter of factly. She was thankful that he had called to her from the hallway and that he had not seen her face. And she was doubly thankful that he had told her as he was leaving rather than as he had come home.

When she heard the front door close behind him, she went into the hall and picked up the journal and carried it into her bedroom; she shut the door. It was a fortunate thing, she told herself, that for the afternoon Rosemary would have the responsibility of caring for little Gordon.

2

The *grande dame* of the Gunn textile empire picked up the speaking tube. "Stay on the circle but stop as close to the steps as you can, James," she instructed the chauffeur. "I want to go inside and look around awhile."

"Yes, ma'am, Miz Gunn."

The black Packard limousine purred around the asphalt driveway and stopped noiselessly in front of the stone steps leading up to the verandah of the old Osborne mansion. The chauffeur slid from his seat and came around behind the sleek car to open the right rear door. He took off his leather-billed cap and peeped inside. "Can I he'p you out, Miz Gunn?"

"Here. Take my stick. Now let me catch hold of your arm, James." She extended a heavily ringed hand to grasp the gray whipcord of his uniform sleeve, and with the other hand clutching the door frame, she got her feet to the ground and stood erect. "Now give me my stick back. And I'll want to hold to your arm, James, while we go up the steps." She stopped to study them. "They don't look as high as they used to, when I lived here, James, especially when I was a child." She smiled, a rather apathetic smile. "But that was a long time ago." Then she caught his right arm with her left hand and, holding the walking stick firmly in the right, she mounted the steps to the verandah. Turning about, she released her hold on the chauffeur's arm and pointed. "The circular driveway looks nice, don't you think, James?" He promptly agreed. "I think a great round bed of mixed flowers in the center would look good. I'll talk with the landscape man about it." She turned to face the chauffeur, her face beaming, her eyes alight with quick fires. "James, won't little Charlie be surprised when he gets home from his honeymoon?"

"He shore will, Miz Gunn. He don't know nothin' 'bout it, does he?"

"I don't think he does. All I told him was that he and Ann wouldn't get their wedding present from me until they got back it done over, James?"

"They shore oughta, Miz Gunn. They bound to. Wouldn't nobody who was used to seein' it 'fore you fixed it up know it was the same place. I bet, Miz Gunn, it's finer now than it was back when you were a little girl here, don't you reckon? With all this here paved driveways and such and the paintin' and plasterin' inside, and the water and lights and all?"

"Yes, James, I suppose it is, though to me as a child it seemed mighty fine, of course. But we had no running water and no electricity, just oil lamps and, before them, just candles, I suppose. But the candles, except sometimes for big dinners and such occasions, were before my time." She turned toward the door. "I'm going inside to look around, James. Everything ought to be about finished. Unlock the door—I gave you the key, didn't I, James?"

"Yes'm; I got it right here." He took a large iron key from his pocket. "This here's the biggest key I ever seen." He went up to the door, inserted it in the lock. "Anyhow, I ain't never seen one no bigger."

"It's the original key, James, as far as I know. You don't see locks like this one any more."

"No'm, Miz Gunn. I ain't never seen but one like this here one."

Her interest was evident. "I didn't know there were any other locks like this one still being used around here any more. Where's the house?"

" 'Tain't so far from here, Miz Gunn." He nodded his head to indicate the direction. "Over yonder to'ards the river, 'bout eight or nine miles from here, I guess it is."

"What sort of house is it, James?"

"It's a great big old brick house, Miz Gunn, 'bout three stories high, I think. I ain't been there in a long time, but I mind it's a big one."

"Who lives in it, James?"

"It's some colored folks named Cardell lives there now, Miz Gunn, but long time ago it b'longed to white people."

230

no   p ace you re ta   g   ,   se to go
there when I was young. But I haven't been there in a long
time. I guess it's pretty rundown now?"

"Yes'm, when I was there it was. I guess it's in worse shape
now."

James had the door open; he stood back for her to enter. But
for the moment she did not go in. "I'll be here half an hour, I
expect, James. I want you to go down to the stables while I'm in
here and see what they've got done down there. Take your
time. If I get through going over the house before you come
back to the car, I'll blow the horn for you."

"Yes'm."

He went quickly down the steps and around the house. She
stood at the door, and the years fell away, and it was night and
a full moon shone through the trees to dapple the verandah ın
shifting patterns of woven moonlight and shadow. ˎ

. . . we sat together right over there on the joggling-board. I
wonder what ever became of it. So long ago. We sat on the joggling-board and he leaned back against the bricks and pushed
his long legs out into the moonlight. He praised Mother's meal,
and then like a simpleton I had to ask him about his cook. He
resented my prying, and I resented his deprecating Charlie. He
left soon. He did kiss me good-by—right here, on this very spot,
so long ago, so many, many years. But that night his heart wasn't
in his kiss. I knew it

She went inside and closed the door behind her. She stood in
the middle of the wide hall and studied the new wallpaper, the
freshly trimmed doors and door frames, the molding, the base-
board, the gleaming white banisters and beautifully turned walnut handrail of the stairway; she looked up to the elegant
bronze chandelier with its cluster of round rose-tinted globes.
From the hallway she moved into the parlor, and then back
across the hall to the dining room, the kitchen behind it, and
at the rear of the parlor, the bedroom of her parents that had
been transformed into the library-den of the surprise gift awaiting the return of her grandson and his bride.

. the architect and contractor have done well. The house

231

never looked this elegant even in my earliest childhood when it was still comparatively new. Wouldn't Mother have loved those panels of French wallpaper, reproductions, of course, but authentic, on the parlor walls and above the dining room mantel? And how Father would have sat back with his friends and his bourbon before the open fire and f ught the War Between the States over again had he possess . . . ach a den as little Charlie will have.

With her stick in her right hand and her left sliding along the handrail she mastered the stairway and went along the upstair hallway to her old bedroom at the right front corner of the house. For a moment she stood just inside the doorway and surveyed it from wall to wall, floor to ceiling.

. . . lovely, just lovely. Charlie and Ann should take this for their bedroom. It's the best one in the house. Cozy in winter, with the sun from the east and the south warming it most of the day. But cool in the summer, too, the coolest room, in fact, because it always gets a cross breeze if there's any stirring at all. . . .

This had been her room since childhood as long as she lived in the house. Though in recent weeks it had been completely redecorated and though it was now emptied of all furnishings, she could visualize it plainly as it had been through the long years—early girlhood, the summers home from Salem College, the first months of her married life with Charlie Gunn before they had moved over to Alamance for him to get his initial training in textile manufacturing; in this room Charles, junior, was born, and here for years afterward they lived while Charlie was getting established in his business. The walnut-top bureau all those years stood over there against the front wall; the bed sat in the corner between the front and side windows; above the washstand with the big china bowl and pitcher and soap dish a picture in a carved frame crossed at the corners illustrated "The Seven Ages of Man" on steps ascending from a mewling infant to a mustached and muscled bridegroom and descending again to a doddering, bent old man with a gnarled walking stick.

But of none of these nights and days with Charlie was she thinking as she crossed the room to peer out the front window toward the old driveway now discarded and bulldozed into the lawn and supplanted by the circle of asphalt. She stood back a little way from the window, and a suddenly venturesome stirring of air caressed her wrinkling but rouged cheeks. She stood just inside the shadows that are bent up to touch the broad band of ight from the full moon, and her walking stick and her arthritis d fifty years and her textile plants and her mink stole and all her clothes in one remembered, rapturous moment were gone; erect, and with the sweet juices of youth, unclothed, she stood responding while the deliciously wanton little breeze toyed; and once again, clearly across the fled years, came up to her from the packed earth of a long plowed-over dirt road the clomp-clomp, clomp-clomp of retreating horses' hoofs.

She turned away from the window and the cadenced sounds of the ghostly horses faded into silence and, against the returned years and the stole and the wool-silk of her suit and her bracing stays, the shy, small breeze had not a chance.

In the hallway she stopped precipitately.

. . . I was sitting right here that morning when he came from Charles, junior's, room. He couldn't see me for the walnut commode and the sheets and things stacked on it, the things for Charles, junior, and the lighted lamp between us, beside the things on it. He didn't see me until I stepped around the commode, and I startled him.

h. had been there four days, and he was haggard and worn and he needed a shave. "Thank God! Thank God for you, Claiborne!" I said to him, when he told me Charles's fever was broken and he would live.

. . . I had offered to wake Charlie and let him get one of the nigras to hitch up the buggy, but he told me not to wake Charlie. He had said he would be back, and as he started to leave, I ran up to him and kissed him, full on the mouth. Because he had saved my boy's life? Yes. But, actually no, no, no

. Melissa, you're a fool. Yes. You married a man and he

made a million dollars and his son doubled and tripled and quadrupled that, the son whose life Claiborne saved, and little Charlie will likely double and triple and quadruple what his daddy added to the Gunn fortune. But, Melissa, you're a fool nevertheless. You didn't marry the man you wanted to marry. You didn't marry the man you should have married. . . .

She crossed the hall into the other front bedroom, and from there she came back into the hall and along it to the rear bedroom across from Charles, junior's, old room. Then she peeked into it. But her examination of the refurbished rooms was cursory now. She had lost contact with the present and interest in the future; she was living in the irrecoverable past.

What if I *had* married Claiborne? What if I hadn't acted so damnably stiff-backed, so holier-than-thou, that night he came here to ask me to marry him? He freely confessed his error, his sin, as I saw it and so told him. He had made plans to send the woman north somewhere where she and the baby that was coming could pass for white people—and why shouldn't they? Heaven knows, that Sarah Gordon was a pretty woman, and looking back now after half a century, how can I blame Claiborne for getting involved with her? If I'd been a man, I suspect I'd have done the same thing—living out there at Holly Grove with nobody close around except that good-looking quadroon. Claiborne had hoped I hadn't heard about her being pregnant, but I had; Charlie had seen to that. And so I had to throw it up to Claiborne and put on a pious, long face. But he had confessed everything, and I could have, I should have, forgiven him. If he just hadn't said cutting things about Charlie.

Charlie, of course, *was* a model husband. Just too model. Charlie's eye was always on the main chance. Conservative and practical, that was Charlie, and hard working. He died too young, too, but he made it past sixty-five and he saw the war over and the Allies victorious and himself richer perhaps than even he had ever dreamed he would be—all that olive drab and all those blankets he sold to the Army; Charlie had been smart in switching a part of his production to blankets, for heaven knows how many blankets the government bought for the servicemen and then used up, lost, had stolen, and finally sold for a song after Armistice Day. And Charles, junior, had been too old for that war and little Charlie, thank God, too young, and you could almost believe Charlie planned the thing that way, he was such a man to plan and then to push his plans to completion. Charlie was woven in the pattern of following precedent, doing things as one would expect them to be done, and seeing to it that they were done in spite of hell or high water—and then collecting the check. Charlie didn't look like him and he didn, have that Yankee twang, but I always thought that, under the skin, Charlie was very much like Cal Coolidge. And Cal got there, too, didn't he? He beat John W. Davis and Bob LaFollette four years ago and he'd be re-elected this fall if he hadn't decided last summer he didn't choose to run again. Coolidge is safe. Yes, and that's it—Charlie was safe and sound and solid, yes, and stolid. When Charlie looked at me—forgive me, Charlie, for though you're dead and gone these nine years, I can't help but feeling that way—when he looked at me, I had the feeling that he was seeing right through me into a textile mill, that he was listening to the whirring frames and the clacking looms, yes, and fearing one of them would break down. But when Claiborne looked at me, I felt like a woman being looked at by a man.

I wonder how it would have been if I *had* married Claiborne. Different, for a certainty. Different for me. Different for him. I suspect Claiborne would have become a famous doctor, a tremendous figure in his profession. Claiborne had the brains, and he had the bedside manner. And he was no dull precedent follower; he would have forged out for himself, and he would have ranged wide and far. I suspect he wouldn't have gone to his grave in old Bethel churchyard in his fifties, beaten down, worn out, not so much by the labor of his doctoring as by the heaviness of the heart burden he was carrying.

and I? Certainly I wouldn't have been rich. I would never

have become chairman of the board of a great manufacturing empire and mother of its president. No. Maybe the best automobile I'd ever have owned would have been one of those little one-cylinder Brushes. But we would have lived well, comfortably, happily. I'd have been the mistress of Holly Grove—poor Holly Grove, why did James ever have to mention it? I couldn't bear to go back there and see it being swarmed over by those nigras, *his* children and grandchildren. But there would have been no nigras in Holly Grove if I had married Claiborne; *I* would have been mistress there; I'd have been Mrs. Claiborne Cardell! If on that long-ago night, that night never to be recovered, I hadn't been such a prude, such an insufferable damn prude. .

She glanced at the diamond-studded tiny wrist watch, last year's gift of her Stonewall Jackson chapter of the United Daughters of the Confederacy on her retirement as national vice-president-general. "Good heavens!" she exclaimed aloud. "I had no idea I'd been in this house so long "

At the head of the stairway she transferred her walking stick to the left hand, with the right grasped the handrail that many a time as a child she had slid down. Carefully she descended the stairs and went out on the verandah. James, waiting in the car, sprang from it and came up the marble steps to assist her.

"I didn't know I was staying in there so long, James," she aid apologetically. "I was just looking around and I got to thinking of old times."

"Yes'm. A little while ago I started to go in and see if anything had happened. Then I figured you just got to studyin' 'bout old times and clean forgot what time it was gettin' to be. But then I says to myself I didn't reckon you was in no hurry to leave; you 'bout as much at home here as you are at your house."

"Yes," she agreed, as she half turned at the foot of the steps to look again at the restored great house, "that's right, James—maybe more so."

4

HOUSE OF
THE MENDED HEART

As he turned into the parking area, the big plane was roaring down to the runway. He sprang from the car, dropped his nickel in the meter, and broke for the airport terminal.

"Eastern Air Lines' *Golden Falcon,* flight five-o-nine nonstop from Washington now arriving at gate nine, north concourse," Operations was singing out as he shoved open the glass door and burst into the lobby. He glanced at the clock on the wall as he dashed past passengers coming in from another arriving plane. "Six-thirty, right on the button!" As the glass panel opening on the north concourse swung wide behind an entering passenger, he darted through and ran down the concourse's covered way toward gate nine. Already he was meeting passengers disembarking from flight 509. "If she gets into the lobby before I spot her she'll likely take a taxi into town," he said to himself. "I wonder what she looks like." All the time he was scanning the women in the throng surging from the plane. "If I just knew how old she is, what she's wearing, anything—" He spotted a tall, angular woman in a severe gray suit, wearing horn-rimmed glasses and with a large handbag on a strap slung over her shoulder.

"Pardon me, please," he stepped up to her, "are you Miss Vicente?"

"No," she said, almost petulantly, hardly turning her head and without checking her stride as she bolted for the terminal building. He looked after her and shrugged.

"Did you ask if she were Miss Vicente?"

239

Turning, he saw the girl as she came through the narrow gate. She was laughing. "I heard her. And that's what I thought I heard you ask her."

"Yes, and she was saying she wasn't—thank heavens." He grinned. "Are you—I hope?"

The passengers pressing behind spilled her from the single-file runway into the concourse and she stepped to one side out of the pushing traffic. "I'm Sarah Gordon Vicente. Were you looking for me?"

"Yes. But I can hardly believe it." His eyes traveled over her appreciatively, and he suddenly realized it. "Excuse me, I've hardly recovered. I'm Osborne Gunn. Mr. Hinson, my good friend, asked me to meet you. Did you have a pleasant flight down?"

"Wonderful, thank you. It was good of Mr. Hinson to have me met," her blue eyes lighted, "and nice of you to come." Then the eyes narrowed. "But why can you hardly believe I'm the one you came for?"

"I suppose I was looking for somebody like her. You know, somebody rather formidable, grim; you sort of expect that of missionaries." He pointed along the walkway. "It's air conditioned inside. You have much baggage?"

"Two pieces. A big bag and one of those plastic suit things. I expressed the rest."

"They'll be unloaded in a few minutes. We can get 'em after we've eaten. There's a nice place on the mezzanine—the Dogwood Room—good food, music, sometimes a small floor show."

"Dogwood. That's the state flower, isn't it?" She grinned coyly. "I've been reading about North Carolina." Then she was apologetic. "But I've eaten. We had a lovely dinner coming down."

"Oh, I might have known. I've been on that flight. But say, you can have some coffee and dessert, can't you? And you'll let me eat, won't you, since I haven't, and I'm getting a little hungry?"

"Of course. And I'll have some coffee with you. But no dessert."

"What you mean, no dessert?" His tone was scornfully reproving.

She laughed. "Calories, you know."

"You?" He shook his head. "Well, I'm right on one score, and maybe both."

"What do you mean?" Her eyes showed she was puzzled.

"It would take a long speech to explain, and right now I'm too hungry." He caught her hand, tucked her arm under his, and they started up the stairway. "I'll tell you while you're having your coffee."

They turned left on the landing and left again to mount the next flight. The lobby, in marble and tile and chrome, with long couches and individual chairs in modern styling, and wide corridors running out like fingers to the various service areas, lay below and in front of them.

"This is a gorgeous airport," she said. "And the long runways and the huge paved area, and that tremendous electric sign in red lights—I had no idea you had anything like this in—"

"In the South. Go ahead and say it." His eyes sharpened. "Say, did you know that this airport handles one of the greatest volumes of traffic on the eastern coast and in proportion to the city's population one of the biggest in the country?" Then noticeably he relaxed. "I didn't mean to be giving you a chamber of commerce pep talk. But what you were about to say makes me all the more certain I was right."

The hostess was approaching them, and Osborne motioned. "Over where we can see the planes coming in, if there's a table, please." She smiled, nodded, led them across the room to the glassed outside wall. He seated the girl as a waitress approached. He took the proffered menu card. "Coffee now, please." The girl was glancing over hers. "Won't you change your mind and have something?" he asked. "How about a fruit salad? Not many calories in that."

241

"It does sound good. Well, all right." She smiled at the waitress. "But no mayonnaise, please."

"Would you mind if I had a small steak?" He grinned. "I know it's hot, but I've been stirring around this afternoon and I'm pretty hungry."

"That sounds wonderful. I wasn't talking about calories for you. Why not some French fries too, and tossed salad? And hot biscuits?"

The waitress, smiling, shook her head. "No hot biscuits. Hard rolls, French bread, with a little garlic butter if you like it, rye, whole wheat. Sometimes we do have hot biscuits, but not tonight."

"French bread will be O.K.," he said. "And make the steak medium. And say, could we have the coffee now?"

The waitress nodded, disappeared.

"Now maybe you have time to make the speech." She leaned forward, looked him in the eyes. "Just what did you mean by those several remarks?"

"Oh, the speech." He bent nearer, studied her inquiring eyes. "Did anybody ever tell you that when you struck that pose you were quite attractive?"

"I'll have you know I'm not striking any pose." She said it evenly. "And I'm not withdrawing my question. What did you mean when you said you had expected me to be grim, you know, like you'd expect a missionary to be? And when I said I didn't want any dessert, you said you knew you were right on one score and maybe both? And out there on the stairs, when I commented on the airport, you flamed up like that welcoming electric sign outside."

"Now, you listen," he demanded with mock sternness, "and answer me. Has anybody ever pointed out how your eyes snap when you make speeches of—of righteous indignation?" He was laughing now.

She sat back and shook her head sadly, so that the dark curls beneath her tiny black hat lifted and swirled. "I surrender. Now will you please tell me?"

"The Yankee invader surrenders so quickly? Do you throw yourself on my mercy?"

"The Yankee invader?" She leaned toward him again. "Now maybe I'm beginning to catch on. Do you expect Yankee girls to be grim, formidable, with saddle shoes and bags slung from their shoulders?"

"Only the missionaries among them, and I'm not speaking of religious missionaries." He was enjoying the challenge in her eyes. "But you? Yes, frankly, I did."

"But why?"

"Well, deduction. When Ham Hinson asked me to come by and pick you up—I'd told him I had to be in town this afternoon —I naturally asked him to tell me something about you. And it was on what he told me that I arrived at my deduction."

"What in the world did the principal tell you?"

"Well, he said you had an M.A. from Columbia, I believe, and that in itself gave me a pretty definite opinion; he said you were Phi Beta Kappa, I recall—" He asked the confirmation with his eyes, and she nodded slowly. "But the main evidence was that you had been teaching in Washington, and that your subject was sociology. And then, your last name—"

"What's wrong with Vicente? Is it grim and formidable?"

"No. I'd say rather that it's musical, friendly sounding. But it's not exactly North Carolina Anglo-Saxon or Scots-Irish, you must agree."

She laughed again and affected a shrug of futility. "Interesting—perhaps. But I don't read you."

"I haven't finished. He said you were from Philadelphia. And there's that item of the Supreme Court's decision integrating the public schools." He grinned. "Is the light breaking?"

"Oh-h-h. I do begin to see—"

"There's one more in my bill of particulars. A school teacher— and I know how much they make—comes south to her new teaching mission," he paused on the word, "aboard a super-duper Golden Falcon, paying excess baggage—didn't you?—when she could have come on the train or bus—"

"But it's not so much more than the train or bus fare, considering the free meal on the plane."

He shrugged. "I'll concede that's a small item, but it helps fill in the picture."

"Now let me see if I read you." She assumed a serious attitude. "A Yankee woman—a rather ageless old maid, you probably presumed—reared in Philadelphia, educated in northern colleges, gets a position teaching in Washington, sees at first hand the values of democracy practiced as opposed to democracy preached, and feels herself called to go—or be sent by the NAACP—as a missionary to carry the gospel of sweetness and light—a foreign woman named Vicente, a Spanish female or maybe Eyetalian, she is—this dedicated, grim soul in a fervor of determination comes south to bring the glad tidings of the brotherhood of man as enacted by that great legislative body known as the Supreme Court of the United States and as practiced in Washington, D.C., Levittown, Pa., Detroit, Chicago, et cetera, et cetera; in holy fervor this female evangel comes to bring these revised glad tidings into that vast region of blight and hate and destitution known as The South, USA." Solemnly she paused and regarded him with steady, boring eyes. "Do I read you?"

He reflected her solemnity. "You overread me."

They burst out laughing. Then, as the waitress set down the two cups of coffee, the girl lifted hers, but held it, halfway to her lips. "I was on the right track, even if I clowned a bit?"

"Yes, I'll admit it. You really don't look like the woman I was expecting to meet. But even now I don't know why you decided to come south to teach."

The waitress had brought their food.

"The salad looks good," she said. "And so does your steak. And it's still sizzling." She speared a cube of pineapple. "Um-m-m; it is good. How's yours?"

He swallowed, licked his lips. "They usually have good steaks here. Won't you change your mind?"

She shook her head.

"Just a small one? Or a bite of this anyway?"

She studied the steak. "Just a bite. It does look so good."

He cut a square; she caught it up on her fork. "Um-m-m."

He cut off another segment. "One more?"

"No. Don't tempt me. I'll be popping when I eat this salad." She tasted a bit of pear. "Good." She set down her fork. "Honestly, did you think I'd be like that?" She leaned nearer. "Really, did you, Mr. Gunn?"

"Well," he gestured with palms up, "let us say that I wouldn't have been much surprised. You remember, I did pick that somber sister, you know. And you aren't at all like the person I had pictured you'd be; you don't look and act like her, I mean. But, say, my name's Osborne, remember; usually I get Oz. We call people down here by their first names—if we like 'em. It's just an old—"

"Old southern custom, eh?" She laughed. "Well, it's an old Yankee custom, too—or new one. Anyway, we do too. And I'm Sarah Gordon, remember. I usually get the double name. And that's an old southern custom, isn't it—the double name, I mean?" With her fork she neatly halved a peach slice. "But say, you know all about me, though you didn't do so well on the foreign name implication; now, how about you? I suppose you're from this state?"

"Yes, for a couple of hundred years. My people came down from Pennsylvania about 1750—Lancaster County, I believe."

"Well, that must have been about the time old Alfredo Vicente came to America from Spain. He was my father's grandfather's father." She smiled saucily. "That's as near as I get to being Spanish and foreign. On my father's mother's side we were already living in the South when your Yankee forefathers moved down—farther south, in fact, down in the South Carolina Low Country."

"Whew! How wrong can I be! I'd already figured you got your black hair and that touch of Spanish peaches-and-cream complexion—don't tell me it's just suntan—from a father or at least grandfather who was a Spanish count or something and a mother or grandmother who wore a gorgeous mantilla and diamond-encrusted high silver combs—"

"And who danced the fandango to the clicking of castanets!" She sat back laughing. "And whatever tinge of swarthiness I do have, though what you have noticed is pretty much all suntan, doesn't come from the Vicentes; it comes from the other side, the South Carolina side. They say I get it from my grandmother Cleo, whom I can just barely remember; she died when I was four or five. Her name was Cleopatra Gordon."

"Hm-m-m," he said wryly, "Egyptian."

She put down her fork, laughing. "Just plain South Carolinian. Grandmother, Daddy said, named me for her mother, who was Sarah Gordon. She must have been a remarkable woman. She was probably widowed early; I don't know anything about her husband, my great-grandfather, though there's a family tradition that he was the son, perhaps, of some old South Carolina planter who in his travels had married an Indian woman—East Indian, I mean. So the peaches-and-cream maybe comes from farther east than Spain—like Bombay or Calcutta." She nibbled at a ripe olive. "But we were talking of you. You have filled in all the blanks—school, fraternity maybe, family? Or should I ask the last first and skip the fill in?"

"Take 'em in order. Carolina—that's North Carolina, then North Carolina State; Beta; father, mother, one brother."

"That's all?"

He nodded.

"Well, I can't be charged with husband-stealing designs." She was lifting her cup. She set it down. "I'll bet that's what you meant when you said you were right on one score if not on both." She wrinkled her forehead.

"It's what?"

"You meant that I got this schoolteaching job down here to campaign for integration and/or capture a husband. Now didn't you?"

He reached across and caught the hand that had just put down the fork. "Look me in the eye," he said, grinning. "Didn't you? And/or, I mean?"

"I emphatically deny the integration business." She leveled eyes with him, and hers were dancing. "On the other I plead *nolo contendere*. No woman should be expected to do more. After all, sometime I might see somebody interesting down here."

"*Sometime* you *might* see somebody." He released her hand and tapped the back of it lightly. "Lady, you're fast on the rebounds."

When they had finished eating they walked down to the lobby. "Your bags are over this way." At the counter he gave the checks to the attendant. When the man handed the luggage over, Osborne slid him a coin and nodded to a redcap. "Help us out to the car with these." He turned to the girl. "Imagine a school marm paying an excess-baggage charge. It must have been three or four bucks, eh?"

"It's paid for," she said.

He grinned like a reproved schoolboy. "The car's out this way." They went along the corridor, crossed the lobby, and walked out through the main entrance. "Say," he directed her toward the right, "I'm still not entirely satisfied as to why you came south to teach." He turned to confront her, his eyes narrowing. "It still looks a little suspicious. A Philadelphian, by way of Washington, comes down to North Carolina to teach, of all things, social science. I just don't—"

"Do you object?"

"Oh, no. No indeed. Based upon all the facts I have before me, I am very much in favor." He caught her arm as they stepped down to the driveway. "But, really, how did you happen to come down here to teach?"

She laughed. "Well, Mr. Sherlock Holmes, it's quite simple. I just decided I didn't want to teach any longer in Washington I've been there two years, which is the sum total of my teaching experience, incidentally—and I thought I'd like it in the South."

247

She shrugged, gestured with palms flung out. "Nothing complicated—all very simple."

"But how did you happen to get to Hortonsville and Alexandriana High?"

"Oh. That. Well, that's very simple, too. No clever infiltrating. It so happens that the first year I was in Washington I had a good friend who was teaching with me. She was from Charlotte. She decided to return home. So she applied to the city superintendent of schools and also the county superintendent. She got the county job; it happened that there was a vacancy in her subject at Alexandriana and the county superintendent telephoned her to hire her before the city superintendent could answer by mail. She came down last fall, a year ago, and she wrote me that she liked the place. So when I decided I'd had enough in Washington, I wrote Mary Lou—"

"Mary Lou Jenkins?"

"Yes. Do you know her?"

"Very well. Sometimes I play bridge at the teacherage."

She paused in her striding along the driveway toward the parking area. "Say, are you one of the teachers?"

"No." He laughed and caught her arm. "We'll get run over." He led her to the side of the drive. "But I live at Hortonsville, Miss Sherlock Holmes. I'm with the textile plant there."

"Whew-w-w!" she exclaimed a moment later, when they came up to his car. "Cadillac convertible! Must have cost you three or four bucks, eh? Or did you borrow it—the car, I mean?"

"It's paid for," he said.

"I led with my chin." She shrugged.

He tipped the redcap and helped her in. They drove out to the highway.

"Say, would you like to drive into town? It's only a couple of miles out of the way. And you're in no hurry to get to the teacherage, are you?"

"I'd love to. Let's do."

"Good. Just so we get to Hortonsville in time to see 'em lynch a nigger, Miss Livingston. I haven't been to a good lynching in three or four months."

"Still unconvinced, eh? Well, Mr. Stanley, you're belaboring a point you don't have. There hasn't been a lynching in this state, according to the Tuskegee reports, since—well, since either of us were born, I'd say."

He ventured to take his eyes momentarily from the highway. "I withdraw the remark, which wasn't too good. I was trying to be clever, but I wasn't. Maybe it's because lately we have a chip on the shoulder. Maybe down deep it's a southern-guilt complex."

"Maybe so," she agreed, "though I wouldn't know about that. But if you have it, then very likely I do, too—my southern blood, you know, and I'm proud of it. Maybe that had something to do with my determination to get away from those Washington schools. I wasn't fired, you know."

"You left because you couldn't any longer endure teaching in those integrated schools, eh?"

"Exactly." She was entirely serious now. "And I have an idea— I'm pretty sure of it, in fact—that you people in the South, and this may surprise you—are more tolerant in problems of race than we are in the North."

"I don't know; I've heard that, and from northern people. But we should be more tolerant, you know. We've lived with the problem. And we understand—as many persons living elsewhere apparently don't—that only tolerance and patience and good will, will solve it."

In town they crossed the principal intersection. "This is Independence Square. They call it the crossing point of the Carolinas. We're almost exactly in the center of the two states."

"But why that name?"

"It goes back to colonial days. In a little log courthouse that sat at the crossing of two muddy roads—the square back there— the citizens of this county—Mecklenburg—on May 20, 1775, adopted a declaration of independence from England. That was more than a year before your Philadelphia convention. And five years later they fought Cornwallis on the same spot. The only significance now, I suppose, is the fact that it shows they were pretty independent-minded people, and so are we today. We don't stand for being pushed around."

"You like history, don't you?"

"Yes, I do. I like to get behind the scenes, you might call it. You know, they say history repeats itself, that there's nothing new under the sun—all those old clichés. And the remarkable thing about it is that it's true; history really does repeat itself. And if you want to understand what's happening now and what will be happening later, you've got to know and understand what happened in years past, and why. That's a cliché too, but it's also true, I'm convinced of it."

"So if you look back you can see events and situations that parallel events and situations of today—like, for example, this integration problem?"

"Definitely. And what happened as a result of those past situations provides clues as to what will result from our present situations, so that we can offer pretty accurate forecasts. But let's don't." He mopped his face with the handkerchief he had pulled out folded from his coat pocket. "It's too hot already—the weather, I mean, without discussing the Supreme Court."

"But just between us southerners," she twisted about to face him, serious despite her joking, "are they really so terrible, the Negro schools in the South, I mean—one-room shacks, with the stovepipes hung on wires and passing over the pupils' heads, like you see in *Life*, you know?"

"There must be such places, of course, or *Life* couldn't make those pictures. But I have never seen any. Let me demonstrate." He turned left at the next intersection and drove west. He pointed out churches, the Federal building, and, shortly, a tree-filled campus. "That's a university for Negro students, and it's a very fine institution."

"Do any whites attend it?"

He was thoughtful a moment. "Well, I suppose not. It has never occurred to me that any white boy or girl would want to.

Probably could, though, if the school's authorities, Negroes, were willing to enroll him."

A dozen blocks north, Osborne Gunn pointed off left. "That's what I wanted you to see. Have a look at that one-room shanty."

"*That!*" she exclaimed incredulously, "is a Negro school?"

"Yes. That's one you aren't likely to see in the national magazines. That's the city's newest Negro high school—the most recently built and finest school plant in the city, in fact. It cost more than a million bucks. They come here from all over the country, school people—even Philadelphia, everybody except the magazines' photographers, in fact—to study it for the latest ideas in school-plant designing."

"It looks like a very modern and fashionable girls' college."

"It isn't representative, I'll admit, either of Negro or white schools. But all over the state there are many Negro schools equal to or superior to the white schools. That's true in many communities in other states, too. And it's not unusual; such schools are being built month after month, or certainly they were until the Supreme Court hurled the monkey wrench. But I'm preaching. I'm sorry."

Soon they were in the country, and the twilight was deepening. "It's a wonderful time of day, isn't it?" She leaned her head back against the seat.

"Particularly when the company's charming—and intriguing."

"Thanks. You can say nice things, too. And I reciprocate." She sat up. "How far now to Hortonsville?"

"Another six miles or so. We're halfway there from town. Pretty soon we'll be going by Alexandriana High and you'll see where you'll be teaching."

"Will we have any Negro students? I understand North Carolina has a new state law that permits integration, and that this year for the first time some white schools may have some Negro pupils."

"That's right. The General Assembly passed a law under which integration was legalized under certain set-out circumstances provided the voters should approve amendment of the state constitution to permit it, which they did. The law leaves the question of school enrollment in the hands of the various local school boards, both city and county." He glanced her way, his expression quizzical. "And the local board having oversight of your school has assigned a Negro pupil to it this fall. But why did you ask in the first place?"

"I remember reading somewhere, maybe in *Time,* that North Carolina was the only southern state whose school law had a chance of surviving federal court tests."

"That's what a lot of folk—state officials, lawyers, and school people—seem to think. But it remains to be seen. If the law is reasonably and fairly complied with, I have the feeling that perhaps the courts will let it stand. And that means, the way I see it, that we'll have some integration in various communities —token integration, you might call it, has already been provided for this fall in two or three of the larger cities—and there'll be more before long, I suspect."

As the car rounded a curve, he pointed out his window. "There's your school. It's getting too dark to see it very well; but it's a good plant—well-designed classrooms, labs, a big auditorium, cafeteria, tremendous gym, athletic fields. It's modern, too. But say, you should see the Negro high school a mile above here. It's even more modern; they've just completed a half-million dollar addition. That plant has everything."

A few minutes later they drew up to the curb in front of a two-story, red-brick Georgian residence. "Here we are. Your new home."

"Looks nice. Do all the teachers live here?"

"Most of the single ones, I think, and some of the Hortonsville Junior High teachers." He was opening his door. He came around to her side to let her out. "O.K., Carrie Nation, get your ax and I'll take you inside."

"I told you I was no missionary." She slid from the seat. "And I'm no crusader either; I'll thank you to get no such rumor started!" But her pout manifestly was contrived.

2

"If you ask me, Sarah Gordon—" Abruptly she stopped, slid up in her bed, pushed the pillow under her ribs, and thrust a pert forefinger toward her new roommate in the other single bed. "But why ask me? I'm just an old-maid school teacher. You're a—a sociologist, and from Washington. Can there be anything that a Washington sociologist doesn't know, pray tell!"

"But you're an economist, Mary Lou, and likewise from Washington. Remember?" She affected earnestness. "Economists, I'm sure, know much more than sociologists."

"Sure, I'm an economist, all right. I teach cooking and sewing, simple stuff telling you how to have something on your table to eat and something on your back to wear. But you, my dear, are a sociologist; you deal with the broad aspects of society, its functions, institutions," she paused, laughing, "sure, institutions, and that takes in schools, integration—"

"Yes, and I'm just that much more confused than you, having had one more year than you in Washington."

"That's pretty good. You'll get along down here, gal." But then her demeanor changed. "To be frank with you, about this school situation, it's my feeling that if both sides quieted down and the newspapers and radio and TV—"

"Both sides?"

"The extremists, I mean. Those who are pushing integration, like the NAACP, and those who are fighting it, like the white councils, the Patriots, and such groups. If they would all calm down and if the news services would stop playing up the question so much—headlines and letters to the editor, generally from crackpots on both sides, and the radio and TV interviews—I believe that the situation pretty soon would work itself out. But if everybody keeps on agitating the situation, I'm afraid it may really get bad, you know. You can't pick up the paper without seeing an interview with this Dr. Claiborne Henderson, Jr."

"Who's he?"

"He's head of the NAACP around here—a Negro doctor. And

he must have a million patients by now, with all the free advertising he's getting. It's one of his cousin's daughters, I understand, who has been assigned to our school. One of the newspaper reporters dug that out."

"Oh, I'm beginning to see."

"Sure, the poor little Negro is being shoved into a situation that can't be pleasant for her. I feel sorry for the child; it's none of her doing; she's just a pawn. Yet she's had her pictures all over the papers, and all that. Many Negroes consider this Henderson fellow the dedicated champion of their race; some, white and colored, think he's just an opportunist. I'd hesitate to give an opinion."

"And it's the same way, isn't it, with those who are determined to keep the schools segregated?"

"Yes. Some are sincerely opposed to integration, the far greater number are, especially the older people; they feel that if whites and Negroes are permitted to go to school together it will be utterly disastrous, and they may be right, too. But then there are some who are waving the Stars and Bars and filling the newspaper open forums with frenzied letters for selfish reasons of one sort and another. And the great danger is that in the commotion the voices of level-headed, sensible people, the moderates who counsel patience and tolerance, simply won't be heard."

"That's the gist of what Osborne Gunn was saying when we were coming—"

"Oz? You've already been talking things over with our jackpot prize?"

"Jackpot prize? Is that what you call him?" Sarah Gordon sat up straight. "He met me at the airport and brought me here. I remember now that you weren't here when we came. But why do you call him a prize?"

Her roommate registered astonishment. "He's male, isn't he? And single. And good looking and quite evidently healthy. And smart. He was one of the top Phi Betes in his class—" She hrugged. "Well, isn't that enough? What more do you want?"

"He didn't tell me about the Phi Bete key. But that isn't such an exclusive club, you know."

"Neither is the masculine gender, dearie, but it's in great demand, and when you get to be thirty-two without having acquired one of the specimens, then your appreciation of the entire breed begins to multiply in—well, in geometric progression." She held up her hand, palm forward, in emphatic gesture. "Now don't get me wrong. Oz is too young for me even if otherwise I had a chance. I'm not warning you to be hands-off; I'm encouraging you to get busy, my dear." She beamed; but then suddenly her expression was questioning. "But, honestly, you don't know about Oz?"

"No more than the little I picked from him."

"You rode in his Cadillac, didn't you?"

"Yes, I asked him if it was his or if he'd borrowed it, and all he said was that it was paid for."

"Brother-r-r!" Mary Lou slapped her thigh a resounding smack. "You asked him if it was paid for?"

"Oh, not seriously, of course. He knew I was kidding. He had been kidding me about taking the plane down from Washington."

"But, listen, Sarah Gordon, didn't the name ring any bell?" She pointed to the blanket folded neatly at the foot of the bed. "Don't you ever read ads in the magazines?"

"Gunn? Gunn blankets." Sarah Gordon's eyes lighted. " 'Every night the world sleeps tight under a Gunn blanket.' And that picture of the world tucked under a huge blanket. Of course. And Oz did tell me he was with a textile plant here." She leaned forward, forehead wrinkled. "Just what has Oz got to do with Gunn blankets?"

"What has he got to do with 'em? I guess Oz *is with* the mill here. He runs it." Mary Lou's frown was scornfully reproving. "And Oz's old man *is* Gunn blankets!"

3

The next morning the teachers of Alexandriana High School met with Principal Hinson in the school library. He presented each teacher, since several of them, like Sarah Gordon, were new; he expressed his appreciation of those returning,. welcomed cordially the new ones, and without waste of time and words outlined the policies of the school, discussed developments since the spring term's ending—particularly improvements in the physical plant—and several new courses of study that were being added to the curriculum.

"And now," he said, with a wry smile, "we come to a discussion of the problem that likely has been uppermost in your minds ever since the recent action of the school board." He paused, studied the crepe myrtle in bloom beyond the window, turned back to face his teachers. "I assume that you all know that the board has assigned a Negro girl to this school, one of the six Negroes, I believe, assigned to white schools in this county. I assume, too," his smile was grim now, "that you aren't too enthusiastic over it, and neither am I. But I presume also that we will all accept it and act on it in good faith."

He looked toward the window, cleared his throat, turned back to face his faculty. "As you know, the Supreme Court has held that the segregation of public-school pupils on the basis of race alone is illegal. Many people contend, and I am frank to say that I share that view, that the Court went beyond its constitutional authority to interpret the law; they feel that the Court actually assumed legislative authority and *enacted* such a law. But however that may be, the Supreme Court is the nation's highest judicial body and it has differed with all the past courts and held that segregation on the basis of race alone may not be permitted; and our school board, acting under the authority of the newly enacted state school law, has assigned this Negro child to our school."

For a moment the principal studied his teachers. "I don't know yet to whose home room this girl will be assigned or what courses of study she will have, but I trust that those teachers under whom she will study will co-operate in our determination to follow as best we can the school board's rulings and instructions." He paused a moment, but no one offered to comment. "I wonder," he then invited, "if there are any questions or observations at this point."

"Mr. Hinson," one of the returning teachers ventured to ask, "how do you think the students themselves will react to this Negro girl's coming into the school?"

"I think it will depend to a great extent on how the parents and teachers act," the principal replied. "If they remain calm and do nothing to excite the students to act disorderly, I look for little or no difficulty. I think we must realize that the present-day school boys and girls do not look at this integration problem even as we look at it, just as we do not have the same view of it as our parents had and, particularly, our grandparents. For example, there are several Negro students at the university—just how many I don't know, and that in itself is a commentary on how the situation has changed in the last few years. I understand no one pays much attention to Negro students any more. In fact, some of the students told me recently, unless he happens to be in a class with you, a Negro student is likely to be taken as a janitor or any of the other Negroes you'll find on a big college campus. And few of the white students, this one told me, care whether he's student or janitor."

"Mr. Hinson, that's true," one of the younger men teachers spoke out. "I know it from having been there so recently—I finished, you know, a year ago this past June. But if a Negro had tried to enroll at the university when my father was at Chapel Hill, there would have been a riot. In fact, he told me, the students of his day were opposed to permitting co-eds to enroll." He shrugged. "Times and people change, you know."

"Of course," Principal Hinson agreed. "But there are only a handful of Negroes enrolled at Chapel Hill, most of them in the professional schools. And that makes a tremendous difference in how you look at this business. If they constituted a sizable group, a third or half the student body, it would be different. And that's where the danger is pointed up in the integration of grade and high schools, proponents of segregation declare."

Suddenly Mr. Hinson's eyes lingered on Sarah Gordon Vicente. "Miss Vicente, as I told you, taught last year at Washington. She certainly got an unobstructed view of integration in the public schools. Tell us, Miss Vicente, what was your reaction? And since you're from the North, too, perhaps you have a calmer—let us say—view of integration than we do. How do you look at it after seeing it in operation?"

"Do you want me to speak frankly, Mr. Hinson?" The other teachers twisted in their chairs to face her.

The principal nodded. "Of course. Say whatever you want to; we'll be glad to have your viewpoint."

"Well, when I was going to school in Philadelphia we'd have now and then a Negro boy or girl, maybe two or three, in our classes. But nobody paid much attention to them, and not often did they enter into our school's social activities. But in Washington," she paused, "well, I was re-elected, but I knew I wouldn't be teaching there another year. That's why I came south," she added, "to get away from it." She laughed.

The teachers and the principal laughed, too. "But actually, how is it working out in the capital?" Mr. Hinson pursued his questioning.

"It is fast lowering the schools' standards; that's one effect, I'd say, that can't be denied. But perhaps the most noticeable result is the moving away of the white people from the District, virtually all who can get out, in order to send their children to other schools. That is true particularly of the politicians who are shouting most vociferously for integration."

When the laughter had subsided, the principal thanked her. "I must say that your observations are most interesting," he commented, "and perhaps surprising and even startling to some of us. But let me say that I have heard similar views expressed by other northern people engaged in public-education work." He studied the crepe myrtle again, then turned with furrowed forehead to his faculty members. "I fear those who are pushing integration so zealously may be sowing the seeds of a whirlwind, but on the other hand, I have the feeling that those who are advocating massive resistance to the Supreme Court's decision may be calling down a storm that would do our entire nation untold damage and utterly wreck our public-schools' system in the South." He shook his head slowly. "It's a shame that always there are those who in order to hasten what they think is progress are willing to jeopardize it." But quickly his manner changed. "Actually, though, in my opinion, many of the difficulties we are foreseeing will never materialize. It's my feeling that it will be many years, if ever, before the public schools in the South will be integrated beyond the token stage. When the Negroes find that they can go to school with white boys and girls, I think they'll begin to discover more and more that actually they don't want to. They'll be happier in their own schools, I am convinced.

"The Negroes, as a matter of fact," he continued, "have much to lose in the integrating of the schools, particularly Negro teachers. For instance, Miss Vicente," he glanced again toward Sarah Gordon, "did you know that in this state the Negro school teachers—and there are some nine thousand teaching in the public schools—average higher salaries than the white teachers?"

"I've read that somewhere. How do you explain it?"

"All teachers, white and Negro, are paid by the state and on exactly the same basis. But salaries advance in yearly increments and Negro teachers as a general rule teach longer than the whites —more white teachers get married and leave the profession. So the Negro teacher has more teaching experience and is earning a larger salary. And if integration becomes general, it will mean that more and more Negro teachers will lose their jobs, and Negro teachers are among the highest-paid workers of their race. So, I would think, few Negro teachers really favor integration."

"Then you mean, Mr. Hinson," one of the teachers inquired, "that if we do become integrated on a pretty broad basis, very few Negro teachers will be employed to teach in these schools?"

259

"Exactly. Do you think school boards will employ Negro teachers to teach white pupils?"

"They don't do it in states where there is no segregation," 'another teacher answered, "not on a large scale, I mean."

"That's right. Miss Vicente, more Negro teachers are employed in North Carolina alone than in some dozen states in the North and East combined," Mr. Hinson declared. "That is one of the practical arguments against integrated schools. But the Supreme Court, in my opinion, paid little attention to practicalities. They seem to have based their decision on philosophical and psychological studies; at any rate, many of the Court's critics so contend."

The teachers' meeting was concluded shortly before noon with the principal's giving renewed emphasis to his hope that all the teachers would co-operate with school authorities in carrying out the orders of the school board.

In mid-afternoon Osborne Gunn came to the teacherage and asked to see Sarah Gordon.

"Well, how'd the teachers' meeting go?" he asked, when she came down to the living room where he was waiting.

"Very well, I suppose, except that I'm beginning to tire already of this integration-segregation business. It seems to be the only thing people are thinking about."

"It is a pretty lively subject. But say, Sarah Gordon, I thought maybe you'd like to take a little ride with me. I've got a small errand to do."

"For your boss? That's how you got away from the job in the middle of the afternoon?"

"Yes," he said. "You guessed it. And I can't be off very long. Say, you'd better get a scarf to tie over your hair. The top's down."

"Is it to see more Negro schoolhouses and hear another lecture on mixing in the schools?"

"No. I promise not a word."

"I'd love to go, Oz. It is a lovely day for driving."

"There's something I want to show you."

"You promised—"

"Oh, this has nothing to do with schools. It's an old house—"

"With a history, no doubt."

"Sure, quite a history. And intriguing. I intend to uncover more of it, too."

4

In bright September sunshine they drove north along the four-lane highway. The slipstream—up and over the windshield and above their heads—slashed at the ends of her scarf and sent them dipping and darting.

"It's a truly gorgeous day. Just like summer."

"It's hotter, as a matter of fact. September weather down here is usually warmer than August. But October's the choice time. That was Tom Wolfe's month, and it's mine." He risked a look her way. "Do you like him?"

"Yes, very much. But he was a strange one, wasn't he?"

"Not as strange as you would judge from his books, my dad says. He was in school with him at Carolina before Dad went to State College for his textile engineering."

"You said you went to State, too, didn't you? To study textile engineering, I presume. But why did you go to the university first?"

"Well, I had thought I might go into history, maybe as a college professor, but, well, the spindles and the looms got me. Actually, Dad and Charlie were needing help; things were getting so spread out, you know." Suddenly he pointed off left. "Look. Over there in that grove. You can't see it very well for the trees."

"Oh, the house." She turned sideways for a better look. "It's brick, isn't it? And two stories?"

"Three stories, one under the roof, with dormer windows. And basement."

"You've already been there, of course?"

"Oh, yes, several times. By now I'm an old friend of the family."

"Who lives there?"

"Negroes now. That's where Ophelia lives."

"Ophelia?"

"The Negro girl who has been assigned to your school. Everybody knows Ophelia now. She's in the headlines; since the school board assigned her to a white school she's been a public figure. In fact, she's the reason for my getting interested in the house."

"But how did that cause you to discover the house, Oz?"

"It didn't cause me to discover it; it was re-discovery, I suppose you'd call it. I knew about the old place. In fact, I went there once with my great grandmother; she must have been past eighty-five when she died. I was six or seven when she took me there. She was too old and twisted with rheumatism to get out, but she had me go inside and come out and report to her. And she told me the story of the house. But I hadn't been back there until this stuff came out in the papers about Ophelia." He looked around, his expression inquisitive. "Does this interest you, or am I just boring you?"

"No, you aren't boring me. It sounds wonderful, like it might be leading up to something spooky or horribly gruesome, like some old English castle on the moors, you know, with fog and fierce dogs—"

"Well, it's not that good." He laughed. "But, to get back to my story, one of the newspaper stories about Ophelia showed her standing in front of the house, on the verandah steps, in fact; it showed the front door behind her, and that front doorway caught my eye. As a child that day I went there with Granny Melissa I hadn't noticed it, of course. Then the newspaper account went on to tell about the house, even some of its history."

"So you went exploring?"

"Exactly. And knowing what I did from what Granny Melissa had told me—which had so impressed me at the time that I hadn't forgotten it—I was able to find out things the reporters hadn't uncovered." They were turning left on a paved belt road.

"You did? Golly, this *is* getting exciting! What?"

"Well, she had told me that the place was owned by a country doctor who wanted to marry her. But she jilted him, though she never forgot him and all her life continued to love him; at least, I got the impression that she was recalling him even then with a sort of romantic tenderness. She told me as we were driving away from the old house that she was going to buy it and leave it to me; Charlie would get her old home, the old Osborne place, she said, since he was the older son. She had had it restored and she gave it to my father and mother as a wedding present, and they lived there until they built the place in town; Charlie is living there now."

"And did she? Buy this old house, I mean?"

"No. She died a short time after we came out here that day— just a few months."

She sat up straight, and the slipstream over the windshield dallied with her black hair pushing out above her forehead from beneath the restraining scarf. "Golly, Oz, this sort of history *is* intriguing. I had an idea you were interested in heavy stuff, like wars and the movements and forces that caused them, that sort of stuff, you know, and integration and segregation, the whys and wherefores."

He laughed. "This history goes integration and segregation one better."

"It does! What do you mean?"

"Miscegenation." He was turning onto the dirt road that led to the house. "It's an amazing story. I'll tell you about it the first chance I get. But right now I want you to have a look at the house. Of course, it's in pretty foul shape, but it's not past restoring." They drove between two heaps of moldering bricks. "This evidently was the gateway between brick columns that very likely held a gate," he said, pointing. "I'll ask Uncle Lem about it. There he is, up there on the front porch."

They drove toward the house, past a huge water oak, and stopped near a tremendous magnolia. The old Negro got up from his chair, shuffled down steps at the end of the porch, and picking his way between huge but misshapen boxwoods, came up to the car.

"Howdy, Uncle Lem," Osborne greeted him. "How're you feeling?"

"Tol'ably." He peered at the white man behind the steering wheel. Then his dark face broke into a broad grin. "Lawd, that 'ere's Mist' Gunn, ain't it? I didn't know who you was right off when you driv' up."

"Yes, and this is Miss Vicente, Uncle Lem. She's one of the new teachers at the high school."

Sarah Gordon beamed. "How do you do?"

"Tol'ably, ma'am." He was smiling and bowing. "Won't you all git out and come in?" He looked Osborne in the eyes, and his own were teasing. "I guess you wants to show it to the lady, don't you, Mist' Gunn, and see how she likes it?"

"Yes, I would like for her to see inside." He got out, went around to her side and helped her from the car.

"Jus' walk right in," the Negro directed. "Ain't nobody here but me. My granddaughter and her ma's down at Claib Henderson's office, and Jim he's off on a trip; he's helper on one o' them big trucks."

"I guess your granddaughter's still planning to go to the whites' school?"

"I reckon so, Mist' Gunn." He shook his head slowly. " 'Tain't none o' my business, I guess, but I'd rather she'd keep on at the colored folks's school. But Claib's set on Feelie goin' to the white folks's."

"This Dr. Henderson is some of your people, isn't he, Uncle Lem?"

"Yes, sir; his daddy and me was first cousins. But his daddy's dead."

They walked between the boxwoods to the front porch. As they approached the verandah, Oz pointed upward. "Notice the iron balustrade, Sarah Gordon. It looks a little beaten up, but actually it's in pretty good shape. A little sand-blasting would get the rust off, and the missing balusters can be duplicated.

You know, I've come to the conclusion that this iron work was done across the river at a place owned by Major John Davidson and his son-in-law, Captain Joe Graham—those names mean nothing to you, I know, but they fought the British when Cornwallis invaded this section. After the war they prospered in iron manufacturing; they called their ironworks Vesuvius Furnace. There's an iron heat reflector in the back of the parlor fireplace in there that has molded in it the initials of the ironworks and the date it was made."

"More history." She turned teasing eyes to him. "But not the sort you promised to tell."

"I will; just have patience. And look at the house—that doorway, for example. Isn't it a gem? Even some of the original panes are still in—amazing. And they can be matched."

As they crossed to the door, the Negro man opened it. "Step right in and make yo'selves at home. Jus' go 'round anywhere you wants. It don't look much; ain't been took care of too good and things is mighty dirty, but it's still strong and stu'dy. Been always had a good roof on it and it ain't rotted out nowheres."

They went inside.

"Oh, Oz! The stairway! Isn't it gorgeous!" She strode along the hall to the foot of the stairs and looked up through the well to the ceiling of the third floor. "No supports. It just seems to float upward around the walls."

"I knew the stairway would catch your eye. As a matter of fact, it's not only beautiful; it's also an engineering marvel. And the balusters and handrail are hand-carved walnut and also the scroll work at the ends of the steps." He ran an appraising hand along one of the balusters. "Uncle Lem, how did you manage to keep the stairs in such good condition? Usually in old houses the balusters get knocked out, sometimes for firewood; but I doubt that there's a half dozen missing in this whole stairway."

"I al'ays tried to take care o' this house, Mist' Gunn," the old man replied. "I was born on this place and I been livin' in this house a long time, ever since pretty soon after Doct' Cardell died back when I was a little chap. And my daddy and his daddy and my daddy's granddaddy and farther back, I reckon, was born right here on this plantation—course it was a lot bigger back in them days—and my ma—"

"Her name was Ophelia, wasn't it, Uncle Lem; she's the one your son's daughter was named for, wasn't she, the one who's going to the whites' school?"

"Yes, sir, Mist' Gunn, like I told you t'other day, I named my son Jim's chap—Jim was named for my daddy—I named Jim's chap for my ma."

"And your mother was the doctor's daughter, didn't you tell me?"

"Yes, sir, Doct' Cardell he was my granddaddy on ma's side. That's howcome we got aholt o' this place, you see, Mist' Gunn. When Doct' Cardell died he didn't have nobody but his chil'en to heir the place—they was mulatto chil'en, Mist' Gunn, like I told you, you mind—and wasn't nobody livin' on the place then but my daddy and ma, and the rest o' the heirs sold out to them. And when my daddy died, it come down to me. Course, it's a lot o' the land been sold off, but they's still more'n a hund'ed acres left in the home tract."

"The doctor's wife, Uncle Lem, who—"   ɔw bɪ

"He didn't have no wife, Mist' Gunn. He just sórta look up with my grandma; she was a mulatto woman pretty nigh white. You mind, I told you—"

"That's right, you did. And what did you say her name was?"

"I don't mind hearin' none of the old folks call her name, I don't think. She died 'fore I was born or when I was too young to mind 'bout her, and my ma died when I was still pretty young. So I never heared much talk 'bout my grandma. But my daddy's folks had been slaves on this plantation 'fore the Civil War, I mind my daddy used to tell 'bout."

They went into the large front room on the left. "This here was the parlor when Doct' Cardell was livin'," Lem told them. "You can still see them places on the wall up there," he pointed, "where they had pictures hangin' up. They was pictures o' the old folks, the doctor's folks, my daddy al'ays said. My daddy knowed a lot 'bout the place; he was raised up right here and he rec'lected the doctor mighty well. I've heared my daddy say his granddaddy was Doct' Cardell's daddy's body servant in the war." He rubbed his grizzled head with the palm of his hand. "It was my daddy told me 'bout them pictures. He rec'-lected seein' 'em hangin' up there."

"Wonder what ever happened to them? You hadn't told me about the pictures."

"I took 'em down a long time ago. They was gittin' dirty and flyspecked, and I was scared somethin' might happen to 'em."

"So you sold 'em to some woman hunting antique frames, eh?"

"No, sir. I wropped 'em up in some old sheets and put 'em up there in that big room over the attic, which my daddy said was the ballroom in olden times, and I locked the door and ain't nobody been in there in many a year, I guess; it's got some old furniture in it, too; I just hated to see them spindly legged chairs and things git broke up and I knowed they would if I left 'em down here, with the chaps playin' on 'em, and every-thing."

"Could we see the pictures and the furniture some time, Uncle Lem?" Sarah Gordon's eyes betrayed her interest, con-siderably increased now with the Negro's revelation. "They must be over a hundred years old, aren't they?"

"Yes, ma'am, Miss. I guess they's nigher two hund'ed. I heared my grandaddy Lem when I was a chap tellin' 'bout them pictures; he said they was painted, some of 'em, 'fore this here house was built, and some o' that furniture was handed down from folks in the old country, he thought maybe." He paused and rubbed again his grizzled dome. "You wants to see them things right now?"

"We won't have time this afternoon," Osborne answered. "We'll come back some day when we have longer, maybe some Saturday, and have a good look. We'll just take a quick peek at the house now, if you'd like, Sarah Gordon."

"I'd love it. This is quite an experience for me." She turned to Lem. "Were the doctor's children brought up in this house?"

"Oh, no, ma'am, they didn't live in the mansion house, which this was called in them times. You see, they was colored chil'-en."

"But where did they live?"

"They lived with my grandma back there in the kitchen house what burnt down long time ago. It was back behint the mansion house, over to the left sorta. They's still bricks out there showin' where it was at."

"But you've been living here."

"Yes, ma'am. But you see when the kitchen house burnt down, which was pretty soon after Doct' Cardell died and while I was still a chap, that's when my daddy and ma bought out them other heirs, and then they moved in here. But that was a'ter the old doctor died, you see. And then when my daddy and ma died the place it come to me, you see, ma'am."

The girl nodded. "I'm beginning to understand."

"But you still can't remember your grandmother's name?" Osborne asked.

"No, sir, I shore can't. Seems like I mind hearin' some of the old ones sayin' something about her name was Sal, but I just plumb disremember; it was a long time ago she died, and like I told you, my ma died when I was just a chap like."

Lem guided them about the old house. "This here room was where they et, I mind my daddy tellin'," he revealed, when they went into the room behind the parlor.

"You mean, your grandmother and the children lived in the kitchen house but they all ate together here in the dining room?" Sarah Gordon was trying to follow him.

The Negro turned to reply with evident determination to make himself understood. "No'm, not her and the chil'en; you see, they was colored; they et out in the kitchen house where they lived at. I was talkin' 'bout Doct' Cardell and his folks, them white people. When the doctor lived here a'ter he got to be a doctor, his folks was dead—that was a'ter the war, you see—

and he was jus' batching like; he didn't have no wife." His forehead was furrowed with his effort to make himself understood. Osborne moved to relieve the old man.

"But you do remember—you were telling me the other day, you recall—that your father did say something once about the doctor's having been in love with a young woman who jilted him?"

"Yes, sir, I do mind tellin' you that, and I jus' can mind somethin' 'bout my daddy talkin' 'bout it one day when I was a chap. Him and my granddaddy, old man Lem, was talkin' 'bout one day a'ter old man Gunn had done went home—"

"Old man Gunn?"

"Yes, sir; he was the one they said cut out Doct' Cardell with the lady, I mind hearin' it told. He wanted to buy the plantation; he told them he used to run it for the doctor when they was both real young men and he'd al'ays had a hankerin' to buy it; he was gittin' pretty rich by then in the cotton mill."

"But your folks wouldn't sell?"

"No, sir, they wouldn't sell out, and a'ter he left they was talkin' 'bout how he cut out Doct' Cardell; I think that's how it was, but I was still just a chap then. But I mind seein' Mist' Gunn. He was gittin' to be a pretty old man by then."

"He was my father's grandfather."

"Yes, sir, I mind you said that t'other day."

"That's right, I did. Now did you ever know my grandfather, the son of the Charlie Gunn you've been talking about? His name was Charles, too, Charles Gunn, junior."

"No, sir, I don't think so; I do mind hearin' tell o' him, but I don't think I ever seen him. I don't mind any o' the Gunns comin' over here a'ter my daddy and ma wouldn't sell out to Mist' Charlie." He rolled his eyes. "But I al'ays heared tell them Gunns was mighty rich folks."

They crossed the hall into the kitchen, which smelled of kerosene; Osborne saw that the odor came from the decrepit oil-cooking stove in the far corner of the room. Across from it was a table loaded with a hodgepodge of pans, pots, dishes.

"This here used to be Doct' Cardell's office," he explained. "Them shelves," he pointed to shelves burdened with jars of canned fruit, cereal boxes, lard cans, bulging paper bags, "was where he kep' his medicine and stuff. But when the kitchen house burned down and my daddy and ma moved over here, they turned the old doctor's office into the kitchen and it been here ever since."

Osborne had been studying the walls. "Notice the paneling, Sarah Gordon. Wouldn't this make a wonderful library or den, or maybe combination of the two? What is this wood, Uncle Lem? Pine?"

"No, sir, it's walnut, Mist' Gunn. It was big trees it was cut from."

"You mean that all this is walnut?"

"Yes, sir, and it's a lot more walnut boa'ds in this house. It musta been pretty plentiful 'round here when they built this house, more'n it is now'days."

Quickly they climbed the stairs to the second floor and went into each of the four large rooms.

"It wouldn't be any trouble to build a bathroom between the bedrooms on each side of the hall, and another downstairs," Osborne declared. "In fact, a good architect like Walter Loye— he's one of my friends in town—could completely modernize this house, I'm sure, without spoiling its original design inside or out."

Lem was shaking his head glumly. "I couldn't do nothin' like that, Mist' Gunn," he said. "It'd take a lot o' money to fix up this house and I can't hardly make enough to keep the taxes paid up."

"I didn't mean for you to fix it, Uncle Lem. But if somebody should come along and offer you a reasonable price for the place—"

The colored man still was shaking his grizzled head. "It'd take a powerful lot o' money; I don't know anybody'd be willin' to spend it on this old house, even if he had it." He looked Osborne in the eyes. "And I'd hate to have to leave this place,

Mist' Gunn; I was borned and raised right here; I been here all my life."

"But if somebody made you a good offer for the house and let you keep one of the tenant houses to live in and maybe gave you the job of looking after the farm and the yards around the house, cutting the lawn, and that sort of thing." He said no more, for Lem's eyes clearly were speaking his mounting interest.

"If I could stay on the place, and they'd give me 'nough money for the house and whatever land they wanted to go with it," he appeared to be debating with himself rather than with Osborne Gunn, "I've a notion I just might sell out." He paused, his dark forehead wrinkling, and then he smiled. "I'll just tell you the truth, Mist' Gunn. For a long time Jim has been wantin' to move to town so's to be closer to the place where he works at, and I reckon the only reason he ain't went already is because Claib Henderson's been arguin' with him to git him to stay on here awhile longer until they sees if Feelie'll stay in that white folks's school or if she'll git th'owed out or quit or somethin'." He paused, and then, more serious, he began again. "But the main reason I might sell out, I reckon, is so somebody what's got money could fix this old place up like it musta been when the doctor's daddy and them old folks was livin' here. But I don't b'lieve I could stand to move off somewheres."

"You really love this old house, don't you, Uncle Lem?"

"Yes, ma'am, I reckon I does. But I ain't never been nowheres else much but right here, and I ain't never lived nowheres else. And it was my folks's place, you see, white and black. The Cardells is been here a long time. I don't reckon I could live contented nowheres else."

"You ought to stay right here, Uncle Lem. And if you ever sell it, you should have an agreement with the person who buys it that you can stay on as long as you live, like I said. By the way, has anybody ever tried to buy the place recently?"

"Last year a man come here and said he wanted to buy it, but when he started talkin' 'bout tearin' down the house—"

"How was that?"

"Said he wanted the place for the farm mainly; it's got some good creeks and branches on it and he said he wanted it to raise some o' these white-face cattle on; said he'd put his son to raisin' them cows; he'd build him a house right here on this spot, he said; said he'd tear this here house down; it was too big to keep up if he had the money to fix it up, he told me, so he'd jus' tear it down and build his boy one o' these here bungalows, he called it." The old man was shaking his head sadly. "When he say that, I backed up; I told him I didn't want to sell. Mist' Gunn, I jus' couldn't stand to see this here old house tore down."

"I don't blame you, Uncle Lem; you did the right thing. But if somebody came along who loved it the same way you do and wanted to fix it up like it was in the old days, maybe even better, and fix up the grounds around the house, and the farm—"

"Mist' Gunn, if somebody would do that, and let me keep on livin' on the place," Lem's black eyes were ablaze, "I'd shore live happy and die happy, too!" Suddenly his demeanor was more matter of fact. "Like I told you, my boy Jim and his wife they wants to move to town; they wants to sell this place and git they part o' the money. So if somebody come along and wanted to fix it up," he paused and a wide grin overspread his naïve countenance, "Mist' Gunn, would it be you all—" he glanced toward the girl and then quickly back to Osborne "—what wants to buy it and settle down right here?"

The two looked at each other and burst out laughing. That prompted Lem to press his questioning. He turned again to the girl. "But ain't it you all Mist' Gunn was talkin' 'bout?" His friendly black face was beaming.

Sarah Gordon pointed to Osborne. "He's the one who was doing the talking," she answered, her blue eyes dancing. "Ask him."

272

5

Sarah Gordon and her teacherage roommate, whose home rooms happened to be adjacent, had come out into the large brick-and-tile lobby between the auditorium and the classrooms section. They entered it just as Principal Hinson was stepping forward to grasp the microphone. From the portico, which was actually an extension of the lobby that in cold weather could be closed off by sliding glass doors, the principal had been surveying the throng of several-hundred students and a sprinkling of parents and other patrons massed on the esplanade below; Sarah Gordon and Mary Lou had spoken to him as they had entered a few minutes before.

"Your attention, please! Please let me have your attention!"

The milling throng faced him, quickly quieted.

"Today, ladies and gentlemen, as we begin our fall term, I wish to welcome our returning students and give a special welcome to those others who are entering our school," the principal began. "Also I welcome those parents and others patrons who are with us. As is our custom on the opening day of school, however, we will have no chapel assemblage this morning, but instead the students will go to the various home rooms for registration. In a moment then I shall ask the students to move quietly to their rooms, and I cordially invite you others to return for a visit after we get the new term under way. You are always welcome. School will be dismissed today at noon.

"This morning," he paused and his demeanor was serious, "is a significant and critical time in the life of our community and state. As a result of action recently taken by our school board and in accordance with the law, this school today is enrolling a Negro student—" He held up his hand, for a low muttering, he sensed, was threatening to swell into an uproar. "Please give me your attention another moment!" he called out sternly, and again the crowd quieted. "The authorities of this school, I assure you, have had nothing to do with this decision. It was made by the school board after long and careful and, I might say, prayerful study. But though we have had nothing to do with the decision arrived at, we are determined to carry out to the best of our ability the instructions and orders of the board."

"To hell with the school board! To hell with the Supreme Court!"

Sarah Gordon saw a long-necked, red-faced man on the fringe of the crowd as he shook an upraised fist and shouted his denunciations.

"Oh! There's going to be trouble, Mary Lou, I'm afraid. I wonder—"

The other girl caught her arm. "Look! Maybe not."

Looking again in the direction of the angry heckler, Sarah Gordon saw him being escorted aside by a policeman. She turned again to face the principal, who momentarily had been interrupted.

"So I want to appeal to all students and patrons of this school to be calm and orderly; don't do anything to agitate the situation, and I am confident that if we follow such a course we will have little difficulty in adjusting our school to the new policy." He caught the arm of a man standing beside him. "And now, ladies and gentlemen, I am glad to present to you Chief Watson of the county police, who wishes to say a word. Thank you."

There was a sprinkling of applause as the police chief stepped to the microphone.

"Ladies and gentlemen, I want to endorse what your principal has just said and to tell you that we are going to have law and order here today, and from now on too. I want you to understand that your county police are not taking sides in this argument, one way or the other. We are not here to enforce integration or prevent it. We're just here to see that order prevails, and that's what we're going to do." The loud-speaker blared his words.

"Now we aren't expecting to have any trouble; we are expecting you boys and girls as well as you grownups to act like ladies and gentlemen. But," he smiled grimly as he paused for emphasis, "we are going to see to it that you do. My men have orders to arrest anybody who gets disorderly, and that applies to you students, too, understand. This Negro girl will be coming to school any minute now, and when she does, I want nobody to molest her in any manner. I hope that's clear to everybody."

Television newsmen with hand cameras, and reporters and photographers from the newspapers and press services in the city—scattered in the throng on the esplanade—had been covering the talks by the principal and the police chief and making crowd shots and getting interviews; the crowd, too, had been facing the speakers, who had continued to stand near the school entrance, and consequently the automobile now drawing up to the curb had approached virtually unnoticed. But the chief had been watching for it.

"All right now, boys and girls," he spoke sternly into the microphone as the automobile stopped, "open up a way so she can get through!"

Instantly the throng whirled about. The cameramen dashing to get into position to film the girl provided a signal for the others to surge toward the thin Negro now advancing alone up the wide concrete walkway.

"Nigger, go back to your school!" a boy near her shouted. "We don't want niggers here!"

"Yeh, nigger, go home! Yeh, nigger! Nigger! Nigger!" Others were joining now in the jeering. "We don't want you! Get gone, nigger! Go home, black gal! Nigger! Nigger! Nigger!"

The throng had surrounded the girl; boys and girls pushed and jostled each other to stay beside her as she walked steadily, eyes straight forward, toward the school.

"Open up, I tell you!" shouted the chief into the microphone. "Get back! Give her room!"

But the surging mob of students and the sprinkling of adult hecklers swarming about the advancing girl were giving little heed to the police officer's commands. Sarah Gordon, who with Mary Lou had eased out to the portico with other teachers and some of the students, saw a leathery individual, with slumped

275

shoulders and a heavy beard darkening his pasty face, dart around the outer fringe of the crowd and sidle up to a pimple-faced youth nearing the steps to the portico. "You don't have to let no nigger go to yo' school!" she heard the fellow say to the boy. "Git in thar! What you waitin' on, boy!"

In that same instant a big boy with a large white block-A numeral on his blue sweater was clambering up the steps. "Let me give 'em a load, Chief," he said, as he stepped up to the microphone. The police chief stood aside. "Hey, listen!" the youth bellowed. "What kind of sports are you all! Six hundred to one against her." He pulled the microphone closer. "Get back! Leave her alone! She's not bothering you all!"

"We don't have to listen to your nigger-lovin' gab, Jake Miller!" the pimple-faced youth shouted defiantly. "Just because you're a football big shot don't mean nothin' to us! We ain't gonna have no nigger goin' to this school!" He ran toward the girl and with a quick lunge knocked her pocketbook from her hand. It fell with a thud to the concrete and snapped open, and some of her things rolled out; as she bent to recover it, the boy kicked the pocketbook, and guffawed contemptuously as it sailed across the esplanade, further spilling the contents as it spun away.

But the chief had seen. "Arrest that boy!" he shouted. "Take him to town and lock him up for assault!" A patrolman stepped forward and grabbed the boy's arm with one hand and clutched his belt with the other. "Come on," he said. "Let's go to the car."

The boy, his eyes wide, his defiance suddenly vanished, twisted around on tiptoe as the officer tugged at his belt. "Pa, ain't you gonna—where you, Pa?" But the bearded fellow with the stooped shoulders had lost himself in the crowd. The patrolman swung the youth around and walked him on tiptoes toward the police automobile.

Once more the police chief pulled the microphone to him. "I warned you that we'd have no disorder this morning," he said calmly. "Now I'm telling you for the last time; stand back and let that girl through."

As the crowd split quickly, one of the girls advanced into the opened lane. "Here, Ophelia," she said, as she bent above the scattered contents of the purse, "let me help you pick up your things."

6

Late in the afternoon Osborne telephoned Sarah Gordon at the teacherage. He had to run down to the city before their office closed for the day, he explained, and he wondered if she wouldn't like to go with him. They could have dinner, and go to a show afterward, if she liked, or they could ride around awhile through the residential sections; he would like to take her by to see his parents, but they hadn't returned from their home at Blowing Rock in the mountains.

And, he said, he'd like to hear how she got along at school and just what actually had happened; all day the radio had been telling, hour after hour on the news broadcasts, about the unfortunate incident that morning.

"I'd love it, Oz," she said. "Can you give me time to get a quick shower and put on something fresh?"

"Sure. If I can get down there a few minutes before the office closes at five it'll be O.K. How about thirty minutes?"

She was ready when he came by. In fact, she had already glanced over the front page of the afternoon paper which the boy had thrown on the porch just as she was coming down from her room.

"Well, how'd it go?" he asked, as they drove off. "You don't seem to have any black eyes. Did anybody offer to take a crack at the Yankee teacher?"

"No," she said, "and Ophelia's in my home room, too."

"She is? Did you have any excitement in the room? The radio said she was assaulted as she was going up the walkway to the school and also struck by an eraser thrown by someone in the crowd."

She sat up. "I'll never understand the radio and TV and the newspapers, I'm sure," she declared, with emphasis. "The paper —I was looking at it just before you came—had big headlines about this morning's incident, and you say the radio's been broadcasting it all day, and the TV, too, no doubt. And what really happened? Some students jeer a little and make some catcalls, little of it in anger actually, and one boy knocks her pocketbook out of her hand. And as far as the eraser, I hadn't even heard about that—and I watched the girl all the way from her car up to the school and I thought I saw all that happened —it was only a little rubber eraser, like those you get in pencil-box sets, you know, I found out later—in fact, the girl told me what it was; said it hit her on the shoulder and didn't hurt her. And the paper puts it in a headline, and I suppose the morning paper will do the same way, or worse." She sat back again. "I don't understand it, Oz. Haven't millions of school children had their pocketbooks, lunch boxes, books, footballs, caps, knocked out of their hands before? Haven't millions been hit with rocks, apples, books, eggs, sticks—heavens, Oz, is that worth a big headline across the front page of a newspaper, is that proper news to be sent all over the country, perhaps all over the world?"

"I think the papers must have misinterpreted that eraser business; they must have thought somebody had struck her with a blackboard eraser."

"Maybe so. But would it have been worth such a headline if she'd been hit by a—a flying saucer from Mars?" She laughed. "They couldn't have played it any bigger if that's what had happened." She leaned out again, faced him. "And there was a long story—I didn't have time to read it all—that told everything the girl did during the two or three hours we were at school— that reporter followed her into my room and watched every move she made, I remember. It even had what she ate for lunch. And my picture in the paper, too, as *her* home room teacher. I shall never get it in the paper again, I'm sure, short of murdering and dissecting the principal." Her forehead furrowed. "How do you explain it?"

"It was the first time a Negro ever enrolled as a student in a white school in North Carolina, my dear lady. And that is news. The newspapers—and the radio and TV, which do the same way, of course—say that the people want it. So you can't blame them. Or can you?"

"I don't know, I'm sure. But it does seem that the news media could lead people into an appreciation of more important things. After all, does it matter particularly whether *Miss* Cardell ate two rolls or one, or drank all her milk?"

Osborne laughed. "Perhaps it's just another manifestation of this how-silly-can-you-get age we're living in. And now this race business is getting all mixed up with the rest of the goofiness. For example, do you ever watch the fights on TV? Do they ever refer to a Negro fighter as a Negro? Of course not. They go to great pains to identify 'Butch Bongo-Bongo in the lavender trunks with the purple stripes' and 'Kid Pusho Fisto in the purple trunks with the lavender stripes,' when the best possible way would be simply to refer to the white boy and the Negro boy. But no, they think it insulting to call a Negro, a Negro. And why?" He gestured with left hand outthrust. "And do you know, the radio and TV have actually murdered one of the most beloved characters in American tradition, Old Black Joe, along with about everything that Stephen Foster ever wrote. And worse, it is destroying some of our most wonderful Americana."

"I agree. And look what is being given us in place of them."

"Sure. Elvis. What else can you say of an era, except that it's goofy, that pays a fellow like him forty-thousand a week—a week, mind you—but pays school teachers, even college professors, one-tenth of that a year?"

"Miss Cardell, the story in the paper said—I did see that—has as her number-one song choice that beautiful and inspiring offering, 'Love Me Tender.'"

"It's likewise the choice of many millions of white American teen-agers." He grinned. "It is my considered opinion that were

Presley and some half-dozen American Negro singers, men and women, and two or three others—and I'm not including such great ones as Marian Anderson, you understand—were these suddenly to lose their voices and all their records were to vanish, the American jukeboxes and record players would go silent —happy thought—and the disc jockey would become an extinct breed—more happy thought."

"You do say the funniest things, Oz. But I agree. And have you found a parallel in history? You must have."

"I'm not very familiar with the history of American music. But we've had parallels in other fields, haven't we? There were the abominable styles in women's dresses—I've seen pictures and even some of Mother's surviving ones—of the early nineteen-twenties, and there was gingerbread architecture, for instance. I suppose you could call them comparable to rock and roll." He drove along in silence, and then he ventured to risk his eyes off the road long enough to face her. "By the way, was there anything in tonight's paper about the situation in Little Rock, Arkansas? The radio announced that the Governor of Arkansas had called out the National Guard out there; said he claimed that implementation of the school board's decision to enroll nine Negro students in the high school would cause a riot. And now the troops are keeping the Negroes out."

"There was a box about it on the front page." She reflected a moment. "But didn't that North Dakota federal judge order the school authorities to proceed with the integration? Couldn't what the Governor did lead to trouble?"

"Well, I suppose it could. But I don't believe it will. The Governor of Arkansas is on the defensive. He's opposing the federal courts, he's opposing the school authorities of his own state, and he's opposing the calm, thinking, law-abiding citizens of his state. At least, that's how I see it, and it seems to be the way the commentators dope it out. The people of Arkansas generally oppose integration just as they do in this state, but they also favor upholding the law, as we do; in other words, the moderates, I'd be willing to wager, are preponderant in Arkansas too."

"But he's still got the National Guard at the school keeping the Negroes out."

"That can't last. It's just a phase. He's on the defensive and he'll have to make the first move. In a few days he'll send those boys home and the situation will settle down. If they can just keep things calm, if nobody starts throwing monkey wrenches, it'll be running smoothly in another week or so. The people in Little Rock are just like us here, and we've had no trouble, nothing of any consequence. But say," his demeanor suddenly was relaxed, "I've been preaching again. And already I've heard enough today about schools and integration and Negro students and Little Rock. Let's talk about something else, and—oh, yes, Sarah Gordon. The family will be closing the house at Blowing Rock for the summer pretty soon. Would you like to ride up there this weekend?"

"I'd love it, Oz. I'd like to meet your parents, and I'd like to see the mountains too. They must be beautiful this time of year."

"They'll be gorgeous in another few weeks, when the leaves start turning. But we can go back for that. Then we can leave after school on Friday and stay up there until Sunday night?"

"Wonderful!"

"Good! Then that's settled. Now for the next item, food. As soon as I get through at the office, and it'll take only a few minutes, let's go eat. There's a little French restaurant— You like French food?"

"Mais oui—beaucoup."

"Good. Then we'll go to Henri's. And afterward—well, we can decide while we're eating what to do next. O.K.?"

"O.K." She snuggled down into the cushions and the slipstream let go of her scarf.

They were finishing their dinner on the terrace of the Gunns' summer place which clung precariously to the cliff overlooking the gorge of the St. Johns River. They had placed Sarah Gordon's chair with its back toward the stone and chestnut-bark house so that she would be looking off west across the gorge toward Grandfather Mountain.

"It was delicious, Mrs. Gunn. And with such a view, too, it's heavenly—everything! I'm having such a wonderful time! I'm so glad Oz brought me."

"We're so glad you could come, Sarah Gordon. We want you to come again, any time you can. We will be coming up for an occasional weekend during the fall. It's gorgeous in October, when the leaves begin turning. We get the frost up here, you know, before we do at home. And it's nice in the winter, too, with open fires and snow on the slopes; it's a different world, and cold!"

"I'd love to come." She looked toward Osborne.

"I'll bring you," he said, laughing.

"And we want you to bring her to see us at home too, Oz," his mother said. "We'll be down there in another couple of weeks, maybe before."

"Thank you," the girl said. "We rode out to your home the other night and circled the driveway. It's a lovely place."

The sun was barely peeping now above the Grandfather and a sheen of golden light was beginning to outline the long, irregular summit of the great mountain, and already the shadows had deeply purpled the forests carpeting the floor and sides of the gorge.

Osborne saw that Sarah Gordon was studying the sweep of the mountain. "But why is it called Grandfather Mountain?" she wanted to know. "Because it's so old?"

"Oh, I'm sorry. I thought I'd explained. It is quite a mystery until you see why." He stood up, caught her hand. "Come over to the edge of the terrace and I'll show you.

"He's a sleeping giant, you see," he said, when they stood against the heavy railing. "He's lying on his back. Now look. His head is this way and his feet off down there. That's his head. See his forehead and nose, and his beard lying along the top of his chest? And his hands folded across his stomach. See?"

"Oh, yes, I do! It is amazing. It's just like a tremendous sleeping giant, as you said. And there are his knees," she pointed, "aren't they? And his feet?"

He nodded. "You see him now, don't you?"

"Yes. And is Grandfather Mountain really one of the oldest in the world?"

"You can't prove it by me, lady. But that's what the geologists say, so I've read. The old gentleman has been lying there on his back a long time though, I think it's safe to say."

Charles Gunn came over to them. "Young lady, I'm sorry that we have to run off this way, but the other day we promised Dr. Harrison and his wife that we'd play bridge over at their house tonight. But you and Oz—" He stopped suddenly. "By George!" He snapped his fingers. "That's it! I knew I'd heard that name!" He saw that the other three were awaiting an explanation. "It's your name, young lady. It's been bothering me ever since I heard it, subconsciously, I mean. There was something mighty familiar about it, even though it's most unusual. Now I've got it. Dr.—" he paused a moment, "Dr. Vicente, Dr. Gordon Vicente. That's it—Dr. Gordon Vicente of Philadelphia. Is he any kin of yours?"

She smiled. "He's my father. Do you know him?"

"Well, I'll be durned, girl. Talk about coincidences."

"Tell us," she said, her eyes eager.

"Well, it was four or five years ago—I guess it was longer, maybe; time passes so quickly now—anyway a group of us from this section had been to a meeting in New York of the American Cotton Manufacturers' Association and were driving home. We had stopped for the night in Philadelphia and one of our fellows became violently sick. We got the house physician and he said he had an acute case of appendicitis; said he'd have to have immediate surgery. He called up the hospital and made the arrangements, got the surgeon—"

"That was my daddy?"

"Yes, ma'am." He grinned broadly. "I remember one of us asked the hotel doctor if the surgeon was all right. 'All right?' he said. 'Hell, there's none better.' "

"I hope Daddy did a good job."

"He did. Tom was home in a week. And he's never been sick a day in his life since, as far as I know. And you're Dr. Vicente's daughter, what d'you know. You must be proud of your daddy, eh?"

"Yes, sir, I am."

"Listen, young lady, and please excuse me if this is a little personal, but I wondered at the time, I remember, is that name —are you all Spanish?"

Osborne laughed, but waited for her to reply.

"Originally, yes sir. My grandfather's grandfather, I think that's the way it was, came over from Spain as a child or young man, and the Vicentes have been in Philadelphia ever since."

"And tell him about the other side of the house," Osborne said, grinning.

"That was South Carolinian—some old Colonel Gordon— that's where Daddy got his name—from down around Charleston."

The elder Gunn shrugged. "Well, I'll be durned." He started toward the door, then turned around. "We won't be out too long—probably see you before bedtime. Look after her, Oz. Can you beat it—Dr. Vicente's daughter. And say, you all might want to ride over to Mayview Manor after awhile. There'll likely be a bunch of your friends over there, Oz."

When his parents drove off, they went inside and watched television. Then they stacked some lively numbers on the record player and danced until the stack was played out. She went over and stopped it. "Let's go out on the terrace again," she suggested, "and see how Grandfather looks under a full moon. It must be lovely out there."

They sat in the glider. The chasm below them and the Grand-father beyond it and the wisp of a feathery small cloud, motionless and dreaming, lay under the spell of the bright disk suspended above. Off to the right and down, from some mountaineer's cabin in a cove perhaps, came the barking of a dog, not raucous and disturbing but rhythmical and soothing and musical, while up to them from their left arose, as of an orchestra accompanying a singer, the softened, distant, supporting music of a college band playing a summer's dance. They sat back silent against the cushions of the glider; for a long moment they were still and silent.

Then she leaned forward and turned to look into his face. "Listen. Time has stopped, Oz. Don't you hear it? Time has been called."

He laughed, restrainedly. "I think I know what you mean. I never heard it put that way before though."

"It's fantastic! I tell you, Oz, time has stopped. Can't you hear it? Can't you feel it?"

"Yes, lady, I read you. But time's still ticking and the law of gravity is still in effect." He laughed. "If you don't believe it, throw something out into the gorge. But I know what you mean. I get that feeling sometimes up here. It's the mountains, Sarah Gordon, the thin air, and the brilliant moonlight and the silence and the great distances one can see."

"Yes, I suppose so; it's the spell, I guess." She settled back, her eyes lifted to the shining circle high above the coves and the tiny stream lost far below in the great gulch. "I can see why the ancients said she drove men mad. And, Oz, I believe—I dare think—I can understand, I can feel just one tiny bit what eternity's like. The absence of time. Up here above the gorge, looking across to old Grandfather sleeping away fifty-million years or five-hundred-million—who knows or cares?—under a bewitching moon," she thrust out her hands into the brightness, "I have the distinct feeling that time is unreal, imaginary, non-existent—"

"Well, don't the scientists say something like that? Isn't time only relative—'a thousand years are as but a day,' you know?''

"Yes, I believe so. Oh, I don't know. But, Oz, oh, isn't it wonderful? Isn't it a gorgeous night?'' She leaned closer. "I'm having such a wonderful time. And, oh, Oz, I like your dad and mother very much.''

"They like you, too. And say, wasn't it a coincidence, Dad's friend being operated on by your father?'' He laughed. "And that surely fixed you solid, eh?''

He sat up. "Would you like to run down to the Manor? We could dance. And maybe we'd run into some people.''

In the moonlight he could see the little pout. "Do we have to?''

"Of course not,'' he laughed, "if you'd rather stay here. But we can go inside, or I can get you a wrap. Aren't you getting a little chilly? Do you need a little something around your shoulders?''

She snuggled close. "Yes, I do. I want something.''

He looked into her moon-filled eyes. "My coat?''

"What must I say?''

His left arm about her shoulders, gently he pulled her down to cradle her head in the crook of his right arm, so that now she was looking up, wide-eyed and waiting, into the blaze of the watching moon.

"I see moons in your eyes,'' he said.

But in the same instant the moons were gone, lost in the shadow of his head as hungrily his lips sought hers.

8

Osborne Gunn pointed toward the gap in the iron balustrade. "I have an idea we could get that foundry in town to make us a section that would match the rest.''

" 'Tain't no use to see 'bout that, Mist' Gunn,'' Uncle Lem said. "You can put the old one back; it's out there in the ca'-iage house, and the big i'on front gate's out there too.''

"Good! How'd they happen to be saved?''

"Them bolts that holds the sections together got rusted out and it was leaning out bad, and I jus' took it down. I been aimin' to git some new bolts but I jus' ain't done it. And the gate was draggin' bad, so I took it down, too. But if you built some new brick posts, 'twouldn't be no trouble to hang up the gate agin. And 'fore I fergit, Mist' Gunn," Lem's excitement was mounting, too, "it's some cream bricks in the old ca'iage house what musta been left over when the big house was built; you could take them bricks and fix up that crack in the heart at the end o' the house. And it's plenty red bricks from the burnt-down old kitchen house you could use to fix the crack in the house wall too."

"Uncle Lem, I believe you really want me to buy this place."

"I ain't gonna tell you no lie, Mist' Gunn; I do wish you'd buy it and fix it up, and let me stay on the place and help look after it. You see," he paused, "Jim he wants to move to town and buy him a little house. It'd be nea'er to his work."

"But then Ophelia would have to transfer from her school."

"I know it, yes, sir. But that's another reason Jim he wants to move."

"Isn't Ophelia getting along all right?"

"I don't think she's doin' no good. Them white chaps is too far ahead o' her."

"But she could drop back maybe and catch up."

Lem shook his head. "I don't think she'd want to do that. It'd hurt her pride. But if she went to a colored-folks's school in town she could keep up all right." He looked across the disordered yard sweltering in the late September heat. "Mist' Gunn, Feelie ain't never wanted to go to the white-folks's school nohow. It was Claib Henderson pushin' 'em mostly's why she went. She's been goin' 'bout three weeks now and she ain't doin' no good." He turned troubled eyes to Sarah Gordon for support. "Ain't you her teacher, Miss? Ain't that right 'bout her?"

"I'm only her home-room teacher, but I'd agree that she is somewhat behind the others."

Lem nodded his head. "And another thing, she's away from her friends; she jus' ain't where she b'longs, Mist' Gunn."

"But maybe Henderson wouldn't want her to change schools."

"He wouldn't want her to go back to the colored-folks's school up here. He'd figger that'd be backin' down. But if Jim moved to town, that'd be diffe'nt."

"I can see your point. But, listen, Uncle Lem, if I bought this big house and fixed it up—" his grin overspread his face, "what in the world would I do with it?"

The Negro studied Osborne a moment and then the girl. He turned back to face his questioner. "I 'spect you done figgered 'bout that."

"But it takes two to figure that sort of a proposition, you know."

Lem glanced at the girl again. "You right, yes sir. But I sorta 'spect you both done been figgerin'."

"You think so, eh?" Osborne, laughing, glanced at Sarah Gordon. "But if we should want this place, could you give us a good title to it?"

"As clear as yo' hand, Mist' Gunn. You can go down to the cou't house and look it up. Ain't nothin' 'g'in' this place nowheres."

"But what ever happened to the heirs that sold out to your folk, Uncle Lem? In fact, what ever became of the doctor's children, besides your mother, I mean?"

"Well, sir, I don't reckon none of 'em done much good. Of course, I never knowed much 'bout 'em. The only one I knowed besides Ma was the one they called Julie, but she died when I was jus' a chap, 'bout the same time Ma did. The baby boy, I heared tell, went to town and died pretty young; he never got married, I don't think. The other two boys got killed, one of 'em in a fight and t'other one got hung for killin' a white man, I heared tell when I was a chap. Wasn't none o' them married neither and didn't leave no heirs is the way I heared it told; that left Ma and Aunt Julie and one daughter which went north and ain't never been heared from."

"But maybe she had heirs and that would put a cloud on the property."

"I don't know 'bout no heirs she mighta had. But that wouldn't make no diffe'nce because the doctor had done give the one that went north her part 'fore he died. And my daddy and ma bought out Aunt Julie—she was Claib Henderson's grandma—and so when my daddy and ma died, the place come to me clear as yo' hand, with nothin' 'g'in' it."

Osborne turned to the girl. "Sarah Gordon, we'd better be getting back; it'll soon be your suppertime." He faced the Negro. "I'll tell you what, Uncle Lem. I'll try to find out if I might need this house and then I'll be back to see you; in the meantime, don't you let anybody else have it."

"No, sir. I want you to git it; I want it fixed up fine, like it musta been way back yonder 'fore I was borned."

They drove out between the moldering bricks that once had been the proud gateposts. At the highway they turned south, and the lowering sun was still warm on their cheeks beneath the air stream over the windshield.

"You really intend to buy the house, don't you?" she asked, as she snuggled lower.

"I really do. It'll take some money, but it can be made a gorgeous place, finer even than Charlie's; it was more pretentious to start with than the Osborne house."

"You want it, too, because it could have been yours anyway, don't you?"

"I suppose so. I should have been the old doctor's great grandson."

"But then you wouldn't have had the blankets, eh?"

"Meaning I'd probably be sticking thermometers into young-'uns' mouths and some other fellow's family would be making blankets?"

"I don't see how you could legitimately be the great-grandson of two men with the same wife."

289

He laughed. "Remarkable reasoning. Sarah Gordon, you're a genius."

"But if you had been the doctor's great-grandson and inherited it, you wouldn't have had enough money likely to fix it up."

"But I wouldn't have let it get rundown in the first place." He looked her way, slyly. "Won't it be a wonderful place to live? Close to the mill here and less than half an hour from the main office in town—if I ever have to be there, heaven forbid—running it, I mean."

He had been watching an approaching transport truck, and now it roared past; he could turn to her momentarily. "You know, Sarah Gordon, if you—I don't mean just you, I mean anybody—really knew the story of that old house back there, if he knew it and comprehended it, really appreciated it, he'd know the South." He gave his attention to the road, but he continued to talk. "If he knew the story of the old Cardell place, he'd really understand, for instance, the desperate earnestness of those who are fighting integration in the public schools, the sincere, dedicated persons, I mean, not those blatant opportunists who grab segregation as a banner under which to advance themselves politically or economically, you know."

A car filled with teenagers was coming up behind; he let it speed by and returned the wave of several grinning youngsters who had recognized their teacher. "Yes, sir, the whole Southern story is wrapped up in Holly Grove—had I told you that was its name in the doctor's day and before? It's a fact," he hadn't waited for her to reply, "the whole romantic, fearful, tragic, desperate, earthy and idealistic, promising, violent, ugly and glorious, hopeless, despairing and yet eternally hopeful story," he was punctuating his adjectives with taps of his right fist on the steering wheel as he drove with his left hand, "has happened and is happening and will happen right back there in that old brick house. A fellow who could write could tell the South's story, make it comprehensible, I do believe, by relating the story of Holly Grove. What an article or series of articles maybe for, say, *The Atlantic*, or better, what a novel—"

"Why don't you write it, Oz?"

"I? I'm no writer."

"You've just shown that you're a poet." She grinned. Then she was serious again. "And miscegenation, I suppose, would be the theme, the framework?"

"It would be a big part. And it should be. It's a big part of the Southern story."

"But isn't miscegenation now more bugaboo than fact? Isn't talk of the dangers of miscegenation mostly talk, excuses—"

"Yes, and no," he interrupted. "But I'm afraid it will take a long speech to clarify my answer, if I can. Are you prepared to endure it?"

"I'll try."

Her frankness amused him. "Well, I'd say that miscegenation *is* more bugaboo than fact. I think that it can be shown that percentagewise there is far less mixing of the races now than there was, say, immediately preceding the War Between the States and even in Reconstruction times and later. But on the other hand, I believe that the *fear* of miscegenation is growing in the South. Certainly many people sincerely feel that the danger is increasing, and integration in the public schools, they honestly believe, will bring about a widespread increase that will grow with the relaxing of segregation. I do myself."

He turned to her to hear her comment. "Go on," she said.

"You see, in the old days, much of the race mixing was a white-master-and-slave-wench affair; it came about usually as the result of the slave woman's being in the master's home as a servant or in a slave cabin close by, so easily available, you might say, and she was his slave; she had to submit whether she wanted to or not, though, I suspect, she was usually quite willing. And in those days, too, it was not frowned on to the extent it is now. I have an idea that the Holly Grove story was something like that. This mulatto woman, who was probably the daughter of some slave owner, was likely the doctor's house servant; she very probably was attractive physically—"

"I don't see how—" the girl shuddered. "I just don't see how any white man—" She stopped, her eyes fixed on the road ahead.

"But some always have, my dear," he said, "and when they begin going to school together and then after awhile to school parties, and a Negro boy gets to be the star halfback or the best dancer or singer of rock and roll—which he likely would be, well—" He shrugged. "That's what the South is seeing now in her nightmares."

"But, Oz, Southern white boys and girls wouldn't—"

"Wouldn't they? Huh. Already they are having conferences of one sort and another, youth movements in education, international relations, and so on, whites and Negroes together, in the South, mind you, on college campuses where they stay in the same dormitories—they still keep the sexes separate, of course, in the dormitories, I mean—they eat at the same tables, they loll about on the campus lawns together." He turned perplexed eyes upon her. "Would it surprise you to know that right here in this state they had a conference of representatives of the various colleges and universities, a number of them, and passed a resolution favoring the repeal of the state law forbidding the intermarriage of whites and Negroes?"

"Heavens, Oz, you don't mean "

"I most certainly do mean it. It was spread all over the newspapers. Some grownups dismissed the incident with the explanation that the college students were merely kidding, having fun at the expense of their elders, trying to shock them. Whereupon the college students declared solemnly that they had been entirely serious." He slowed for a car entering the highway ahead. "So—well, what are you going to do about it?" He was silent a moment and so was she. "Maybe the answer is to do what the students advocated, throw out all laws that would tend to put a check on race mixing. Is that the answer—a hybrid citizenship? What do you think?"

She was shaking her head sternly. "I can't see that, Oz. I have a horror of mixed blood. I cannot imagine anything more terrible."

"Many liberals, so called, are advocating it. They say to let everybody marry anyone he wishes to. They argue that very few mixed marriages actually would result. Maybe not, but I wonder. Some of them say it would be better that way. Let the races amalgamate and thereby end the race problem." He shrugged. "But races have been going pretty strong since the days of Ham, eh? And I figure they'll continue in pretty definite patterns. Heaven knows, I hope so." He turned his head to face her. "Remember, Sarah Gordon, this is no Southern problem alone; it's national. The only reason it's always hitting us between the eyes is because we have the Negroes. As they begin to migrate North in increasing numbers you'll understand it up there. And the difficulties will be worse. Look at Detroit, or Levittown, look at Chicago, where they're rolling in by the thousands. You'll have it worse because you don't understand them. You haven't lived with them. And you don't have as much sympathy for them; you don't love 'em. You pass laws and write editorials and you go to school with 'em and eat with 'em—in some places but you really don't give a merry damn about them, do you, as people, I mean, friends, even beloved friends, do you?"

"You're right, Oz, I agree. But don't say you, and so viciously."

"I didn't mean to be vicious. And I was only saying you, well, editorially." His solemnity vanished in a wide grin. "We aren't vicious in the South. It's just that sometimes we get impatient at the refusal of our critics, who don't understand us or our situation, to be patient, to help us work the problem out —actually, the only solution is for it to work itself out, and that takes time. We get impatient when they refuse to hold back their rocks and monkey wrenches while we're trying to oil the machinery." He visibly relaxed, settled back. "It's nice riding this time of day, isn't it? And say," he was quickly serious again, "I hope I don't sound completely pessimistic. As a matter of fact, I'm not looking for any monkey wrenches to be thrown.

Everything being considered, people are keeping pretty level-headed, don't you think?"

"Maybe, in this state. But how about Little Rock?"

"Oh, that's already blown over with the governor's pulling out the National Guardsmen. All he was waiting for was a way out, and the judge's injunction gave him one. There may be a little disorder, but the Little Rock authorities will be able to handle the situation, just as ours did. If people keep their heads, not only in Little Rock but all over the country, and let the steam blow off, the situation out there in a week or two will be as calm as it is around here."

"But if you are right about that, won't it upset your theory about history's repeating itself. In Reconstruction times, remember, there was a victorious soldier in the White House and he let the hotheads and vengeance-bent and the political opportunists get control, didn't he? And now there's another soldier, tremendously popular—"

"But Ike's no Grant. I didn't vote for him, but I have a high respect for him as a man. I believe he's a dedicated leader, and he's patient, not quick to jump the traces—"

"But how about his advisers? Doesn't the President depend on them a lot—too much maybe?"

"Well, he was brought up on the Army system of operating through staff, and that's not good, I think, in politics. But in this matter Ike has staked himself out. You remember when the civil-rights issue was going red hot in Congress and some of the southerners warned of the possible use of federal troops in upholding civil-rights laws should the proposed legislation be enacted, the President declared emphatically that he couldn't imagine any set of circumstances that would ever induce him to send federal troops into any area to enforce the orders of a federal court?"

"Yes, I remember reading that. But—"

"You can depend on Ike, lady. He'll keep his head. He'll never paint himself into a corner like Grant did." He was turning into the driveway at the teacherage. "The lecture's over. Well, you asked for it."

"Stay and eat with us, Oz," she invited.

"No, thanks, not this time," he said. "But I will run in with you and use the phone, if I may."

As he entered, Mary Lou handed him the evening paper. "They've been raising the devil out in Little Rock," she said.

"Funny, Sarah Gordon and I were talking about that as we drove up." He scanned the black headlines. "Pretty rough, eh? Well, it'll all blow over in a day or two."

"Some of the columnists claim that the governor's actions have actually invited the disorder today."

"Could be. But whatever his motives, he's played out his hand now. The local authorities will have the situation under control; the citizens out in Little Rock, like ours, are against integration but they believe in upholding the law. They won't flout the law and the courts."

9

The next morning Osborne telephoned Walter Loye.

"I'm pretty excited about an old house I've discovered up this way, Walt," he revealed. "I believe you'll be, too, as soon as you see it. I want your advice about it, and if you agree with me that I've got on to something good, I'll want you to do the restoration job for me. I wonder if you couldn't run up late this afternoon and let me take you over there for a preliminary look?"

By four o'clock Loye was at the plant, and Osborne drove him out to the old Cardell place. For an hour they went over the house, floor by floor; they went into the great chamber on the top floor, where Osborne saw the sheeted furniture. "I want to have a good look at it the first chance I get," he told Lem Cardell. "And this goes with the house, if I buy the place?"

"Yes, sir, Mist' Gunn. It wouldn't b'long nowheres but right here in this house."

The three walked around the house and into the basement, where they carefully examined the walls, the interior supporting brick pillars, the huge sills and joists. With his pocketknife the architect pecked at the hand-hewn timbers. In the same way he had examined the rafters. He closed his knife and pocketed it. "Well, Oz, I've seen all I need to. You want to go out to the car and talk it over?"

"Yes." He caught the Negro's arm. "Much obliged for showing us around, Uncle Lem. I'll probably be back to see you pretty soon."

They climbed into the convertible. "Well, Walt, what do you think of it?"

"I just wish I'd found it first—and had the money to buy it and fix it up the way it should be done. Oz, it's fabulous. The timbers are sound as a dollar, and the walls, too, except for that crack in the south wall; and it's nothing serious, structurally, I mean. That earthquake must have been sixty or seventy years ago—"

"Eighteen eighty-six, I think."

"Well, you know the house has done all the settling it'll ever do. And with that old brick out there it can be fixed so you'd never know there'd ever been a crack."

"What'll it cost me, Walt?"

The architect laughed. "I thought you'd be getting around to that. Well, Oz, it could cost very little to do an adequate job of restoration, or it could cost a lot. It depends on how far you want to go. If you went all the way, like getting authentic reproductions of those bits of wallpaper we found—"

"Could you do that?"

"Yes, it can be done—if a fellow's willing to pay for it. You'll have to install plumbing, of course, and that means a drilled deep well, and, if you want to go all out, designing fixtures to harmonize with the period of the house—special stuff, of course. And the same way with the wiring, which will have to be done over throughout and concealed; you can have fixtures of any price you wish. This house can take them, Oz, those gorgeous chandeliers with cut-glass prisms," he was gesturing, as his enthusiasm grew with his envisioning "skillfully worked-out, indirect lighting that dims or goes up with the touching of an ingeniously concealed switch, well, any number of interesting features, Oz." He looked his friend in the eyes. "But, fellow, it would take a lot of blankets."

"But I'd have something when I got through, eh?"

"Listen, Oz, it would cost a lot of money to do it that way, but you'd have a mansion, really a mansion, when we got through with it. There's nothing comparable to this house in this part of the country, as far as I know, except Cedar Grove."

"Cedar Grove?"

"It's over west of here. It's another federal period house, built in the 1830s, I think. The great grandson of the builder is living there now and he has been restoring it. It's three-story, brick, with basement, too, and it's a beautiful house. But what amazes me about this one, Oz, is how well it has been preserved, even though Negroes apparently have been living in it a long time. Usually, as you know, they let a house go down mighty fast."

"Old Lem loves it; that's the reason. You see, Walt—well, it's a long story and some time I'll tell you the details—but his mother was the illegitimate daughter of the country doctor who owned it, he had a houseful of mulatto children by his quadroon Negro housekeeper and cook; the woman and her children lived in the kitchen house which was back there," he pointed, "and years ago was burned. By the way, Walt, could we duplicate that old house? The foundations are still there and Lem very likely remembers it well."

"Why not? That would complete the Holly Grove layout as it was originally." He reached over, slapped Osborne lightly on the knee. "It would just take more blankets, Oz."

"O.K. When you starting?"

"I can start any time. But hadn't you better buy the place first?"

"I'm going to do that in the next few days."

quate restoration—plumbing, new wiring, patching up the plaster, replacing banisters in the stairway, sanding the paint off that paneling, you know, that sort of job, or a really de-luxe one? I've got to know before I start, of course. You'd better be thinking about it."

"I want you to do it the way you'd do it, Walt, if," he grinned, "if you had the blankets. But I'm not inviting you to soak me, understand."

The architect's forehead wrinkled. "There's just one thing, Oz, that's got me a little puzzled. You know, the restored Holly Grove will be a mighty fancy place, with that superb stairway and gorgeous ballroom, and all the rest, and a mighty big one, for one lone bachelor to be living in all by himself."

"Well, it just might turn out that I'll have that problem solved before you have the house ready."

"Really, Oz?" His eyebrows lifted. "Who is she, this time?"

"This *is* the time, Walt. She's a little Yankee gal from Philadelphia."

"Wonderful! I hadn't heard."

"I've just known her myself since the first of September. She's one of the new teachers at the high school. But this is it, Walt. And say, by the way, I want her to be in on this house-planning business, too. She loves the old house; it has a tremendous fascination for her as well as for me. I wonder," he paused, reflecting, "Saturday morning we'll both be free. Could you meet us and the three of us look over the place again? Sarah Gordon will have some good ideas. And I want you to meet her anyway."

"Saturday morning? Sure, I can do it; I'll be glad to, Oz."

At the mill office Walter Loye changed to his car to return to town, and Osborne drove on to the teacherage.

10

She was coming toward him along the hallway. "Say," he called out excitedly, "I've just made a deal with the architect to do meet him Saturday." He stopped, his enthusiasm suddenly lost. "You don't seem very interested," he added glumly.

"Oh, but I am, Oz." She ventured a smile, and immediately was serious again. "But have you had your car radio on lately?"

"No, Walt and I have been talking about the house. Why? What's happened?"

"The President has ordered federal troops into Little Rock."

"No!"

"Yes. He's federalized the Arkansas National Guard, and the Army is flying in the 101st Airborne."

"The paratroopers!"

"Yes. The troops will escort the Negro children into and out of school and they'll stay in Little Rock as long as necessary, the radio's been saying. The President is speaking on TV tonight to explain."

"I don't get it!" His scowl was more of bewilderment than passion. "It hasn't been more than a couple of months since he declared he couldn't imagine any circumstances that would cause him to call out troops to enforce a court order. We were talking about it yesterday, remember."

"Yes. But, well, he did."

Osborne declined their invitation to remain for dinner; he explained that he had to go back to the office to make some telephone calls. He made a date with Sarah Gordon for Saturday morning's visit to Holly Grove.

At the dinner table the President's drastic action was the subject of lively discussion. One girl was sarcastically critical.

"But do you think the President should have sat back and let that mob flout the judge's orders?" a teacher across the table asked her.

"Are you going to call out federal troops every time somebody disobeys a federal judge, for heaven's sake? Why couldn't he have waited a few days, to say the least, and given the local authorities a chance to restore order? They had Faubus in the crack; now he's not only let the governor out, but he's made a hero of him with a lot of folk in Arkansas and throughout the

South. Why'd he risk starting another War Between the States just to make sure that nine little niggers got to go to a white school?"

"It's not that simple, Jane. I don't understand it all, of course—"

"Who does?" Mary Lou interjected.

"That's it, who does? But Jane isn't laying out the issues right, I know that much. And the President wouldn't have taken such a serious step if he hadn't thought he was right."

"Sure. He *thought* he was right, of course," Jane persisted.

"I think he got a bum steer," one of the men observed. "He's too disposed to operate through staff—the Army way, you know."

"Well, all his experience has been in the military."

"Sure. But a President can't run the country like a general runs a division. A general doesn't have to listen to anybody under him; a president has to listen to everybody under him; in fact, nobody's under him; everybody's over him really, and on election day everybody has his say, you know."

"That's right," another teacher agreed. "But, still, don't you think it'll all settle down without any great violence—like another Reconstruction period and a new set of South-haters and all that—and that the common sense of both the President and the people of Little Rock will come out on top?"

"Then you're supporting the invading of Arkansas by federal troops?"

"There you go again, Jane," heatedly declared the girl who a moment before had challenged her. "Twisting things, oversimplifying. Who said federal troops had invaded Arkansas?"

Jane smiled icily. "Well, the Governor of Arkansas, for one. And thousands of other folk. What would *you* call it? The troops came from the outside, didn't they? And they came forcibly, didn't they? What, dearie, would you call it but invasion?"

"There you go, twisting, twisting. I don't see—"

"And I wasn't addressing you anyway," Jane interrupted. She turned to confront the man who had been giving his observations. "Jim, you think he got a bum steer, you said. Do you think he was deliberately steered wrong?"

"Oh, I wouldn't say that at all. Certainly I'm not supporting him or those who advised him to take such action, any more than I was supporting the governor in using troops to keep the Negroes out. And I'm not saying that the governor wasn't sincere in contending that he was trying only to preserve order. I'm making no charges and I think we Southerners particularly should make none. I do think the President acted hastily, and probably illegally, and certainly out of character; I believe he blundered tragically. But I think he was misled, and furthermore, I am sure he thought he was taking the right course; I'm certain no leader in the world acts with more sincerity and more dedication." He relaxed into a broad grin. "And, Jane, I didn't vote for him either time."

11

"As I see it now," Walter Loye told Osborne and Sarah Gordon after Saturday morning's room-by-room examination of the Holly Grove mansion house and visits with Lem to the stables and carriage house, "this restoration project involves four distinct jobs—five, if you include landscaping of the grounds. Check with me."

Osborne nodded. "Go ahead."

"Well—and this isn't necessarily in the order they should be done, of course; in fact, much of the work can go on simultaneously. But there's the restoration of the mansion house, which, of course, is the major item, and potentially the costliest, though in the case of the house the amount you spend may vary a great deal, as I said the other day; it's according to whether you want an adequate job or an all-out one. Well, that's number one. Then there's the building of the old kitchen house as the guest house; that's a completely new structure, of course, from foundations to roof. The building, or rather renovation and enlargement, of the carriage house to serve as garage and servants' quarters is still another job. And last, there's the renovation of the stables. Is that the way you see it, Oz?"

"Yes, and the fixing up of the grounds, as you suggested, after the building part is finished."

"That's right. Now I can get on the plans right away, and how long it will take me to finish them depends upon how far you wish to go into this restoration business. If you give me a little time, and the contractors, of course, it won't cost as much, naturally. But," the beginning of a smile lifted the corners of his mouth and his eyes narrowed as he looked at one and then the other, "that depends, too, on when you want to have this place ready for occupancy." His gaze fixed on the girl.

She laughed, but nevertheless colored a trace. "Ask Oz," she said. "He's the one who's planning to buy the place."

"*I'd* like to have it ready as quickly as possible," Osborne declared, grinning.

"I don't blame you, Oz." Then he was serious again. "There'll be no difficulty about the stables. Actually, there'll be little to do to them except repair them. I should think you wouldn't want to make many changes. The lines are excellent, I think. You agree?"

"Yes, I wouldn't want them changed. And I'd like to preserve the present lines of the old carriage house as much as possible."

"Sure, Oz. I agree. It will have to be enlarged somewhat to accommodate the cars and to provide adequate servants' rooms above, but that can be done with a little careful planning so that the general effect will be the same. And that won't be any difficult job." He paused. "That leaves us with the rebuilding of the kitchen house and the restoration of the mansion house itself."

"Can we get brick for it that will match the mansion house?"

"Sure, Oz, so close to it that you could hardly tell the difference. The problem will be aging them, of course. But ivy will help do that trick." He considered a moment. "And one good thing about it—the kitchen house was burned fifty years ago, wasn't it? So nobody living, outside of Lem maybe, even remembers it. We can plan it to fill your needs; all we have to look out for is keeping it contemporary with the mansion house, you see."

"Then we can have more rooms than the kitchen house—" She stopped, her cheeks coloring. "Editorial *we*, I mean, you know."

The architect laughed. "When have I seen a girl blush? Say, you know, Sarah Gordon, that's the restoration of a lost art. It'll be in perfect keeping with the restored house, eh, Oz?" He turned back to face the girl, serious again. "That's right, we can have whatever we want in the guest house, so long as we keep it in the period and in proportion, of course. For instance, a living room with open fireplace, three or four bedrooms, baths, a small kitchen so guests can make their coffee, midnight snacks, maybe breakfast."

"That would be wonderful! They'd like that, I know."

"And we wouldn't have them under our feet all the time," Osborne added. "I'd like that."

"That leaves the big job—the house itself," said Walter. "It won't take so much work and time to put the house in good shape, as I said. There will be the wiring and plumbing, plastering, a great deal of sanding, of course, papering and painting—the big things. But that can go along pretty fast. The things that will slow us—if you want to do them—will be the special touches. And, frankly, they'll make the house."

"Like that wallpaper you were talking about the other day, eh? And lighting fixtures? They'd have to be specially made, would they?"

"Very likely, Oz. But sometimes we run into a piece of good luck and locate matching wallpaper, for instance, or maybe a fixture like we want or so nearly like it that it will do. I deal with an interior decorator in New York who is an authority on wallpaper. We can steam off a section of that paper in the parlor near the ceiling—I notice that a bit of the border's still there too—and send it to her, and it may be that she'll have enough of that very pattern to do over the room. But if she hasn't, she can send to France and have it duplicated."

"But wouldn't that take a mighty long time?"

"Several months, if it has to be made. But we could be virtually finished, with the exception of the papering, when we did get it." He was thoughtful a moment. "I believe we can be through with the whole business in late spring, Oz—if I get right to work on it."

"But it will be a few weeks, maybe longer, before you'll have the plans done and ready to let them out for bids, won't it?"

Loye's forehead crinkled, his eyes narrowed. "I could do that on the guest house, all right. But on the others, and especially the mansion house, I think it'll be best for you to let me do it on a cost-plus basis, if you want me to do it, of course."

"Sure, I want you to do it; you know that, Walt. And I can see how that's the most practicable way to handle it, since we'll probably be adding things and changing them around as we go along. So—well, Walt, consider yourself hired, and let's get going."

12

During the remaining weeks of the fall and early winter the work moved fast. Osborne and Sarah Gordon spent several afternoons each week, when he was not away on business for the mill, out at Holly Grove. His parents had closed their mountain home and opened the town house early in October, and on an occasional pleasant Sunday he had driven her down for Sunday dinner with the elder Gunns. And Osborne and Sarah Gordon had joined young Charles and Janet for the Thanksgiving Day festivities at their parents' home and afterward had gone to the football game at the stadium.

By the first week in December the stables were finished and the carpenters had almost completed their work on the carriage house.

"The stables apparently were never painted, Oz," Walter pointed out one afternoon as the two were inspecting the work. "I think they should stay that way. I had in mind treating all the exposed wood with a colorless preservative to which we'd add a touch of grayish-brown stain to give it a weathered effect. For one reason, I don't want it to compete in any sense—as it might do if it were painted white or barn-red, for instance—with the mansion house itself."

Osborne quickly had agreed. "But we ought to paint the carriage house, don't you think," he had hastened to suggest, "since it's near the front gate—sort of a porter's-lodge appearance—and is really a part of the house, you might say?"

"Oh, yes, of course, though it should also be given a slightly weathered look, I feel. We want it to be in tone with the house, but somewhat subdued; it ought to be white, but not a glistening, resplendent white, if you see what I mean. Everything must contribute to making the mansion house the jewel in the setting."

The masons were making progress on the construction of the guest house; by the time they had to stop for an occasional below-freezing day, since freezing of the mortar would destroy its bonding qualities, the one-story walls had reached to the tops of the window openings.

They had decided on three bedrooms, each large and with a commodious walk-in closet; two baths; a small kitchen with stove and refrigerator; and a big pine-paneled living room with a wide, open fireplace.

"It'll be a dream," Sarah Gordon exclaimed when she first saw Walt's drawings. "And it certainly should be large enough to accommodate all the guests anyone might ever have."

"I should think so," Osborne agreed. "But there are still three extra bedrooms in the mansion house—and the ballroom, which we could fill with army cots." His eyes were teasing. "I don't think we'll need any more room, surely for a long time, eh?"

Lem and his wife were living now in the tenant house that Osborne, in purchasing Holly Grove, had reserved to him for his lifetime, and Jim had moved his family to town, where Ophelia had quietly transferred to the new Negro high school Sarah Gordon had seen that first day on her ride up from the airport. "She's gittin' on fine," Lem had reported when Osborne inquired; "she's with her own crowd, Mist' Gunn; she ought never left 'em nohow; but it weren't the child's fault; it was that Claib Henderson pushin' Jim and his wife."

Installation of the plumbing and the rewiring of the mansion house were started soon after the Negroes moved out, so that this phase of the restoration would be completed before the carpenters, masons, and decorators should begin their renovating. Then one Saturday morning, a few weeks before Christmas, the architect brought good news.

"That interior decorator in New York has discovered enough of that floral pattern—in the parlor, you know—to do the whole room, including the border. It'll likely be here before we're ready for it. And she wrote also that the French manufacturer to whom she sent that swatch we steamed off the dining-room has assured her he can supply us, though he'll have to make it, and that will take time. We should get it by late spring, she thought." He evidenced his delight. "I was certainly glad to get that information. I was afraid we might run into considerable difficulty getting those particular patterns. And that leaves us with only one other hurdle, a pretty big one. And that's the matter of electrical fixtures. What do you have in mind?"

"Walt, you're the architect. What do *you* have in mind?"

"Well, this is what I'd like to do. We've been faithful to the old house thus far, even to the wallpaper. But we cannot be faithful in the matter of light fixtures, since the house had none to begin with. But we can be faithful to the period and select fixtures that wouldn't do it violence. What I'd like to do, then, would be to install fixtures similar to ones that have been installed in other great houses that have been restored, houses of the period of Holly Grove, I mean."

"What, Walt?"

"Well, naturally I've been studying houses of that era. The other day I was looking through Pratt's book on early American homes, checking particularly on lighting fixtures in the houses illustrated. I saw several that I think would admirably suit Holly Grove's requirements. Some of them may be in houses a few years older than ours, but that will make little difference. Houses of that day didn't have electric lighting, of course, so there is no authentic fixture for that period. But of course we can provide electric chandeliers, for instance, that look very much like the actual chandeliers used in that era of lighting. There are houses, for example, in Charleston and New Orleans and Natchez, up in Virginia around Charlottesville, in Richmond and up and down the James River; there's the Read house in New Castle, Delaware, built in 1801, I believe, and probably about the same age as Holly Grove—I'm thinking of the gorgeous candle chandelier in the dining room there, and, incidentally, the scenic wallpaper in that same room might give ideas for the wallpaper I'd like to put up the stairway all the way to the third floor. And in Fairmount Park, Philadelphia, there are some palatial old houses—"

"Of course!" Sarah Gordon exclaimed. "I've been in them! That beautiful candle chandelier in the great music room of Strawberry that hangs above the circular, red-satin sofa, for example. And another one, less ornate but more graceful, also candled, in the Lemon Hill drawing room; and a beautiful one in brass, it must be, simple and with only four candles, but dignified and impressive looking, in the drawing room of Woodford, where, they told us, Benjamin Franklin often came to tea! Oh, Oz, one like that in dark bronze would be just lovely in the library, wouldn't it?"

"Great!" Walter Loye was sharing her enthusiasm. "I'd forgotten about your being from Philadelphia. Now if you'd have another look at those houses and select the types of fixtures you'd like."

"But Oz will have to do that!" She faced him, her eyes flaming. "Oz, you'll just have to see them!" For support she turned back to the architect. "Walt, don't you think he should? It's his house, and the library den will be his own retreat, you know. I've been trying to get him to promise to run up at Christmas to visit my parents. Now, he just must!"

Walter, nodding solemnly, winked. "Yes, I agree. It's highly important—necessary, I'd say—for Oz to have a look at those houses in Fairmount Park."

13

The county schools closed for the holidays on the Friday afternoon before Christmas, and Osborne drove Sarah Gordon down to the airport to catch the four-forty-five plane for Philadelphia.

The schools would reopen the day after New Year's. Osborne would drive up for her on the Saturday or Sunday after Christmas. He'd get a three-day visit with the Vicentes and then the two would leave early on the morning of the first and have an easy drive south.

At the gate he kissed her good-by. "Sure, I'll be there," he promised. "And I'll be careful. Now you have a wonderful time!"

And he had fulfilled his promise. He had driven up on the Saturday after Christmas—he hadn't been able to wait longer—and immediately on his arrival he and the girl's parents had found themselves on an old-time friends' basis. Sarah Gordon already had told her father of Charles Gunn's having remembered about the appendicitis operation, and Dr. Vicente in referring to it had inquired about the manufacturer's health.

"I hope my repair job on him has held up," he had commented.

"It evidently has, sir. The last time my dad saw him, which was this past fall, I believe, he was thriving."

They had made a hurried trip about the city. "I thought you'd surely want to visit Independence Hall, since you're so crazy about history," she had observed.

"No, I don't care to see it again," he had declared. "I'd rather spend more time looking over those houses you and Walt were talking about. We might get some good ideas, you know."

So they had gone out to Fairmount Park. And now, armed

with notes Sarah Gordon had taken, and pictures and souvenir booklets they had purchased after talking with the various curators and guides, they were returning home.

"Oh, Oz," she said suddenly, "we aren't but a few blocks from it. I'd like for you to see the old house." She pointed quickly. "Turn here. And at the next intersection, turn left and it's just two or three blocks. It's not far out of the way."

He followed her instructions. At the second street crossing after they had turned left, she pointed again. "Slow up, Oz. There. That's the old Vicente town house."

Osborne saw a narrow, three-storied house of red brick and weathered, smoke-stained brownstone quoins and window sills, standing forlorn in its faded grandeur; a small, gasoline-service station squeezed between it and the side street on the left, and hulking row houses leaned against it on the right, flaunting vulgarly on their ground floors a pawn shop and an unkempt restaurant from which was pouring juke-box rock-and-roll. He didn't look farther along the blighted row.

"Of course, it's terribly deteriorated now—the neighborhood," she hastened to explain. "But when Grandmother Cleo lived here as a bride and in the years before that this was *the* neighborhood. But places, like people, you know, go up and down, don't they?"

"Yes," he said. "But you can tell that once it was a fine place —solid and stern, and righteous, or maybe pious." He regarded her with narrowed eyes, quizzically. "Were the Vicentes like that?"

"I don't know," she said. "I hope not. Certainly they aren't now."

"Who owns it now?" They had driven past. He indicated with a backward nod. "The old house, I mean?"

"Oh, I'd meant to tell you. In a way, it's still in the family. Daddy couldn't see to disposing of it. So he deeded it to the Vicente Foundation. That's a foundation to promote medical research, help charitable projects—you know, that sort of thing. The old house is now the Cleo Gordon Home."

"Home for what?"

"For unwed mothers. You know, a place where girls can go while they are waiting. And stay after the babies are born, until they can get adjusted. Daddy named it for his mother. I guess it's his particular pet; he gives a lot of personal attention to it."

He looked toward her and all the teasing in his eyes was gone. "Sarah Gordon, you must be mighty proud of your dad. You should be."

"I am," she agreed.

Late that evening they were sitting alone in the library. She snuggled close against him, caught his hand in her left palm, with her right forefinger traced the veins on the back of his hand. "Oz," she said coyly, "I'm afraid to—to— I've been putting it off. I'm just afraid."

He clasped his free hand over hers. "What you mean, afraid?" His eyes mirrored his sudden concern. "What's happened, honey?"

"It's—it's about my Christmas present, the one Daddy and Mother gave me. I don't know whether to accept it."

"What d'you mean? You haven't already got it? Christmas is over, remember?" His countenance revealed relief but no understanding. "For heaven's sake, what did they give you?"

"You see, Oz, I hadn't told them—about us, I mean, about the wedding, you know, in June, I mean," she paused, smiling shyly. "I was waiting until you got here, you see. And when they told me about the present, I still didn't tell them about us. Oh, Oz, I—I don't—"

He looked her in the eyes, sternly, and squeezed her two hands between his. "What did they give you? Lady, for heaven's sake, what's the present?"

She was on the verge of tears. "A two-month trip to Europe this summer!"

"Hell's bells!" he exclaimed, a sudden grin overspreading his face. "The way you were acting, you'd have thought it was a nest of rattlesnakes!"

"But, oh, Oz—"

"You don't have to go to Europe if you don't want to." He lifted her chin to look her in the eyes. "Or do you want to go?"

"They said that judging by what I'd been writing them this fall, and everything, your coming up here, and all," she evaded his question, "I might be getting married sometime and they wanted me to have the trip before I did, because if I waited, it might be a long time—"

"But do you want to? You haven't said."

"Oh, Oz," she looked up with shining eyes. "I—I want to do both."

He laughed, the tension relieved. "But obviously you can't do both."

"But we could get married, and you could go, too."

He shook his head. "Not this summer. I won't be able to get away that long, I know. And I don't see how I could wait until you get back, either—for the wedding, you know. Gosh, that would make it August or even September, wouldn't it?" He was sober faced a moment, and then he relaxed, and pinched her chin. "But, say, you don't have to decide right now. Your dad and mother will keep their offer open, won't they, and you'll have all spring to decide, eh? And you know—I hate to admit it," he shook his head dubiously, "but it just might be that they've got a good idea." Suddenly he was glaring. "If you don't go over there and fall for some playboy prince or count or something!"

14

He was glad, looking back now, that Sarah Gordon had gone to Europe. They had been busy with the house during the late winter and spring months, and time had passed quickly, almost too quickly, they had agreed. And during the weeks she was abroad he had been deluged with work at the mill; while all the time he had been keeping an alert eye on Holly Grove and pushing Walter Loye, as tactfully but as vigorously as he knew how, to get the restoration completed before Sarah Gordon's return.

He had written her twice a week and had had that many or more letters from her, and he had reached her in Paris on the telephone and three weeks later she had called him from Rome. The days had rolled fast.

And now she was home. She had wired him from New York, after she had failed to get him on the telephone, that she was leaving for Philadelphia. He had given her time to get settled a bit from her flight, and then, excited, his whole frame tingling, had called her.

Already now they had been talking for long minutes. "But, honey, you're just got to come!" he insisted. "I can't wait to see you. And I want you to see Holly Grove. Sure, I know it isn't but one month more, but that's a long time. And say, we'll live in the guest house—"

He paused. "Oh, it'll be perfectly proper, and all that, tell your dad and mother. Charlie and Janet will be out there with us, and they're bringing their cook. Honey, we'll have a wonderful time. And, listen, there may be some few little things Walt will want to talk to you about, you know, finishing touches here and there."

Suddenly he guffawed. "You weren't thinking of whether or not it would be proper, eh? You were thinking about how much you have to do to get ready for the wedding? Well, you'll just have to let that go for a few days. Just don't have such a big wedding."

He listened another moment. "Good." He nodded his head. "I'll meet you at the airport, honey. And give my love to your dad and mother. And, say, hurry." He gave her a long telephone kiss and hung up.

15

They were turning in between the tall brick gateposts.

"Oh, Oz. The brick columns, and the gate! They look like they'd always been here!"

"I was wondering if you'd notice them. The posts were built with old bricks, you know."

But already she was looking at the lawn. "And the grass, Oz! And those flowers we set out in the spring, the plants, look! They're blooming. And the rose garden. Oh, they're lovely!"

They drove along the newly graveled driveway and stopped near the big magnolia. "Say!" She had noticed the boxwoods filling the gaps. "They're new, but they look like they'd always been here, too."

They had got out. "Charlie and Janet will be back before supper. They had to go home for awhile. But they left the cook, which is the important thing." They started along the box-bordered path toward the steps at the end of the verandah. Suddenly he stopped and pointed up toward the eaves of the mansion house. "Look."

Her eyes followed his pointing. "Oh, the crack's gone! You'd never notice there'd ever been one if you didn't know it already, would you?"

"You're right," he agreed. "Those masons did a good job." He studied the great repaired heart. "Fixing that heart and the wall would have pleased the old doctor, I know."

They went up the stone steps and onto the wide verandah. The ironwork, which had been repaired before she had left early in June, had been sanded and repainted, she noticed, and at the door she saw that the few glass panes that had been missing had been replaced.

But it was on the inside, as she stepped into the wide hallway and faced the spiraling stairs, that she was all but speechless.

"Beautiful, utterly beautiful," she said, when she had recovered her breath. "The most beautiful entrance hall and stairway I've ever seen. Even in Fairmount Park, Oz, I'm sure there's none the equal of this one." She caught his arm, and her eyes were ablaze. "Oz, we'll just have to have a daughter so that she can get married at the foot of these stairs!"

They went into the downstairs rooms one by one, the parlor first, the dining room, the music room across from the parlor, and she marveled at the transformation two months had brought. She hadn't seen the wallpaper nor the lighting fixtures.

"Aren't they wonderful, Oz? It's amazing how everything seems so perfectly right for the house, as if it had been made just to be put where it is. Oh, I do love it all!"

But she was ecstatic when she saw the library. "Let me sit down awhile and just look," she said, after her first moment of studying the room that had been transformed from Lem's kitchen after having for many years Dr. Claiborne Cardell's office. They sat on the Empire-period sofa that Lem had brought down with the other stored furniture from its sheeted long exile in the ballroom.

"Maybe you'll want to put this sofa in the parlor," he said. "But that can be done later; there'll probably be a lot of furniture shifting. And some of the stuff may need re-doing. But it's been well kept, and it's the very type for this house."

This room was the most changed one in the house, they agreed; perhaps it was because it had been the one most abused through the years. But now the smoked, dirty walls, the shelves —gaudily papered for the dishes and cans of fruit and kitchen utensils and countless other odds and ends accumulated since the moving in of the Negro's family—were happily gone. The walnut-paneled walls had been sanded and rubbed to a satin finish, and the shelves, repaired and sanded and finished like the walls, awaited their burdens of bright-jacketed books, and pottery pieces, and brasses and pewters.

"Let's go upstairs and have a look at the bedrooms," he said, as he stood up and caught her hand to help her to her feet. "I want to see how you like the decorating job. Of course, they'll all look better when you get the curtains up."

They had just gone into the southwest corner room, the one that looked out on the big magnolia and, through the west window, on the guest house, when they heard a car in the driveway. Osborne ran over to the south window, peered out. "Charlie and Janet are here," he said. "Good. Let's go down and greet our guests. And pretty soon we'll be having supper. I'm famished, too."

16

A full August moon, high above the old carriage house and lifting slowly westward, defined on the verandah floor a gradually retreating junction of light and shadow. In the water oak near the iron gate to the driveway a solitary cicada suddenly blasted the night's stillness with his rising, shrill-cadenced calling.

"I love to hear those rasping things," he said from the shadows that engulfed them on the wide chaise longue. "The Negroes call them dry-flies, claim they are calling for rain. But to me it's a peaceful, time-suspended sort of sound. Maybe it's just an association of ideas, a bringing back of the old, slow, summer days of childhood—" He paused. "You asleep, honey?"

Her answer was to snuggle closer.

"Maybe it's not a dry-fly anyway; maybe it's one of those heavenly choir angels with a saxophone that needs tuning. Anyway, if heaven is any more wonderful than this, I don't see how I'll be able to endure it. Insects singing in the trees, a gorgeous moon, a wonderful old house, and in my arms—" he gave her an added little quick squeeze "—the most intriguing, cleverest, prettiest, most stunning, most utterly gorgeous girl."

"And you value them in that order? The insects most, the girl least?" She lifted her head from the rounded dip between his right shoulder and his chest, and as she sat up into the silvered square of moonlight and turned her head to face him, he saw mischievous small moons dancing in her eyes.

"In inverse order," he countered, as he sat up and swung his legs to the floor. "I was climbing the heavenly stairs."

"You always have the answer." With her right hand she gently slapped the back of his left, cupped over hers on his lap; then she leaned against him again and he snuggled his face into her hair. "But I love it."

They sat silent, watching the moon.

"You know, this has been an amazing year," he said, after a long minute. "It has been a tremendous epoch, the twelve months—it will soon be—since I met you that first afternoon, tremendous in the life of the nation, and for me," he held her close, "incomparably the greatest. So much has happened: first, you; and that little Negro girl Ophelia and the hullabaloo about integration, and Little Rock, and the Sputniks, and, of course, all the time the house—"

She twisted her head around to look him in the face. "And in inverse order of importance?"

"No, silly." He pulled her ear. "In order of importance, with the first a million-times more important than all the others combined."

"You're sweet." And then her tenderness was suddenly a questioning seriousness. "Tell me, Oz, are you frightened? About the Sputniks, I mean; you know, Krushchev and his crowd?"

"No," he said. "Not of them. Sometimes I've been afraid about us. But now I feel much better about us than I did, well, about the time that Little Rock business turned so hot." He was silent again, his eyes on the disk above the old carriage house, and she did not offer to interrupt his thoughts. "Maybe I'm just an incurable optimist," he said after awhile, "but I don't think that's entirely it. I'll confess I was pretty scared when I saw history repeating itself, a new Reconstruction period looming with a new set of Thad Stevenses and all that terrible business.

"But it didn't come off, thank God. The administration took another look, a long, calm look, and so did the South and so did the whole country, and everybody calmed down. Nobody tossed the match and the potential big blast didn't come off. And I don't think it will." He lowered his eyes from the moon to turn them upon her. "And maybe this Sputnik business was a good thing for us. Maybe it got us—the whole country—to thinking; maybe it focused our attention on the things that unite us rather than divide us; maybe it got our minds and our hearts running on the same track again—and when the people of this country get together, I mean really together, in their thinking, their working, their fighting, their praying, well, dear lady, you've got a power that no Krushchev or anybody else will challenge, I'm thinking." He leaned back on the lowered pillow of the chaise longue, pulled her down to him. "But I've been preaching again. And you started me. And I don't want to think about anything but us now—you and me, and the house." He eased her head into the hollow of his shoulder. "It seems so right, Sarah Gordon, our having this old place. And tonight I somehow can feel old Dr. Cardell's presence and approval. He probably sat many a summer night here in the moonlight, with his mulatto mistress and his children back there in the kitchen house, and wondered how it would have been if he had married Melissa Osborne instead."

He felt her shudder. "Don't, Oz; don't talk about it. I just can't stand to think about it. After all, he wasn't your great-grandfather; certainly you owe him no loyalty. And that woman—" She paused. "Oh, it's—it's so repulsive. Let's don't think of them, Oz, ever, any more; the house has been completely renovated, cleared of them. Oh, Oz, I can't bear to think of that man, the way he did. And that woman and her frightful brood—oh, Oz, let's never talk—"

"Sure! Sure! We won't." He was nuzzling his nose in the fragrance of her black hair. "Don't let it upset you, honey. As far as we're concerned, it's just a story, a tale out of days long past. Forget it. Forget them. We won't talk about 'em any more. In fact," she couldn't see his face, but she knew he was smiling in the darkness of the shadows, "I had started out to talk about us, remember?—you and the house, mainly, how you were made for each other. To me, you and the house look alike, the way I see you both—poised, gracious, elegant but enduring, feminine."

"A house feminine, a big house?"

"Certainly. To me Holly Grove is irresistibly feminine." He pushed her up and sat beside her. Then quickly he stood up. "Say, Sarah Gordon, you haven't seen the chandelier up in the ballroom, the one copied from the Strawberry House music room, you know." He reached down, caught her hand, pulled her to her feet. "Let's have a look."

They went inside, and at the foot of the resplendent stairway he flicked the switch. Instantly the stair well to the third-story ceiling was flooded with soft light from the graceful bronze lantern suspended halfway down. They climbed the stairs, entered the ballroom, switched on the chandelier, and a thousand small lights blinked at them from the curving cascades of prisms encircled by a great band of flaming, yellow candles.

"I love it! Oh, Oz, it's perfect. This room—it's unbelievable!" But he was not looking at the chandelier or the room. He was watching the tiny shining circles of candles in her eyes.

But after awhile he pointed to a row of oils, framed in ornate gold-leaf, ranged along the floor at the other end of the great chamber. "There are the Cardells," he said. "We'll have to figure where to hang them."

"Formidable-looking folk," she said.

"They probably were," he agreed. "But they'll likely look more human when they're cleaned up."

They had turned to leave and were at the door when he noticed the stack of books on the floor near it.

"Wait a minute, honey. Let me have just one peek at these books. They must have been the doctor's, or his folk before him. There may be names of the owners on the flyleaves. It just might be that her name's—" But he said no more, for he was opening one of the books. "Hmm-m-m, medical books. 'Property of J. Claiborne Cardell, M.D.'" He dropped one after another back on the stacks. "Here's a Fenimore Cooper. And Dickens. Say, you know, there could be some first editions in this bunch of books. And here's a *Complete Works of William Shakespeare*." He opened it. "Say, Sarah Gordon"—he walked nearer the chandelier, squinted at the inscription in faded ink, written in a precise feminine hand. He read aloud: " 'Presented by Eliza G.—to Sarah'— Gosh," he said, "it's a shame the page is torn across the last two names—'June 3, 187—' it was in the eighteen-seventies some time."

"Hadn't we better be going, Oz? If Charlie and Janet are still awake, they'll be wondering if we're ever going to bed. And after flying down, I'm a little tired."

"Sure, honey." But he continued to stare at the mutilated fly-leaf. "You know," he said, his forehead wrinkling, his eyes boring, "I'd bet my neck this was her book. If somebody hadn't torn out this half of the page—Sarah—Sarah— Well, the world turns on small things." He shrugged. "If some youngster, probably one of her little bastards, hadn't torn this page, I might right now be uncovering one whale of a story."

"Oz, I'm really tired."

"Coming, coming." He shut the book and dropped it on the stack.

They walked down the stairs and out the front door. He led her along the boxwood path to the guest house, went into the front room on the right, and switched on the lamp beside the bed. The house was dark, silent. Listening, he caught the rhythmical sound of Charlie's snoring.

"I'll be in the room next to this one, honey," he said. "I think I'll go sit on the verandah a few minutes, while you're getting to bed. Oh, it's wonderful to have you back again, precious; it's the most wonderful thing in the world." He held her a long moment, and then kissed her. "Good night." He pinched her chin. "Sleep tight."

He walked back up the box-bordered path and sat down in an ancient hickory armchair. It had been the old doctor's veran-dah chair, Lem had explained in bringing it down from its long storage on the third floor. He sat at the end of the verandah, near the steps that went down to the path that led to the guest house, and he lifted his tired legs to the iron railing of the balustrade; he leaned back in the chair and closed his eyes.

In the water oak up near the gate a cicada shivered the si-lence with his shrill, cadenced cacophony. Startled, he opened his eyes, and pulling his feet from the railing, sat up. "I must have drowsed, and—" A light on the freshly painted wall of the carriage house cut a bright rectangle from the deep shadows. In the rectangle a silhouette moved.

CPSIA information can be obtained
at www.ICGtesting.com
Printed in the USA
LVOW10s0022290417
532640LV00031B/1183/P

9 780243 485833